BRIGHTER THAN BEFORE

ALSO BY COURTNEY WALSH

STAND-ALONE NOVELS

The Summer of Yes

The Happy Life of Isadora Bentley

Things Left Unsaid

Hometown Girl

Merry Ex-Mas

ROAD TRIP ROMANCES

A Cross-Country Christmas

A Cross-Country Wedding

NANTUCKET LOVE STORIES

If for Any Reason

Is It Any Wonder

A Match Made at Christmas

What Matters Most

HARBOR POINTE NOVELS

Just Look Up

Just Let Go

Just One Kiss

Just Like Home

PAPER HEARTS NOVELS

Paper Hearts

Change of Heart

SWEETHAVEN CIRCLE NOVELS

A Sweethaven Summer

A Sweethaven Homecoming

A Sweethaven Christmas

A Sweethaven Romance (a novella)

Praise for Courtney Walsh

"I loved this heartwarming and delightful story of a woman reinventing her life after a crushing loss. I particularly enjoyed the plucky heroine, Claire, her second chance romance with a swoony love interest, and so many yummy baked goods all set in Chicago! I was smiling 'til the very last page."

—Rachel Linden, bestselling author of *The Secret of Orange Blossom Cake*

"This sweet, slice-of-life romance from Walsh (*The Happy Life of Isadora Bentley*) kicks off when overworked associate book editor Kelsey Worthington is hit by a curb-hopping car and taken to the hospital, where she meets Georgina Tate, the formidable owner of Tate Cosmetics . . . Walsh delivers just enough introspection to make her heroines' journeys believable without slowing the pace. The romance, when it comes, is gentle and sincere rather than steamy. Readers looking for G-rated love stories will want to snap this up."

—*Publishers Weekly* for *The Summer of Yes*

"Courtney Walsh is an incredible storyteller. She has a magical way of weaving hope and happiness into every story she writes. If you love books by Denise Hunter and Rachel Linden, then say yes to *The Summer of Yes*!"

—Melissa Ferguson, bestselling author of *How to Plot a Payback*

"Two unlikely women come together for a summer that will change their lives in Courtney Walsh's latest perfect page-turner. Full of heart, humor, and, oh yes, a happy ending, *The Summer of Yes* reaffirms why Walsh is one of my favorite writers. This feel-good novel is her absolute best yet—and the beach read that everyone will be talking about!"

—Kristy Woodson Harvey, *New York Times* bestselling author of *A Happier Life*

BRIGHTER THAN BEFORE

A Novel

Courtney Walsh

THOMAS NELSON
Since 1798

Brighter than Before

Published in Nashville, Tennessee, by Thomas Nelson. Thomas Nelson is a registered trademark of HarperCollins Christian Publishing, Inc.

Thomas Nelson titles may be purchased in bulk for educational, business, fundraising, or sales promotional use. For information, please email SpecialMarkets@ThomasNelson.com.

HarperCollins Publishers, Macken House, 39/40 Mayor Street Upper, Dublin 1, D01 C9W8, Ireland (https://www.harpercollins.com)

ISBN 978-1-4003-5289-0 (epub)
ISBN 978-1-4003-5288-3 (TP)
ISBN 978-1-4003-5290-6 (audio download)

Library of Congress Cataloging-in-Publication Data

Printed in the United States of America

26 27 28 29 30 LBC 5 4 3 2 1

For the women who've lost themselves along the way.

CHAPTER 1

It was the mac 'n' cheese that brought me here.

I didn't know that mac 'n' cheese would result in impulsive lunacy.

Leading to the parking lot of the country club where I'm sitting, unshowered, wearing my favorite oversized gray sweatpants and slightly matching gray sweatshirt. It's my favorite outfit, or "groutfit" as my daughter, Minnie, calls it, which is probably why I've been wearing it for three days straight.

Beside me, on the passenger seat of my Jeep Cherokee, is a crumpled bag of cheese puffs (half eaten and *delicious*) and a box of Swiss Rolls ripped open and missing two. The smeared wrappers next to the box, leftover traitorous evidence.

I'd gone to the gas station for milk—to make the mac 'n' cheese—but the Swiss Rolls were calling to me.

Not the most nutritious dinner, but I think they have flour and milk and eggs in them, right? That totally counts.

Lately, I'm not picky.

I'd forgotten that today was the annual One Voice charity gala until I saw Dana and Tad Mathison pull into the gas station. I was parked in one of the far spots opening the cheese puffs when I spotted their Lexus. Instinctively, I sank down in my seat, pulling the Cubs cap down a little lower over my brow. These days, I don't leave the house without some kind of cap and a big pair of sunglasses.

It's dramatic and probably unnecessary, but I've taken to doing what I can to *not* stand out.

But you do what you have to do for the mac 'n' cheese.

Tad was wearing a tux, and Dana was decked out in an off-the-shoulder fitted blue formal gown. That's when I remembered.

The gala.

Had it really been a year since the last one?

I watched them in my side mirror as he filled their car with gas and she reapplied her lipstick.

He made a face at her through the windshield as he squeegeed it off. She puckered her lips in a kiss, and he raised his eyebrows and nodded enthusiastically.

Flirting. I vaguely remembered flirting.

They looked like a normal, happy couple.

That's when it really hit me. It *had* been a year. A year since I'd organized the last charity gala. A year since my life fell apart and I became a very public, very viral spectacle.

I sank lower, until only the brim of my cap was raised enough for me to peek.

I held my breath and they drove off, thankfully oblivious that I was here at all.

Where was this unbridled anonymity a year ago?

I thought on that for a moment until a crazy idea waved at me.

For a reason that I still don't fully comprehend, I waved back.

The thought was simple.

You should follow them.

And I did.

I didn't go home, where a new crime documentary was cued up.

That would've made too much sense.

Instead, I dropped the Jeep into gear and peeled out of the parking lot, following Tad and Dana down State Street all the way to the country club.

I've binged enough TV shows to think I knew what I was doing, keeping a distance and driving casually.

The second I saw the club's familiar exterior, a wave of nausea rolled through me. It'd been a year since I'd been here, and there isn't one thing about my life now that even remotely resembles my life then.

Because of John, everything changed.

I kept my head low and navigated to the back of the parking lot.

Which is where I am now.

A voice in my brain is shouting: *What are you doing here?!* But the insane part of my brain shushes that voice and puts duct tape over its mouth.

I have a clear view of the front entrance. It's a ways away from the numerous expensive cars parked closer to the door. Without looking away, I slowly reach over and snag the cheese puffs.

Last year, I wore a simple but elegant navy blue gown, and I showed up early to tend to last-minute details.

Little did I know there was something *else* on my husband's agenda that I had apparently overlooked.

Blond hair. Silver sequins. Cleavage for days.

She was tossed into my world like a grenade with the pin pulled, and I'm still digging out shrapnel from the edges of my life.

I shake away the memory as John's new black Porsche drives into the lot.

The nausea I was feeling is immediately replaced with anger. The hurt kind of anger that feels rage-y but helpless.

Of course he was still invited to the gala. He's the one with the money. And the family name. I'm the outsider, no matter how many hours I dedicated to this charity or how many years I dedicated to him.

I look down and realize I'm death-gripping the bag of Cheetos, and my hand is covered with the orange dust. I unclench my fist and am gluttonously (and depressingly) pleased that there are still a few good ones left in the bag.

One by one I stick them in my mouth, still watching as the lights of John's car turn off. I reach for the fountain Dr Pepper in the drink holder and take a drink.

And that's when I see him—tall, broad, simultaneously attractive and nauseating in a well-fitting tuxedo. The one I picked out. The one I had dry-cleaned after every event just like this over the years.

Who's handling his dry cleaning now?

He closes the door and pulls out his phone, types something on it, then sticks it back in his pocket. When the passenger side door doesn't open, I think maybe he's come alone, but then he walks around to the other side and opens the door, and as if I'm watching a movie in slow motion, I see a pair of Jimmy Choos step out onto the pavement.

John reaches for her hand, guiding her as she stands, their bodies only inches apart like two people emerging from a secret tryst in the coatroom.

Or behind a stairwell.

John clearly spared no expense on the forest-green formal gown with a slit that practically goes up to her armpit. This year, she looks the part. Not a department store sequin in sight.

I stifle a groan, reach for the box of Swiss Rolls, and absently wonder if I could accurately throw a brick from this distance.

I also try to remember how long it had been since John opened the car door for me.

Years and years, you dummy, the struggling voice of logic whispers through the duct tape. *Can we get out of here now?*

Shhh, another voice says. *We're busy.*

I pull open the cellophane wrapper and stick one of the cakes in my mouth. I'll eat this whole box before the end of the night, but desperate times call for desperate chocolate.

John leans in and kisses her cheek (*gag*), closes the door (*jerk*), then places a strong hand on the small of her back (*homewrecker*), ushering her out of the parking lot and toward the front door.

They smile and wave at Roxie and Garrett Cartwright like they're old friends who vacation together. They all walk through the door, a happy little foursome, and it makes me want to vomit.

But my anger is just a front. Because what really strikes me is how easily replaceable I was. It's like I never existed at all.

What lies did John tell our old friends? What did he say to stop them from reaching out? Did any of them feel even a twinge of guilt as this new woman slipped right into the vacant seat I'd left behind?

I finish the pair of Swiss Rolls with a Dr Pepper chaser.

More familiar faces arrive, dressed to the nines and ready to donate. They smile and wave and hug and air-kiss as they make their way inside.

I stupidly thought it would be hard to find someone to chair the gala in my absence, but I was obviously wrong. The gala, like everything else in my life, has gone on without me.

We'd talked about a new direction for the decor this year. We were going to go for a brighter, happier theme instead of the usual pastel palette. It had been my idea, mostly because we'd been doing the same dusty-pink roses for over a decade. Change is good, I'd argued, and my co-chair, Marcie, had eventually agreed.

I feel differently about change now.

Change used to be flowers stretching their colors in spring. Butterflies emerging from chrysalises. The warm ochre hues of a park in the fall.

Now? Change feels like a tornado. A wildfire. Sudden and violent destruction without sympathy or warning.

My life is completely unrecognizable thanks to change.

But I do still wonder if Marcie went with the brighter palette.

Not that it matters, except . . . if the decor is all brighter, then there's still a little bit of my influence left on this gala, an event that genuinely meant the world to me. To some of the women in our circle, it might've been about fancy dresses and expensive dinners, but to me, the gala was about one thing: raising money for the children's hospital.

Many people, all walks of life . . . but coming together with one cause, one goal. *One Voice.* Hence the name.

I reach into the bag of cheese puffs and find it empty as I see my former in-laws' Cadillac pull into the space directly in front of the door.

I catch a glimpse of my pinched brows and downturned mouth in the rearview mirror.

When Marilyn, John's mother, found out about her son's affair, she actually had the nerve to look me in the eye and say, *"This never would've happened if you'd taken better care of your husband."*

If only I'd been ready with one of the many, *many* comebacks I've since thought of.

"This from a woman who can't keep a houseplant alive."

"Really? Well, maybe if you hadn't done your best to raise a selfish, self-important waste of space, I could've done a better job."

And my personal favorite, *"John has found discount Barbie, someone pretty and shallow with no morals and no fashion sense. People say boys end up marrying girls just like their mom, so . . ."* And then I'd just shrug and smile.

And regret it immediately. Because it's not in my nature to go low.

Or to be quick with a comeback. In the moment, the comment left me dumbstruck. Silent.

Which was often what happened when I was around John's family. I always felt like a guest who'd overstayed her welcome. An underdressed stranger who won a ticket to a party.

They made no secret about the fact that I was absolutely not who they'd hoped would end up with their precious son.

Usually when the husband cheats, there's an outpouring of sympathy toward the wife. In this case, it must've been my fault he was driven to such a decision.

Not attentive enough. Not social enough. Just plain not *enough.* I was Princess Di in Buckingham Palace, at least the version depicted in *The Crown.*

Sure, there was plenty of pity, but mostly what this affair taught me about my social circle is that it's full of people who are really interested in staying in the good graces of John Sr. and Marilyn Wellesley.

I can practically hear Marilyn's posh tone: *"I warned him this would happen if he married that girl, but did he listen? No."*

She was pretty forthcoming with her disapproval from the start. She didn't know about Amelia at the time, of course, but I have to wonder if it would've made a difference. She never made much of an effort to know her granddaughter, and when she did find out, my pregnancy only gave her "proof" that I was trying to trap John.

I wish I'd been trying to trap him. All of this might've been less horrible if my feelings hadn't been involved. Back then, John and I were smitten with each other. He made me feel wanted and loved. He didn't care that his mother didn't approve; he was committed to me. When did that change?

Up until that fateful night a year ago, I'd been doing a pretty good job of fitting in. At least I thought I was. I had the right clothes. The right shoes. I attended the right dinners and events. I drove the right car and I knew all the right people.

But still . . . deep down . . . I knew the truth.

I never belonged here.

The doors open again, and I wish I had a pair of binoculars so I could get just a tiny peek inside. Did Marcie play it safe with the dusty-pink roses?

Maybe you should go and find out, my lunatic brain prods. *Just quick—no one will even notice.*

And I'm convinced.

The sun has begun to set, I reason. The impending dusk will provide enough cover for me to sneak around the back of the building and take a quick look inside. The back wall of the ballroom is all windows that open to a two-story deck and patio leading out to the golf course. Holes one and eighteen have plenty of trees and bushes for me to go undetected.

I grab the handle to open the door when I look down at my feet.

I'm wearing flip-flops.

Because gas station. Because milk. Because mac 'n' cheese.

Hmm. This could be an issue. It's February, and it snowed yesterday.

You'll be so fast, your toes won't even have time to get cold, I think to myself.

I pull the baseball cap down lower and shove my oversized sunglasses on my face, making it twice as dark as I step out of the car, lock it, and dart off into the trees.

I channel my inner Tom Cruise in *Mission: Impossible*, crouching as I move.

If I were self-aware, my movement would be more Bond and less baboon.

I quickly move from one tree to the next, feet slipping in the plastic shoes. I stop with my back against the tree and peek around to make sure the coast is clear before racing to another when the back of the building comes into view.

Yellowish light spills out onto the brick patio, illuminating the big stone fountain John's parents donated to the country club a few years ago. The waitstaff weave their way through formally dressed men and women milling around, and I squint to try to see what they're serving.

Probably shrimp. They always start with shrimp.

I never liked shrimp.

I see the string quartet on the small stage, and I'm glad Marcie decided to hire them again this year. The violinist is a sweet young mom I met a few years ago at a wedding, and I was so happy to give her foursome a little more exposure. I know they'd booked several holiday parties as a result of this gala over the years, and it made me feel good that I got to pass that on.

I miss that part of this life. Having the means to help other people was huge to me.

I huff out a breath as I move in a little closer. If I angle myself just right, I might be able to see what big-ticket items Marcie was able to score this year. Last year we had two sets of Nuggets tickets and a pair of box seats to a Broncos game, but those had been my contributions. Maybe it's wrong, but I want to believe that the gala is a little worse off without me.

From where I stand, though, it doesn't seem to have missed a beat.

Which is good, Claire. This event is about sick children, not your pride.

I see John and *the other woman* standing in a group with Roxie and Garrett and two other couples I can't make out from here. The men are on one side, and the women are on the other. And everyone seems perfectly comfortable with my replacement.

I dart out from behind my hiding place and run in the direction of a small patch of bushes, wondering how often my old friends see this woman socially. Do they invite her to spa day? Do they go shopping together?

I squat down and look at the group just as one of the women, who I now see is Lainey Russell, reaches out and takes *the other woman's* hand the way you do when . . .

My stomach clenches.

The women lean in, and *the other woman*—Misty—throws her head back and laughs. She reaches her right hand out, and John takes it, sharing with her a knowing look that anyone could see from a mile away.

Is my ex-husband engaged to this woman?

Maybe I didn't see what I thought I saw.

There's still a lot of commotion around their group. Marcie—who was *my* friend, not John's—walks up to them as Bill Russell moves toward his wife, blocking my view.

Instinctively, I rush onto the patio and hide behind the fountain, certain that with the light of the ballroom, nobody looking out into the darkness is going to be able to see me out here. I inch out from behind the fountain, but as I do, the motion lights from up above come on, lighting up the whole patio like searchlights from a helicopter.

The sudden burst of light is like an instant shock, and without thinking, I hide in the only place I can think to hide.

The cold water of the fountain is another shock, and it almost burns as I dunk myself down behind the statue. My right foot slips on the slick, wet floor, and I topple over, losing a flip-flop. I instinctively let out a yelp as I splash, and I flounder to stand up straight, slipping again. I find my footing, slap my hand over my mouth, and press my body into the back of the stone statue, hoping it's big enough to keep me hidden, even in my oversized sweatsuit.

I screw my eyes shut as I hear the door of the ballroom open. Heels click on the brick patio as someone steps outside.

Cold water seeps deep beyond my sweatpants, and I'm struck by a frigid wave of panic and the sudden urge to pee.

"Claire?" I don't have to open my eyes to recognize John's voice, but when I do, I see he's not alone.

He's standing there with a small group of my once-closest friends, staring at me in a frumpy sweatsuit that's soaked from the waist down as I stand with flip-flops in a fountain at a formal function in the middle of February.

Even alliteration has given me an F.

I close my eyes, wishing with every fiber of my being to be whisked away like Dorothy Gale or teleported like Marty McFly—zapped back in time to right before I made the decision to follow the Lexus here.

I wait. I wince. I mentally plead. But nothing happens.

I open my eyes and see that now a larger crowd has gathered.

Their expressions range from disgusted to amused to horrified, and I can't even blame them. Because if I didn't know it before, I know it now—*this* is what rock bottom feels like.

CHAPTER 2

I still don't have any milk.

I grumble that thought to myself as I push open the door to my house, blaming John for that fact too.

The door closes behind me, but it does nothing to shut out the competing feelings of embarrassment and red-eyed anger.

"Go back to your stupid party with your stupid, fake friends and your fetus of a girlfriend, and stop pretending to be the bigger person here!" I had shouted at him from the fountain.

He thought I was drunk.

He told me to move on.

I told him I would drive away right now if he would stand in front of my car.

Everyone was watching, looking down at me from their perfect little perches, sharing whispers about the crazy lady in the fountain.

I shut my eyes, my fists, my whole body tight, and hold it, trying not to scream at myself for being *so. Incredibly. Stupid.*

I kick off my soaked shoes, then peel off my wet sweatpants right there in the mudroom and fling them down the hall at the washing machine in the laundry room. They land with a mucky squelch a good three feet from the open lid, and I think, *Great. Now I have to mop that up.*

That's your fault too, you idiot.

I head upstairs to find new clothes, feeling the footprints I'm leaving with my wet socks. As I pass the bathroom, I catch a glimpse of myself in the mirror. I stop, move back a bit, and stand fully in front of my reflection. I take my baseball cap off and my wavy brown hair falls out, somehow wet *and* greasy at the same time and in dire need of highlights.

I look like I've been strapped to the hood of a car that just went through the Super Suds.

I spent years carefully keeping up my appearance—going to Pilates with Roxie and Dana and Marcie, eating only the allotted number of calories each day, visiting the salon every six weeks like clockwork to keep myself from ever knowing my hair was possibly turning gray. I got my nails done every other week, waxed my eyebrows, and went for a spray tan regularly.

Misty, the new flavor of the month, looks exactly like that.

And Marilyn looks exactly like a wrinkled version of that.

When we got married right out of college and John insisted we move back to Colorado so he could work at his dad's advertising agency, I didn't put up much of a fight, even though I'd always had my heart set on living in Chicago. But John wanted the stability of a job that was a sure thing. It seemed like an easy compromise—I was sure I'd end up loving Denver.

But from the very early days, John's mom was an ever-present force in our relationship. What started as suggestions turned into expectations. From big things, like furniture choices in the den, down to the little things, like which stamps I put on an envelope—she had opinions and expectations about everything.

And she made it clear that my appearance was to be taken *very* seriously.

So I did exactly that. For the entirety of my twenty-three-year marriage. Because I wanted her to like me. Plus, I never really had a mother of my own, so I was excited at the idea of having her guidance in my life, especially as a newlywed and, eventually, a new mom.

Never mind that when I got really quiet, the voice I heard guiding me wasn't Marilyn's—it was my grandmother's.

The woman who raised me.

Life in my small Midwestern hometown was *very* different from here. Slower. Less flashy. More personal.

New man, new city, new life. I had a lot of changes to get used to. But I was determined to fit in. Even after John's parents made it very clear that I didn't. And wouldn't. Ever.

I'd been determined I could change their minds.

I grit my teeth at the image of John's mother in my mind. It's so incredibly frustrating to feel completely helpless, with no retribution, no recourse. It's like the villains are getting away with their crimes, and I'm screaming into the void.

I shake my head clear of the headache-inducing thoughts of revenge.

And I sigh. Heavily.

I became the kind of wife and mom I thought I had to be, all the while listening to the many, many ways I was lucky John had chosen to marry me in the first place.

Funny, I don't feel so lucky anymore

* * *

In lieu of mac 'n' cheese, I make myself a cake.

Because you don't need a birthday to eat cake.

And I plan to eat the entire thing by myself.

For as long as I can remember, baking has always been a way to relieve my stress. I have Gram to thank for that. I always carried a lot of stress, even as a little kid. I understand now that giving my mom "one more chance" to raise me led to a lot of confusion on my part.

Because she got one too many chances, and because they never seemed to work out.

It led to a sort of limbo of living for several years in a row. A few solid months with Gram, a few disastrous weeks with Mom. That was the pattern, and it took a toll.

But baking helped me cope.

Something about the act of mixing ingredients, stirring them all together to create something new—it calmed me. Something about not having to make decisions—since it's all right there in the recipe—is settling. Relieving.

As I pull the flour from the cupboard, I remember the first time Gram popped into my bedroom and tossed me an apron. I'd barely said a word since I'd moved back into the old farmhouse, but what eight-year-old who'd just been abandoned by her only parent would feel like chatting?

"Pops brought home some fresh strawberries, and I'm making Strawberry Shortcake," Gram said. "I need some help with the biscuits."

In hindsight, I realize Gram didn't really give me a choice.

My mother and I didn't bake. Some nights we didn't even eat dinner. When we did, it was often cereal or something from a box. I'd find out later that my mother didn't abandon me so much as my grandma saved me.

If I'd stayed with my mom, I would've ended up like her—and Gram knew she had to intervene. She'd given her daughter a chance to turn her life around, but there was only so much time she'd let her have when my well-being was on the line.

There were a lot of feelings to sort through over the years, but somehow, Gram always knew pressing me wasn't going to work. Instead, she gave me something to do and the space to do it. As I measured and mixed and kneaded, inevitably I'd make peace with the feelings I was trying so hard to bury.

Which is maybe why I still bake when I'm confused, stressed, sad, or lonely.

Tonight it's Texas sheet cake.

Lots of leftovers with a Texas sheet cake.

My mind clears as I pull out the rest of the ingredients, grab a few bowls, and get to work.

It's a calm, blessed relief, the muscle memory of mixing, and soon I'm pouring the batter into a shallow pan.

While it bakes, I turn a circle in the too-big-for-one-person kitchen.

"Frosting." I say this out loud, then walk into the pantry. When I flip on the light, I see the ticks on the wall marking Minnie's growth.

Some have exclamation points next to them. All different colors of marker and pen.

I breathe, stiffen my spine, and turn away.

I walk into the living room and flip on the television just to have some background noise.

The house is so quiet. Too quiet.

I walk into the den and look around. The built-in bookshelves are full of books, mostly mine, but I haven't read anything new in months. I sit down in the armchair, and when I lean back, I feel something hard behind me. I reach behind the pillow and grab it. I don't have to look at it to know what it is.

A journal.

My journal.

The one thing that was supposed to "help me heal."

It hadn't been my idea. My therapist, Dr. Lydia Baskin, recommended it in the weeks following that fateful night at the auction. I was seeing her religiously up until two months ago when she looked me straight in the face and said, *"Claire, nothing about your life is going to change if you don't change it."*

I might've rolled my eyes at her because I *know* that.

But also because I don't know *how* to actually do it.

She said to start with small changes. I've tried small changes. All they do is bring me closer to having to make big changes.

I open the journal and thumb through the pages, momentarily proud of myself for taking her journaling assignment so seriously. I'd been a faithful journaler for months.

But my pride is short-lived when I notice that almost every entry is a rehashing of the one before. Page after page of bitter diatribes from a woman who is angry. Devastated. Terrified. Hopeless.

A woman who, even all these months later, is still exactly the same. Well, *mostly* the same, but now with a smattering of heartbreak mixed in.

I flip to the last page before a series of blank ones.

There, in bold black letters, are the same words Dr. Baskin had said to me. *"Nothing about your life is going to change if you don't change it."*

I'd written it down, underlined it, *and* circled it, and I have no memory of doing so.

Those words had not been well received, but some part of me, the part that wants to heal, must've known they were important.

And while everything about my life has changed in the last year, none of those changes were ones I'd made. They'd been made *for* me. They'd happened *to* me.

Under that quote, in the same bold lettering, is a question. One I *do* remember writing.

My mind spins back to that day in therapy, sitting in the chair opposite her—me, cross-legged in my black leggings and worn-out CSU sweatshirt, and her in her pantsuit and stilettos.

The journal is open in my lap, and Dr. Baskin says, "I want you to write down a question, and then I'm going to give you some time to answer it. Then we'll talk through it together."

I look down at the journal, back in the present.

The question is simple, but the answer is definitely not.

It reads, *"What do I really want?"*

The rest of the page is blank. I never answered it.

And I also haven't been back to see Dr. Baskin since.

I pick up a pen from the desk nearby and settle back into the chair.

"What do I really want?" I tap the end of the pen on the open journal.

Over the past year, I haven't changed. Over the past year, I haven't moved on. Over the past year, I've listened to a very specific, very loud voice in my head that is angry and hurt.

This time, though, I listen to a different voice. Not the angry one, not the vengeful one, not the hurt one or even the lonely one.

This voice, strangely, has a twinge of hope in it.

I sit up.

I look down at the journal . . . and I start writing.

Day One of My New Life:

My New Life. I actually like the sound of that. New. Fresh. A do-over. Underneath I write . . .

What do I really want?

What did I want before everything in my life went pear-shaped? I close my eyes and inhale a deep breath, remembering, and when I open my eyes I write:

1. I want a job or career I love.

I want to feel creative and helpful and alive again. Which makes me think of the second thing I want.

2. I want friends. Real ones.

Being lonely sucks. Worse than that is being told who your friends need to be, or what kind of "friend" to be to fit in. Enough of that. I just want friends.

I think of the things I sacrificed when I moved here. Things I was happy to give up at the time.

3. I want to live in a new city.

I stare at that one, pen hovering over it like I'm ready to cross it out. It's thrilling and terrifying at the same time. I press my lips together, but a smile sneaks through.

What if I moved to a new city? My stomach flip-flops at the idea.

But then I think of something else I've always wanted . . .

4. I want a dog.

Not a big dumb one. A smart one. One that sits with me and doesn't bark at leaves blowing past the window.

A more serious thought hits me. I move the pen with purpose.

5. I want to figure out who I am—apart from a wife and a mom.

This feels big but it feels right to add it to the list. This feels like actual decisions are being made. I'm writing these as if I'm already doing them.

The last thing I write is simple.

6. I want a place where I fit in. I want a place where I belong.

The timer on the oven goes off, and I bring the journal with me into the kitchen. I set it down on the counter, grab a pair of oven mitts, and pull the sheet cake from the oven. I lightly press on the top, and it springs back.

"Perfect."

I read over my list again. It's unfiltered and raw and vulnerable, and there's no one in my life I would share it with . . . but maybe that's what makes it important.

Because maybe identifying the things *I* really want is the first step.

And the next step is to actually do them.

CHAPTER 3

One month later

I slide the key in the lock of my new apartment but pause before I open the door.

I pull out my phone and open the camera app. With the apartment door in the background and the number 6 on the door clearly visible in the frame, I snap a photo and send it to Minnie with a caption that reads: **I made it!**

She's doing a postgrad seminar at Oxford for a few months, but when I told her I was moving to Chicago, I swear I heard her cheer from the other side of the ocean.

She did make an offhanded comment that if I really want to "get my groove back," I should move somewhere tropical and have a torrid affair with a Michael B. Jordan look-alike.

Minnie is twenty-three now, and I love that she's old enough to be my friend, but some subjects are still just too weird to discuss with her. My nonexistent love life is *definitely* one of them.

Finding my journal that night unlocked something in me. I finally understood what Dr. Baskin meant—nothing is going to change unless I change it.

So this is me. Changing it.

I'm terrified—but strangely excited.

Dr. Baskin told me once that bravery isn't the absence of fear. It's feeling the fear but doing the thing anyway.

This feels brave. It also feels a little crazy.

I secured the apartment before I even sold the house—something that happened in record time—and with Minnie's help over FaceTime, we went through everything, keeping things we wanted and selling or donating everything else. It was sad, and hard, and stressful, and nostalgic.

I had my neighbor help me remove the trim piece where we'd marked Minnie's varying heights so I could take it with me. That stuff was never important to anyone else, plus John's mother hated that I marked up the trim.

I did it anyway. One tiny rebellion. It was—and still is—important to me.

Once we were done, and once I shut the door behind me for the last time, I felt . . . free.

I always wanted to live in Chicago. When I was in college, this city was always supposed to be my next step. After a twenty-four-year detour, I've finally arrived.

I've only seen the apartment in photos, and now that I'm here, I take it all in. It's an end unit in a horseshoe-shaped brick building and there's a beautiful courtyard in the center that's clearly been well-tended. You'd never know that on the opposite side of the building is a partially obstructed, distant view of Lake Michigan and a close-up view of the skyscrapers that populate Chicago's famous skyline.

My new apartment building, The Bexley, is only two stories tall, and each of the apartments has an exterior door facing the courtyard. Flower pots and welcome mats and benches and chairs are neatly positioned around the space, and there's a patch of grass in the center, making the whole area social and private at the same time.

It's the middle of March, not quite spring, and there's a crispness in the air despite the sunshine beaming down into the courtyard.

I don't know what I expect, but I'm struck by a wave of something that feels a lot like . . . possibility.

Well, that's a feeling I haven't felt in a long time.

My plan isn't overly fleshed out. More of a loose outline.

Honestly, it's still just number three on my list in my journal: *"I want to live in a new city."*

It's not even, like, 12 percent of a plan.

A point John was quick to point out when he found out I'd sold the house. He'd shown up as I was hauling a giant box down the stairs, and because he didn't seem to remember—or care—that he no longer lived there, he let himself in.

Instead of helping, he stood there watching.

When I finally reached the bottom of the stairs, I blew out a breath and looked at him. "Wow, thanks for the help."

"Just want you to see what it's going to be like when I'm not around," he said.

I rolled my eyes and walked toward the kitchen. "Right, because you've been so reliable since you moved out," I said over my shoulder.

As expected, he'd followed me into the kitchen. "What are you thinking, Claire? Amelia told me you think you're moving to Chicago?"

"No," I said, aware and annoyed that he'd used our daughter's given name—the formal one that suited his family—and not the nickname I'd given her practically since the second she was born.

"No?"

"I don't think it," I said, vaguely gesturing to the rest of the boxes strewn about. "I'm doing it."

"That's a bad idea."

"I didn't ask your opinion."

"The crime there is *terrible*," he said. "It's like the Wild West."

"It's really not."

He continued as if I was just there to listen to him talk and not be a part of the conversation. "And it's expensive. Really expensive. Especially in the city—are you going to get a job?"

I smiled right at him and shrugged.

"Do you have a budget?" he asked. "My alimony check will only go so far."

I stopped briefly. "Here's the great thing about divorce, John. You don't have to care. You don't have to wonder, or worry, or have an opinion about anything I do anymore, ever."

He crossed his arms over his chest and studied me. "You haven't thought this through."

I sighed and pulled a bottle of water from the refrigerator.

"I'll figure it out," I'd said, with far less conviction than I intended to. But honestly! I'm forty-six years old. A competent, capable woman. I steeled my jaw and leveled my gaze. "Everything is figure-out-able."

He'd stared at me like he couldn't believe what I was saying. "Did you read that on a poster somewhere? You're making a huge mistake."

A plaque in HomeGoods, actually, but I didn't tell him that.

What if John's right? What if this whole plan is going to crash and burn?

I shake myself into the present. I'm still holding the key in my hand.

The house sold in record time. The sale set me up for at least a year to make things figure-out-able.

I'm here. With a new apartment. In a new city. In a new state.

In a new life.

The thought is equal parts terrifying and exciting, but I shove all the feelings aside as I push the key into the lock and turn it.

The door swings open, both in front of me and metaphorically.

I breathe in and look around.

It's my new place.

Mine.

I'd rented the apartment after finding it through a simple internet search. The photos made it look so gorgeous, I started to write my next chapter right there in the living room of my suburban house in Colorado.

But the photos didn't do the apartment justice. I stand in the open doorway, gawking at the hardwood floors and the exposed brick walls, admiring the rustic wood beams and all the natural light.

I can feel a smile spreading across my face. It's even better than I imagined.

I take a few steps inside, suddenly energized despite the fact that I've been driving for almost two days straight, a pared-down version of everything I own packed in a small trailer attached to my Jeep Cherokee.

"Oh, you made it!" A short woman with glasses and a rounded bob of sand-colored hair strolls in through the still-open door. She's wearing loose jeans and a striped pink button-down shirt with a pair of white tennis shoes, and her whole face lights up at the sight of me.

"I heard this unit had been rented, and when I saw you walk in, I thought, *That must be her! Our new neighbor.* I know because I know everyone around here." Her Chicago accent is thick. I expect her to tell me about "da Bears" and pronounce the word *caught* like *cot.*

Wasn't it only yesterday I'd worked hard to get rid of that same accent? Yesterday and a million years ago.

"I'm Lorraine Ashby"—(*Lah-rain,* she says it)—"and I live across the courtyard in apartment 2." She turns and points outside, indicating the apartment that sits kitty-corner from mine.

When she looks back and smiles, I note the wrinkles around her eyes and across her forehead, wondering if it was years of laughter that put them there.

"I'm Claire," I say. "Claire Karadec." It's strange using my maiden name now, but a new season called for a new name.

"It's nice to meet you, Claire." She closes the door, steps over my suitcase, and walks into the living room. "Do you need a tour?"

It occurs to me that I can probably find my way around the two-bedroom apartment on my own, but then I think about number two on my list: *I want friends. Real ones.*

I'm guessing Lorraine is at least two decades older than me, but that could be a good thing. Wisdom comes with age, and my first impression is that she's outgoing. Maybe she can teach me how to make friends, because I'm pretty sure I've forgotten. Without the common ground of my child's activities or my husband's work, it feels hard.

How do I make friends as an adult?

"Claire? Still with us?"

I look up and find Lorraine's eyes fixed on me, her expression bright and inviting. I must've zoned out. I've been doing that lately—the danger of overthinking.

It's like I'm trying to calculate where each choice I make will lead so I don't end up in a country club fountain with my wet sweatpants falling down.

I fix my face with a kind smile and say, "Yes. Sorry! Ugh, I get lost in—" I wave a hand in front of my forehead. "I'd like that." I prop my suitcases against the wall and turn toward her.

"Good! Thought for a second you checked out." She laughs. "So! This"—she gestures to the room we're standing in—"is the living room. Probably the space you'll be spending most of your time in entertaining friends and family and so on, so eye-wise, this is the best blank canvas you've got." Lorraine quirks a brow in my direction.

If only you knew the truth, Lorraine . . .

I used to entertain. Heck, I used to plan galas. I used to have the means to care about things like that, but my budget these days is exceedingly more modest. I have money, thanks to the sale of the house—nothing to sneeze at—but I'm trying to set up a whole new life here.

Also, right now the only person I know in this city is standing in front of me.

I nod but stay quiet and follow Lorraine as she moves into the kitchen, spanning her arms out.

"Don't you just love the space? It's so open. Apartments are often cut up into little boxes." She scrunches her nose in disapproval. "I'd rather see everyone and be able to hold a conversation without shouting from one room to the next!"

I smile. I immediately like Lorraine.

"Did you see the courtyard on your way in?"

"Yes," I say. "It's beautiful! It's one of the reasons I was attracted to this place."

"It's a shared space," she explains, "where all the residents gather, meet, mingle. We're a friendly bunch."

I smile at that. I like the idea of knowing my neighbors.

"We have Miles to thank for how it looks. He lives in apartment 1, right across from you. Before he moved in, it was little more than a patch of dead grass, and he took it upon himself to turn it into—well, what you see out there. I think he needed a project to keep himself busy." She says it as if I already know the backstory there and doesn't give any more details.

Well, that's intriguing.

Lorraine opens a drawer. "Watch this," she says, as if she's about to reveal a magic trick. She gives the drawer a hard push, and it slows down halfway, then softly pulls the drawer front flush.

"Soft close! They're all like that." She smiles. "Modern conveniences with historical charm."

Lorraine breezes through the space, showing me the small laundry room at the back of the apartment with an exterior door that leads to a walking path.

"We're just a short walk to the lake, so if you're the fresh-air type, it'll be great for you. Personally, I take my fresh air sitting down." She chuckles to herself and continues on up the stairs.

"Each unit is two stories. Two bedrooms, one full bath, one half. And then there's a linen closet." We're standing in the hallway outside the bedrooms, and she looks at me. "Lots of space, don't you think?"

"It's actually a lot smaller than I'm used to."

"Oh?" Her eyebrows shoot up. "Where'd you move from?"

I hesitate for a moment, then say, "Colorado." I don't offer any details because I don't know how to share everything that led me here without getting into the weeds with it.

"Ooh, Colorado. Where God vacations," she quips.

I chuckle. It's not the first time I've heard that. She's not wrong. Parts of that state are divinely carved.

Too bad the majesty of the mountains was overshadowed by the emotional valley I was living in.

"Well? What do you think?" Lorraine asks as we walk back downstairs and into the living room.

I look around the cozy space and smile. "It's perfect."

And it is.

Well, I did it.

I'm here. Moved halfway across the country to a city I've always wanted to live in.

It's a place where, so far, only one person knows my name.

Maybe I'll get to the place where I can walk into a room and everyone calls out, "Claire!" like I'm a regular.

Cue the Cheers theme song.

I didn't mind being known before.

But then my life imploded.

I'm having trouble sleeping. New place, new bed, new noises, but that's not it.

I'm replaying the moment I first found out about John and the other woman at the gala.

It takes no effort to put me right back in that

bathroom stall, listening. Roxie and Lainey are blathering on and on about someone's husband having an affair.

It's like it's happening again. In the present. My heart races and my stomach feels hollow. My palms start to sweat, and I have to get up and walk around just to remind myself that it's not happening in the present.

It's not now. It's then. Rearview mirror.

I lived through that. I drove away.

I'm still alive. I survived.

And I'm determined to move forward.

My wounds are healing—one day at a time.

I met my first new friend.

Her name is Lorraine, and she's older than me. A little bit of a busybody, but in a good way. I already like her and would love to meet some of the other people in the building. Maybe she can introduce me.

She said the man across the courtyard is Miles. I want to know what made him work on the outdoor space. It's beautiful. Is it his job? Or a hobby?

How do I get a hobby?

Am I a person who likes art? Collecting ships in bottles? Do I love rock climbing? I want to find out.

I want a hobby. (Add to list.)

Maybe it'll help me get to know myself better.

CHAPTER 4

One week later

I added another thing to my "What I Want" list.

It's a biggie. It's probably going to have its own list underneath it. My "What I Want" list, so far, is—

1. *I want a job or career I love.*
2. *I want friends. Real ones.*
3. ~~*I want to live in a new city.*~~
4. *I want a dog.*
5. *I want to figure out who I am—apart from a wife and a mom.*
6. *I want a place where I fit in. I want a place where I belong.*
7. *I want a hobby.*

And now, the last and latest one is . . .

8. *I want to do the things that scare me.*

When I wrote it, I wasn't thinking of cliff diving in Acapulco, or lying in a coffin while arachnologists dump buckets of tarantulas on me.

I was thinking of simple things. Going out to dinner by myself. Striking up a conversation with a stranger. Trying new foods.

No big deal, right?

I've eaten alone before—unfortunately, it was junk food while stalking. After everything that happened, I did everything I could *not* to be noticed.

Not anymore. Time to figure out what I want, and I'm hoping stepping out of my comfort zone will lead me there.

Or I'll hate it.

But at least I'll know, right?

The weight of the past year suddenly comes crashing in on me, and I'm momentarily mentally paralyzed.

I can't do this.

Then, just when I expected it the least and needed it the most, I get a text from Minnie.

It's a selfie of her on the London Bridge, grinning so wide it makes my heart skip a beat.

I *love* her in this photo, and my heart aches to be around her. I reach down with two fingers and zoom in on her face when my phone vibrates again.

Minnie: Living my best life!

I stare at the words, marveling at how I managed to raise a daughter who doesn't seem to be afraid of anything, and I wonder what she thinks of who I've become.

Claire: It's so beautiful! Are you having fun?

Minnie: The best time, Mom!
You should come visit!

Claire: Maybe I will!

Minnie: How's Chicago? Have you
seen a lot of the city yet?

Claire: Not yet, but I'm on my way to eat right now.

Somewhere I've never been.

Food I've never tried.

I'm terrified.

And I am. Lists are great and all, but they're on paper, and you can cross them out or rip them up, no damage done.

Doing the things on the list? Actually *doing* them?

Terrifying.

Minnie: Good. You deserve to have an adventure of your own.

Those words hit. Do I *deserve* it?

Yes, my relationship fell apart in an epically awful way, but I don't know if the universe owes me some great debt.

Claire: I've had plenty of adventures this past year . . . What I need now is a little bit of calm.

My phone buzzes in my hand, and Minnie's face pops up on the screen. I answer the FaceTime call with a smile. "Hey, you!"

"Mom," Minnie says in a stern voice. "We need to redefine 'adventure.'"

"I'd rather hear about Oxford."

"I'll tell you all about Oxford, but first we need to talk about you."

I groan. "You know that's not my favorite subject." I prop the phone up and pull on my jacket, then stick my AirPods in my ears.

I know what's coming. I've had many pep talks from my daughter over the last several months, and it's not how I want our relationship to go. She doesn't need to be taking care of me—it needs to be the other way around.

"Finding out your husband is cheating on you and then hiding in your house for almost a year is *not* an adventure."

"I know, Amelia," I drone. I pick up the phone, then open the door of the apartment to step out into the courtyard. "Look, I'm on my way to have an adventure right now!"

Minnie squints, like she's trying to decide if this counts, and finally relents. "Okay . . . So, how's the new place?"

I flip my camera around to show Minnie the courtyard and the building.

"Ooh! Nice!" she says. "There's a spot right in the middle to sit? Do they let you grow things out there? What kind . . . *Whoa.*"

Her tone changes, and I see on my phone's screen that as I was panning over, the door of my across-the-courtyard neighbor opened and a tall brunette stepped out. There's a man with her, and judging by his bare feet and unkempt hair, he's the one who lives there.

Miles.

"Scandal!" Minnie whispers.

I click the button to turn the video back around, eliciting an "Aww, come *on* . . ." from Minnie. I face the phone in a different direction to give the impression that I'm not filming them, aware that I might be creeping on a private moment. Still, I can't help but toss a sideways glance in their direction.

The man I assume is Miles gives the woman a quick hug—not a romantic one—and then lifts a hand in a wave. The whole scene turns awkwardly platonic.

"Is that your neighbor? Did you just film a walk of shame?"

"It's 5:00 p.m.," I say. "So I hope not."

She giggles. "He looked kind of hot?"

"Amelia Joy!" I glance back up and find the man standing in his doorway, watching me.

I hear Minnie quip, "Yikes, whipping out the middle name, that's bold . . ." as the man lifts his hand in that same lazy wave.

I wave back, feeling conflicted about whether to go introduce myself.

I'm almost thankful when he doesn't give me the chance. He closes his door, and the woman disappears through the front gate.

"You know, since we're talking about you having adventures . . ."

I groan, worried I know where this is headed.

"You're going to start dating again, right?" Minnie asks. "Because I—"

"Minnie—"

"What? It's not like Dad's wasting any time moving on."

"Dad moved on while we were still married," I say dryly, then hold up a hand as if to suggest I'm taking that back. "Sorry. I'm not trying to be ugly about your dad. Not to you anyway."

"He cheated on me too," she says plainly.

That revelation stops me.

"He did, didn't he," I say, almost to myself.

There's a sadness behind her smile, and I recognize it because I feel it too.

I'd much rather connect with my daughter over literally any other subject . . . but for now, this is where we are. Someday, hopefully, we'll both get past it.

She's sitting on her bed in her little dorm room in England, and I wish I could jump through the screen and hug her.

"I'm proud of you, Mom."

The words catch me so off guard, I stop moving. I'm frozen on the sidewalk just a few yards from the front gate, staring at her face on the screen in my hand. "You are?"

"Yeah. You've had a lot of crap to deal with in the last year. But this change? This one's good," she says. "It's the first one that feels like a choice."

A choice. *My* choice. I smile at that, suddenly emotional.

"That means a lot to me, Min. Thank you." I blink to keep the tears from falling. "And you know that me being here and starting over or whatever—it's not because I regret anything. I don't regret having you or raising you or choosing motherhood over any career I thought I'd have." A career that never felt like the right fit anyway . . . Advertising may have been the plan, but it was clear that was John's world, not mine.

"Duh. Because I'm awesome."

I smile. "Yeah, you really are."

She leans in toward the camera, her face filling my screen. "But, Mom, you launched me. Your job here is done. When I get back, we can go shopping and hang out like friends . . . but for now, you can be a little selfish, you know? You've never done a selfish thing in your whole life. You've earned the right."

"So basically you're telling me to get a life?"

She makes a show of snapping her jaw shut and looking back and forth, as if to say, *I'm not saying a word*, even though she's said plenty.

"Okay, I have to go get ready," she says.

"Wait," I say, doing a quick calculation. If it's a little after 5:00 p.m. here, then . . . "Isn't it after eleven there?"

"Yes, Granny, but this is when things are happening."

I grimace, suddenly uncomfortable knowing that my daughter is going to be out late in a foreign country with people I don't know. It's so much easier to launch a child when you're still a little in the dark.

"Before you go—what I was going to say before, about dating—"

"I thought we'd moved off that subject," I say, *wishing* we could move off that subject.

"I just thought you should know that"—she inhales a deep breath—"I created a dating profile for you. I'll send you all the details so you can log in! Love you, bye!"

"Amelia Joy!"

The power of the middle name has no effect. She's hung up.

Seconds later, a link to an app, along with login details, shows up in my text messages.

A dating app? Really?

I stare at Minnie's text and scrunch my lips together. Why am I moderately curious about this? Is it because I've never even opened a dating app? Because this is how so many people meet their partners these days? Or because deep down, there's a part of me that wonders if maybe one day I might actually fall in love again?

My finger hovers over the link, like I'm about to pull the trigger on something that can't be undone.

And before I can talk myself out of it, I tap it.

A website pops up, prompting me to download the app: Matched.

And that's when my sense of adventure turns cold. I'll have to add this to my list later—but right now? It feels a little too scary.

I click my phone off and tuck it into my bag, then look up at the neighborhood in front of me. It rained recently and is unseasonably warm. The kind of weather that makes sun-starved Midwesterners rush to be outdoors, probably in shorts, saying things like, "Yeah, the rain's a lot, but boy, the grass sure needed it. Ope, lemme scoot right past ya."

I turn the corner and find myself walking straight toward a group of young women, probably in their late twenties. There are four of them, dressed like they just got off work, and my knee-jerk assumption is that they have everything all figured out.

They're a visual representation of *confidence*, and for some reason, mine shrinks at the sight of them.

They're young. They've got years stretching out in front of them, and they can do *anything* with those years.

I'll never be able to go back to the days when the world seemed to be mine for the taking. The years I spent in college, mapping out my life plan, and the years of watching every aspect of that plan break off in a detour are still too fresh for me to ignore.

But more than that—these women have no idea yet how cruel life can be.

And I don't have that luxury. The luxury of *not knowing*.

How do I start over with the aftertaste of fresh failure so prominent on my tongue?

The truth is, you can plan all you want, but you can't account for the curveballs. The one pitch I still haven't learned to hit.

I reach the corner at the same time as the group of women, and my eyes snag on the patio of a local restaurant across the street. I scan the tables while I wait for the light to change.

A toddler screams and tosses a toy on the ground. A group of guys let out a loud laugh, like they've all just gotten the punchline of a joke at the same time. A man and woman sit on the same side of a table, engrossed in only one thing, in spite of the busyness around them—each other.

There are no single diners at this restaurant. Everyone is paired off or in a group.

Everyone has someone.

And I'm on my own.

Suddenly, eating alone doesn't feel brave.

It feels embarrassing.

My pulse quickens and my face heats, the way it does sometimes when I start to feel anxious, and as the light changes, a small crowd of people, including the group of women, maneuver around me to cross the street.

But I don't move.

I can't move.

What if I can't figure out how to make it here? What if city life isn't for me? Why did I think this was a good idea?

The light cycles through, and a man walking a beagle gives me a sideways glance. His dog stops in front of me, wagging its tail, pulling on the leash, excited to meet someone new.

I can't even muster a "who's a good boy" and a pat.

I can't even meet a stranger when that stranger is a friendly little beagle.

I shake my head, step back onto the sidewalk, and bolt in the direction of my apartment.

John's voice plays on a continuous loop at the back of my mind.

"You're making a huge mistake."

What if he was right?

What if I was wrong?

What if . . . ?

Then Minnie's voice cuts through the noise.

"I'm proud of you, Mom . . . It's the first one that feels like a choice."

A choice.

My choice.

"No, Claire," I say to myself quietly as I pass a young mom pushing a stroller. "You can do this. You just need more time."

Right. That's it.

Tomorrow will be better. Tomorrow, I'll feel ready.

I hope.

CHAPTER 5

I'm muttering under my breath as I make my way back into the courtyard, a mere ten minutes from when I left it, when I see a tall, beautiful woman with long blonde hair standing outside the apartment directly across from mine.

It's the barefoot guy's apartment.

The same apartment where I just saw a different woman leaving when I was on the phone with Minnie.

Multiple women makes me think of John. And automatically makes me despise Miles, even if he did create this beautiful courtyard.

This woman must've already knocked because the door opens and Miles, no longer barefoot, appears. At the sight of her, he smiles, opens his arms, and pulls her into a tight hug.

As he does, his eyes meet mine, and I force myself to look away. What do I care if my across-the-courtyard neighbor is a middle-aged man who has a thing for much younger women?

Still, I dare one more glance in his direction, and I'm pretty sure I'm doing a bad job of hiding my annoyance.

Knock it off, Claire. This is none of your business.

I unlock my door and duck inside, close the curtains, and exhale a long breath.

I walk over to my table, grab my journal, and add a new item under number eight.

Now the list reads . . .

8. I want to do the things that scare me.

- *Have a meal by myself. In public.*
- *Strike up a conversation with a stranger.*
- *Try new foods I've never had or can't pronounce.*

And the new one . . .

- *Download dating app.*

I don't have to open it or anything. I just need to put it on my phone. That feels like plenty. Because if I *do* ever fall for someone again, it's not going to be anytime soon.

I walk into the small first-floor bathroom and flip on the light. I'm slightly disheveled after my walk, my hair windblown and my cheeks pink.

I look at my reflection, smoothing my hair and thinking again how badly I need to get to a salon. "That's what you should do, Claire. Something nice for yourself. You deserve it." I lean forward, noticing my skin could also use a refresh.

When John and I were married, my appearance was a part of my job, but now I can take care of my hair and skin simply because I want to. For me.

I can even change my look if I want to.

I'm thankful to learn that with some diligent plucking and my new best friend—root cover-up—I've been able to keep the gray away, and as I stare at myself, I think maybe Claire 2.0 will be less fussy. More natural. More relaxed.

And just like that, I know how to spend the night. To rescue it from the feeling of failure that followed me home.

Maybe I'm not ready to go out to eat alone, but I can still cross one thing off my list.

- *Try new foods I've never had or can't pronounce.*

God bless Lorraine. After I met her the first time, she showed up at my door the next morning with a stack of takeout menus and said, "Life's too short for bad takeout."

As I grab the stack and flip through the menus, I realize how narrow my food experience has been. I've never had Indian, or Thai, or Mediterranean, or numerous other kinds of food represented by this pile of menus.

John was a bland, boring, picky eater, so I was too.

I bristle at that thought. *He did X, so I did X.* I can practically hear my grandmother asking about bridges and jumping off.

What if I love spicy food? Or find Moroccan to be amazing? What if falafel becomes my new favorite meal or I discover I could happily eat hummus on everything?

A risky thought hits me, totally in line with this rush of "newness" I'm feeling. I spread out all of the menus on the counter, close my eyes, and mix them up like a pile shuffle before a game of Go Fish.

Keeping my eyes closed, I fumble around until I land on one, pull it out of the pile, and open my eyes.

MingHin Cuisine.

On it, there's a sticky note on which Lorraine has written: *Authentic and delicious!* She's circled the Dim sum in permanent marker.

MingHin Cuisine and Dim sum it is.

I tap the Grubhub icon on my phone and order three times as much food as I'll be able to eat. Chaozhou dumplings with pork. Mongolian beef. Chiu Chow marinated duck. Mixed vegetable lo mein. Pan-fried taro cake.

Probably enough to feed the whole building. Frivolous? Maybe. But I've never heard of any of these and I'm conquering fears here.

And maybe once I trust myself with these silly little decisions, I'll trust myself with big decisions too.

I add instructions for the driver to leave my food at the door, pour myself a glass of wine, and walk upstairs. There, in an opened box that is still half unpacked, are products I purchased at the spa the last time I went. They're probably all expired, but they were too overwhelming to use and too expensive to throw away, so they got a first-class ticket to Chicago in the back seat of my Jeep.

I pull the packing tape off a smaller box and find bath salts and lotions, a moisturizing mud mask and a deep-conditioning hair treatment.

"Jackpot."

Less than an hour later, I'm standing in my short pink robe, a coating of deep conditioner in my hair, and a thick, green mud mask hardening on my face when my phone dings.

Your food has been delivered.

On cue, my stomach growls, and I'm inexplicably excited about the smorgasbord of new dishes to try.

I creep down the stairs and peek outside, and when I'm sure the courtyard is clear, I open the door a crack.

I kneel down and start feeling around, like I'm blindly searching for a contact lens in the dark, but the only thing there is my welcome mat. I open the door a little wider and poke my head out, looking for the bag of food, but there's nothing here.

I stand, tighten the belt of my robe, and step outside. I do a quick search of the area and see three large white bags by the entrance to the courtyard.

I groan. They brought the food as far as the building but decided it wasn't necessary to actually set it in front of my door. Perfect.

I look around. I'm not going to go back inside and get dressed when I still have to shower and wash the conditioner out of my hair, so I opt for the quick dash to the front gate instead.

I pull the door to my apartment closed and run toward the front gate. I pick up all three bags, then turn and rush back, doing my best to keep the belt of my robe secure while carrying enough food to feed the entire offensive line of the Chicago Bears.

I make it to my apartment, but when I twist the doorknob, it doesn't turn.

I crank it again. Nothing.

The door is locked.

Stupidly, I try it a third time, as if I somehow operated the doorknob wrong the first two times.

Not surprisingly, it's still locked.

One of the bags slips, and as I go to catch it, my hand catches on the belt of my robe, loosening it just enough to take the whole scene into rated R territory.

At that exact moment, I hear the sound of a door opening across the courtyard.

Because *of course* now is precisely when my womanizing neighbor has decided to say good night to his second (third? fifth?) date of the day.

I duck around the side of the building, behind one of the bushes, clutching the bags and doing my best to hold my robe together while my fingers tangle in the plastic loops of the takeout bags.

I look around, frantic, trying to find a way back inside.

But I freeze when the man—Miles—walks the beautiful blonde out to the front gate. They're chatting happily, unaware that only yards away, there's a semi-naked, green-faced woman with three bags of pork dumplings in the bushes.

The memory of the night in the fountain rushes back. I should be used to getting caught in compromising situations, but I'm not.

Sweat gathers along my brow and upper lip, and I feel a piece of the green mud mask crack and fall right off my face.

I've *got* to get back inside.

The bushes scratch my bare legs as I move toward the back door, the one in the laundry room that opens to the small garbage area. I know the door is locked because I double-checked it before I left, but I try the handle anyway.

It doesn't turn.

I step back and study the exterior of my apartment, wishing the window in the laundry room wasn't so high or that I was the kind of person who knew how to scale the side of a brick building.

Unfortunately, it is and I'm not, which means I'm completely, wholly, and 100 percent stuck.

And the one person who might know how to get me out of this mess is in the apartment that's the farthest away from mine across a fairly well-lit courtyard where a potentially handsome neighbor with questionable moral character stands.

I sneak back to my previous hiding spot and check the front gate again, just in time to see the young, perky woman wrap her arms around Miles and hug him. He pats her back in another surprisingly platonic gesture, and she walks away.

Two awkwardly benign send-offs. Weird.

One of the bags starts to spin and slip, and I grab haphazardly to get a better grip, throwing off my balance. My foot catches on something hard—a rock maybe—and I let out what can only be described as a yelp.

Because I'm the perpetual butt of a giant cosmic joke, this happens just as Miles is turning back. He freezes, eyes trained right on the spot where I'm standing, which I only now realize is right underneath an exterior light. A familiar sense of dread threads through me as I step out of the beam of light, hoping that the bushes conceal my hiding place in spite of it.

I go still, pressing my back into the brick wall of the building, and screw my eyes shut, praying that this guy has the eyesight of a T. rex, and if I stay still, he won't be able to see me.

The traitorous belt on my flimsy robe slips.

Eyes still shut, I slowly raise the bags higher. Noodles and egg rolls are now all that stands between the world and my naughty bits.

I slowly count to five, then open my eyes.

I exhale a long, slow breath of relief, because all I see in front of me is an empty sidewalk. Maybe my luck in these situations is finally starting to turn.

Never mind that I still have no idea how I'm going to get back inside my apartment.

I listen for a few more seconds, and when I'm satisfied that Miles has gone inside, I step through the bushes, robe loose and bags clutched, out onto the walkway that runs parallel to the building. I stop short when I find myself standing right in front of my very casual, very amused, very *handsome* neighbor.

I scream and drop all three bags, which snag on the belt and pull it all the way out of the loop. My robe does its best impression of those inflatable blow-up men outside a car dealership, just waving wherever it wants. I frantically clutch the thin fabric around my body as Miles takes a step back, looking away, his hands up in front of him, as if to let me know he comes in peace and isn't trying to catch me in a compromising position.

I grimace, and another chunk of face mud cracks and drops to the ground with a comically soft *thump*.

I tighten my belt, clear my throat, and try to act like I'm supposed to be there.

He smiles. "What are you doing in the bushes?"

"I . . . locked myself out," I say, straightening up a little, trying to act nonchalant.

"Oh, you *live* here," he says. "I didn't recognize you with the—" He swirls his hand around his face, then points at mine, and in a weird move, he reaches down and grabs the cracked chunk of mask and tries to hand it back to me. "Does this go back on somewhere, or . . . ?"

I stare, feeling like this whole scene is happening to someone else.

He tosses the chunk to the ground again. "Yeah, right, that

was . . . I mean, it probably can't stick back on . . ." He takes a step toward me. "Claire, right? I'm Miles. I live across the courtyard." He sticks a hand out in my direction, but then decides against it when he realizes both of my hands are clinging to my decency.

In any other situation I might find him endearing.

"I would've introduced myself sooner, but I've been out of town."

I'm still struggling to find a foothold in this scene, so I don't say anything.

"How are you liking it so far?" He doesn't seem to notice that I'm still practically standing in the bushes, surrounded by enough takeout to feed a whole suburb, wearing a very thin, probably see-through pink floral robe with enough mud on my face to prevent my phone from opening at the sight of me.

"I'd like it better if the door didn't lock behind me," I finally say with a weak smile.

"Oh. Yeah. Safety feature." He scratches his head. "Kind of like a hotel. I mean . . . it's usually a good thing." He gives me a quick once-over. "Though, maybe not in this case."

I wince. "Yeah. Maybe not."

He's smirking now. "It's in the welcome email—did you read the welcome email?"

"Of course I read the welcome email," I lie.

"There was no welcome email."

Crap. "What—?"

"I'm just teasing." He chuckles.

"This isn't funny." I cinch the robe tighter and reach down to grab the bags.

"Oh! Here, let me . . ." He moves toward them, and I instinctively flinch at his closeness—which tips my balance again, and I lean, having to put a hand down on the ground to keep from falling.

He stands, bags in one hand and offering me his other one to steady me.

"It's *kind of* funny," he quips.

I look at his hand and decide it would be better if I didn't fall over again, so I take it to stand back up, quickly dropping it as soon as I'm upright.

"It would be funnier if it were happening to someone else," I volley back at him, trying to emote, but without the use of my eyebrows it's not very effective.

"You'll laugh about it one day," he says. "When people ask us how we met, I'll tell them the story of the half-naked woman stalking me in the bushes." He looks down at the bags. "Oh my gosh, is this MingHin? I love this place."

He's acting like we're old friends. What the heck?

"I am *not* stalking you!"

He squints at me. "Aren't you, though? A little bit stalking?"

"They left my food at the gate," I say, as if the explanation will help any of this. "I was halfway through a facial, and I'm trying new things, so I ordered all of this food I've never heard of, and then it came but not to my door, and I didn't think it would be any big deal if I—" I wave a hand in the direction of the gate.

"Hid in the bushes in your bathrobe."

I ignore him and hold out a hand to take the bags.

He extends one toward me but keeps the other two. "I can help." Then, in a fun way, he adds, "Looks like you'll need the other hand to keep things . . . you know."

I stiffen again, pulling the robe tighter with my free hand. "And nobody is going to ask how we met."

He gestures to the walkway back to my apartment. "They will if we become friends."

Before I can stop myself, I make the connection between my experience and my assumptions and blurt out, "You probably have enough female *friends*, huh?"

He holds eye contact for a long beat, then raises an amused brow. "Did you say you're 'trying' new food?"

I take a few tentative steps toward my apartment. He dodged the accusation, or just didn't give it any mind, which is good because it was a jerky thing for me to say. "Yes."

"But this is Chinese food," he says, nodding at the bags.

"And?"

"You've never had Chinese takeout before?"

By his face I can tell he doesn't mean this to be insulting. Just curious. In a vulnerable slip, I admit, "My ex-husband didn't like it."

He gives me a slow nod, like he's sorting something out about me, and I shift because I don't like feeling like I'm in his crosshairs.

"Let me know how you like it," he says. "The dumplings are *so* much better with the ginger sauce."

He smiles. And that's that.

I'm having trouble reconciling how he's acting with what I've decided about him. For me, it's not a leap to look at a man apparently dating two younger women and immediately think of my own history. But my experience isn't everyone's experience.

And this man is not John.

It's an unfair conclusion to jump to.

As I'm mentally debating, he walks over to a large flowerpot on the opposite side of my door. He fishes around in the center of the plants and pulls out a small black box. He opens it and holds up a key.

"What is that?"

He frowns. "It's a key." His tone says, *Duh.*

"To my apartment?"

"Everyone has one hidden somewhere," he says.

"And you just happen to know where mine is?" I ask.

"Lucky for you, yes."

"How?"

"Because I'm the one who put it there." He pauses. "You're welcome."

I shift. "Why did you hide a key to my apartment in the plants?"

"Because people lock themselves out all the time," he says, moving toward my door. "The safety feature is great . . . until it's not." He sticks the key in the lock and turns.

"But why did *you* hide them?"

"Oh, uh, because I own the building." He shrugs.

"You *own* the building," I say.

Realization sets in.

"You own the building."

"Yep."

He turns the key and opens my door, motioning with one arm for me to walk through.

I step inside my apartment in a daze, then turn back. He sets the other bags just inside the door.

"Ginger sauce. I'm telling you."

He turns to leave, and I blurt out, "Thank you!"

He glances back.

I shake my head, hoping it will sift out the lunacy and keep the sane parts of my vocabulary. "Thank you. For helping me. I really didn't know what I was going to do about getting back in."

He nods. "Anytime, Claire."

And I realize that even though I never told him my name, he knows it because *he owns the building*.

"That's what friends are for." He holds my gaze for a beat too long, then turns and walks away.

* * *

Minnie: Did you download the app?

Claire: No.

Minnie: Mom.

Claire: Amelia.

Minnie: I found someone perfect for you. He loves Chicago sports and tavern-style pizza.

Claire: That's literally the entire South Side.

Minnie: Mom.

Claire: Amelia.

Minnie: You love pizza.

Claire: Everyone loves pizza.You can't build a relationship on pizza.

Minnie: It's one date, you're not going to marry the guy.

Claire: I'm not comfortable with dating apps. It feels like shopping for people.

Minnie: I mean . . . kind of. But it's a great way to get out and see your new city. And maybe meet a hot guy.

Claire: Amelia.

Minnie: Mother.

Claire: Mother? 

Minnie: Check it out. And your profile. And hey . . .

Claire: Yes?

Minnie: Have fun! 😉

CHAPTER 6

The Dim sum was better with the ginger sauce.

And everything was *amazing.*

The next morning, I've got a Chinese food hangover, but I'm feeling empowered to cross something off my list.

I grab my journal and a pencil and scan down to the list under number eight.

8. I want to do the things that scare me.

- *Have a meal by myself. In public.*
- *Strike up a conversation with a stranger.*
- ~~*Try new foods I've never had or can't pronounce.*~~
- *Download dating app.*

I hover my pencil over *"Strike up a conversation with a stranger"* because of my surreal chat with Miles.

I decide against crossing it off because semi-nude conversations in hedges don't count. It wasn't intentional, after all.

But the last one—*"Download dating app."*

Hmm.

There's nothing on this list about actually *using* it. Download it and cross it off.

Boom. Done.

I navigate to the App store and find the little icon with two cartoon hearts woven together—Matched—then click the button to download it.

And then I stare at it. My finger hovers over the icon, and I'm curiously aware that if I tap on this tiny little square, I'll open up a whole new semi-scary, semi-exciting world.

Is this really how people date these days?

Never in a million years did I think I'd be back in the dating pool. I haven't looked at another man with any kind of attraction or interest for over twenty years. I pledged myself to my husband, and that was that. Because I'm a promise keeper.

John, however, is not.

In an *okay, fine* moment, I quickly tap on the icon. My heart races as the app opens, the two little animated hearts dancing while a cute, jaunty song plays.

I enter the login info that Minnie sent, and when I hit Done, the edges of the screen fold over into a heart, then reopen to my profile.

There's a photo of me laughing, looking away from the camera. I've never seen the image, but based on what I'm wearing, I know it was taken the day of Minnie's college graduation. I was just so proud of her. It's a nice photo.

I look happy.

Underneath, it says:

CLAIRE—FLIRTY, FUN, AND FABULOUS 40-SOMETHING

"Oh geez," I groan.

Starting over. Looking to make new friends and explore my new city.

One rule: No boring dates!

No boring dates.

Huh. I like it.

I have to hand it to my daughter—she's doing everything she can to push me out of my comfort zone.

I click around on my phone for a few minutes, then find a way to scroll through images of men on the app. And as I do, I'm overcome with a strange sense of dread.

It feels so . . . weird.

For years, I taught Minnie not to go anywhere with a stranger, and now I'm swiping right to go *out* with one? On purpose?

My phone pings, and a message pops up on the screen.

Rob has hearted your profile.

"Uh. Okay, Rob."

What am I supposed to do now? Like his profile back?

I click on his photo.

ROB—LATE 40S, LOOKING FOR ADVENTURE

Outdoor enthusiast

I frown. Outdoor enthusiast?

A message pops up on the screen.

Rob: Hi Claire! You're gorgeous! We should go out and see if we have anything in common! I can promise our date won't be boring! 😉

So! Many! Exclamation points!

Without responding, I click the phone off and tuck it away. I'll think about that later.

Today, I have other plans.

Today, I'm going to go find a job.

It's number one on my list, and I haven't really thought about it yet.

Selling the house set me up to be able to do what I'm doing—

but not forever. Plus, I'm not naive enough to think that I can just live off that with no income. It'd be gone in six months.

I need to find something. Something for me. Something that fits like a glove.

I always thought I'd end up in advertising, like John. However, my creativity, he reasoned, would be put to better use planning charity functions and dinners, serving on boards, and doing anything I could to keep myself busy. And I was good at those things, even if they weren't what I'd originally planned—or wanted—to do.

Maybe that's where I'll start.

Last night, MingHin's Dim sum and I searched the job sites for ideas. While I do have a degree in communications, the last time I had a paying job I was in college working at the library.

It seems everything about my degree is outdated as well.

When I was in school, social media marketing was not a thing. Heck, social media wasn't a thing.

I'd been a sounding board for John and had even been a frequent idea generator for some of his most successful ad campaigns, but I can hardly put "helped my husband come up with ideas" on my résumé. And while a younger version of me romanticized the idea of taking control of a room full of ad execs in my slick black power suit, that life doesn't appeal to me anymore.

Who do I want to be? And shouldn't I know this by now?

I won't figure it all out today. I'm determined not to let anything deter me. For now, I just need a job.

I made a list of places within walking distance, and I'm starting with those first. Walking to work, at least in nice weather, sounds sort of dreamy. And very much a perk of living in the city.

I drove everywhere in Colorado. Things were spread out, making walking anywhere nearly impossible.

I get dressed—a simple pair of black chinos with a lightweight sweater and a black jacket that hits me at mid-thigh. One of the benefits of having wealthy friends all these years is that one of them, Dana, taught me how to accessorize. Never mind that I don't live a wealthy life anymore—I can still look put together. At least until everything I own goes out of style. Claire 2.0 is a little more casual than Colorado Claire, and I think I like it.

I fix my hair, using a healthy dose of root cover-up, apply my makeup, then give myself a quick once-over. I walk over to the full-length mirror hanging next to the door of my bedroom and snap a full-body photo and send it to Minnie.

Claire: Heading out to find a job! Think anyone will hire an experienced woman with no work history?

Minnie: Heck yeah! They'd be crazy not to!

Thank God for my daughter. I can't rant about her father or drag her into the depressing parts of starting over, but she's an excellent cheerleader.

And currently my only friend.

In return, she sends me a selfie of her standing outside a gorgeous old brick building at Oxford.

Minnie: Do you believe I get to go to class here?

I smile and tap the photo.

Claire: That is stunning, and so are you! Have an amazing day!

I tuck the phone away, grab my bag, keys, and the giant sugar cookies I baked this morning, and walk outside. I pull the door shut behind me, and yep.

It locks.

Across the courtyard, Lorraine stands. "Claire!" She waves and rushes toward me, holding up her phone like she's recording something. I look around the courtyard and behind me, wondering why in the world she's putting me in her video.

"This is my neighbor Claire," Lorraine says to the screen. "Smile and wave!"

I do as I'm told with an "Uh, hi!" unsure how to politely excuse myself because I really don't need to be in on this call to her grandkids or whoever she's talking to.

Lorraine smiles at the screen, holding it a little closer. "For any gentlemen out there, Claire is recently divorced, new to the city, and looking for a good time."

"What the . . . ?!"

"Not *that* kind of good time," she says, holding the phone closer. "I just meant you want to explore Chicago." Then, back to the screen, "In case any handsome fellas out there want to be her tour guide."

She pans the phone at me, up and down. "Isn't she *adorable*?!"

"*Lorraine*," I hiss. "Who are you talking to?"

"YouTube," she says gleefully.

My frown deepens. "Who are you really talking to?"

"I told you." She flips the phone around so I can see the screen. "Smile! We're live!"

I stare at her phone, slack-jawed. "Live?!"

"Yes, I have a channel," she says, turning it back around.

A serial dater who owns the building and an elderly YouTuber. Who am I going to meet next—a brother and sister who lead a soul funk band? A quirky child prodigy attending Columbia at age twelve? This building could be a half-hour sitcom.

"What are those?" She nods down at the container I'm holding.

"Oh, I, uh, baked cookies," I say.

"You bake?"

I nod. "Helps relieve stress."

She looks at the screen. "And she bakes!" She flips it to face me, and I smile weakly, holding up the cookies.

"Ta-da," I manage with a shrug.

What am I doing?

"I have to go," I say. "I'm going to find a job."

Lorraine beams. "Oh! Maybe someone on my channel can help you find a job!"

"Oh! I mean . . . sure? Maybe?" I hold up a hand and wave to who I'm envisioning are a handful of people watching this video, then smile at Lorraine. "Have a good day!"

"You too! Keep us posted on the job hunt!"

As she turns around and starts back toward the bench nearest her apartment, I hear her say, "If you're interested in my sweet new neighbor, just send me a message . . ."

I smile. I like Lorraine. Even if I might need to establish a stronger boundary.

As I walk over to Miles's door, I'm struck with an unexpected wave of nerves. Why am I nervous?

Also, why did I bake him cookies?

He's going to think I'm weird.

Though . . . last night probably already solidified that.

He's a very good-looking guy. The first one I've even noticed since my divorce was final nine months ago. Maybe subconsciously, I want him to see me without the dumpling bags and the green face. Maybe I want to give a better second impression to make up for the nightmare of the first.

But that's *ridiculous*. From what I've seen, he could be dating between two and four different people at the same time.

What do I care what this man thinks of me or the way I look?

Then, suddenly, the door of his apartment opens, and Miles appears. He's wearing jeans, a dark green henley, and an expression that seems to ask what I'm doing out here.

I never knocked on the door.

Which means that while I stood out here mentally spiraling for at least two minutes straight . . . Miles witnessed it all.

Just doing my part to solidify my status as the resident weirdo.

"Hi . . . ?" he says after a beat.

"Hi," I say.

His eyebrows go up in a question.

"I made you these"—I thrust the container in his general direction—"to, uh . . . thank you."

He looks at it, then at me. "For what?"

"For helping me get back into my apartment last night."

"Oh, you're *Claire*," he says, drawing out my name, exaggerating. "I didn't recognize you without the green face." He smirks and reaches for the container.

He's got jokes, I see.

I pull it back. "Never mind."

He changes his tune immediately. "No, no! I'm kidding. I promise." He motions for me to hand it over.

I make a show of pretending to think about it, then finally give it to him.

He takes the lid off, picks up a cookie, looks at me questioningly. *These good?* he seems to ask.

I raise my eyebrows to answer, *Eat it and find out.*

I realize I'm nervous to share my baking with him. It's . . . vulnerable, in a way, because there's a story behind everything I bake. A memory of my grandparents or of my childhood. Every cookie is personal to me.

Which, I realize, is a little ridiculous.

He nods in capitulation and takes a bite. His face changes, looking pleasantly surprised.

"You made these?" he asks with a mouthful.

"Yes."

He closes his eyes, nodding, like this will enhance the experience somehow. "That's good." He looks at me.

"Thanks." The nervousness melts away, and I'm oddly proud that he likes them.

In another weird moment of honesty, I say, "I'm not used to needing people's help." A pause. "So, thanks."

The irony of that statement isn't lost on me. *I'm not used to needing help* implies I'm a strong, competent woman.

Which is, of late, the opposite of how I feel.

There's an awkward pause, so I give a little wave and turn to go.

"Oh, wait, Claire." He stops me. "I wanted to . . . There's something I should, um, probably tell you . . ."

He screws up his face and points to the corner of the building over my shoulder. I turn, not knowing what he's indicating, but then my eyes focus on something mounted to the side, just above the awnings over the windows.

It's a camera.

My eyes dart to the other corners of the courtyard.

There are cameras on every corner of the building. I count at least six.

I whip back around to him, eyes wide, panicked. Did some security guard see my nearly nude escapades last night? Was I half naked on a bank of screens somewhere? Did someone take that footage and is now uploading it to . . .

He immediately holds up a hand, seemingly knowing what my distressed face is silently screaming.

"I erased it."

I stare into his eyes, looking for a joke or a dig. I find nothing except honesty.

"You—" I start.

He nods. "It's fine. No one saw anything. I didn't even rewatch it." He pauses and smiles slightly. "Three times, tops. But no more than that."

I burst out a nervous laugh, shaking my head. "You're the worst," I say, and then after a pause, "but seriously . . . thank you."

He smiles.

I smile.

We stand there for a beat too long, and then I start to walk away, but he follows me, stepping barefoot onto the rug in front of his door.

"Where are you headed today?" he asks. "You look, you know, done up."

"Job hunting," I say, chagrined. "In an unfamiliar city with a nearly blank résumé." I scrunch my nose, aware this might be a fool's errand. The best I can hope for is that someone will take pity on me.

"Wait, you're not from here?"

I wince. "No. Moved from Colorado."

"Wow, you're a long way from home."

"Oh! No," I say. "I lived there for a while, but I'm not from there. I grew up in Illinois."

He leans on his doorframe. "Just not the city."

"No, not the city."

He folds his arms, and he seems fully engaged in this conversation. I can't remember the last time I had a meaningful conversation with a guy.

Oh, wait. I do.

I was in a fountain.

"Are you just, like, popping in and asking for applications?"

I stop. "Is that a bad idea?" My stupid insecurity, and possibly my age, is showing.

He shrugs. "No, not at all. It just depends on what kind of job you want, I guess. Mostly everything's done online."

"I'm not looking for a career here," I say. "Just a job. A coffee shop, retail, or maybe the Lincoln Park Zoo?"

He chuckles. "The zoo?"

"Yeah." I smile. "It looked kind of fun. And, I don't know, different."

"You're looking for different," he says. Not a question but a conclusion.

My gaze falls. "I don't have a lot of work experience. And I . . ." I look for a way to say something without saying *everything*. "I maybe just don't know exactly what I want. Yet."

He seems to consider this. "Hmm. Well, okay then. I'm coming with."

"What?" I gasp. "No!"

"I'll just put my shoes on." He starts to back away. "Don't leave."

"You really don't have to do that!" I call after him.

He disappears inside, leaving me standing there trying to decide if I should wait or run.

I'm thinking the latter.

After all, I'll be the third woman in the past two days he's walked to the gate.

CHAPTER 7

Miles joins in on the job hunt. It's a little unnerving having him there, but in a way, it breaks the ice everywhere we go.

Because Miles is a people person. He has this easygoing way about him that instantly disarms people, and everyone seems drawn to him. Which is why I shouldn't be surprised that he also disarms me.

The next day, when I leave my apartment, he *happens* to be leaving at the same time and comes along, this time with a list of places I hadn't thought to apply. We stop for coffee and walk around our neighborhood, and he patiently waits as I fill out job applications in person or online.

Most of the managers in charge of hiring are Minnie's age, which is its own kind of humiliating, but if Miles is embarrassed for me, he doesn't say so.

This goes on for the rest of the week, and while most of our conversation is surfacy, I'm getting a sense of who he is. Sort of. And I have to admit to myself that maybe my first impression of him was a little skewed. Biased. Judgy.

Not the kind of person I want to be.

I haven't shared too many personal details, just that I'm divorced, have a daughter, and I'm originally from rural Illinois and just moved here from Colorado. Beyond that, we keep our conversation about the city, our apartment building, our neighbors.

Benign topics with zero feelings attached.

On Friday, I step out into the courtyard with a basket of fresh-baked muffins for Lorraine. I've decided this is the kind of neighbor I want to be—one who bakes for people just because.

But also? Stress baking is going to lead to stress eating if I don't start giving some of this stuff away.

Spring has descended on the city, and the tulips in the courtyard are starting to bloom. The space is like an advent calendar with secret surprises every time I step outside.

As I close the door behind me, I see Miles sitting on the stone bench in the center, talking on the phone.

I don't want to eavesdrop, but I do catch the "I love you too" as he ends the call, and I wonder if I've earned the right to a personal question or two. But when does a casual, platonic friendship earn the right to go to the next level?

And if I ask him personal questions, he's bound to ask me personal questions, and I'm not sure I'm willing to share.

He looks up and sees me, then gives me a quick wave. As I approach, his eyebrows shoot up. "More cookies?"

I tilt my head and make a face. "No, that was a onetime thing."

"Dang it."

I nod toward Lorraine's door. "Muffins for Lorraine."

"Is it her birthday?"

I frown and look down at the basket. "No, they're just because . . ."

"'Just because' muffins," he says, like he's trying the phrase on. "She'll love them. Although you *might* need a taste tester. You know, for purely academic purposes. You'd hate to hand them over and find out they're bad."

"They're not bad."

He holds out his hand and motions for me to give him one.

Slowly I relent, then sit on the stone bench beside him.

"New recipe," I say. "Let me know what you think."

He unwraps the paper around the bottom and, without hesitating, inhales half of the muffin. He closes his eyes and nods, letting out a little hum of approval.

It's embarrassing how happy it makes me to see that he likes it.

"Why haven't you applied at a bakery?" he asks around the

bite. "This is the best thing I've ever had in my life." He presses his lips together and then pops the other half of the muffin into his mouth. "I need more homemade muffins in my life."

"You're dating in the wrong age range for homemade muffins," I say dryly.

The comment is out before I can stop it.

He looks at me funny. "What?"

My muscles tense. I didn't mean to say that out loud. I really need to be better about keeping my sarcasm to myself. While I have many thoughts about Miles's dating life, none of them are actually my business. Up until now, I've done a good job of keeping them to myself.

I hold up a hand, trying not to squirm. "Sorry. Didn't mean that. Who you date is your own business."

He still looks confused. And who can blame him? I've been having multiple conversations on this topic for almost a week now, but only in my own head. He has no idea what story I wrote for him that first day.

A story I only now realize may very well be fiction.

Though . . . I can't ignore what I saw with my own eyes.

Not. Your. Business. Claire!

I scramble to change the subject. "I don't have any formal training, you know, in baking, so I'm not sure anyone would hire me."

His expression shifts. "Sometimes experience is enough, don't you think?"

I shrug. "I'm just out here winging it, really."

He smiles and reaches for another muffin. I shake my head but hold out the basket. "I'm telling Lorraine you're stealing her treats."

He leans back against the bench. "The only thing that would make this better is a cup of coffee."

He drinks his black. Usually two cups a morning. I glance over at him. "You're kind of my first friend here."

His eyebrows shoot up. "Oh? Are we actually friends now?"

"Aren't we?" I ask.

"I mean, I think so," he says. "I'm just shocked you're admitting it."

I huff out a laugh.

"With a 'how we met' story as good as ours, we *have* to be friends." He takes another bite. "You should eat one of these."

"I already had two before I walked outside."

He chuckles softly to himself and swallows his bite.

My phone simultaneously dings and vibrates on the bench between us. The noise is so loud, we both look at it.

I pick it up and silence it, but not before we both see the notification for the dating app, which happens to show up in a bright pink bubble.

"Is that . . . ?"

I hold up a hand to silence Miles, who snaps his mouth shut, obviously wanting to comment on the app.

I let out a dramatic sigh. "My daughter made me a dating profile."

He pulls out his own phone, clicks around, then says, "'Flirty, fun, and fabulous forty-something.'" He glances at me, eyebrows raised.

I snatch the phone from his hand and see my profile pulled up on the screen. "Of course you're on this app."

"It's a nice photo," he says. "You look happy."

I glance at it. "I was happy." I click the phone off and hand it back to him, aware that the air between us has shifted.

"Do you want to talk about it?" he asks. "I mean, now that we're *friends* and everything."

I half smirk but roll my eyes. "You're going to keep bringing that up, aren't you?"

"Of course."

I shake my head. "I don't want to talk about it."

"That's fair."

"But . . ." *Maybe I should?* I think the words but don't say them out loud. Maybe I should because maybe it'll get easier to say it out loud if I do.

"But . . . ?"

"I'm newly divorced," I say.

He tilts his chin upward. "Ah."

"But we've been apart for over a year."

A quiet nod.

"So . . . my daughter is trying to help me, you know, get back out there."

"I see." He turns the phone over in his hand. "Well, if I could be so bold—you know, as your *friend*—I would say that the first few dates back can be awful."

I laugh. "Sign me up."

"But—" He holds up a finger. "I think it gets easier."

I pull a face. "Yeah, you don't seem to be having any issues."

Confusion spreads across his face. "What makes you say that?"

The image of John and the silver sequins assaults my mind—and I wonder if I'll ever be able to erase it. As it is, it has a tendency to pop up when I least expect it. Like now. When John is nowhere in sight.

Or maybe there's a protective mode of my brain that's intent on reminding me of the similarities between my new neighbor and my ex.

"Two different women in two weeks?" I widen my eyes at him, letting my expression speak for itself. "I'm not stalking you, but maybe don't make it so obvious."

"Two different women . . . ?" His confused look changes to what looks like realization, then amusement. He actually has the nerve to laugh.

"That's funny?"

"I mean . . . you're assuming a lot, but it's fine," he says. "I'm not in the habit of worrying about what other people think."

I sit with that for a second, noting the pang of jealousy that he can so freely let go of someone else's opinion. If I'm wrong, he doesn't correct me, but he has no need to. It's an interesting approach.

I wonder if I could try that for myself.

"I'll just say this," he says. "I'm good with people."

"Mm-hmm." I quirk a brow in his direction. "I've noticed."

"Really?" He side-eyes me. "Thanks."

I get the feeling he could turn anything into a compliment. If only that made me like him less.

"And we're friends, so I can help with this."

"With what?"

"The dating," he says, like it's obvious. He props his ankle on his opposite knee and opens his phone. "You don't know anyone here, and I've already navigated this minefield, so let me help." He pops the last of his second muffin into his mouth. "Maybe I can even help you realize that not all guys are pigs."

I scoff.

"Some of us really are decent, Claire," he says. "I'll help you find the decent ones."

"You think you know which guys are the decent ones?" My tone is skeptical, but it does nothing to deter him.

Instead, he opens the app, clicks around for a second, then holds it up. "Let's take Hunter B. for example." He flips the phone around and swipes through a series of group photos. "What do you notice about Hunter?"

"Uh . . . I'm not sure," I say. "I don't know which one he is."

"Exactly. Is he the tall guy who just completed the 5K or the short, bald guy holding the sign?"

I shoot him a look, which he ignores. He holds the phone up

again. "And let's take a look at Chaz." His eyes jump to mine. "First of all—Chaz?"

I laugh.

"Second of all"—he glances down and reads—"'My ex was crazy' with three exclamation points."

I wince.

"There's a whole language out here, and I can teach you."

"Like a dating mentor."

"Or like a *friend*." He clicks the phone off. "You're new here. You're fresh off what I'm assuming was a bad divorce, and I want to make sure you aren't going out with guys who are only going to make it worse."

I frown. "Why would you do that?"

He squints over at me. "Let's see if I can get this right . . . You're recently divorced, haven't been on a date in, oh, maybe"—he pulls a face—"twenty years?"

Longer, but who's counting?

"You don't understand why the real-life meat market has now moved to the little device in your hands, and it feels a little"—he scrunches his nose—"gross. But also? You're mildly curious if you can figure out a way to navigate it."

I start to respond, then snap my jaw shut.

"Well, shoot. Yeah, that's exactly how I feel," I admit.

He purses his lips. "Despite what you think, I'm actually a nice guy." He leans toward me. "And I know what guys are looking for."

"I know what guys are looking for too," I say. "To sleep with as many women half their age as they can."

He whistles. "This is worse than I thought."

I cross my arms. "Experience is the best teacher."

"Not all guys are like that," he says.

"Oh, really?" My tone challenges.

"No. Some guys even want relationships." He whispers this, like it's a secret he's sharing against his better judgment.

I chuckle to myself, thinking of the irony. "Do you know any of these guys?"

He leans in slightly. "I was married once too."

"Oh." In a blink, the story I'd written about him shifts and changes. Again. What if I've pegged him all wrong?

"So, I think to start, you just need to play up your very attractive qualities," he says, unaware that I'm inwardly chastising myself for being so judgy and bitter.

My stomach swoops without my permission, but I quickly right myself. I shift the basket of muffins on my lap. "My 'very attractive qualities'?"

He shrugs. "Yeah."

"And what would those be?" Did that sound as desperate as it felt?

He leans back and studies me for a beat too long, making me feel like I'm onstage in a spotlight. Naked.

Or in a robe in the bushes.

"First of all, you're a knockout," he says simply, like it's obvious. Then he looks at me like he's judging a sculpture in a juried art show. "You could stop traffic with those eyes alone."

Warmth spreads through my body like I just swallowed a heating pad. But then I return to my senses and hold up a hand. "Oh please. Stop right there."

"What? I'm being sincere here," he says. "I don't know what your ex was thinking, but he screwed up letting you go."

My breath catches in my throat, but I'm too caught off guard to respond. I search his face, but I honestly don't think he's flirting. It's like he's stating a fact.

He thinks I'm a knockout.

And he's not looking at Colorado Claire, the made-up, perfectly groomed woman who put effort into her appearance. He's looking at the dressed-down, casual, more *natural* person I've started to become. It feels hard to believe, but I suppose we all have different ideas about what makes a person attractive.

I'm still pondering this when Miles grins. "Trust me. I can help."

I grip the handle on the basket of muffins a bit tighter. "What's in it for you?"

Without the slightest hesitation he points at my lap. "Baked goods."

"Baked goods," I repeat.

"Baked goods," he says. "I'll offer my services in exchange for baked goods." He leans in. "To be honest, I really miss homemade food."

I shake my head. "You're ridiculous."

"Probably," he says. "But at least you won't be getting back out there alone." He gives his head a quick shake. "I don't like that idea."

I frown, trying to figure out why Miles would feel protective of me and also why I kind of like that he does.

"What do you say?" He sticks out his hand in my direction, and I stare at it.

I sigh, and for reasons that will never make sense to anyone, especially me, I slip my hand into his and squeeze.

"Deal."

I feel like I should start with "Dear Diary" with the way I've been feeling lately.

It felt good to cross out "Try new foods I've never had or can't pronounce." It's gotten me on such a kick that I've tried something new at least four times in the past week.

Plov with chicken in a cast-iron kazan? Yes, please.

Oodkac breakfast from the Mogadishu restaurant? Sign me up.

Haven't tried Thai food. I heard it's super spicy, so I've been avoiding it so far.

But there is just so. Much. Deliciousness.

I never knew.

It feels good to choose. And discover.

If only someone would discover my résumé.

After a week of visiting businesses and dropping off applications—with Miles's help—I still haven't gotten one single interview.

That doesn't feel great. I feel . . . outdated. Obsolete. Past my prime.

It's so close to the feeling I get when I think about how John so easily replaced me.

Maybe a "filler" job is selling myself short, but if I can't get one of those, then how am I ever going to find one that makes me want to get out of bed in the morning?

Three coffee shops, a clothing boutique, two museums, and an art gallery.

Nothing.

On the other hand, there are other "interviews" I'm getting.

The dating app. Ugh.

Why did I give Miles access to the dating profile Minnie set up for me?

I regret that decision.

Somehow, he and Minnie connected through that app and have been discussing me and my profile.

Every time I get a new message or someone "likes" my profile, my phone dings. I'm guessing there's a setting in the app to turn off notifications, but I haven't figured that out yet. In my defense, I also haven't opened it.

Like, if I pretend it's not there, it will just go away. Like not wanting to hear the dinging can make it magically disappear.

Three guys. They picked out three guys. Together.

How is this my life?

CHAPTER 8

I have no idea what to expect from a Miles-Minnie collaboration.

I'm cautious, because if he is as . . . prolific at dating as I think he is, he'll weed out the players. Plus, Minnie will be there to keep him in line. Of that I'm sure.

Yesterday, after another unsuccessful round of dropping off my résumé at area businesses, Miles showed up to tell me he and Amelia had some good options and that he wanted to discuss them with me.

"We did a lot of vetting, and I think we cleaned out most of the messy ones," he'd said, like I was supposed to be grateful and not what I really was.

Terrified.

But then he said, "Your kid seems great."

And I had to smile because, "She is great."

"You call her Minnie," he said—a statement, not a question.

"Yes. That's her nickname. It's short for Amelia."

"How is that—"

"It just is." I cut him off because I know it's not the first nickname people think of when they hear her given name. The truth is, I wanted Minnie to be her given name, but John said no one would ever take her seriously. I suppose calling her that all these years was my tiny attempt at having some control.

"Right." He looked confused. "So what do I call her?"

I smiled. I found his uncertainty amusing. "She'll answer to either."

"But we're still strangers, so I should probably stick to Amelia." There was a hint of a question in the statement.

"Co-conspirators, more like," I said. "So Minnie would be appropriate too."

"Right." He started to walk away.

"Can you just show me these dating options now?" I'd asked. Because yes, fine. I'm curious.

He pulled a face. "Not a chance. We're going to do this right."

I still have no idea what he meant by that, but I assume he's going to make a big production out of it. Probably Minnie's influence.

She once made a PowerPoint presentation to try to convince John and I that our family needed a dog.

It was very persuasive, and two weeks later, we got Samson.

I loved that dog.

John did not.

I should've seen that as a red flag. I mean, who doesn't love dogs?

I spent the rest of yesterday filling out more online job applications and baking pecan bars just like my grandma used to make. The great thing I've discovered about being in the city is that there are lots of specific, even imported ingredients I can find here—like fresh milled flour, Lyle's Golden Syrup, and the freshest fruits in any season. I'm happy to report that Chicago is a foodie's paradise.

Baking gave me some much-needed stress relief and also the reminder that while none of these businesses seemed to want me, my grandparents always did.

Gram was a constant in my life right up until the time she passed away when Minnie was five. She never wrote her recipes down, and she rarely measured anything. I'd asked her about it once because I'd grown to like rules and structure, but she'd winked at me and said, *"It's better when you've got some skin in the game."*

John didn't even go to her funeral with me. Didn't help pack up the farmhouse for the estate sale we'd had because my grandpa was also gone by then. He knew how much she meant to me—I'd told him many times—but he claimed he had to work and couldn't get away.

I'd agreed to move to Colorado after we got married because it was practical and John needed a job, but I would've hesitated if I'd known it would mean I'd only see my grandma a few more times. I still regret that.

I realize this as I turn on my KitchenAid mixer and watch all the ingredients come together. I stand like that for a few long seconds, processing.

Baking therapy. It's cheaper than the alternative.

Were there red flags all along that I chose to ignore? After I found out about Misty (blech, even her name in my brain tastes like plastic), I tried to answer that exact question.

How could I not have known?

"You know what I always say—if she isn't paying enough attention to know about an affair, she's probably the reason he cheated in the first place."

The memory of the overheard comment in the adjacent bathroom stall smacks me in the face with the same force it did the day I heard it, once again conjuring a gnawing question—*Was the divorce my fault?*

John and I *had* been happy once . . . hadn't we?

The knock on the door is a welcome distraction that thankfully takes me out of my own head.

I open the door to find Miles standing outside holding three large brown paper bags. I hold in a smile.

"Where's your robe and your mud mask?" I ask, a callback to the night we met.

He grins. "Speaking of that night—"

"Oh, let's never speak of it again, please," I cut him off, half joking.

He chuckles. "That night you said that you hadn't ever tried Chinese food."

He remembered that?

He holds up the bags. "I figured then you probably haven't tried Indian food either."

I'm not sure how to respond, other than to wonder if he somehow broke into my apartment and read my journal.

Also, I didn't expect him to be so thoughtful.

"It seemed like trying new foods was maybe something you wanted to keep doing . . ." He shifts, and there's a flicker of doubt on his face that almost gives him away. Maybe Miles isn't the always-confident charmer he pretends to be.

"No, yeah, it is." I step aside so he can come in.

He laughs. "Spoken like a true Midwesterner. 'No, yeah' means 'yes,' so I'll take it."

He steps past me, but close enough to brush up against me as he enters. Either he doesn't notice he did it, or doesn't react, but the brief touch shoots electricity from my spine to my fingertips. Which is ridiculous. I'm not a teenager, for Pete's sake.

He sets the bags down on the counter. "This okay?"

I gather myself and manage a "No, yeah, totally," and then groan at myself for repeating the same thing I just said. "I'm kind of on a mission to try a bunch of new things."

I didn't mean to admit that, but it's out there now, and it seems that Miles is intrigued.

"Really?" he asks. "Like what?"

"Um, like"—I shrug, trying to avoid answering—"Indian food."

His eyes narrow. "Okay, fine. Don't tell me. But I already know dating is on that list, and that's why I'm here." He starts to unpack the bags on the counter, then looks up.

I'm still standing awkwardly by the door.

There's a man who isn't my husband in my apartment. A very good-looking man who has, on more than one occasion, made my insides swirl.

I suddenly feel strange about this whole scenario.

"What's wrong?" he asks. "Am I being too pushy? I do that. I tend to act like I've known people a lot longer than I have." He takes a step back from the counter like a chef on *Chopped* when time's just been called.

I walk over to the kitchen and stand on the opposite side of the counter from him. "Why are you doing this?"

He looks down at the bags on the counter. "Uh . . . because I'm hungry?"

"Not the food," I say. "The dating app. Minnie said you guys have been texting back and forth and that you're taking this very seriously. Like you're serious about making sure I go out with decent guys."

"I told you. The first date after a divorce is a serious thing," he says with an air of confident experience.

"But it's not your job to watch out for me."

He nods. "You're right. It's not."

I move my hands to indicate, *So?*

He holds my gaze for a three-count, then his eyes go wide. "Can't a guy do something nice for his friends?"

"It's just a lot of trouble to go to for someone you don't really know."

He shrugs it off. "What can I say—I'm an all-in sort of guy."

I cock my head and study him. "Judging by your relationship status, we both know that's not true."

He looks like he's about to protest, but then he smiles and doesn't say anything. He just reaches in and takes out the food, opening a few foam boxes.

It smells *amazing*.

He must notice the look on my face, because he says, "Yeah. I know. Just wait till you taste it." He glances at me. "And just so you know, you don't have to know someone well to do something nice for them."

Well, shoot.

Miles might be one of the good ones.

"Why'd you pick Chicago when you moved?" He opens a drawer, then another one, clearly looking for something. "Silverware?"

I nod toward a third drawer, which he opens, pulling out three large spoons.

"I always wanted to live here," I admit. "I've never really lived on my own."

"Never?"

I shake my head. "I went from my grandparents' farmhouse to my college dorm to John's house in Colorado."

"His name is John?"

"Yeah, why?"

He inhales a sharp breath. "Oh, just trying to get a picture of the guy."

"Think Bill Pullman from *Independence Day* mixed with a used car salesman and you'll be close."

He laughs, and I find I like the ease of the conversation.

I shake my head, thinking about things. "It's a little more intimidating than I expected."

"It's a lot," he says. "I get it."

And somehow, I think he really does.

"I remember how it felt to start over," he says. "It felt . . . oddly unfamiliar and familiar at the same time. Like 'I should know how to do this' but also, I had no clue."

He pops open the last lid. "Maybe that's part of it. Like, I feel like I might be able to help you acclimate a little easier having been through it myself."

It strikes me then that even though we are very different, Miles might really make a decent friend.

Which is why I shake the heaviness away and force myself to lighten the mood. "Okay then, let's hear it. Who do you and Minnie think I should go out with? And where is he taking me?"

"We'll get to that. But first, let's eat."

"Oh, they labeled everything," I say, noticing that Miles has left each labeled lid near the dish, arranging everything neatly as if we're at a potluck.

"I asked them to," he says. "I figured you'd want to know what to order next time, if you like it."

The thoughtfulness is like a pinprick to my heart. It's unexpected, and it catches me off guard.

When I don't respond, he looks up. "What?" He frowns.

"Nothing, it's just . . . you're being really nice."

He laughs. "It's concerning that this surprises you."

"Maybe I'm just not used to it."

He holds my gaze for a beat, but I have to look away. Because it's another admission I didn't mean to make. And one that tells him a little more about me than I want it to.

He picks up a plate and hands it to me. "After you."

I load up a plate—naan, samosa, bhel puri, keema matar, along with a small bowl of something called dal—like lentil soup, maybe?—and we sit down on the floor in the living room, food on the coffee table, laptop between us.

"I can't believe you've been texting my daughter about my love life," I say, my mouth full of naan.

"She's hilarious," he says. "And she loves you like crazy."

"She is. And I love her too." I smile. "Do you have kids?"

"I've got two daughters," he says. "Zoey and Ava. Pretty much grown now. They don't need me for anything until a sink breaks or they forget to get the oil changed in their cars." He laughs. "And stop changing the subject."

"Was it that obvious?" I grin. "This dating app is not my favorite topic."

"I promised I wouldn't let your first date be a dud, so—" He touches a key on the laptop and it comes to life.

"Bachelor number one," he says, affecting a game-show announcer voice. "Meet Tom. Tom is a data analyst at a software engineering company."

"Hmm. I don't think I could hold a conversation with Tom."

"You didn't let me finish."

"Sorry." I nod. "Please continue."

"Tom loves to play racquetball, go to museums, and play *Pokémon GO*."

I stare at him. "Please tell me this is not the best you have for me."

He smirks. "You actually have lots of interest on this app."

"I do?" My eyes go wide.

"You can't be surprised," he says.

"I can't?"

"I mean, you know what you look like." When he smiles, the tiniest lines crease at the edges of his eyes, and somehow they make him even handsomer.

I shove another bite in my mouth because, again, I don't know how to respond. John wasn't the complimenting type. If he thought I was pretty, he rarely said so, and I just assumed that's how it was after you'd been together awhile.

I never dared to wonder because I had a whole lot to be thankful for.

"You really didn't look at all?"

I chew the bite, then take a drink. "No. If I had, I would've figured out how to mute the notifications." I take a bite of something that had been labeled *biryani*, a rice dish with flavors so deep and complex, I have to pause to give it my full attention. "You've got to be kidding me. This is amazing."

"Have you tried the butter chicken?" He scoops up a bite on his fork and holds it out in my direction. It's an innocent yet oddly provocative move, and after I swallow my bite, I meet his eyes.

He nods toward the fork, paused in the air between us, and I lean in while he feeds it to me. The creamy flavors of the tomato curry hit my taste buds, and I cover my mouth, nodding at Miles as if to communicate, *Oh yeah, this is really good.*

"Right?" he says, a satisfied smile on his face. Then he's back at the computer. He clicks a button and another photo fills the screen. "This is Henry. Henry is an investment banker, which means he's probably very rich—or on cocaine—"

I laugh so hard I almost spit out the rice.

"Okay, let's stay positive and say he's rich." He angles his head, studying me. "I get the sense you don't care about that, though."

I take a sip of wine. "I don't. John was . . ." I catch myself. I really don't want to talk about John, and I wish he would stop taking up so much real estate in my mind. "Money is fine, but I'd rather be with someone I can trust." I look over and find Miles watching me like he's collecting these tiny personal details I share in bits and pieces.

Miles turns his attention back to the computer. "Okay, well, Henry *looks* trustworthy, but you know, time will tell. No immediate red flags is all I can promise."

I take another bite as he clicks over to a third photo. The man on the screen looks perfectly nice, if a little bland. If I were to describe him to a sketch artist, I'd say, *"A little round with a receding hairline and very dad-like features. A rounded nose and eyes that seem kind and close together. His ears stick out a little more than average, and he's clean shaven."*

Then I realize that description would have the sketch artist drawing practically every character from the Guess Who? kids' game Minnie used to love to play.

"This is Roger," he says. "My personal favorite for your first date."

"Your favorite? Why?" I frown. Henry was the best-looking option, not Roger, but in my experience, men with money are used to getting whatever they want.

"He seems like a decent guy," he says. "He's divorced with two kids—both in college—and he's on staff with a minor league hockey team, volunteers for a youth hockey league . . . You know, decent."

"I don't know anything about hockey," I say.

"You don't *have* to know anything about hockey," he says. "But maybe he could teach you."

I shrug noncommittally.

"Look, Claire, this is just your first date back," he says. "You don't want to date anyone who might be a real contender."

"Why not?" I ask.

He turns to me. "You want to rush back into a serious relationship without seeing what's out there?" One could argue that I already did that once. Sometimes, in hindsight, I wonder if I was so taken with John in those early days because I so desperately wanted independence. Not because I needed out from my grandparents' rules, but because I didn't want to be a burden to them for a single second longer than I already had been.

John had a plan, and when he started to include me in it, I bought in. We were going to work at his father's ad agency until we could take it over. It sounded like a dream.

If Minnie hadn't come along so early, maybe I would've realized how incompatible we were, but she did come along, and our plan shifted into overdrive. I don't regret it, but I do wonder if Miles is right—I should take all of this slow.

I'm not that girl anymore.

I narrow my eyes. "Is that what *you're* doing? Seeing what's out there?"

"No," he says matter-of-factly. "I have a pretty good idea of what's out there. But I'm different."

I dab the corners of my mouth with my napkin. "How so?"

"Because I'm never getting married again," he says simply. Again, like he's stating a fact.

"Never?"

"Nope."

"Ever?"

"Been there. Don't need to do it again."

"Interesting."

He scoops up a bite of butter chicken and shovels it into his mouth. "It's really not. I had something, and then I didn't. I'm not interested in that again. I'm perfectly content to date women I have no intention of marrying."

"Meanwhile, you're leaving a trail of brokenhearted women in your wake," I conclude, fascinated by his take on relationships, given that it's so different from mine.

"No, they know."

I frown in disbelief. "You tell them this before you go out with them?"

"Yeah. I'm pretty up front about it. It's in my profile." He clicks around on the computer and pulls up an image that would definitely make me stop scrolling.

MILES—40S, LANDSCAPE ARCHITECT

Nice guy looking to have fun.
No strings. No baggage. No drama.

I pull a face. "And women go for this?"

He gives me an amused shrug. "I do okay."

"They probably think they can change you," I say, rolling my eyes as I focus all my attention on my plate.

"What?"

"Nothing, it's just—"

"It's just . . . ?"

"You were married once," I say. "So obviously you're a guy who sees the benefit of a relationship—"

"But I'm also a guy who sees that relationships eventually end."

"Not all relationships," I say. "My grandparents were together for sixty years."

His eyebrows shoot up. "No way."

"Yeah," I say, sadness washing over me at the realization that if they were still here, they'd be so disappointed that my marriage ended. I feel like such a failure.

"It's a nice sentiment, but it's not reality for most people," he says.

I meet his eyes. "That's because too many people look at other people like they're disposable. The apps make that worse. You swipe through people the same way you shop for a new winter coat."

He goes still and then nods slowly. "Yeah, I think you're right."

I go back to eating, unsure how the conversation led us here. "I know I'm still a little bitter about the way my marriage ended." I look up at him. "But I don't want to get so jaded that I swear off marriage forever. I have to believe there's someone out there who is honest and kind and good." I pause, then add, "And not a total jerkface."

"All right," he says, chuckling softly. "I hear you. But you won't find him if you don't see what's out there." He clicks off his profile and back to Roger's. "Plus, I have the perfect not-boring date idea for you and Roger."

That night, while I'm lying in bed, I open the Matched app on my phone. I ignore my messages, and for reasons I hope to never have to explain, I navigate to Miles's profile.

I open the photo and stare at it. He has a kindness about him. Perfect blend of well-groomed meets messy hair and just the right amount of stubble, with sandy-blond hair and genuinely piercing eyes that crinkle at the corners when he smiles.

But then my eyes find the words he's written under the photo, and I reread them again in hopes they'll bring me back to reality.

Nice guy looking to have fun.

Judging by who I've seen him with, a forty-something divorcée is the opposite of what he's looking for.

I'm definitely a "swipe left."

* * *

Claire: Guess who got a job!

Minnie: No way!

Claire: <insert photo of me in my barista hat and apron>

Minnie: Wait. You're working at a coffee shop?

Claire: Yes! I just got done with orientation.

I think the girl training me is twelve. 😆

Minnie: Are you having an identity crisis?

Claire: No! I'm giving myself the summer to have a fun job until I figure out what I want to do with the rest of my life.

Minnie: I give it a week.

Claire: What? Why? I'll be great at this!

Minnie: You're WAY too used to being in charge. You are SO not going to be okay taking orders from teenagers and serving coffee to professional people going off to do jobs you could do in your sleep.

Claire: What happened to Cheerleader Minnie?

The girl who tells me I can do anything?

Minnie: She's still here. She just knows you can do more than make coffee.

Claire: Well, she will also be happy to know I also have my first date tonight.

Minnie: WITH ROGER, WOO-HOO

Miles told me.

Claire: He did?

Minnie: 👍

Can we talk about Miles for a second?

Claire: No.

Minnie: Why don't you date him?

Claire: Miles is not interested in a relationship.

He's playing the field, dating like three women who are all half his age at the same time.

Minnie: Huh.

Claire: Huh, what?

Minnie: He just doesn't seem like the type.

CHAPTER 9

The following Saturday morning, I wake up with what feels like a flock of geese in my belly.

And it feels like they're fighting with each other.

Today, I'm going on my first date in twenty-five years.

With Roger.

His name is Roger.

Before he left last weekend, Miles told me to think of Roger as "practice," which felt very strange. And maybe a little wrong. But then he explained.

"You're not going to get everything right the first time," he'd said. *"Give yourself some grace to feel things out."*

I'm not sure I want to feel things out with Roger.

Miles, in all his vast wisdom, told me that the more practice I get, the easier this whole "going out with strangers on the internet" thing will become.

I don't have high hopes.

When I started dating—approximately a million years ago—it was different. You'd see a guy in class, maybe, or at a frat party or on campus. You'd make eye contact. Talk. Exchange numbers. Go to dinner. Study together. Make out in the library. Get engaged. Get married. Get pregnant. (Not in that order for some of us . . .)

Blink and twenty years later find out he's in love with someone else.

Huh. Maybe Miles is onto something, never wanting to do any of this again.

Suddenly, I don't want to do any of it either.

I pick up my phone to text Miles that I'm backing out when a knock on my door interrupts my train of thought.

I open it, phone in hand, and find him standing there.

"You're thinking about backing out, aren't you?"

I frown and look at my phone. "How did you know that?"

"I'm a little bit psychic," he says. "Or . . . you're a little bit predictable."

I groan, roll my eyes, and walk back inside. "I don't want to do this anymore. I have no interest in meeting Roger or anyone else."

He holds up his hands, making a T shape. Time-out.

I fold my arms like I've been put on the naughty mat.

"Let's go get coffee," he says.

"I just made coffee," I grumble.

"Oh, come on. The fresh air will do you good," he says. "My treat."

I only stare.

One of his eyebrows rises so slightly I almost miss it.

I huff out a long grunty breath like a toddler who does *not* want to obey. "Fine." I pull on my shoes, grab my jacket, and step outside.

I start to walk toward the front gate when Miles puts a hand on my arm. "Just wait a second."

I go still. "What am I waiting for?"

"Peace."

I glare at him. "If you tell me to take a deep, cleansing breath, I'm going back inside."

"No," he says. "Nothing so hooty."

I stifle a laugh. "Hooty?"

"Quiet. Don't interrupt."

I clamp it down.

"Just . . . wait. Don't start your day in a panic. You're overthinking this. Right now, just take a second. Enjoy the sunshine and the warmth. We just survived a brutal winter, and look at us—we're still here."

"I don't know what you're talking about. Winter in Colorado was really mild this year."

Now he rolls his eyes. "You know what I mean."

I inhale an exaggerated breath, then huff it out dramatically. "Fine."

"There you go," he says in a slow, condescending tone.

I shoot him a look and take another breath.

Well, dang it.

It's working. The sun feels good. The air is crisp. The world settles.

Pfft. Whatever.

I start walking. "Can you at least tell me what the date is?" I ask, because he and Minnie conspired about that too. Who knows what they've said to Roger. "Also, does Roger know I haven't been the one messaging him?"

"You didn't read the chat?"

"I try not to open the app." I shrug over at him.

"But . . . how will . . . you didn't even . . ." He starts and stops three times. Then, clapping his hands and rubbing them together, he says, "You know what? It's great. It'll all work out. And be fun. Promise."

We reach the end of the block, and I notice how busy it is. Just like the first time I left my apartment to try to eat somewhere by myself—there are couples pushing strollers, people walking dogs, a man jogging, a woman biking, and groups of friends doing the kinds of things people do in the city on a Saturday morning. Shopping. Eating. Drinking coffee.

I glance over at Miles and find him watching me. "What?"

"Nothing, you just seem really engrossed in, you know"—he waves a hand out in front of him—"everything."

The light changes and I step out into the street. "Sometimes I just have to take it all in. I still can't really believe I live here."

"It's brave what you did," he says.

"Brave. Ha. It was self-preservation," I say, not wanting to get into all the reasons I didn't feel like I could show my face back in Colorado.

"It was still brave," he offers. "Don't downplay that."

I try to absorb the words, but it's hard to accept compliments. I shrug. "I didn't feel like I had a choice."

"I get that. If my ex hadn't moved to Arizona after our divorce, I would've been tempted to leave the city," he says. "Or the country."

I smile.

"Work would've made it hard, though."

I know from our past conversations that Miles is a landscape architect who owns his own firm. "Your business ties you here."

"Good thing I love this place," he says.

He slows as we reach a cute coffee shop on the corner of the next block. He opens the door for me, and I step inside. I look around at the space—sleek and modern, exactly like you'd expect a coffee shop in the city to look.

"Have you tried this place before?" I ask.

He nods as we get in line. "The coffee is amazing, but their pastries don't hold a candle to those pecan things you made the other night."

My cheeks flush at the comment, even though they absolutely shouldn't. He's complimenting my pecan bars, for Pete's sake. "Oh, please."

"I'm serious," he says. "You have yet to bake something that I don't love."

I ignore him as I step forward and order an oat milk latte. Miles orders a black coffee and pays for both of our drinks. We move to the end of the counter, and there's a beat of silence as my gaze lands on a young couple in the corner. "What do you think? First love?"

He follows my gaze and squints, clearly deep in thought. "Maybe. Or maybe . . . he's in the military. Leaving tomorrow to serve overseas."

"They've spent one bliss-filled week ignoring the world and falling in love . . ."

"And she's going to ghost him in three months when she meets someone else at a club."

I frown. "Whoa. That took a dark turn. She would at least let him down easy."

He shakes his head. "Nah, she'd ghost him."

"Maybe he isn't actually in the military at all," I counter. "Maybe he says he is to get girls to fall for him, spends a few nights with them, promises he'll stay in touch, then never talks to them again. He's used a fake identity so she can't track him down, and he's already moved on to his next victim."

Miles looks at me, eyes wide. "Now who's the dark one?"

Our drinks appear on the counter, and I grab them both, handing Miles his cup of coffee and turning to walk back outside.

He starts off in the opposite direction of our apartments, but I don't ask why. I get the sense that we're out for a morning stroll and that maybe he's going to share a little information about my date. But minutes go by, and Miles hasn't said a word, seemingly content to soak up the sunshine and the scenes of the city where we both live.

Up ahead, I can see Lake Michigan, and a few minutes later we're walking toward the water.

"Have you been down here yet?" he asks. "By the lake?"

I shake my head, drinking in the view. I understand why they call Chicago the "Third Coast." If I didn't know I was looking at a lake, I could easily confuse this with the ocean.

The skyline stretches all the way up the shoreline as traffic weaves through the city streets, creating an energetic backdrop of noise. Miles leads the way over to a wide sidewalk that's situated next to the lake, and I see a giant shoal of huge boulders stretching out into the water like a dock or a natural sidewalk. There are two boys way out on the end, one looking like he's trying to pose *Karate Kid*–style while the other takes his picture.

"I want to walk out there," I say absently.

"On the groyne?"

I stop. "The what?"

He laughs through a wince. "In landscaping, you learn a lot of weird names for things. It's called a groyne—it breaks waves and blocks sediment, extends the life of the beach actually."

I pretend to push up fake glasses on my nose, then hold up one finger. "Um, *actually*, it's called a *groyne* . . ."

"You know what they say about nerds," he says. "We'll rule the world."

"I've never heard anyone say that." I toss him a smile.

Am I flirting? What am I doing?

"So? You want to?" He nods toward the groyne.

I look out at the rocks. "Let's do it."

We walk out over the sand, and when we reach the boulders, Miles steps up first, then reaches a hand out to help me up. I accept his help, aware of how his strong hand wraps around mine, his other on my arm just above the elbow, steadying me as I take a step.

I take a second to get my footing, and when Miles doesn't let go of my hand right away, my skin prickles.

I take a step onto another large flat boulder, and he holds up his other hand as if to say, *You got it?* then lets go of me.

He steps, one stone at a time, alongside me as I slowly start out on the misshapen, unsteady boulders, heading a bit farther toward the lake. I smile as an older couple holding hands passes by, headed back to the shore.

"See?" I say, a bit of bite in my voice. "They made it. What's their secret?"

Miles tosses me a look, but his tone is light. "You have no idea what their story is. They could've met yesterday."

"True." I shrug. "I guess I just wish my story were different."

"I don't," he says without hesitation.

"What? Why?"

He looks at me, right in the eyes. "Because if your story were different, you and I wouldn't be on these rocks."

My breath hitches, but I—hopefully—catch myself before giving away that my stomach just did a cartwheel.

"And who knows?" He laughs. "Maybe you'll get lucky, and Roger will turn out to be the real thing."

I frown. "You told me I didn't want the real thing my first time out."

He bends over and picks up a large oblong stone, then tosses it out into the water with a big *kerplunk*.

"Let's just hope your date doesn't go like *that*," he quips.

I laugh and absently think that if my date with Roger goes anything like this impromptu walk, I won't be sad.

CHAPTER 10

I'm on a date.

Well, technically not yet, because he's not here, but still.

It's hours after my walk with Miles, and I'm on a date.

The thought sits sideways in my mind, and I try not to linger there. It's the kind of thing that's better if I just do it, like jumping into a cold lake. If you think too much about it, you're bound to chicken out.

I'm wearing ankle-length, slightly flared jeans, my favorite neutral Nike tennis shoes, a simple black top, and a khaki-colored trench coat, and I'm standing on the Ogden Slip dock on the Chicago River near Robert's Pizza waiting to meet a man named Roger.

Who I'm hoping won't be a *kerplunk*.

I'm not pre-judging him, but when I got home from my walk, I read the messages between Roger and Miles/Minnie-pretending-to-be-me. I wondered if this counted as some twisted version of catfishing but decided that since I'd signed off on the communication, it's okay.

Mostly because the entire exchange started with Miles/Minnie writing: **I prefer to get to know each other in real life rather than over text messaging. Would you like to get together Saturday?**

Forward, but hey, it worked.

It meant that Roger didn't get any false information about me. It also meant that I know almost nothing about Roger except that he's recently divorced, has two daughters, and included in his profile lots of pictures of himself with different hockey players that might be impressive if I had any idea who they were.

Now, as I shift my weight back and forth on the riverwalk, stopped near a sandwich board sign with the menu for Robert's Pizza handwritten on it, I pull out my phone to look at the photo one more time. Roger isn't the kind of guy who would turn a woman's head. But in my experience, sometimes those are the men most worth knowing.

Like Miles said—this is just practice.

I blow out a held breath and look around the riverwalk. There are boats in the water and a few diners willing to brave the chilly spring weather scattered around the tables and chairs on the restaurant's outdoor patio.

I glance at my watch. The tour starts at 1:30 p.m. and it's 1:29. I scan the area again, wondering if maybe I got stood up. I pull out my phone and see a text from Minnie:

Minnie: Date day!! Let me know how it goes.

I text back:

Claire: If he doesn't show up in the next sixty seconds, he's late, and you know how I feel about people who are late.

"Claire?"

I look up and find Roger standing in front of me. He's wearing a brightly colored Hawaiian print shirt, khaki pants, and white tennis shoes with the thickest soles I've ever seen.

"Uh, yes, I'm Claire," I say. "Roger?"

He gives me a little bow. "At your service."

My eyes dart around the riverwalk, and I laugh to myself, but when Roger stands up from his bow he stumbles, and I reach out a hand to steady him.

"Oopsie," he says. "Lost my footing there."

Oopsie?

"I think the tour is about to start," I say. "Should we go in?"

"Yes. I'm starving!" He starts walking, and I have to jog a few steps to catch up. When we reach the door, he opens it and walks in, letting it shut halfway on me.

It's fine. Maybe he's not into stereotypical gender roles. I'm perfectly capable of opening my own door.

Inside, I pause in the doorway to look around. The brick walls and wood-planked ceiling are a modern industrial style. Small tables line the window looking out over the river, and there's a long bar with tall, wood-backed chairs running parallel to them.

Roger is standing near the hostess stand. He looks flushed and a little sweaty, and he doesn't say anything to the young woman at the stand.

I frown. "Are you okay?"

He scrunches his face. "I might've had a little too much to drink before I left," he says through gritted teeth, holding up his thumb and forefinger on the word *little*.

I lean in closer. "Are you . . . *drunk*?"

He shakes his head. "No. *Pssh.* What? Noooo, not drunk. Just needed a tiny bit of liquid courage." He reaches out and his beefy hand lands on my shoulder. "I haven't done this in a really long time, and you're just so pretty."

My eyes dart over to the hostess, who gives me a stunned but sympathetic look.

I glance back at him. I guess I understand where he's coming from. Sort of. But this was an ill-advised way to handle the nerves.

"I'm fine." Roger waves me—and what I assume is the double of me that he's seeing right now—off. "Cup of coffee, and I'll be fine."

"Are you sure?" I ask. "We can reschedule this." *Or not.*

"No! No, no, no, we already got the tickets, and you look hungry, so—" He slams a hand down on the hostess stand, and I flinch.

"We're here for the tour!" he says, much louder than necessary.

He gives a thumbs-up to the woman behind the stand, who is not three feet from us.

"Uh, sure, follow me," the woman says.

She leads us through the restaurant, back to a section where several small tables have been pushed together to form one long one. A group of people are already seated, and a tall, lanky guy stands to greet us when we walk in.

"Hey, guys! Here for the tour?" he asks.

I look over at Roger. He's blinking so slowly I wonder if he's trying to stay awake.

I look at the man and plaster on a smile. "Yes. Here for the tour."

"Great, we're just about to start." He motions for us to sit down, and when we do, Roger nearly misses the chair. He catches himself—barely—and I wince, fire rushing to my cheeks.

I grit my teeth. Minnie is my flesh and blood, so I won't kill her. But Miles?

Miles is getting pushed off the rocks.

I resist the urge to tell everyone at the table that this is a first date and this man is essentially a stranger to me. Instead, I give the tour host my full attention.

"Welcome, everybody! My name is James, and I'm your host for the very best walking pizza tour in Chicago. I'm going to tell you a little about the history of different pizza places here in the city," James says. "You'll get to taste four of my favorite Chicago pizzas in four very distinct styles, starting with the brick oven, thin-crust artisan pizza of Robert's."

As if this is a play they've rehearsed and that was their cue, the waitstaff appears with several pizzas, which they set on the tables in front of the group.

I glance over at Roger, whose chin is resting on his hand, and I know there is no way this man is going to make it walking around the city for three and a half hours.

I lean across the table. I have to whisper-shout his name twice to get his full attention. "Roger. *Roger*? Are you sure you're—"

He burps and covers his mouth, and the woman next to him shoots me a look. I try to apologize to her with my eyes, when Roger picks up a plate and hands it to her. "Hey, can you get me two slices of that one down there? The one with everything?" He motions to a pizza at the other end of the table.

The woman slowly takes the plate, glances at me, and I look away, pinching the bridge of my nose.

All I hear on a loop in my mind is *kerplunk*.

Roger looks at me. "Aw, c'mon, sweetie. Don't tell me you're one of those women who doesn't eat."

I feel like an animal trapped in a corner.

"No, I eat," I say, trying to stay as sweet as possible.

He looks at my plate. "Then why is your plate empty?"

"I was waiting for other people to get their food," I say, biting back the words, *which is the polite thing to do.*

The woman next to him hands his plate back, and he doesn't say thank you. "You know what they say, 'God helps those who help themselves.'"

God never said that, I think to myself.

I draw in a breath as Roger takes a huge bite of pizza. The waitress comes around with water, and he grabs her arm. "Can I get a beer? Is that allowed?"

"Of course, sir," she says. "We have several beers on tap—"

He cuts her off with a loud "Nah—Bud in the bottle is fine."

I take a slow, steadying breath and take a slice of pizza from the pan and set it on my plate.

"So," Roger says. "You're divorced."

I'm mid-bite when he says this—not quietly—and I cough a little as I chew. "Uh, yes. I am."

"Let me guess. He found someone better. Ain't that always the way?" The waitress hands Roger his bottle of beer, and I really wish she didn't. The last thing this man needs is more alcohol.

"Uh . . . your profile said you work with a hockey team?" I say, desperate to change the subject. "What do you do with them?"

He looks at me condescendingly and mutters, "Oh, babe, it's not anything you'd understand," he says, mouth full. "I'm divorced too. Married for nineteen years. She kicked me out last month."

Last month?! This guy should not be dating if his marriage just ended a month ago.

"Said she was tired of doing everything alone." He scoffs. A chunk of pizza falls out of his mouth. "Kept talking about socks or something on the bathroom floor, dishes in the sink, who knows. Like, I work all day. Right? And I gotta come home to that? Nah. Better off. More fish in the sea, right?"

He drops the half-eaten slice of pizza onto his plate. "Excuse me, Eileen, if I forget to pick up my socks once in a while. I'm forgetful. She knows that."

And then—because just when you think a date can't get worse, it absolutely will—Roger starts crying.

The other people at the table stare at him. James stares at him. I stare at him.

And Roger starts sobbing.

He's quiet at first, muttering something about how he "promised to do better if she'd just take me back and let me try again." But the sobs get progressively louder.

"Roger, maybe we should go outside for a minute," I say. "Just until you, uh, get ahold of yourself?"

He covers his face with his hands, shoulders shaking, and lets out what I'd call a wail.

The others at the table are either looking away, like they don't want to impose on this private moment Roger's having—or looking at me, like *I'm* supposed to do something.

There's just one problem. I have no idea what to do. I don't know this man.

I lean a little closer, and in my kindest, most nurturing voice, I say, "Hey, Roger, why don't we take a little time-out?"

It's like I'm negotiating with a toddler.

In response, Roger looks at me. "She's dating a guy named Geoff. Did I tell you that? Plus he spells it like the stupid way with a *G*! Is your name Jeff or Gee-off?! What does *Gee-off* have that I don't have?"

I'm imagining so many things . . .

"I don't know," I say, realizing there's no way I can sit here and keep eating while he's having a literal meltdown at the table.

There's a long, awkward pause. James moves in his seat, and I wonder if he's worried how the other people on the tour are going to review this experience.

Finally, I shift into a different gear, clap my hands in front of Roger, and say, "Okay, Roger. That's enough. It's time to get it together. Come on. Time to get your big boy pants on."

He stops moaning and looks at me. His cheeks are stained with tears, truly the epitome of pathetic. He drags the back of his hand across his face, wiping his nose.

I think of how unsuitable I was for company during the first few months after John moved out, and I'm overcome with sympathy for him.

"We're going to stand up and walk outside. I'm going to call you an Uber, and you're going to go home and sleep this off." I stand up, fully aware that everyone is watching. "Let's go."

Miraculously, he does exactly what I say, and a few minutes later we're standing on the street waiting for a driver named Sheila to roll up in a black Toyota Camry.

While we wait, a still teary Roger looks dejected and slightly embarrassed.

"Look," I say. "You shouldn't be dating right now."

"But she's dating—"

"Right," I say. "But you need to give yourself some time to get over this. Hang out with friends. Play video games. Watch dumb movies. Eat junk food."

"Does that really help?"

"Absolutely not."

He looks up and chuckles.

"You'll feel like crap," I say honestly. "But eventually, you'll get tired of feeling like crap. And then maybe you can figure out how to make yourself better. Get a hobby. Find some friends. Change your life."

He looks sheepish.

The irony of me giving this pep talk is not lost on me.

The black car pulls up, and I open the back door and help him pile in.

"I'm really sorry, Kate," he says.

I nod ruefully. It's a perfect end to this date.

"It's Claire."

"Oh, right." He nods. "Claire. I'm sorry, *Claire.*" He over-enunciates my name, then his eyes flutter closed.

"Roger," I say, one hand poised on the door.

He looks at me.

"For heaven's sake, pick up your socks."

* * *

Claire: NEVER AGAIN.

Minnie: Oh no! What happened with Roger?

Claire: You don't want to know.

Minnie: I absolutely do.

Claire: He showed up drunk and sobbed at the table. About his ex.

Minnie: He WHAT??

Claire: I called him an Uber after twenty minutes and told him to pick up his socks.

Minnie: His socks?

Claire: Long story.

Minnie: OH NO! Okay, I'll confer with Miles. We'll do better next time.

Claire: See screenshot of above text with NEVER AGAIN circled in red.

Minnie: Ignoring you.

I'm really bummed you didn't get to do the walking pizza tour.

Claire: Oh no, I did the tour.

I went back inside, and everyone at the table applauded me for handling a bad first date like a boss.

Minnie: Yoooo! Go Mom!

Claire: And we all swapped bad first date stories and bad breakup stories, and it ended up being a really fun day.

I got to walk around downtown Chicago and made some notes about things I want to come back and see later.

WITHOUT A DATE.

Minnie: So what's the verdict on the pizza?

Claire: Oh. Deep dish all the way.

Minnie: That's the correct choice.

We'll eat it together when I'm back from England.

Claire: Can't wait. Xoxo

CHAPTER 11

Sunday morning, I try to sleep in.

But the loud knocking on my door won't let me.

I throw off the covers, pull on a giant oversized Colorado State hoodie over my shorts, plod downstairs, open the door, and glare at Miles.

His eyes go wide. "I can't believe you didn't call and give me the first date breakdown. I waited up."

I groan and walk over to the kitchen. I start a pot of coffee and pull out the lemon blueberry streusel cake I baked yesterday after I got home from my ill-fated date.

A few hours later, I got a message from Roger on the app. It was a photo of him on the couch, holding a pint of ice cream in one hand and making a thumbs-up with the other, and it made me smile.

It gave me a great first date horror story, and in the end, maybe some good will come of it. Maybe Roger will start to heal.

After I returned to the group, I found myself making excuses for poor Roger. After all, I've made some pretty stupid public mistakes myself. We all agreed to cut him a little slack, then a woman named Trish told the entire group her worst breakup horror story. Which led to a guy named Mike sharing his story on the way to the next pizza place, and by the time the tour ended, we'd all chimed in.

I even shared the fountain story—but left out the night of the silver sequins. Some wounds are still a little too raw. Somehow, it brought us all together.

The pain of rejection is a universal one.

"So?" Miles sits on the tall stool on the opposite side of my counter. "How was it?"

While I go over the events of the date, I cut a slice of cake, put it on a small plate, and slide it over to Miles without even asking if he wants it. It's payment, after all. A deal's a deal.

Then I serve myself a piece and grab two forks. "It was quite the unforgettable first postdivorce date," I say when the coffee finishes brewing.

"Geez, Claire, I'm so sorry," Miles says. "He seemed more stable than that."

"I think he was just sad," I say sympathetically. "And it ended up being fine. I had a great time once Roger was gone."

At that, Miles laughs. "Single in the city, huh?"

I shrug. "Things could be worse than that, I suppose."

"We'll do better next time."

"What about you?" I ask. "I'm sure you didn't stay home alone last night."

"Uh, no," he says. "I went out with a lovely woman named Hailey."

"Blond?" I quip.

"Redhead."

"Ooh . . ."

"Took her home early. She was kind of . . ." He pulls a face. "She talked a lot about TikTok."

"How old is this woman?" I pin him with a glare.

"You made this cake?" He makes a show of chewing his bite.

"Smooth change of subject," I say with a pointed roll of my eyes. "And yes, I made it. It was my grandpa's favorite. I used to make it for him every Saturday night."

"You two were close," he says. A statement, not a question.

I nod. "He and my gram. They raised me."

"And your parents?" Miles asks, and it occurs to me that he

might be the first person I've met in a long time who seems more interested in getting to know me than finding reasons to criticize me.

"Uh, my mother was in prison when she had me," I say plainly. "Never knew my dad."

I find it's easier to state those two things outright. Again, like jumping into a cold lake. Best not to emotionally connect to it—it's just a minor detail about my past.

His eyebrows shoot up, and he stops chewing. "Oh! Um . . ."

I nod. "Crazy, right?"

He swallows. "That's heavy."

I shrug. "It's in the past. It was *always* in the past. Until I met John."

"The ex," Miles says.

"Yep." I pause, thinking about him for a brief second. I feel the familiar hurt and anger start to bubble, so I move on. "His family is really wealthy, like, *really* wealthy, and when they found out about my mom . . . it was an issue."

"But you got married anyway?" He takes a drink. "He must've really loved you."

"I was pregnant."

"Oh."

There's a quiet pause, and I fill it by taking a drink of coffee. It feels good to be open about my past. It is what it is, and I can't change it. If it turns people off, then I suppose they aren't my people.

But I'll never find my people if I'm pretending to be someone I'm not. I learned that the hard way. I'm not sure if it was a conscious decision to adopt this attitude or if it just happened when I opened the door to this new life, but here we are.

"Is your mom still . . . ?" He trails off, like he's not sure how to ask such a personal question, which is appropriate because I'm really not sure how to answer it.

I shrug. "We lost touch. After my grandparents died, it seemed like any hope of reconnecting died too."

The lines in his forehead deepen in a frown. "That's a lot—"

"I'm okay, really," I say. "I had two loving parental figures in my life. They just had more gray hair than my friends' parents." I smile, hoping my nonchalance puts Miles at ease.

His return smile seems tentative.

"So," I say, ready to change the subject. "Since we're dissecting my dates, I feel it's only right we also dissect yours."

"Uh, pass."

"No, sorry," I say. "You don't get off that easy. Plus, I might be able to help you too, you know."

"Nah, I'm good," he says. "My system is working really well."

I tilt my head and look at him. "Tell me you didn't just say you have a *system*."

He tips his fork at me. "Got it down to a science."

I squint at him, trying to decide if he's really as shallow as he wants me to think he is. "Don't you get lonely?"

"I'm hardly ever alone," he says.

I wince.

"Okay, not like *that*. I'm not out there sleeping with anyone who has a pulse. I just like to go out. Meet people. See the city." He takes another bite. "Did you hear me when I said this cake is amazing?"

I wave him off. "It's just lemon cake."

"Claire," he says seriously.

"Miles."

"It's not just lemon cake. It's like . . . an experience."

I scoff.

"No, really," he continues. "It's like I've had this exact thing before, but not since I was a kid. This cake?" He points to it with his fork. "This literally transports me back to summers in my backyard. We'd leave in the morning, play in the neighborhood all day, and my parents would have *no* clue where we were or what we were doing. We didn't come back home until the streetlights came on, and there'd be a home-cooked meal and *this cake*. Sometimes my mom would let us spread a big blanket on the trampoline and eat dinner there. Then my brother and I would swat lightning bugs with one of those big plastic Wiffle ball bats." He takes another bite.

I can't help but smile. "Sounds perfect. Except for the bug killing." I pause. "Only . . . we'd make jewelry out of them, so I can't really criticize." I look at him. "You grew up in a small town too?"

He nods. "It's about two hours from here." A pause. "Nothing quite like summer in a small town." He picks up the coffee mug. "I feel sort of bad for people who only ever lived in the city. They don't have a clue what they're missing."

I look down at my half-eaten cake, thinking about all the ways I miss my own small-town life.

It was simple. Not frivolous. Nothing we owned was new, or fancy, or brand name. And that old farmhouse was all I knew of home.

Still, I always dreamed of living in Chicago and making Gram proud. After the way my mother disappointed her, I wanted to give her that.

I still do.

But Miles is right. The people who've only ever lived in the city should experience a little bit of the magic of a small town too.

"What are you thinking about?" he asks.

I shake my head. "Nothing." And then after a pause, I add with a shrug, "Everything."

"Like Roger?" He smirks at me, and I ball up a napkin and throw it at him. He catches it, though, because of course he does.

"I don't even think you deserve cake after the terrible date you sent me on."

He finishes the last bite and smiles up at me. "I promise the next one will be better."

Guess I'm not cut out to be a barista.

First day, and I spilled coffee all over a guy who turned out to be a very important French diplomat or something.

I don't remember much from my high school French class, but I do remember the swear words.

He used them all, and a few new ones I didn't quite catch.

He was shouting that he was going to ruin the shop on social media and send the bill to me personally to replace his designer suit because, and I quote, "Cette tache ne part pas, espèce d'idiot!"

Another learning experience? Maybe.

But I'm gutted. Completely humiliated and embarrassed. AGAIN.

First the date and now this. Getting fired from a job that a monkey could do.

I told Miles. He laughed.

Thought it was hilarious. Did an impression of the French diplomat that was spot-on considering he wasn't even there.

But then he said, "Claire, that job was never going to make you happy."

He's right. But that's not why I got that job. I got it because I need something to do with myself during the day.

Something that makes me so tired that I fall asleep before my brain can start spiraling.

I guess I'll send out another round of résumés and see if anything new has shown up online . . .

And yep. I'm also preparing for date number two.

A guy named Scott.

Here's hoping he's better than Roger.

Then again, if Scott turned out to be a potted plant, it would be better than Roger.

* * *

Minnie: I heard about the job. Are you okay?

Claire: You heard?

Minnie: Miles told me. Said we had to make your next date extra special because you were down about it.

Claire: I don't think I like you talking to him so much.

It's weird.

Minnie: We're not having conversations—just plotting for you. On the app, which you can read.

He's a really nice guy.

Claire: If you lived here, he'd probably try to date you.

Minnie: I'm not the one who should date Miles.

Claire: I need a job.

Minnie: Smooth change of subject.

But seriously. You shouldn't be

working at a coffee shop anyway.

Claire: I'm not sure what I should be doing.

Minnie: You should bake.

Claire: I don't think cookies will pay the bills.

Minnie: They might . . .

What I wouldn't give for your oatmeal butterscotch cookies right now . . .

Claire: I could teach you how to make them . . .

Minnie: It's not the same.

The day I get back, I'm expecting a whole plateful.

Claire: You got it. 👍

CHAPTER 12

I'm holding my vibrating phone in my hand, staring at the screen. It's John.

Really, universe? Right now, right at this second?

It's Thursday afternoon, after a full morning of dropping off résumés and checking in with the places I've already been, and John is the last person I want to talk to.

I just left a microbrewery that's apparently looking for a hostess. After going in with my brightest, happiest face screwed in place, the manager, who could not have been a day over twenty-five, took one look at me, leaned over and said something to the young woman standing next to him, and left.

It was obvious that "middle-aged mom" was not the vibe they were going for.

Something about this particular rejection felt . . . personal.

So there's that.

Now, John.

I take a deep breath, put on my mental armor, and click the green button.

"So you're still in Chicago," he says, forgoing any kind of greeting.

"Hello to you too." I sigh.

Silence.

"You're still there?" he repeats. "How are you even surviving?"

"Yes, John, I'm still here," I deadpan. "I'm doing just fine. I actually live here now."

The condescending noise he makes has me wishing someone

would invent a new type of phone where a person—say, me—could reach through and slap someone with their own hands on the other end.

"I'm calling to make sure you legally changed your name back to Karadec," he says.

"Why?" I ask. "Are you concerned that a woman over the age of forty might be running wild with your family name?"

"No, it's just that . . . Misty wants to be the only Mrs. John Wellesley," he says.

"Ha!" The laugh/scoff is out before I can stop myself.

I stop at a crosswalk and wait for the light, the sound of traffic and conversation filling the air around me. On the other end of the line, it's completely quiet.

"Has Misty met your mother?" I ask, annoyed. "*Mrs. John Wellesley*?"

John starts to say something, then pauses like he hasn't actually realized this, then says, "You know what I mean, Claire."

I'm downtown on the Magnificent Mile, and I pause to admire the thousands of tulips blooming on Michigan Avenue. They're so bright and cheerful, I almost forget it's my ex-husband on the other end of this call. If it were anyone else, I might switch to FaceTime just to share the view.

The light changes, and I join the foot traffic crossing the street like I actually know where I'm going.

"You can tell *Misty* she can have your name," I say. "I got rid of it months ago." She can also have his snoring, his cigar smoking, and his inability to put dirty clothes in the hamper, but I don't say that part out loud.

"Great!" he says, like we just finalized a low-interest loan at a bank.

Silence.

I absently wonder if they've set a date for the wedding but decide I don't care enough to ask.

I shift my weight. "Is that all?"

He sighs. "Uh . . . how've you been?"

I bite the inside of my cheek to stop the dammed-up reservoir of choice words pooling at the front of my brain.

"Seriously?"

"Well . . . yeah," he says. "You know, I'm just . . . wondering how . . . it's all . . . going. There. With you."

The last bit of my patience is about to hop on a plane. I know there's more. Something he's not saying. Something he undoubtedly needs.

"John, just say what you want to say."

There's another pause. And then, "I, uh . . . I need a favor."

I slow my pace, trying to figure out if I heard him right. "I'm sorry—did you say you need a *favor*? From me?"

"It's work, Claire. Don't make a thing of it."

I half laugh. Is he serious?

"Are you serious?"

"We're trying to land that company—Oleander? You remember?" he asks.

"Oh. I remember." It's a high-end line of women's spa products. The kind I can no longer afford.

"Well, the pitch isn't coming together."

"Let me guess," I say. "There's not a single female ad exec at the table, is there?"

"I mean, no, but the guys have all talked to their wives about it," John says.

I don't need him to say another word. I know what he's saying, and it's shockingly empowering. Because even though he'd never admit it, he's realizing that I contributed a whole lot more to his success than he ever gave me credit for.

And now he's stuck.

"I just wondered if you'd think about it," he says. "We were really good about kicking around ideas together. I don't know, somehow you always said the right things to jump-start my creativity."

I refrain from correcting him. I said things and he wrote them down verbatim and then passed them off as his own ideas.

"I can send over the talking points," he says. "Maybe we can spitball, you know? Brainstorm? Like old times?"

Right. Old times. Back when I thought we were a team.

Back when I thought he was faithful.

I hear his office phone beep in the background, then the voice of his secretary says, "Mr. Wellesley, Misty is on line one."

"Babe, I gotta go."

My muscles tense at the "babe," and John stutters almost immediately.

"I m-mean, uh—shoot. I'll send that info over and talk to you later? We'll figure it out—okay, bye—"

He doesn't wait for me to say goodbye. Just hangs up.

I stare at the phone in my hand as the screen goes black. Everything about that phone call irritated me.

The *most* frustrating part is that I have yet to make John understand what a jerk he really is. He's simply too entitled. Every attempt I've made to explain the pure, unadulterated rage I feel toward him and *Misty* is always overshadowed by bigger, more present emotions.

Sadness. Frustration. Disappointment.

Shame.

Why can't I just lay into him and hang up the phone?

Why can't I, just this once, take a detour off the high road? Indulge in a little verbal vehicular manslaughter?

I'm still gritting my teeth at my phone when I look up and find I'm standing in front of the upscale mall I visited when I first moved here. It's several floors of designer shops, full of clothes and shoes and bags I can no longer afford and no longer wish to buy.

I never got used to spending money the way the Colorado Wellesley crowd spent money, even when I had it at my disposal. Probably because I grew up clipping coupons and making my own jam.

Which tastes *way* better than what you get in the store. Just saying.

I didn't—and don't—see the point in a five-thousand-dollar pair of shoes.

Not that I'm judging how anyone else spends their money—it was just never my thing.

Window shopping, though? That I can do like it's my calling. With the exception of baking, nothing is more calming, more interesting, or more daydreamy than walking around looking at mannequins, and doing some people watching . . .

But as I step inside the building and take the escalator up to the second floor, my mind drifts to my list.

After that phone call and that non-job interview, I need to cross something off.

So instead of getting off on the second floor and heading into one of the overpriced stores, I ride the escalator to the seventh floor and find myself standing in the upscale food court.

When I say "food court," I'm really not painting the right picture. It's an eating area on the seventh floor of a tall building near Lake Michigan. There's a bar in the middle, staffed with several people in black shirts, and it's surrounded on either side by open-air, watch-them-cook mini restaurants. Aloha Poke Co., Hot Chi, Lucky Cross, and The Fat Shallot sandwich shop, just to name a few. The food looks and smells amazing.

You won't find Sbarro here, that's for sure.

The first time I was here, I didn't even stop to grab food, but now? I'm going to sit, and I'm going to eat.

By myself.

And who knows, I might even strike up a conversation with a stranger.

Two things under number eight crossed off.

Take that, John.

I walk over to one of the restaurants and take a look. The girl behind the counter watches me expectantly, then smiles and points over to a bank of kiosks.

Oh. Everything is high-tech now. You don't give your order to a human—you punch it into a computer. I nod at the girl, feeling old, then walk over and scroll through the different restaurant options. I could order from any of the different places just from one kiosk.

Well, that's dangerous.

There's a *bunch* of stuff on here I've never heard of before, and my recent need to taste new things is taking over my brain.

I swipe through the options, overwhelmed with possibilities, but I finally settle on the Aloha Bowl with pineapple, cucumber, scallions, and Maui onions. But then I add a Ramen Wrap from a place called Art of Dosa. Noodles, sriracha mayo, and something I've never heard of called katsu, plus there's something on it called a black "gunpowder" spice blend.

Sounds spicy. And new. And different.

I scroll to the drinks and select a Dr Pepper, hoping the twenty-three flavors will be enough to handle the gunpowder.

Once I pay, I take my printout and wait over by the ramen counter, scanning the airy, modern space as I do. There's a man on a laptop, diligently working. Beside him are two men who appear to be in deep discussion. In the corner, there's a group of four older women playing mahjong, and beside them, a woman about my age is sitting alone reading a book.

I notice that her plate is full, like she just sat down, and she's at a large table with three empty chairs.

I could eat alone in a public place or talk to a stranger. But as a man calls my number and I pick up the tray with my food on it, I'm still not sure which one I'll choose.

I bring the tray around to the other restaurant's window, and as soon as I've got my wrap and Dr Pepper, I turn around, inhale a deep breath, then start off in the direction of the woman.

Maybe she needs a friend as much as I do.

At that moment, I'm transported to the first day of kindergarten and Gram's advice on how to make friends. Gram was a sturdy woman, and not the warmest person, but she was a fierce friend. She and her best friend, June, had known each other practically since they were born, and I had no doubt Gram would've done anything for that woman. She knew something about making friends—the good kind.

"Don't be afraid, Claire," she'd said. *"You walk up to a table with an empty seat and ask whoever's sitting there if you can join them. Maybe ask if they want to be friends. Ask what they like. It's all about listening to other people. People like to talk about themselves. The only way to have a friend is to be a friend, sweetheart. Remember that."*

It had worked too. I met my best friend, Libby, because I sat down across from her at lunch and found out she loved Strawberry Shortcake as much as I did. We stayed friends all the way through high school.

I study the woman reading alone and wonder if she could be the Libby for this chapter of my life.

I stop next to her table on the opposite side of where she's sitting. "Excuse me? Hi!"

She looks at me, eyebrows drawn downward in whatever expression is one step more abrasive than a frown. "Yes?"

The woman's lunch sits untouched on her tray.

"Hi!" I repeat dumbly. "Do you, uh, mind if I sit with you?"

She looks around the space. "Why would you do that? There are plenty of empty tables."

My grip tightens on the tray, and all at once I'm standing on the stage at the country club again, the bitterness of rejection on full display.

My face is on fire, and beads of sweat gather above my upper lip. "Oh! I'm here by myself, and I just thought maybe you'd like some company—"

She makes a show of putting her bookmark into the crease of her book and closing it. "Did it ever occur to you that some people *like* to be alone?"

She's not Libby.

Embarrassment washes over me as I realize the mistake I've made. I start to respond but realize I have nothing to say.

But she does. "Some people spend all morning at work just counting down the hours until they get one free hour—just sixty pathetic minutes—of alone time. Uninterrupted. Undisturbed. No kids pulling at you. Nobody asking where the report is. I figured the book was enough of a sign, but apparently not."

"Okay, I understand. I'll just—"

"A bit of free time. I have zero, and it's all I ask. But you wouldn't know anything about that, would you?" She looks me up and down. "You're probably *bathing* in free time."

Are people really this rude?

The words hit me and tears spring to my eyes. "I'm really sorry. I—"

"Don't you dare apologize." I hear a woman's voice from behind me loud enough to make me turn around. She's tall and blonde, probably mid-thirties, wearing a gray pencil skirt, white blouse with the top three buttons undone, and pointy black heels. I didn't see her before, but I notice she's sitting two tables over.

She makes her way to my side, and wow. She's tall. She looks like an actual model. And not a catalog model—a runway model.

"If anyone should apologize, it's her," she says to me, nodding at the woman with the book. She looks at the woman. "You didn't have to be so rude. What is wrong with you?"

The woman, clearly outmatched, slowly looks down at her book.

"You could've just politely declined." The blonde motions to me. "This woman asked you to share a meal with her, and you practically spat in her face."

"I didn't want to share a meal with her," the woman retorts. "I don't even know her."

"Well, I want to share a meal with her." The blonde loops her arm through mine. "Come sit with me."

My heart sputters, aware that the mahjong players have stopped playing, the man on the laptop has stopped typing, and the two men in deep conversation have stopped talking. They're all watching this scene play out.

What is it about me being vaulted into publicly awkward situations? The country club stage, the fountain, Roger, the French diplomat, and now this.

"I'm Lennon," the woman says once we're back at her table.

"Like John Lennon?" I ask.

She smiles, probably used to that question. "Yes. My mom was a fan."

There's a cheeseburger and a big bowl of fries, along with what I think is a chocolate milkshake, at her place setting. She sits down and nods at the chair across from her. "Go ahead. Sit."

I slide into the chair as Lennon picks up her burger and takes a huge bite. "Ooh, you got the Aloha Bowl." She nods to my tray. "It's really good."

"It is?"

She nods, mouth full of food.

"I'm Claire, by the way," I say, still sort of dumbfounded. "Thank you for that."

She picks up a french fry and drags it through her ketchup. "No thanks necessary. That woman is awful. Last week she yelled at a young mom because her baby started crying." She shoots a glare at the woman, who seems to be pretending to read her book but is actually watching us. "Who does that?"

"Yeah, I don't know," I think out loud. "Maybe she's having a rough day."

"Still no excuse," Lennon says. "When I'm on my period, I'm miserable, but I'm only mean to the people who have to love me." She picks up her milkshake and takes a long sip. "So. Claire. What do you say . . . do you want to be friends?"

CHAPTER 13

"So, let me get this straight. He calls you. Criticizes you. Then asks you to help him do his work? Who the heck is this guy?"

It's safe to say that I *really* like Lennon.

After she finished eating, she went over to the sweets counter and ordered us two giant chocolate chunk cookies.

Her metabolism must be as fast as an Olympic sprinter.

Mine is not. But I still eat half the cookie.

Not as good as my gram's recipe, though. These taste processed.

I've just told Lennon the abbreviated version of my history with John, ending with the phone call that prompted me to go window shopping in the first place, and her immediate rush to my defense makes me feel warm on the inside.

It's been a long time since I've had a girlfriend. And there's something really special about female friendships.

"You see what he's doing, right?" she asks. "Classic manipulation. Ugh, thank God you're not married to him anymore."

I smile, but it must not come across right because Lennon's face falls.

"Oh, Claire . . . are you still sad about it?" she asks. "I wasn't sure if we were in the pitchfork phase or the tissue phase of your divorce."

At that, I laugh. "A little from column A, a little from column B," I say with a smile.

She laughs back. "Yeah, I get that."

"I'm not sad," I say. "I mean, mad, maybe? Or vengeful? Sad, though? Not really. Only at night." I pause. "I'm trying not to be."

She reaches across the table and puts a hand on mine. The simple gesture surprises me—I don't have touchy-feely friends. "Look, Claire. People who just want to use you are never going to appreciate you for who you are. Trust me, I know."

I want to hear *that* story.

"It's all about what you can do for them," she continues. "You bend over backward to make their life better, but it will never be good enough." She holds her hands up and makes a shooing motion, like she's brushing the air away from her. "Let him go. He's S.E.P."

"S.E.P.?"

She leans forward in her chair. "Someone Else's Problem."

I laugh ruefully, cross one leg over the other, and run my hands through my hair. "He was *my* problem for so long. It's like my whole identity was wrapped up in him and his family, his work . . . I'm having trouble figuring out what to do next."

"But that's the beauty of it!" Lennon exclaims. "You can do anything you want!"

"Right." I thought I'd be a little closer to figuring out what that is by now.

She levels my gaze. "It only works if you let go of all of that old stuff. If you don't"—she casts a quick glance over to the table where The Reader is now packing up her things—"you'll end up like her. Bitter and alone."

The woman tucks her book into a bag, picks up her tray, and walks it over to the garbage area. Even though I felt really embarrassed, I can't help but feel a twinge of empathy for her.

I have no idea what her story is, but maybe she's just trying to figure things out too.

I look at Lennon. "I'm not sure how to let it go. I mean, the man ruined my life."

She polishes off her cookie, brushes her hands together, then stands. "Come on."

I do the physical equivalent of a stutter as I stand, gather my things, and try to keep up with Lennon.

Her stride is much longer than mine, especially in those heels.

We throw away our trash, then take the elevator down to the ground floor, stepping outside into another glorious spring afternoon in the city.

The weather is darn near perfect, and I feel spoiled by it.

I follow her out onto the street, and we start walking past restaurants, shops, and offices. "Look around, Claire," Lennon says. "You're living in one of the greatest cities on the planet, and you can choose to do anything you want, anytime you want to."

The light changes green just as we step up to the curb, and I pay attention to what's around me. There's an underlying bed of noise from the cars. The buildings tower, almost too tall to take in as the sun glints off their reflective windows. And people—lots of people—are moving, talking, laughing, carrying bags from all kinds of shops and stores. There's a group of college kids chatting excitedly as they walk with purpose; there's a couple lifting a toddler by his hands and swinging him every third step. There are three young guys drumming on buckets on a street corner, and it's crazy, but 75 percent of these people have dark hair.

The world ebbs and flows, and Lennon just takes it in stride.

"It's freeing, really." Lennon glances at me. "And look—you made a new friend today!" She holds her arms out to indicate herself. As she does, she accidentally knocks into someone walking past. "Ope! Geez, so sorry." She winces at me with a smile and moves to the side. "Plus, I know the city like the back of my hand, so if you have any questions—I'm your girl." She turns and keeps walking.

"What do you do?" I ask, quickening my pace to keep up.

"I'm a Realtor," she says. "Luxury properties." She pulls a business card out of her purse and hands it to me. "My cell is on there, so you can call me anytime."

I look at the card, then tuck it into my purse.

"What about you?" she asks. "What are you into?"

"Well . . ." I screw up my face and take a breath.

It was easier when the answer to that question was "Strawberry Shortcake."

"I'm trying to figure that out. I haven't actually been here that long."

"You didn't move here for a job or something?"

I shake my head. "No, it was—" I pause, then decide to open up. "I needed a change. I needed to do things that scared me. So I made a list, and 'move to a new city' was near the top of the list." I go quiet for a second before adding, "I always wanted to live in Chicago."

She drops her jaw and frowns in admiration, hitting me on the arm. "Claire! That's *amazing*."

I half roll my eyes because, seriously, it doesn't feel amazing right now. "Jury's still out on that one."

"Are you kidding? It's huge."

I smile. Someone in my corner. It's nice.

"One of my goals is to get a hobby," I say.

She laughs. "That's fair."

"What about you? Other than selling condos to Chicago's elite, what are you into?"

"Mostly my husband, Daniel, and my baby, Eve." She smiles. "And pickleball." Her eyes light up. "Oh my gosh! You should come! We play on Saturdays. I'll text you the details." She hands me her phone. "Here, put your number in."

"This is a big step in our relationship," I joke. "I don't know if I'm ready."

"True." She sucks in a breath. "We are moving fast . . ."

We both laugh, and I wonder why I waited so long to try to make new friends.

I hand the phone back, and she opens a new text. Seconds later, my phone dings.

Unknown number: It's your new friend, Lennon. Save my number.

I talk and type out her contact info. "New . . . Friend . . . Lennon. Got it."

She beams. "I'm so glad that lady was rude to you!"

I laugh. "Me too!"

She sticks her phone in her pocket and looks down the street, then takes off purposefully. "Come on, slowpoke."

Unlike Miles, Lennon does not seem to be out for a stroll. The opposite actually—she clearly has a destination in mind. I'm tempted to ask where we're going but decide to stay quiet and go with it.

She slowly steps off the sidewalk as a silver SUV pulls up. A man rolls down the window. "Lennon?"

She nods.

"Like the Beatles," the guy says, and I realize she probably gets that a lot. I assume this is where she and I part ways, but she looks at me. "Our Uber. You want to come?"

"Where to?"

She smiles wide. "I've got a showing. I thought if you didn't have anything to do, you could come?"

"Oh. Okay," I say. "Yeah. That sounds fun."

She grins, and I slide in beside her, hoping this isn't some elaborate human trafficking ring, and a little relieved when the address she gives the driver is a street I recognize.

"So, you're married," I say, hoping to learn a little more about her as we drive away from the busiest parts of the city and into a residential area. I've been told that these neighborhoods start to feel like small towns over time—but I'm not sure about that.

No one has a yard.

"Yep," she says. "Daniel's a fommy."

I frown. "A what?"

"Father plus mommy," she says. "Fommy. He made it up." She gives a little shrug. "Eve was such a miracle baby that after I had her, we knew one of us was going to stay home with her. Daniel was an elementary school principal, so it was a great fit. He's so good with her."

She doesn't state the obvious—she was making more money as a luxury Realtor than he was in education, so it made more sense for her to keep working. I notice because it's so different from what I'm used to. The people who were in my social circle before *loved* to brag about money.

New Friend Lennon doesn't seem to need to.

"It took us a long time to get pregnant," Lennon says, her perfectly manicured hand wrapped around the strap of a pink Kate Spade purse. "And even longer to keep a pregnancy past three months."

I look over at her. Even behind her sunglasses, I can see she's struggling to maintain her composure.

She sniffs and looks away, trying to laugh. "Wow, I still can't talk about it without crying."

And I realize that no matter how together a person looks on the outside, inside, we're all dealing with something. Just like that, I see the thing that makes this beautiful, successful, confident woman just like me.

Sometimes I think if we chose to focus on the things that make us similar more than the things that make us different, the world would be a much kinder place.

I take a cue from what she did for me earlier and reach over and squeeze her hand. "I'm sorry, Lennon."

She shakes her head and sniffs, lifting her sunglasses to dab at the corners of her eyes. "Ugh. It's silly, really. I should be over it by now, right?"

"I mean . . . no," I say. "Grief doesn't have a timeline. And it doesn't always make sense."

She nods quietly, and I see something settle inside her.

I smile at her, silently thinking about Strawberry Shortcake.

"Oh! We're here." Lennon stops and pulls out her phone as I look around the block. We step out of the car and onto the sidewalk in front of a storefront with a For Rent sign in the window. It's one of many storefronts lining the street in what looks like a very popular area.

Above the stores, there seem to be apartments, and if I didn't love The Bexley so much, I could easily imagine living in one of them. The whole street is charming and quaint in a way I didn't expect Chicago to be—in a way that almost makes you forget you're in the city at all.

It reminds me a little of that quintessential Main Street in every Small Town, USA.

"He's running a little late," Lennon says, tucking her phone away. "Do you want to see it?"

I smile. "The store? Yeah!"

"Great," she says, animated. "There's just something exciting about an empty space—they're always brimming with possibility. Like . . . I can't wait to see what comes to life in each one."

I peer through the large front window. Maybe Lennon's excitement is rubbing off on me—or maybe she's right, and there's nothing but possibility in a space like this.

And that possibility makes me excited to walk through the door.

CHAPTER 14

Doughnuts.

A memory starts swirling as we step through the door.

I'm eight years old, standing at the counter of Pop's favorite doughnut shop, trying to decide between cherry and blueberry while he and the shop's owner, Francis, argue over the weather.

The doughnut shop was small and quaint, but it always drew in a crowd, especially on Saturday mornings. The doughnuts always had the slight aroma of cigarette smoke from the women Gram called "the Chimneys."

In the end, the blueberry versus cherry debate proved to be pointless because Pop always came home with at least a dozen, which always included two of each of my favorites.

My head starts to swirl with memories of family potlucks and farmhouse picnics. Of Gram spending a whole day baking for the church bake sale or the cake walk at my school's annual bazaar. Of long, warm summer nights on the farmhouse front porch with Libby and her family and a few other families.

Always, after everyone left, Gram and I would stay out on the porch, looking at the stars and talking. She'd knit, and I'd make friendship bracelets, and once it got too dark, we'd stare up at the night sky, marveling at how bright the stars were out here.

It's where she told me about the drug smuggling ring that had landed my mother in prison and that they didn't know who my father was. It's where I told her I had a crush on a boy in the ninth grade and where that boy kissed me good night after taking me to the carnival over the Fourth of July. It's where I broke the news that I was pregnant and that John and I were moving to Colorado so he could work for his father.

That front porch was hallowed ground.

It was exactly what I needed it to be when I needed it. It gave me a place to be silly or serious, depending on my mood. And it always gave me a place to belong.

I think I've been searching for a place like that ever since.

"So this used to be a stationery shop," Lennon says, bringing my thoughts back to the present. "I guess nobody writes letters anymore."

"Yeah," I say. "Everything is digital. It's less . . ."

". . . personal," Lennon says, finishing my sentence.

I nod. It makes me think of my grandmother and the handwritten letters she sent when I was away at college. I'd gone to a small, private university almost three hours away, but it might as well have been the other side of the world. I was instantly homesick and stayed that way for the better part of my freshman year.

I eventually made friends and found my groove, but I never stopped missing my grandparents or the farm.

I still miss them.

My thoughts are interrupted when the door opens and a heavyset man walks in.

On cue, Lennon walks over and introduces herself, extending a hand in his direction. The man shakes her hand, and his eyes move from her face down to her pointy heels and back up again. "You're not Martin."

Lennon smiles warmly. "No, Martin's wife went into labor, and he asked me to open the space for you."

He looks annoyed for some reason.

Lennon waves a hand around the space. "What do you think?"

The man hikes up his pants and starts to look around. "Location's good."

"It's right in the heart of the Lincoln Park neighborhood," Lennon says. "Lots of foot traffic and—"

He shoots her a look. "Martin gave me the details already. You don't need to try to sell it to me."

At that, Lennon's expression changes, and I feel the need to duck and run for cover. After seeing her unload on the woman at the mall, I expect her to go off on this man too.

Instead of putting him in his place, she simply smiles and says, "Of course."

"It's small," the man says. "Smaller than I want." He walks past me like I'm not there and pushes open a door, disappearing behind it. "I don't really need a kitchen either," he calls from the other room.

Lennon looks at me and rolls her eyes. "This is why I only list residential properties," she whispers.

The man reappears. "Rip out the kitchen, put in an office. It might work."

"The last owner rented the kitchen out to make some extra income," Lennon says. "She didn't need a kitchen either." She smiles.

"Yeah, well, her business didn't last, did it?" he says, not looking at her.

"What are you going to do with the space?" I ask, mostly because I'm curious, but also because I feel like I've already written the story of this storefront, and he is not in it.

"Medical practice," he says. "Chiropractic. I'm looking to open a second location on this side of town."

"A chiropractor?" I blurt. "Wouldn't you rather be somewhere . . . else?" This space is oozing potential, and he wants to suck all the charm right out of it?

The man frowns, then looks at Lennon. "Is this some sort of reverse psychology or something?"

"Uh, no," Lennon says. She shoots me a look, and I widen my eyes in a silent apology. I walk to the back of the space and push the door open, stepping into the kitchen this guy wants to turn into an office.

Which is a terrible idea, by the way.

I look around the space, mind swirling again, and I overhear him tell Lennon he's got two other places to see, and he'll let her know.

Ideas start to form, coming at me at light speed, the kind I couldn't stop if I tried. I can practically hear the conversation, the laughter, the seating. I can even see the paint color.

And a whole world of possibility.

I haven't dreamt in such a long time.

Lennon appears in the doorway. "You would make a terrible Realtor."

I fold my arms. "You're telling me when you look around this amazing space you think, *You know who should move in here? A chiropractor!*"

She shrugs. "No. I don't. It would be a shame not to make it something amazing. The stationery shop was adorable; they just couldn't make it work. Even with the extra income from a catering company." She takes a few steps into the kitchen and the door swings behind her. "So what would you put in here?"

"A bakery." I say this almost without thinking, like the answer to that question was ready and waiting. "With a small-town theme. I'd call it The Porch. Or The Front Porch. Something . . ."

Lennon's eyebrows shoot up. "Go on."

"It would be like . . . a pause in the middle of all the busyness of the city, you know? A place to encourage real-life interactions. Maybe we wouldn't even have Wi-Fi."

"That's bold," Lennon says.

"The whole idea would be to . . ." I search the air for the right words and find them instantly. "Sit, sip, and stay awhile."

Lennon leans against the metal counter. "Did you just come up with that off the top of your head?"

I shrug. "I'm just making stuff up." I was always good at daydreaming. Or at least I used to be. I'm so out of practice.

"But it's good. No wonder your ex-husband can't do his job without you." She laughs. "And what would you serve at The Porch?"

"Homemade signature desserts." I turn a circle in the kitchen. It's not a large space, but it's big enough. "The kind you'd find at your favorite farmhouse picnic or church potluck. And there would be sun tea and a fresh-squeezed lemonade stand—oh my gosh, my gram made the best lemonade. She always said it was more sugar than lemon, but that's what made it so delicious." I smile at the memory.

I walk back out into the main area, and the pieces of the daydream start to shift, coming together so clearly that I can't believe it's not real. "I'd paint everything white and hang white twinkle lights around the whole space. Maybe install a few porch swings for seating, but I'd make it so everyone felt like they were here with friends. Even if they showed up alone.

"Oh! And I could handwrite little conversation starters right on the sleeves of the drinks or the dessert napkins. The menu would change depending on the season, and I'd really focus on elevated versions of the desserts my gram made. She never wrote down her recipes, but I have them all memorized." I pause, then say quietly to myself, "Sit, sip, and stay awhile."

"The Porch," Lennon says.

"The Porch," I repeat.

There's a moment, a nostalgic, exciting, unsure moment that hangs in the air. The kind of moment where you stay still—or you leap. I inadvertently go up on my toes.

"Interesting," Lennon says, the word drawn out.

Her voice pulls me out of my haze and I smile at her, shrugging softly. "I guess I like empty spaces too. They make me daydream."

"Are you sure that's all that was?" Lennon asks. "Because it felt like something . . . more. Less like a dream and more like a plan."

I look around. The moment is still there, but now it's just out of reach.

The space would be perfect for an adorable little bakery. I'd change the awnings on the two tall windows flanking the front door, and I'd add exterior seating for beautiful days like today. I'd hand out samples, and every Friday, I'd bake a box of goodies and deliver it to someone my customers nominate, someone who deserves to be recognized for being kind or doing good in the city.

Just because.

I'd focus on bringing small-town charm—all the things I miss about home—to this big, beautiful city.

I'd have to spend every bit of my savings to make a go of something like this, and what do I really know about running a business? It would be a terrible idea.

Right?

I look at Lennon, and the moment wisps away. "Just daydreams."

She opens the door, and I follow her out onto the sidewalk, taking one last, lingering look inside the empty shop.

"Okay," Lennon says, a disbelieving tone in her voice. "If you decide you want to go for it, you let me know."

* * *

I made a friend.

I also had an idea.

Something I thought I'd shake but haven't. I haven't been able to stop thinking about it.

A bakery.

It's a pipe dream, really. Obviously not something I'm serious about. It would've been fun to kick around the idea with Gram, though. I wonder what she would've put on the menu.

The Porch Menu

FARMHOUSE LEMON BARS

Pucker up for tart-but-sweet perfection

PORCH PECAN BARS

Topped with brown butter and a sprinkle of flaky sea salt

STRAWBERRY RHUBARB CRUMBLE MUFFINS

Bursting with fruit and sweetened to perfection

OOEY GOOEY FUDGE BROWNIES

A chocolate explosion

THE SCOTCHEROO

Peanut butter, chocolate, butterscotch, and crisped rice—a Midwest delicacy

SNICKERDOODLE SCONES

With a light drizzle

GRAM'S POTLUCK SHEET CAKE

Light chocolate cake with a thick layer of frosting

I know it's crazy.

I know I wouldn't have the first clue about running a business. I mean, I've had ideas over the years—business ventures that would've given me something to do other than drum up ideas for John's campaigns or work with one of his mother's charities. But none

of those ever got beyond the what-if phase. Something always stopped me—that little voice in the back of my mind saying, "Who do you think you are?"

The voice that always reminded me I don't know a thing about running a business. It would never work.

BUT WHAT IF IT DOES?

Even if I never act on it, it feels really good to dream again.

Claire: I went on date #2.

Minnie: Scott! Architectural boat tour!

Tell me everything!

Claire: . . .

Minnie: Uh-oh.

Claire: It started off fine.

I've been wanting to do this boat tour for years—but Scott had done it so many times, he practically had the spiel memorized. He even corrected the guide when he got a fact wrong about the glass buildings in Chicago.

Minnie: He did not.

Claire: He did.

Minnie: Out loud?

Claire: Yep.

Minnie: Ope

Claire: I think correcting people is his personality.

He corrected me when I apparently ordered the wrong wine with my chicken.

Minnie: Shut up.

Claire: And also when I told him I loved how charming my neighborhood is.

Minnie: He corrected your opinion?

Claire: He corrected Google Maps.

Minnie: Oof

Claire: He also showed up with a small Bluetooth speaker with a "first date playlist" and HE PLAYED IT ON THE BOAT.

Minnie: Welp.

Claire: Where are you finding these guys?

Minnie: Hey, Scott was Miles's pick, not mine.

Claire: Miles and I are going to have words.

Minnie: He seemed so great on the app.

Claire: He's had thirty-two first dates, Minnie. And zero second dates.

Minnie: 32?!!

Claire: He bragged about it like he was proud.

Minnie: You should start a TikTok account to talk about these dates. 😂

Claire: Oh, I'm not done.

It started raining. And I was wearing a white dress.

A white dress, Amelia.

Minnie: 😂😂😂

Claire: No, not 😂😂😂

Minnie: So . . . are you going to see him again?

Claire: ???

CHAPTER 15

Someone, somewhere took two seemingly unrelated words and put them together, creating a craze for middle-aged people across the nation.

Those two words?

Pickle and *ball*.

After another fruitless week of job hunting, I get a call from Lennon with the kind of invite I want to reject.

"Oh, you were serious about the pickleball?" I was hoping she wasn't.

"Daniel's mom watches Eve so we can play every Saturday," she says. "We love it. Remind me . . . have you played before?"

"Uh, no," I say, laughing. "I don't really do sports."

"Eh," she says, "neither do I. But it's *super* fun to get to hit something. And every once in a while we make the guys look stupid, so *bonus*!"

I chuckle. Lennon is so great.

Still, I don't tell her that I've walked by the empty storefront every day this week, half hoping, half dreading the day the chiropractor—or someone else—moves in.

I need to find a job because if I have something else to focus on, then maybe I'll stop dwelling on outlandish ideas.

Like opening a small-town-inspired bakery in Chicago.

Named The Porch.

Never mind that I have a menu. And a color palette.

"You'll love it, I promise," she says. "Do you have a fourth we could ask?"

Without permission, my mind conjures the image of Miles. I'm bound to make a complete fool of myself, so why would I want to do that in front of a man who will relentlessly tease me when I do?

"There will be other people there," Lennon says. "So we won't have a problem finding a fourth."

"Will the other people have a problem when they realize how terrible I am at it?"

She laughs.

"No, seriously. I'm not coordinated," I say. "I'm not exactly athletic."

"That's part of the fun," she says. "Pickleball was invented for the nonathletic to pretend they're playing tennis."

I laugh.

"Actually, that's not true," she says. "It was invented by three dads in Australia who were just trying to entertain their kids."

"You know the history of this sport?" I ask, a little surprised.

"I might be a little obsessed," she says. "You might be too after you play."

I pinch the bridge of my nose, certain there is *no way* I'll ever be obsessed with pickleball, but unable to find a good enough reason to decline this invitation.

Am I really going to do this? I let out an audible groan. "I tried playing tennis once when I was a kid, and it did not go well. I whiffed on hitting the ball back, then tripped and skinned my knee so badly it made the court look like a crime scene."

Lennon laughs, like I've just told a joke, and says, "I'll text you the details. Just wear comfy clothes and bring water."

Right.

I'm going to write "pickleball" on my list because it terrifies me, and also just so I can cross it right off.

I'm also done with the app. As in *done*.

After the Scott debacle, I went on two more app dates.

First there was Mark, who does something with the stock market that honestly sounds a bit shady. He took me to one of Chicago's hidden speakeasies, which had the coolest interior—wood beam ceilings, a jazzy burnt-orange color scheme, leather couches, and sketchy paintings of music legends on the wall—Jimmy Hendrix, Ray Charles, James Brown.

There was a live jazz band, which was just as cool as the setting, but was so loud Mark and I had to shout to hear each other. When I opted for a mocktail instead of the Whiskey Lullaby that he suggested, he got a phone call and claimed he had to leave because he "had to take care of an emergency."

He left me there, but I ended up having the best time chatting with the female bartender. I even got to meet the band, sending a selfie to Minnie with the words, "Date bailed but I'm thinking of becoming a groupie!"

A few days later, I met Barry in front of The Second City for an improv comedy show. I laughed the whole way through, but Barry didn't even crack a smile. He looked utterly bored and even groaned a few times like he was offended. Afterward, he told me he studied acting in college and he "wasn't impressed" and "could probably do better himself."

When I didn't come up with a response immediately (I am *not* trained in the art of improv), Barry said, "So, do you want to come back to my place?"

I frowned.

"You just can't stay the whole night," he said.

And that's when I realized Barry was under the impression that I was going to sleep with him.

"Wow. Well, thanks, Barry, but I think I'm actually going to head home," I told him.

"Seriously?" He did nothing to hide his irritation.

"Yeah, I'm tired and—"

"But . . . I bought your ticket."

I could feel my jaw actually drop.

He was serious.

"I got you a drink in there too. What the heck?"

Roger I felt bad for. I even had some empathy for the food court Book Lady.

But this guy?

I thought of what Lennon would say. And I smiled.

But I bit my tongue.

He looked me over, making a show of it, then scoffed. "Probably would've been terrible anyway."

I stood on the street watching as he walked off, my faith in humanity thrown into a wood chipper.

I've gotten into the habit of talking about my dates with Miles and texting Minnie the rundown of each one. But I didn't tell either of them the truth about Barry. Just said it wasn't a good fit and that I wouldn't be seeing him again.

After that, I told both of them I needed to take a break.

Tonight I'm staying home to bake a few things, journal for a bit, and revisit my list.

1. I want a job or career I love.
2. I want friends. Real ones. (Lennon might count, jury's out on Miles)
3. ~~I want to live in a new city.~~
4. I want a dog.
5. I want to figure out who I am—apart from a wife and a mom.
6. I want a place where I fit in. I want a place where I belong.
7. I want a hobby.
8. I want to do the things that scare me.
    - Have a meal by myself. In public.
    - ~~Strike up a conversation with a stranger.~~

- ~~Try new foods I've never had or can't pronounce.~~
- ~~Download dating app.~~

There are so many things left on my list. Big things.

In the midst of thinking about the big things, I start to doodle about The Porch.

I really can't get away from this idea.

While I'm sketching out a logo, I hear voices in the courtyard. When I pull back the curtain, I see Lorraine and Miles standing outside talking. Given the pained look on his face, the conversation is most likely about something Lorraine wants him to fix or change around the building.

After a few seconds of gawking, Miles must get the sense that someone is watching him, because he looks right at me and waves.

I haven't seen him in a couple days, unless you count peeking at him through my blinds, watching him leave last night for what I assume was a date.

Lorraine turns, and when she sees me, she starts waving enthusiastically. I check to make sure she's not filming before I drop the curtain and walk out the front door.

She's marching toward me, but Miles hangs back.

"Claire, we were just talking about you!" Lorraine grabs my arm and leads me back to where Miles is standing.

"About me? Uh-oh." And why does Miles look bothered?

"Well, I heard you've been *dating*," she says, like she's been let in on a big secret.

Miles shoves his hands in his pockets and becomes the picture of nonchalance.

Today he's wearing jeans and a light blue button-down with the sleeves rolled. The blue brings out the color of his eyes—as if they needed to get any brighter. Miles is the kind of handsome that makes women on the street do a double take when they see him.

I force myself not to be one of those women and focus on Lorraine.

"I've been out on a couple of dates, yes," I say as casually as I can. "But I'm giving it a rest. Dating apps might not be my thing."

"Well, then, this is perfect!" she chimes. "Because it's not a dating app. One of my followers wants to meet you."

I frown.

"One of your . . . what?"

She keeps going without answering my question. "He didn't see the video live, but he watches *all* my videos, so when he saw the one I made with you in it, he reached out," Lorraine says. "I was just telling Miles about it because I know he's playing matchmaker."

I shoot Miles a side-eye. "He's not doing a very good job."

"Well, that's because he's a man," Lorraine says.

I grin as Miles rolls his eyes. "That's why I'm the perfect one to help."

"But you are committed to not being committed," Lorraine says. "Not what Claire needs at all."

Miles's eyes meet mine, but he quickly looks away.

"This man—Duffy—is perfect for you." She squeezes my arm.

"His name is Duffy?" Miles asks incredulously.

Great minds, I guess, I think.

"He's a pediatric dentist," Lorraine says, ignoring him. "He's got his own practice, and he's looking for someone who likes quiet nights watching movies on the couch—oh, and he's a *wine* collector. I think he's *very* romantic, Claire."

"His name is Duffy," Miles says drolly.

"Can I give him your number?" Lorraine's eyes are so hopeful. "I told him that if he's going to plan a date with someone as special as you, it had better be a very unique date, and he told me he already has a few ideas."

The compliment embarrasses me, and I feel my face flush. I glance at Miles, who says nothing.

Lorraine hands me her phone. "This is him."

On the screen, there's a photo of a studious-looking man with sandy-colored hair and round glasses and a bright red clown nose. And I get the distinct impression that he is far more decent than Barry, more engaged than Scott, and more sober than Roger.

But it all could be just wishful thinking.

"Oh! The nose is because he works with kids," she says. "Red Nose Day! The fundraiser? Do you know it?"

I nod.

"I promise he's handsome," Lorraine says.

I can see it. He's got a sort of nerd-chic thing going on, but there's kindness in his eyes.

Ten minutes ago, I was done with apps and men and dating. But now? Something inside me gives me a little nudge. I smile at Lorraine and say, "Sure, give him my number."

Out of the corner of my eye I see Miles shift his weight, like he's uncomfortable. Or annoyed. Or anxious to get out of here.

"Perfect!" Lorraine pulls out her phone and rushes off, leaving me standing here with Miles.

"Are you okay?" I ask.

He shrugs in a not-usual-Miles way. "Yeah, it's fine. I'm fine."

I try to joke with him. "Did you have a bad dental experience? Is that why you're—?"

"It's not that," he says, cutting me off. "I just thought you were trying not to have boring dates."

"At this point, a boring date would be dreamy," I say. "A boring date would be bliss. The last few have been a little *too* eventful."

"I had a great next date picked out for you—"

"Well, now you don't have to waste your time with my love life," I say, like *that's that*. "Lorraine is on the case." I nod toward the front gate. "Coffee walk?"

He looks at his watch, then at me. "Sure."

I start off in the direction of the empty storefront. I just like to look—almost like I'm checking on it or something. It's about twenty minutes from my apartment—totally walkable. Another plus.

Not that I'm collecting pluses about a building.

That would be silly.

Miles and I stop for coffee at a coffee truck, and once we have our drinks, I keep going in the direction of the storefront.

"Why are you walking so fast?" he asks.

"Am I?" I slow my pace, only now realizing I'm excited to get back to the empty space. Excited. An emotion I haven't felt in years.

I'm just window-shopping, remember.

He gives me a quizzical look. "What's going on with you?"

"What?" I take a drink of my latte. "Nothing."

"You're acting weird." He shrugs. "I mean weirder than usual."

"Ha ha," I retort, but something is off. His jokes aren't really . . . jokes. There's no lightness to them for some reason. Like he's trying to sort something out.

Like he's genuinely curious.

I bump his shoulder with my own, then think about the object of my affection—an empty building and a daydream.

And for whatever reason, I want to tell him about it.

Instead, I say, "Oh! Do you play pickleball? I got invited and we need a fourth."

"You play pickleball?" he asks.

"Never in my life," I say, chuckling. "But I met a new friend, and she invited me."

"You made a friend," he says. "That's great."

"Yeah, I can cross it off my list." Shoot. I didn't mean to let him know I have—

"You have a list?"

I shrug, wishing it weren't so easy to blurt things out around him.

"Of, like, things to do now that you're here?"

I try to brush it off. "Oh yeah, it's just silly—find a hobby, get a job, try new foods, those kinds of things."

I'm praying he doesn't make the connection that—

"And one of the things on the list is to find a friend?"

"Pathetic, right?" I scrunch my nose and look away. "But it's hard to make friends when you're an adult."

He looks at me sideways, then says seriously, "I think I'm offended."

My eyes widen. "Oh, I meant, like, a girlfriend. Like, you know, for girl talk and spa days and—"

"Braiding each other's hair and talking about boys?" he drones. Then a smile blooms on his face, and it's obvious he isn't actually offended at all. "You know I'm just messing with you, right?"

I give him a soft push. "You're the worst."

He laughs. "I don't care what you call me as long as you feed me."

I look up at him, and he's smiling.

"Well, what would you call me?" I ask.

"Usually I'd opt for Claire," he says.

I roll my eyes, feeling oddly exposed. Like I've just asked the boy I like to declare his feelings for me or something.

"I'm kidding," he says. "I'd call you a friend."

I take a drink. "Well, good, then I guess I can cross that one off twice."

We keep walking, neither of us talking for a bit, the city's energy the only activity between us. And then we stop at the light kitty-corner from the storefront. My insides buzz as I stare at the space. Like there's some magnetic pull drawing me to it.

"So you're a List Maker." Miles says this like it's capitalized and important, playful again.

I'm distracted when I say, "Yep," and I can feel him staring at me, still trying to work out what my deal is today. Because he's right. I'm being weird. Because all I can think about is that empty storefront.

"That's so you can feel like you're in control, right?"

I frown. "No, I just like to check things off."

He goes quiet, like he's considering something. "Yeah, but it might also be about wanting *some* control, right? Like a 'these are things I've written down and accomplished' kind of thing?"

I stare out at the city, so alive and full of possibility, and still, nothing feels certain. I know now that everything can change when you're not looking. "Hmm," I hum thoughtfully. "Maybe." Maybe my lists *are* my meager attempt at reclaiming a little bit of control.

"In my experience," he says, "none of us really has control of anything."

I frown. "I disagree. I have control over my emotions—and my choices. Whether I go out job hunting or spend the day on the couch eating ice cream and watching Netflix."

"Fair point," he concedes. "But good choices can't always guarantee good outcomes. You can do everything right and make all the right decisions. You can hold up your end of the bargain, and still—the world can blindside you with some gnarly stuff."

I go quiet as I take another drink, mostly to fill space. Because I get the sense that Miles isn't talking about me.

He's talking about himself.

And I wonder what "gnarly stuff" he's been through and if it's the reason he's so opposed to ever having a real relationship again.

Which begs the question—who hurt him?

"The world does have a knack for chewing you up and spitting you out," I say. "But I'm not willing to hide anymore. I've done the wallowing thing, and the angry thing, and the can't-get-out-of-bed thing. I don't want to do any of that anymore. I want to feel like I'm alive again."

"And the list helps you do that?" His tone is incredulous.

"Hey, don't knock it till you try it," I say. "The list is a powerful tool. It helps you get really clear about what you want."

"I know what I want."

I look at him. "Do you really, though?"

His raised brow asks a silent question.

"I just think maybe you should, you know, be open—to whatever life wants to bring you."

"I am," he says, lifting one shoulder. "Mostly."

The light changes, and we cross the street. The subject is dropped when Miles asks, "Where are we going?"

I point down the crosswalk. "We're just walking."

"No, we're not. You seem like you have a destination in mind," he says, more perceptive than I had hoped. "It's like you're on a mission."

We reach the other side of the street and I stop, turning to face another red light, the only thing standing between us and the storefront.

I can feel him watching me, and I realize that if I had my journal here, I'd have something else to add to my list.

Because telling Miles about the plans and ideas I've been dreaming up is possibly the scariest thing I've done yet.

Which is why, when the light changes and I step out into the street, I say, out loud, "I want to show you something."

* * *

I make lists.

Maybe that's why I bake. I like recipes.

Recipes are just lists.

Do them in order, follow the instructions, and boom, you have a scone.

Maybe, subconsciously, I think that if I do the things on my list, follow the instructions, then boom, I'll be whole again.

I don't think it's about control.

Miles is in my head.

He's in my head about a lot of things actually.

Like the whole idea of starting a business.

I think he might be more excited by the idea than I am. After I showed him the space and told him about my ideas, we walked back to The Bexley, and he didn't stop talking about it the entire way.

He's in my corner.

It's another feeling I haven't had in a really, really long time.

His idea to make an outdoor porch and put an actual lemonade stand there so people could walk up and order right from the window was crazy good.

He even sent me information about obtaining permits and a business license and everything I could ever need to know about food sanitation.

He owns a building, so it's apparent he's gone through some of it already.

I don't know if I can.

I don't know if I have the money.

I don't know if it will succeed.

I stop writing. I look at the last three sentences. I consider them for a beat, then make a couple of adjustments:

~~I don't know~~ WHAT if I can?

~~I don't know~~ WHAT if I have the money?

~~I don't know~~ WHAT if it will succeed?

Maybe it's delusion that spurs this change. Or Miles's excitement rubbing off. He's a good guy. A good friend. A really good guy friend.

A really good-looking good guy friend.

I scan down to the bottom of my list, and feeling like a teenage girl with a diary, I add one more thing . . . and then immediately cross it out because the second I reread it, a wave of fear washes over me.

9. ~~I want to fall in love again.~~

CHAPTER 16

Saturday morning Google searches:

What do I wear to pickleball?

How likely am I to get injured playing pickleball?

What is a pickleball?

"Why do you look like that and I look like"—I give myself a once-over—"this?"

Miles frowns. "What are you talking about? You look great."

I do not, in fact, look great. I look like a mom who's cosplaying as an athlete.

Miles, on the other hand, looks like he's just been featured in a Gap activewear ad. I'm starting to think this guy couldn't look bad if he tried.

Even when he's disheveled, he still looks sexy. The worst part? He doesn't even have to try.

"I don't really want to go," I say, lamenting my yes. "I'm not good at sports." Also, I've been actively avoiding situations where I might make a public spectacle of myself. Twice is plenty. And if anyone is going to go viral getting smacked in the face by a pickleball ball, it's me.

"Come on, it'll be fun," Miles says. "Make a list, you'll be fine."

I shoot him a look.

"You already made a list, didn't you?"

In lieu of a response, I hand him an apple turnover.

"I didn't earn this. I haven't sent you on any dates."

I grab my bag and keys, then start for the door. "I need an honest opinion. In case I put them on the menu." I turn back and find him smiling.

"You're doing it." A statement, not a question. "The Porch."

I hold up a hand to keep his expectations in check.

To keep *my* expectations in check.

To keep everyone's expectations in check.

"I'm not *doing* it, I'm *thinking* about it. I went over everything you sent, and maybe I'll talk to Lennon about the space. But it's all just talk, you know. Just . . . dreams." John's voice creeps in at the back of my mind, but I quickly shut it down.

He levels my gaze. "You're totally doing it." He takes a huge bite of the turnover. "And this definitely needs to be on the menu. Oh, can you add my favorite dessert? Those chocolate Scotcheroo things. They're—"

"Rice Krispie treats with peanut butter, butterscotch, and a layer of chocolate on top," I say. "I love those too." And I already added them to my menu, but I don't tell him that.

"You'd probably have to make them huge, like the size of a brick, to sell them in a bakery, but . . . I'd buy them."

"Noted," I say as we walk out to his Range Rover. "I'll get right on that."

As I walk around to the passenger side of his car, he shouts at me, "You're totally doing it!"

I shout back, "Shut up!"

But I secretly smile.

Because he's in my corner.

We drive over to the park where the pickleball courts are located. We park the SUV and get out, then make our way over to the courts, where we find Lennon wearing a cute green skirt and matching high-necked tank. Her white Nikes have a green swoosh on them, and she is, as expected, gorgeous. She's got on a cute white visor that somehow makes her blonde bob even more adorable.

I could not pull off that visor.

She rushes over and pulls me into a tight hug, and again, I'm stunned by her physical display of affection. It's so genuine I'm not sure how to process it.

"I'm so glad you're here!" She pulls back and looks at Miles, hugging a clipboard to her chest. "And you must be Miles. Claire's neighbor-not-romantic-partner." She sticks a hand out in his direction.

Miles laughs and shakes it while I search the immediate area for a hole to dive into. "That's right," he says.

"Are you sure about that relationship status?" Lennon squints at both of us.

Miles and I look at each other, then back at Lennon. "Yes," I say, teeth gritted. "Just friends."

"Okay, I just wanted to be absolutely sure before everything kicks off." She pulls two white papers off the clipboard and hands one to each of us.

"What are these?"

"Your numbers," she says.

I look at Miles, who seems as confused as I am. Did we accidentally sign up to run a 5K?

"I think you're both going to be very popular today." Lennon writes something down on the clipboard as a man appears by her side and wraps an arm around her shoulder.

"Oh, hon, this is my new friend, Claire, that I told you about," Lennon says. "Claire, this is my husband, Daniel."

My mind has snagged on Lennon's previous comment, but I don't want to be rude the first time I'm meeting her husband, so I shake his hand, then introduce Miles.

Daniel is a tall guy with a wide smile who bears a striking resemblance to Henry Golding. If I weren't mentally spiraling, I'd probably spend a bit of time admiring what a striking couple they are.

"Sorry, Lennon," I say once the pleasantries are done. "What did you mean we're going to be very popular?"

"You and Miles," she says. "Because you're both so good-looking."

I frown, doing a slow survey of the pickleball courts. And that's when I realize that Miles and I aren't here to play pickleball with Lennon and Daniel.

There's a big banner strung up on the chain-link fence that says: Chicago Singles PickleMixer.

Miles must see the sign at the same time I do, because he busts out laughing, clearly less horrified by this tragic turn of events than I am.

"Lennon?!" I do nothing to disguise the horror in my voice.

She glances up from the clipboard. "Yes?"

"This is a singles event?" My tone still says "horrified."

Her smile is wide, and I briefly marvel at how white her teeth are. "Yes!"

"You failed to mention that!"

She purses her lips. "Did I not?"

"No." My eyes are wide. "You didn't."

So far, every date I've been on has required a certain amount of mental preparation. I didn't do that today. Most of my time was spent worrying about the whole idea of playing pickleball. Because one stressor is enough.

"Daniel and I actually met at one of these events," she says. "So now we help organize them. It reminds us of those early times—when it was all magic and butterflies and not dirty diapers and late-night feedings." She smiles. "I promise it's going to be *so fun*—and so much better than those horrible dating apps." She shudders. "I have to go help Daniel, but we're almost ready to start."

My smile probably looks as forced as it feels, and as Lennon rushes off, I slow-turn back to Miles, who is checking out the rest of the group, completely unbothered by this new information.

He glances at me. "Why do you look like you want to throw up?"

"I thought we were coming here to play a friendly game of giant, life-sized Ping-Pong. I had no idea I was going to have to learn this game in front of strangers who are essentially rating my date-ability."

He smiles like this is no big deal. "Don't overthink it, Claire. Just have fun."

"That's easy for you to say," I spit. "I bet you were never picked last in gym class, were you?"

He pulls a face.

Clearly not.

"Everyone! If we could have your attention!" Daniel calls out from the center of the courts. "Come a little closer and we'll explain how the event is going to go!"

"He is way too cheerful," I groan.

"Come on, Oscar," Miles says, which makes me *wish* I had a trash can I could dive into.

We move into the center of the courts and listen as Daniel breaks down the rules.

"You're a single now, but with any luck, today is the day you're going to find your double!" Lennon says this like she's a cheerleader at a basketball game.

I take a step toward Miles. "I didn't think she was such a cheeseball, but—"

He glances down at me, and when he does, I realize just how close I am to his face. Per usual, he's unfazed, but me?

Even my brain is stuttering.

"Everyone's cheesy when they're in love," he whispers, mouth dipping into that trademark lazy grin.

He's so close I can smell the woodsy scent of him, and my insides tingle at his nearness.

"All players have been given a number," Daniel says. "Attach the number to your chest. You've been divided into brackets based on your age, and my lovely wife is handing out those brackets now. You'll rotate through playing doubles with other singles. At the end of the event, you'll fill out a card with the numbers of any other players you'd like to stay in touch with. We'll go through the cards, and if there's a match, we'll make sure to get you connected."

I groan. "This is my worst nightmare. It's like a public, real-life version of swiping left."

"Wow," Miles says. "Is your glass always half empty?"

"Only when my dignity is on the line," I say as Lennon hands us cards with what looks like a tournament bracket breakdown, complete with court assignments and pairings.

"Just find your number and the number of your partner and get to playing! After the first round, we'll rotate on through." Lennon squeezes my arm, clearly oblivious to the fact that this is my actual worst nightmare.

"Number forty-three?" A perky redhead walks up to Miles.

"That's me," he says.

"I think you're my partner." She giggles. She's wearing an actual pickleball outfit, like Lennon, and I imagine she's done this before.

He glances down at the card Lennon gave him. "I think you're right." He smiles at her, and the woman smiles back.

Ugh. He's probably going to have eighteen phone numbers after this.

I look at my own card as the two of them leave and a very large, very muscular guy with dark hair and a beard walks up to me. "Number forty-two." He nods at my chest. "Are you ready to crush the competition?" He lets out a sound that's somewhere between a grunt and a yell, then starts off in the direction of court number five.

I glare over at Lennon, who responds with an enthusiastic thumbs-up.

"Forty-two!" the Hulk shouts from court number five. "You coming?"

I raise a hand in a wave and start walking toward him. "Yep!"

The Hulk frowns. "Where's your paddle?"

"Oh, right." I jog over to Lennon as my doubles partner lets out a loud groan.

"They put me with a newbie again," he says—and not quietly.

My skin is on fire. What am I doing here?

When she sees me, Lennon's eyes brighten. "Oh! You need a paddle!"

"Or you could take my place," I say weakly. "I'm not going to be good at this."

"You'll be fine," she says, handing me a bright green paddle. "Just hit the ball over the net! Everyone is just here to have fun, so go have fun!"

* * *

Pickleball is not fun.

And do not let Mr. Popular, Miles Westbrook, tell you differently.

Over the course of a couple of hours and not nearly enough water breaks, I played five matches of pickleball. Matches? Rounds? Sets? Whatever they're called.

My partners were as follows:

Partner one: The Hulk. Judging by his wildly competitive streak, this man has never lost a game in his life. He missed the whole point that this was a singles event and not an actual pickleball tournament. He covered the entire court and threw a tantrum if the ball came my way and I didn't return it. At one point, he yelled,

"DO NOT hit that ball!" Zero out of ten do not recommend. I did not ask for his number.

Partner two: Fred. At least twenty years older than me at the very top end of our age bracket. You might be thinking "sweet old man," but Fred is a pervert. He smacked my butt with his paddle three different times (and once without) and refused to call me anything but Sweet Cheeks. At the end of the match, he told me he could "rock my world." Hard pass.

Partner three: Randy. A bit on the younger side. Wore earrings. Invited me to hear his Journey cover band play at a bar in the suburbs. Every time we got a point, he played the air guitar and let out a death-metal-inspired screech that would make dogs cock their heads from side to side. Nope.

Partner four: Neil. Started our match by mansplaining the rules of pickleball to me. Twice. As if I were four years old. Granted, I'm not the Pickleball Queen, but the condescension! Broke down his strategy for "maximum domination," which involved a spreadsheet on his phone. Maybe even more intense than the Hulk. No thanks.

Partner five: Greg. Actually nice. Totally normal. Self-effacing. Equally as bad at this game as I am. Able to laugh at his mistakes, and between the two of us, I don't think we scored one point. I wrote his number on my little card and handed it to Lennon.

And he asked for my number too.

I was not happy Lennon conned me into coming, but she was not about to apologize.

"You left with a number, Claire," she pointed out. "All's fair in love and pickleball."

In a weird twist, when I was making plans with Greg, Miles and his only match of the day, the redhead from *his first game, walked up. She's a bartender named Daphne with an arm sleeve of tattoos, but she had to be at least mid-thirties, so in my mind, that was a switch from his normal fare.*

Still, I didn't like seeing her hanging on Miles.

It bothers me that it bothers me.

We all started talking, and somehow I agreed to a double date.

Tonight.

With Miles and Daphne.

What could possibly go wrong?

CHAPTER 17

Miles and I open our doors and step out into the courtyard at exactly the same time.

I watch as he closes his apartment door, and I find myself wondering what his place looks like. Meticulous? Modern? Messy?

None of my business, but I've developed a nosy streak where he's concerned.

It took me way too long to get ready. I found myself fussing over one strand of uncooperative hair.

I might be a little extra nervous because I've actually met Greg, and there's a little bit of potential there. I settled on black jeans, a cream off-the-shoulder top, and a pair of pointy kitten heels. I added layered gold necklaces and teardrop earrings, and my hair, other than the rogue strand, is in its natural curly state—a little wild, because it does what it wants.

When Miles turns and sees me standing there, his eyes go wide. Is my lipstick too bright? Am I trying too hard?

"*Wow.*" He overemphasizes the word. "You look amazing."

I brush my hands down my jeans and scrunch my nose. "Yeah?"

"Yeah," he says, nodding. "What's-his-name is a lucky guy." He nods at my bare shoulder. "That's going to drive him crazy." His gaze lingers there for a beat too long, and when he meets my eyes, his smile catches for a split second in the charged air between us.

"Greg," I remind him.

"Right. Greg," he repeats. Then, after a pause, he says, "Kind of dumb for us to take two cars, right?"

"Yeah, I was thinking the same thing," I say. "But what if you want to bring Daphne back to your place?"

He shakes his head. "I won't."

"But what if you guys really hit it off?" I ask.

He scrunches his nose. "Still not bringing her back here." Then his expression shifts. "What if you want to bring Greg back to your place?"

I shrug. "He can ride in the back."

Miles laughs, and I smile, curious about his certainty where the conclusion of the date is concerned. The night I first met him, he'd had two different women at his place on the same day—but since then, I haven't seen him with anyone.

I know he's dating—I watch him leave.

But I also watch him come home.

Ugh. I watch him a lot. I'm officially creepy.

"So do you want to ride with me?" Miles asks.

"Actually, sure," I say, aware that it might be strange to show up to a date with a man who is not my date. "I'm still not used to driving in the city."

We fall into step beside each other and walk toward the gate. For a flicker of a moment, I imagine what it would be like if Miles and I weren't meeting other people at this class. If we were going out together, just the two of us.

"This is a sushi class," Miles says as he opens the door for me. "I figured you haven't had sushi before?"

He holds eye contact for a three-count before that lazy grin shows up on his face. Before we left the park earlier, Miles made it clear he wanted to plan this date, but I had no idea he would plan it based on something I want to do.

"No, I haven't," I say. "Thank you."

He closes the door and runs around to the other side of the SUV, and when he gets in, the masculine smell of the car intensifies, sending a wave of desire straight through me.

Desire? What is that?

He starts the car and connects his phone to the speakers. After a few taps, the familiar riff of Journey's "Separate Ways" kicks off. He turns to me, holds up a rock-out symbol with both hands, and bites his bottom lip as he nods comically to the beat.

"You lunatic." I laugh. "But *great* song choice."

He tells me about one of his pickleball partners—a woman named Sheila who, from the sound of it, would be a perfect match for Freddy the Pervert—and we laugh and commiserate about the ridiculousness of middle-aged dating.

It's easy to talk to Miles. I should've crossed off *Find a friend* the second I met him.

Well, maybe not the *exact* second, but not long after. I suppose I wasn't expecting a good-looking man to become my actual friend.

Miles starts to slow down on Lincoln Avenue, another area of the city that is reminiscent of a small town. On either side of the street, there are shops and restaurants, some chains, some local stores—hidden charm among the mirrored sleekness of the Chicago skyline.

"There's the restaurant," Miles says, leaning down to look through the windshield, pointing at a space with a black awning.

"Looks like Greg and Daphne are already there," I say as we pass by in search of a parking spot.

Eventually, Miles finds one at the opposite end of the street. We park and get out, then meet on the sidewalk in front of the SUV.

"It's weird we're showing up together for dates with other people," I say.

"Do you want me to wait so we can pretend you didn't ride with me?"

I laugh, but when I look at him, I'm pretty sure my expression suggests that this might be a good idea.

"Okay, I'll run across the street. It'll look like I came from a completely different place."

"This is so stupid." I laugh. "But okay."

He grins, happy to keep up this charade, even though explaining to our dates that we're neighbors would really not be that big of a deal.

"I just don't want them to feel awkward," I say.

He holds my gaze for a long moment. "You like this guy."

I press my lips together. "He's nice. And he's normal. Which is a huge improvement."

He smirks then. "Got it." He points to the other side of the street and then, in mock-spy fashion, puts fingers on his watch. "Synchronizing. I'm assuming the position. On my mark."

I shake my head, smiling. "She's either going to love you or hate you."

"*Engage.*" He crouches, darts his head both ways, then crosses the street.

What a goof.

But I still watch him as he crosses.

After he makes it to the other side, he gives me two thumbs-up, and I start walking toward the restaurant, hoping that Greg and Daphne aren't awkwardly waiting. But as I approach, it's obvious they don't feel awkward at all. They're laughing and chatting, and they look perfectly at ease.

Which is a good thing because it would be doubly weird if our dates didn't get along.

"Hi!" I say as I reach them.

Greg spots me and steps away from Daphne. "Claire, hi!" He goes in to kiss my cheek, leaving a wet blob behind. "We were just talking about pickleball."

"Oh, fun," I say, trying to think of an inconspicuous way to wipe his slobber off my face.

"There's Miles!" Daphne waves, and I follow her gaze to the street, where I see Miles crossing toward us, trying to tell myself that the slobber is a fluke and not at all an indication of how Greg might be as a kisser.

"Hey, guys! Hope you weren't waiting too long," Miles says with a quick glance at me. "Took me a minute to find a place to park."

"Oh, I got a spot right at the end of the block," I say with a smile.

Miles raises an eyebrow, and Daphne loops her arm through his and pulls him toward the door.

"It's going to start soon," she says. "I've been *dying* to do one of these classes! I am terrible in the kitchen. Making drinks? Totally fine. Making dinner? Eh." She pulls a face. "I just wish we weren't doing sushi. I don't think I'm ever going to want to make sushi at home."

Miles tosses me a look as Daphne pulls him inside the restaurant, and Greg takes the door and politely ushers me through. Once we're inside, I pause to look around the space. The front, near the windows facing the street, is a retail space with shelves of cooking gadgets and books and special sauces and pans.

Beyond that, toward the back of the space, is a large counter that stretches parallel to what looks a lot like the kitchen in any home. There are tables scattered throughout the space, and a well-stocked bar.

A man with a long black apron welcomes us and leads us back to the long counter where the class is held.

We get situated near the end of the counter, putting Miles and Daphne perpendicular to Greg and me. We each put on a white apron, and the class begins.

Daphne grabs Miles's arm, looking at the portioned ingredients on the counter. "Actually . . . can I just watch?" She winces. "I don't like to touch raw meat."

"Uh, sure," Miles says.

"You can make mine." She scrunches her nose in what I think is supposed to be a cute expression, and if Miles is annoyed, he doesn't let on, giving me a peek into how his easygoing personality plays out when he's around other people.

We listen as a man who introduces himself as Chef Mario

explains the steps we need to take to turn the ingredients on the counter into "gorgeous sushi rolls."

Miles becomes Daphne's line cook as she points to the things she wants in her roll, and she watches, sipping wine and touching him.

A lot. There's a lot of touching.

Greg is very focused as he follows each of the chef's instructions precisely, determined to have "the best sushi roll in the class," an accolade that I'm pretty sure would go to Miles if it were a real thing.

He doesn't seem to need any instruction from the chef, moving around the counter with the same ease he seems to carry into every situation—even the ones that might be unfamiliar.

I envy him that.

Thankfully, unlike on the pickleball court, I also know my way around the kitchen, and when we're finished and I present what I think is a pretty perfect sushi roll, Greg makes a face.

"Ah, nuts, yours is better than mine." He says this lightly, just as self-effacing as he was on the pickleball court. It's refreshing.

"Ooh, yeah, buddy. She's got you there," Miles teases, rubbing it in with an amused grin.

Greg turns to me and smiles. "Had fun, though. How about you?"

"So far, yeah," I admit, and I am. It's not terrible.

For once.

"Let's sit down so we can eat!" Daphne picks up the plate Miles made (to her specifications, of course) and leads our little group over to a four-top table near the front of the space. The room fills with chatter as the other students all prepare to sample what they've made.

We sit, and Greg pulls out his phone.

"I'm so sorry, I have to check on my babies," he says.

I meet Miles's confused expression with one of my own. "You have babies?" he asks.

Greg looks up. "Oh! Not the human kind." He laughs. "I just adopted two kittens." He turns the phone around to reveal what looks like a nanny cam video of two cats in a small crib.

Daphne's "awwww" is so long I want to smack her on the back to make sure she didn't glitch. She reaches into her bag and pulls out her phone. Miles, who apparently doesn't care one bit about any of this, pops a roll into his mouth and quietly chews.

He nods and looks at me. "Whoa. That's really good."

"These are *my* babies," Daphne says, showing a photo of her with three cats, all wrapped up around her neck like a living scarf.

Greg takes the phone and zooms in on the cats—or Daphne's ample cleavage, I can't be sure. "You're a cat person too?" He hands the phone back to her.

"Always have been!"

"They're amazing, right?"

"I know!"

Miles and I share a look.

"Are you a cat person?" Daphne asks, looking at Miles.

"No," he says. "I am thinking about getting a dog, though."

"I want a dog too," I say. "A yellow Lab maybe? They're supposed to be such a good breed."

Miles nods. "They are. I used to have a Lab. That's a good pick."

I have no idea why, but this simple exchange makes my pulse quicken.

Daphne rolls her eyes. "You two are crazy. Cats are way better."

"Couldn't agree more," Greg says.

I pick up my sushi roll and take a bite. I have no idea what to expect—this is pretty far out of my comfort zone. As I put all the ingredients together, I found myself watching Miles for which flavors would be best. The end result is a roll that's nearly identical to the one he's eating.

He picks up the soy sauce and pours a little onto my plate. "Trust me."

I take a bite, letting the flavors fill my mouth—fresh vegetables and rice and spicy tuna—and I pause for a second to enjoy it.

Miles raises his eyebrows. "Good, right?"

"So good." My mouth is a little full when I say this, and I have to cover it to keep the food inside.

The corner of his mouth turns up in a faint smile as he takes another bite.

Daphne has angled her body—and her boobs—toward Greg. "What made you want to adopt?" She presses a hand to her chest. "There are so many cats out there that need a good, loving home."

"Honestly?" He inches toward her. "I saw this video on TikTok," Greg says. "It was one of those gut-wrenching stories about this little cat named Boots that had been found on the side of the road. Someone had just dumped her there—"

"How did they know her name was Boots if she'd been dumped there?" I ask, genuinely curious.

Miles snorts, but neither Greg nor Daphne seem to hear me.

Daphne gasps. "No. Way." Her hand is back on her heart. "Did the video show Boots hiding in a cage until another cat went in and got her?"

"Yes!" Greg practically shouts this.

"You aren't going to believe this—" Daphne is clicking around on her phone.

"What?" Greg hasn't touched his food. "You saw it too?"

She turns her phone around. "Was it this one?"

"Wait. *Wait.* Yes! That was it! That's the cat!"

"This is so crazy!" Daphne clicks a few more buttons, then turns the phone around, a pouty look on her face. "That's Boots. She's my cat!"

Miles catches my eye, then slowly reaches over to take a piece of Daphne's sushi roll. I widen my eyes and shake my head no, but then he scrunches his nose and nods slowly at me. I stifle a laugh and try to look nonchalant as he lifts a piece from her plate and slowly eats it.

Neither Greg nor Daphne notice.

"I can't believe Boots's story actually convinced you to save *two* cats, Greg." She studies him meaningfully. "That's amazing. You are a hero."

"Just call him 'Feline Fury,'" Miles quips.

I almost choke on my sushi.

Daphne frowns over at him, clearly unamused, and I have to look away.

"It was a hard decision," Greg says seriously. "But your video really painted a picture of how desperate the situation is. Dire, really. I couldn't *not* help."

She reaches across the table and grabs Greg's hand, leaning toward him, cavernous cleavage on full display.

He freezes, and I watch something silent pass between them.

"You know what"—Daphne pulls her hand back—"I need to run to the restroom." She widens her eyes at Greg for a quick second, and then she rushes off.

Miles picks up his soda and takes a drink, watching with an amused expression as Greg fumbles to put his phone back in his pocket.

"Oh, wow, I have to take this—" Greg pulls his phone back out and stands. "I'll be right back."

He rushes off, and I look at Miles. "His phone didn't even ring."

Miles chuckles.

"Did we just get ditched?" I ask.

He looks past me, out the front window, and nods toward it, making me look.

I follow his gaze and see Greg, arm draped around Daphne, hurrying away from the restaurant.

I look at Miles. "Unbelievable."

He shrugs and eats the last of his sushi. "Man, these are good."

"Aren't you annoyed?" I ask.

"Annoyed? Why?"

"Well . . . because . . ." I struggle to find a reason. It's not like I was looking for a life partner. "They're supposed to like *us*, not each other."

"Nah, I'm happy for them," he says. "They seem like a good fit."

He's not wrong.

I'm not a cat person.

"Is this how it works for you?" I ask.

"How what works?"

"Dating with no strings, or expectations, or interest," I say, like I'm moving pieces of a puzzle around on a table to see what will snap in place.

Miles stops chewing, seemingly considering the question, then shrugs. "Yeah, I guess this is how it works."

"You don't feel rejected?"

"Rejected? Number one, she's not my type. Number two, I'm not that deep, Claire," he says.

"I don't think that's true," I say.

His eyebrows shoot up. "Oh?"

"Nope."

He leans forward, and my whole body is caught by his gaze.

I clear my throat. "I think you go out with these women—random people you're not really interested in—so you aren't stuck at home, feeling lonely or whatever, but you do it to make sure there's no chance you'll ever get hurt again."

He leans back, folding his arms. "Is that your professional opinion?"

I pop another bite of sushi into my mouth and nod. "Tell me I'm wrong."

"You're wrong." He picks up his glass and takes a drink, eyes locked onto mine.

I shake my head, refusing to be the first one to look away.

He reaches for Daphne's plate and sets it on top of his empty one. "What makes you think I've been hurt?"

"Haven't you?"

He shifts, deflecting with humor. "I'm a guy, Claire. We push our feelings *way* down, and we don't ever talk about them."

"Oh, well, *that's* healthy," I quip.

He shrugs, like, *Eh, it works for me.*

He holds up another piece to me, offering. I tilt my head, sigh, and take it.

He then takes the last piece off of Daphne's plate and raises it like a toast.

"To cat people." He nods at the food in my hand with a loose grin.

At that, I smile, and we tap the last of the rolls together in a mock *clink* and eat at the same time.

Two things are true for me in this moment.

First, this is the best date I've been on so far, and it has nothing to do with my actual date.

Second, I want to know his story.

No matter how deep he's buried it.

CHAPTER 18

I read once that dog people wish that their dogs were human, and cat people wish that they were cats.

Like Shaquille O'Neal and Kevin Hart, they'll never see eye to eye.

After we eat, we thank the chef, then step outside into the cool spring air.

Miles glances over at me, and I must be radiating *I'm cold* vibes, because he takes off his jacket and drapes it around my shoulders. The gesture is so simple, I use all my mental power not to make it more than it is.

His hand lingers on my arm, and the lines of friendship go blurry for a second.

I have to look away.

"Thank you," I say.

"Of course." He drops his hand, and we start walking toward his SUV.

"Don't you feel just a little bit rejected?" I ask. "I mean, they ditched us mid-date."

"You obviously do." He laughs softly and sticks his hands in his pockets.

"I don't have a great track record here," I say. "If you count pickle-ball, I'm oh-for-eight. I'm starting to wonder if the problem is me."

"It's not," he says.

I go quiet at his certainty.

"Besides, do you really see yourself with *Greg* and his shelter cats?"

I bark out a laugh.

"You can definitely do better," he says. "You are way out of that guy's league."

The comment seems so easy that Miles obviously has no idea how it lands. I'm sure he's just being nice—a good *friend*—but for whatever reason, it makes my insides scramble.

"Let's get ice cream," he says, nodding to a little ice-cream shop up ahead.

"Yeah, okay," I say, still reminding myself that *we are just friends.*

My phone buzzes, and I pull it out and see a text message from John. I never got back to him about his pitch, and I'm guessing he wants to know if I've thought of anything brilliant that will help him land this big fish of a client. Like I've done so many times before. I click the phone off and tuck it away without reading the message.

I look at Miles, and his expression seems to ask a question without asking.

"Oh, yeah, sorry." I brush it off. "My ex."

"You guys still talk?"

"Not infrequently enough. He only calls me when he needs something," I grouse.

"What's he need this time?"

I explain about John's job and the "favor" he asked me to do for him, and after a beat of silence, he asks, "Are you going to send him ideas?"

"I'm not sure." I sigh. "On the one hand, I could probably come up with something that would work in like five minutes. But on the other hand . . ."

"Why help the guy who broke your heart?"

I catch a glimpse of my own sad smile in the window of the little ice-cream shop we're in front of. "Yeah. Something like that."

It's a weird feeling. I want to be wanted, but not for what I can do, just for who I am. And not by John.

Miles opens the door and I walk in, pensive as I order pistachio gelato, which Miles refuses to let me pay for. "Save your money for The Porch." He nudges me with his elbow, and I smile, trying not to think about John or his favor or the fact that, yes, once upon a time, he broke my heart.

But then I realize it feels a little more distant than it used to. Less painful to remember.

And maybe that's what they mean by "time heals all wounds." The pain is still there, but it's duller than it used to be. Is it silly to hope that one day it might actually disappear?

The bubbly girl behind the counter hands Miles his raspberry cheesecake ice cream with a smile, and we walk back outside. "There's a park not far from here. Ice-cream walk?" he says.

"Sure," I say, not ready for the night to be over.

Something else I choose not to analyze.

"Are you just trying to make me feel better about getting ditched?" I ask.

"Heck no, I just wanted ice cream," he says. But then, even though he's not looking at me, I catch his smile.

I give him a playful shove, and he laughs. "It's too bad you refuse to date anyone for real."

"Why?" He takes a bite and leads me into a park with a big ornate gazebo at the center of it.

"Because you're actually one of the good ones," I say. "Seems a shame to stick women with guys like Roger and Scott and Greg and keep yourself off the market."

He sits on the top step of the gazebo and brushes the space beside him, as if to clear a spot for me. I sit.

"Maybe I'm actually a terrible person," he says playfully. "I could be the absolute worst."

"Are you?"

"Nah." He holds his bowl of ice cream out in my direction. "Trade?"

I look down at my gelato, then at his ice cream. "Fine, but only a few bites."

We swap cups and eat in silence for a few seconds.

My phone buzzes again, and I wince an apology. "I just need to make sure it's not Minnie." I pull it out of my purse and see another text from John on the screen.

Miles sees it too. "Not Minnie?"

I stare at it for a beat. "Maybe I should make sure it's not *about* Minnie."

Miles takes a bite of my gelato as I click the phone open and read John's texts.

John: Hey, C, checking in on the Oleander account. Thoughts?

John: We're meeting the client early next week so if you've got something, I'd love to hear it.

John: Even just a tagline would help . . . ?

John: You there? I really need you to come through on this.

John: I'll be up, just let me know what you come up with.

I groan and click the phone off, but Miles snags it from me. He sticks it in front of my face to unlock it, opens the camera, then drapes his arm around me. "Smile."

"What are you doing?"

"Taking a selfie," he says. "Send it to your ex so he gets the hint that you're busy . . . living your life." He holds the phone up and snaps a photo of the two of us, then studies it.

"Eh. You look weird in that one."

"Hey!"

"We need to take another one," he says. "Get a little closer—like, pretend we're together." He scoots in and holds the phone back up. He looks at the two of us through the camera. "Maybe lean your head on my shoulder? Like, pretend you like me."

"I'm not that good of an actor," I say with a laugh, moving even closer and inhaling his familiar scent. His draped arm tightens as his hand lands on my shoulder, and at the touch, a ball of heat radiates in my chest.

I momentarily forget reason and tip my head down so my face is practically nuzzled right in the crook of his neck. "Aaand . . . there. Perfect. Don't move. Okay, but look at the camera and smile like you just found a cat in a dumpster."

At that, I laugh, and he takes five quick pictures. The air thickens, though it's quite possible I'm the only one who feels it.

"Send him one of those."

I take the phone and look at the photos, lingering on one in particular.

He's got a goofy grin, I'm laughing for real, and we look . . . like a real couple.

We look happy. I look happy.

And while it *would* be nice to prove to John that I'm not pining and heartbroken, I decide against sending it and click the phone off.

"Ah, you chicken. I knew you wouldn't." Miles smirks at me.

"Really? How?"

He shrugs. "You seem like you have your own lane on the high road."

"I've dipped down to the low road a few times." An image of the fountain behind the country club ballroom floats through my mind, and I shiver at the memory of the cold water soaking through my clothes.

I draw in a breath and hold up the cup of ice cream. "Trade back."

We switch again, and I take a bite of my gelato.

"How is it that you still believe in love?" Miles asks between bites. "This guy sounds like a total piece of work."

"Well, for one, I can't believe that one experience is *all* experiences."

He smiles. "Oh-for-eight."

I pull a face. He has a point.

But still. I don't want to believe that it's a "one-and-done, that's it, good night, folks" kind of life when it comes to love.

"In my experience," he says, in a rare glimpse behind the curtain, "relationships end. Badly. Was yours all that different from mine?"

I stare out at the open green space of the quiet park under the dim light of the moon, wondering if I should share this story. Will talking about it make it feel less painful, or will it only make it worse?

I wouldn't know—even in therapy, I never repeated the whole story of the night I found out about Misty, much to Dr. Baskin's dismay. I remember her saying, *"If you don't want to talk about it, then write it all down. Journaling is the cheapest form of therapy."*

I hadn't written it down either. Because the public humiliation felt cruel the first time around, and I had no interest in reliving it.

I didn't like thinking about it because I didn't like the way it made me feel.

It all felt too painful, too . . . *close*.

Plus, I didn't want *the other woman's* name in ink in my journal. It felt like tarnishing something sacred.

I didn't want to relive it, to remember how it felt to realize I was so disposable to the man I'd married and to the friends who meant something to me.

All that day did was prove my greatest fear—apart from the porch of my grandparents' old farmhouse, I had never found a place where I belonged.

I look at Miles and find him studying me with a quiet intensity that contradicts his demeanor.

"Uh-oh. Are we going to trade war stories?" I ask.

He points an ice-cream-filled spoon at himself. "Compartmentalization king over here."

"Yeah, I know. Then I can't unload my tale of woe on you."

He takes a bite. "Sure you can. I'm a great listener."

I look at him. "Well, that's hardly fair."

"I know," he says, smirking. "Isn't it great?"

I shake my head and roll my eyes.

And then, after a beat and out of character, Miles takes on a more serious tone.

"What happened, Claire?" I look up and he meets my eyes. "You can tell me."

I stick the spoon in what's left of the gelato and set the cup on the floor of the gazebo beside me. "Just to prepare you—this story doesn't have a happy ending." I draw in a breath, and I'm back there in a flash. It's amazing how easy it is to feel every detail of the days that changed your life.

No matter how much you'd rather forget them.

CHAPTER 19

A little over one year ago

I'm locked in a stall, trying not to clear my throat or breathe too loudly.

"I cannot believe she actually had the nerve to show up here." I hear the water turn on in the women's bathroom of the country club.

I know that voice.

And I often learn about the pertinent gossip this way. Perks of being a fly on the wall.

"And did you see what she's *wearing*? Ugh. Does she know this is a fundraiser for the children's hospital? She looks like she's auditioning to be a Vegas showgirl."

That's Roxie Cartwright. I can almost picture her face, pumped full of Botox, permanently showing the same expression.

I know exactly who she's talking about.

The young blonde wearing a silver sequin miniskirt and matching tank top—skirt too high and top too low—had definitely made an impression.

"What do you expect from a woman who doesn't think twice about sleeping with a married man?" Laincy Russell, wife of my husband John's business partner Bill.

"But here? Of all the places—" The water comes on. "When Claire is the one who planned this whole event?"

Wait.

Wait. What?

Did she say "Claire"?

"It's like she's doing it on purpose."

"Maybe she doesn't think anyone else knows about her and John."

My heart stops.

My stomach bottoms out.

My fingertips go numb.

What did they just say?

Are Roxie and Lainey talking about *me*?

My heart races at such a clip, an Olympic sprinter wouldn't be able to catch it. My hand reflexively goes to my mouth as I stifle a gasp.

"Shouldn't we tell her?" Lainey says. "John's so brazen about it. You'd think she'd at least notice, but at this point I think she's the only one who doesn't know."

"I'm not getting involved," Roxie says, and I can hear her rip a towel out of the dispenser. "Besides, she'll find out soon enough."

Seconds later, I hear the door of the bathroom open, then shut, and then I'm wrapped in the fluorescent hum of the quiet bathroom.

This . . . can't be right.

There must be a mistake.

I gingerly undo the lock on the stall and slowly walk out, making sure there's no one else there.

I catch a glimpse of myself in the mirror, and suddenly a pit caves in my stomach.

I fear there is a fool looking back at me.

Numbly, I wash my hands and then head back out to the dining room, where the auction portion of the evening is about to begin.

But before I can get inside, something sparkly catches my eye in the corner under the stairs.

Silver sequins.

I walk toward the low whisper of quiet voices, careful not to make any noise, and then I see him. My husband—one arm pressed into the brown brick wall, the other on the hiked-up thigh of the blonde.

They're half kissing, half talking. She's giggling into the nape of his neck, and I can't seem to make myself look away.

I'm frozen, my feet a pair of cinder blocks, wanting to run and hide, to hit the rewind button and pretend none of this is happening, but I can't move.

And then I hear a woman's voice behind me. "Oh, Claire, there you are—" She stops short and my world shifts into slow motion.

John turns and meets my eyes. The blonde's smile fades, but only for a second. The woman behind me puts a hand on my arm. It's Marcie, the other mom who helped organize this fundraiser. She must see what I see because she wraps an arm around my shoulder and gives me a little tug as John moves out of the shadows and into the lobby area where I'm standing.

"Claire, babe, it's not what it looks like—"

I blurt, "Not what it looks like? *Not what it looks like?* What does it look like, John?"

"Hey, let's talk this out. I can explain—"

But he can't explain away what I've just seen. There is no excuse, no reason, no acceptable explanation for any of it. And we both know it.

The world as I knew it is over, and everything about my life is about to change.

Whether I want it to or not.

My pulse kicks up another notch into what I can only assume is turbo speed, and I let Marcie lead me over to the corner of the ballroom. I'm supposed to be on the stage, starting the auction. I'm the one who is announcing each item, taking the bids, raising thousands of dollars for the children's hospital. A cause I care deeply about.

It suddenly doesn't seem to matter much.

Nothing matters much.

I feel like I'm walking in a haze.

"We can find someone else to go up there," Marcie says.

Then . . . cold clarity.

I face her, certain she's been talking to me for a lot longer than I've been listening. I shake my head, grit my teeth, and press the heels of my hands into my eyes. "No. This is my responsibility. I can do it."

"Claire . . ."

"*No.* I made a commitment," I say, voice faltering ever so slightly. "And unlike some people, that means something to me."

I see John walk into the back of the ballroom, and behind him, the showgirl.

"How old do you think she is?" I ask out loud to nobody in particular.

Marcie follows my gaze. "Twenty-seven."

I turn away and wince, but when I meet Marcie's eyes, I realize—she knew about this too.

"You don't have to go up there," she says.

"I'm *fine.*"

I'm not fine.

But I grab the handheld microphone and walk up onto the stage. My legs are wobbly, and I'm thankful I wore *sensible* shoes. No, my simple black dress with cap sleeves and full coverage can't compete with silver sequins and a very short skirt, but at least I'm less likely to fall down.

At the sight of me, the room goes still. I look around the sea of faces, all poised to pledge money to a very worthy cause. John's coworkers and their wives are here. The other members of the school board are here. The entire teaching and administrative staff are here.

And they're all looking at me.

I've known these people most of my adult life. Some of them since the day John started working at his father's advertising agency. The goal was always for him to become the CEO, and he'd done it. Last year, when his father retired, he handed the keys of his advertising kingdom over to John. They'd had a reception to celebrate. I'd stood by John's side, smiling and shaking hands and making small talk like a dutiful wife.

Anything else had never crossed my mind.

Heat rushes to my cheeks, and I start to sweat, my breathing more shallow by the second. How long have I been standing here?

In the back, I see the blonde take a step toward John, whose eyes are fixed on me. But I know he's not watching because he's worried about me—he's watching because he's worried I'll make a scene.

John is very big on public perception.

I've always respected that he has a reputation to maintain. But in this moment, standing here in front of friends and coworkers—I simply don't care.

"Ladies and gentlemen," I say into the microphone. "Before we begin tonight, I'd like to draw your attention to the back of the room where my husband is standing with the woman he's sleeping with."

A collective gasp echoes through the room.

"Oh, don't pretend to be surprised," I say. "I overheard Roxie Cartwright and Lainey Russell in the bathroom and it's pretty obvious that this affair is one of those well-known secrets. At least it is to all of you. Apparently, I'm the only one who had no idea." I laugh wryly, then mutter quietly, "The wife is always the last to know."

A low murmur makes its way around the room, and I look at the faces of the people I thought were my friends. Obviously, there is no way they *all* knew about John's affair, but I'm not thinking clearly enough to make that distinction.

John starts moving toward me. "Claire, honey, maybe put down the microphone? Let's talk about this somewhere else? Somewhere more private?" He's speaking to me like I'm a toddler, and it makes my blood go cold.

"Like under the stairs? Where I just caught you?"

He looks around, shrugs and smiles, visibly uncomfortable.

"I devoted twenty-three years to this man," I say. "*Twenty. Three.* Gave up everything to make sure he had the life—and the *wife*—he wanted. And this is how things end up? Tossed aside for some discount Barbie who, by the looks of it, hasn't even hit puberty yet."

"Claire!" John is standing on the floor right in front of me, wearing a look that used to mean something to me.

"Is she old enough to drink from the bar?" I say into the mic, causing a little feedback.

"Knock it off," he says through gritted teeth.

I take a step closer to the edge of the stage, hold the mic so it's touching my chin, and glare right back. "How long has this been going on?"

"Claire, you're acting like a child."

"How. *Long. John.*" I say this into the microphone, and the sound of my own voice booms through the speakers.

"Come outside and we'll talk about this." He reaches up and tries to put a hand on my leg.

"Don't *touch* me," I snarl, voice quavering.

All I see is red. Hurt and anger are now driving the car.

"I gave you everything." Tears spring to my eyes. "*Everything*, John."

John sighs. Behind him, I can see a whole table of beautifully dressed people, eyes averted like they're witnessing something they shouldn't be.

And they are.

The demise of my marriage.

Behind them, I see multiple phones pointed in my direction. "You're *filming* this?" I shout, throwing down the microphone, making it thump and whine loudly through the speakers. I start making my way down the steps, not in control and not knowing what I'm doing. "Is this entertaining to you?!"

John lunges for the microphone, nodding to Mr. Burrows, the hospital rep, who meets me at the edge of the stage and puts an arm around me to stop me from making my way into the crowd.

He turns me toward Marcie, who's standing helplessly off to the side.

I hear John's voice in the mic.

"Well, hey, everyone, uh . . ." He fumbles a bit. "Let's take a brief couple minutes and then see if we can get this night back on track, shall we?"

Back on track?

I break. The anger and hurt are too much, and I can actually feel my mind snap, and I can't hold in the emotion.

I fold, crumpling into Mr. Burrows's arms, sobbing.

I can't think. I can't see, and the world as I knew it lay in pieces at my feet.

Once the whole story is out there, I can't take it back.

The emotions are as fresh now as they were then, and the tears on my face are proof.

Miles is now the only person I've ever told it to. Obviously, lots of people were there to witness this disaster, but I don't talk about it. Ever.

Until now, apparently.

At first, he doesn't say anything, like he's trying to process all the things he didn't expect me to say. And I go quiet.

All out of words. All out of tears.

He shifts, angling his body toward me, and for seconds that feel like hours, he just looks at me. But more than that . . . he sees me.

And while maybe it should be uncomfortable or unnerving, it's not. It's quiet. And raw. And honest.

And safe.

He reaches over and swipes his thumb across my cheek, letting his hand rest on the back of my neck, seemingly unbothered by my show of emotion.

"You've never been with a man who deserved you, have you, Claire?" he says quietly.

I close my eyes and another tear escapes.

Miles wipes it away, and when I open my eyes, he says, "I'm starting to wonder if there's anyone out there who does."

I'm hyper-focused on the way his hand is cradling my cheek, the way his thumb moves lightly along my face, the way he's looking at me—not like a friend.

Then, at the perfect time, he breaks the sadness. "I mean, you play pickleball like a newborn giraffe, but hey, we can't all be winners."

I laugh through the tears.

He smiles and pulls his hand back. "Can I see your phone real quick?"

I frown, knowing what he's going to do—but I unlock it and hand it over.

He taps a few buttons, then spins the phone around and shows me.

He's pulled up the text thread to John, and he's added the photo that I lingered on before.

The one where I look happy.

Miles then holds up a finger—*wait one second*—and types out a message.

He spins the phone around to me again.

Haven't had time to brainstorm. Probably won't get to it. Sorry!

He moves it ever so slightly toward me, shaking it a little.

I hesitate, then reach over and tap the button to send it.

I cover my mouth to try to hide a smile, because even though it shouldn't, sometimes being just a little bit petty feels really, really good.

* * *

I have never, ever had feelings for someone who was "off-limits" to me. Unless you count Jimmy Ballard in the ninth grade. He was off-limits because he was dating Noelle Fisher, the prettiest girl in school, but in typical male fashion, that didn't stop him from flirting with me. Maybe it was that crush on Jimmy that taught me that off-limits boys are off-limits for a reason.

This is my written reminder to myself that Miles is off-limits.

Miles is off-limits! You hear that, Claire?!

I am not a hormonal teenager. (I am a hormonal, perimenopausal adult woman, which I'm starting to think might have some similarities, but seriously, I know better.)

But tonight, when he said those words—"You've never been with a man who deserved you"—it set off this chain reaction inside me. The kind of emotional domino effect there's no coming back from. The kind that feels like a hangover the next morning.

And I don't want to get all caught up in something that can never happen.

I don't want to get caught up at all. If I'm honest, I'm not looking to be swept off my feet. I'm just looking for someone stable.

Actually, maybe that's not true. John was stable. Until he wasn't. Maybe what I really want is someone who is so in love with me, the thought of cheating would never cross his mind.

Someone who maybe loves me just a little more than I love him.

Gosh, is that terrible to admit?

I deserve to be loved, right? Without the threat of betrayal.

But if I could keep that love from making me lose my mind, that would be best. Because I can't risk everything again—and I can't change myself to suit a man. Not when I'm so close to figuring out who I am.

I want a partner. I want to believe real love exists. But I also want to protect my heart at all costs.

Where do all these contradictions leave me?

CHAPTER 20

The thought of doing something just for me, selfishly, is strange.

It's not in my nature. After years of taking care of everyone else, I'm not even sure how to begin.

But a small-town bakery in the heart of Chicago? That dream is my own. *My* idea.

My plans. My money. All of the risk and all of the reward.

This is the job I want. The one I feel passionate about. The one that will get me out of bed in the morning. Not just because it sounds fun. Not just because it's a way for me to share something I love.

Because I believe I *can* do it.

I pull out my phone and call Lennon.

"Tell me everything," she says. "How'd you and Pickleboy hit it off?"

Pickleboy. Hilarious.

I singsong, "Oh, he ditched me in the middle of the date."

"Oh no!"

"Oh yeah," I say, mimicking her. "But it was fine. He and the redhead—Daphne—hit it off. They bonded over cats."

"Cats? Like the musical?"

"No," I say, laughing. "But that would be so much worse."

She laughs. "Unbelievable. So Hot Neighbor was also ditched?"

"Yeah," I say, reminiscing about the night. "We got ice cream."

"Okay . . . promising."

I squint at the phone. "Promising?"

"Yes! You and Miles went on a date."

"No," I say. Because seriously, if she starts teasing me about Miles, I'm going to turn into that ninth grader with the off-limits crush again. And it's taking everything in my power *not* to let that happen. "We're just friends."

"Uh-huh."

"Seriously," I say. "Miles is not interested in any kind of serious relationship."

"And that's a problem?"

I pause, trying to imagine a world where I'm a casual dater.

I suppose that's what I've been doing, hilariously.

"I don't want to become one of Miles's two-dates-and-he's-out women," I say. "We're friends. Good ones, it turns out. And I still don't have many of those."

"You have me," she says. "I'm a great friend."

I smile. "You are. But I didn't call you to talk about boys. This is a business call." I try to put on my most professional voice.

"Oh, okay. Let me shift gears," she says. Then, lowering her voice, sounding like an announcer, she says, "You've reached Lennon. How can I help you?"

I smile at the change in her tone. "The storefront we looked at—did . . . the chiropractor lease it?" I realize once my question is out that I'm nervous.

Nervous she'll say no.

More nervous she'll say yes.

"Let me check," she says. "Since it wasn't *technically* my listing, I haven't kept track. But . . . why?"

"Oh, you know." I try to sound casual. "Just curious." I'm amazed I can hear her shuffling papers over the sound of my heart pounding.

"Okay, here it is." More shuffling. "No, the chiropractor didn't lease it, but . . ."

I hold my breath as I listen for what's next.

I hear the clicking of her computer keys. "Nope. Still available."

I blow out the breath in one hot stream, shocked at how happy this makes me. "Okay, so . . . what do I need to do to lease it?"

"You want to lease the storefront?" I can hear the excitement in her voice.

"I think so," I say. "If I can swing it. I want to open a bakery."

"No way, Claire! That's a great idea!" Her enthusiasm is like a confetti popper inside me.

"Yeah?"

"Yes! I love this!" She's back to clicking. "Hold on." She must've set her cell phone down and picked up her office landline because I can hear her talking to someone else. "Yeah, I've got a very interested renter." Pause. "Right. Okay, great." Pause. "Sounds good. I'll call when I have more details, but don't show it to anyone else." She laughs, then comes back on the line. "All right, let's figure out what we need to do to make this happen."

And it hits me then that I've just taken the first real step toward starting my own business. In a new city.

Because I want to.

Over the next few days, I work on the logistics of owning a business and opening a bakery.

It's . . . a lot.

There are things I never thought to think of, but thankfully Lennon—and Miles—are both willing to lend their expertise.

I should probably make more of an effort to stop thinking about Miles, but it's hard when he keeps coming around. Last night, after I texted to tell him the ball is rolling, he showed up with a pizza and a six-pack of Dr Pepper. "I'm here to tell you everything I know about starting a business," he'd said.

"What are we going to do after those four and a half minutes are up?" I cracked.

"That's funny," he said dryly. "I mean, I can take my Dr Pepper and go—" He raised a brow and turned to leave.

"No, no, no! I'm kidding. I might actually need some help here. There's so much to think about. I thought it would be about the baking, and it's totally not."

"Yeah, lots of people start businesses to do something they love. The problems start when what they love turns into a job." He walked into my apartment and set the pizza and soda down on the counter, then looked at me. "Do you have a pen? You're going to want to take notes. I'm very successful. A very big deal."

"With a very big head." I smiled at him, glad he showed up, then spent the rest of the night asking questions, making plans, and laughing. A lot.

This was becoming a habit.

"Part two tomorrow," he'd said when he was leaving. "I'll get Mediterranean." He stopped in the doorway. "Unless you have other plans."

I grabbed onto the door, not wanting him to leave. "I don't."

At the sight of his now-familiar smile, my stomach did a little two-step. He stood there for a beat, then finally turned and walked away.

I won't admit how long I stood there watching him walk toward his apartment.

Not out loud anyway.

Afterward, I stalked his website because I had no idea, really, what he does or how he does it.

Sure, I'd seen the courtyard, and I knew that if he owned this building he had to be doing pretty well for himself. But I didn't understand the scope of his success.

He's the owner of a very prominent firm that boasts a pretty incredible portfolio. High-end clients with noteworthy projects.

After looking through the before and after photos of several projects on his website and hearing him talk about a playground installation he's doing for the city with all the excitement of a kid meeting their favorite superhero, I'm more certain than ever that this man is more than a landscape architect. He's an artist.

I spent the rest of the night sketching, journaling, and dreaming, mostly about The Porch, but about Miles too.

The next night, I'm standing at his door holding a glass pan of baklava and trying to calm the nerves bouncing around in my stomach. Before I can knock, he pulls the door open.

"Hi there, *future business owner,*" he says knowingly.

I look up and off to the side and do a little curtsy.

"I saw you walk over. Come on in." He opens the door a little wider, and I walk inside, feeling a little like we're taking our friendship to a new level.

He invaded my space, but he's inviting me into his.

Being in here is a glimpse into who Miles is when nobody else is looking. Who is, if I had to guess, a lot like who he is when we're together.

Still, I'm apprehensive. Guarded. I want things to be honest, and I *think* I'm getting to know this guy . . . but look what happened last time.

I thought I knew John.

Turns out everyone knew him *but* me.

With Miles, my emotions and my logic are struggling to find a balance.

I take a quick look around. The layout of his apartment is similar to mine. The vibe in here is very Nate Berkus. Modern, neutral, masculine. And it smells like Miles, a fragrance that is quickly becoming one of my favorite—and most familiar—scents.

"I made this," I say, holding out the baklava.

As Miles takes it from me, his fingers brush mine and I force myself to silently chant, *He's just a friend* over and over in hopes that the romantic part of me will listen.

"It's celebratory baklava," I say, my hands still on my end of the pan.

"What are we celebrating?" he asks.

I take a breath and hold it. "I know tonight is part two of you sharing your infinite wisdom with me, but"—I wince—"I signed the lease this morning."

He raises his eyebrows and grins.

I make a face that's equal parts excited and terrified.

He beams. "Big first step. *Huge* first step."

"Am I crazy?"

"Yeah," he says, not missing a beat. "But it's way more fun that way."

I let go of the dish and groan. "I'm not a huge risk taker."

He walks over to the counter and sets down the baklava. "Huh. I beg to differ." He waves a hand over the spread on the counter. "You're about to try another new cuisine. That's risky."

I smile and shake my head, then look at all the unboxed Mediterranean dishes that smell like heaven. "You know what I mean."

He puts his hands on the counter and pulls my gaze. "Listen, you moved here to a city where you don't know anyone, with no job, no family, and no friends. I'd say that's pretty risky."

I feel intoxicated realizing that he noticed. Because part of me assumed everyone back home, apart from Minnie, probably thought I was running *away* from something and not *toward* something.

But Miles gets it. And he's acknowledging how hard it was.

"Pretty brave, Claire."

I don't look away. I'm frozen and trying desperately to swallow the lump in my throat. "Thank you," I finally say.

He claps his hands together and looks down at the food. "I don't think we should even use plates," he says. "Grab a fork."

I'm grateful for the change of subject and the levity. "Is that because you hate doing dishes?" I laugh.

"Yes." He holds out a fork and I take it, then sit on the stool next to the counter.

As we eat, we talk. I have about a million and twelve ideas, and even more questions.

Thankfully, the space is in great shape—mostly in need of decorating and not renovating, but there are still going to be some steep up-front expenses. This springboards the conversation into the benefits of getting a loan versus using my savings as an investment versus trying to secure an investor or two.

"I could invest," Miles says as he takes a bite of falafel.

My mouth is full of pita bread and hummus, but I shake my head, humming a closed-mouth "uh-uh."

"Why not?"

I swallow the bite. "It's a bad idea to get into business with friends."

"Who says?"

"People," I say, though I can't for the life of me think of one.

"What if I wasn't an investor, like, technically?" he says. "What if I just gave you some money to buy twinkle lights and tablecloths? Like a gift."

I frown. "Why would you do that?"

He frowns right back. "Why wouldn't I?"

He makes it sound so simple. So obvious. I laugh it off and look away.

Just friends. Just friends. Just friends.

"Plus your idea is so cool, and everything I've tasted so far has been incredible." He pauses. "You know this is a great thing, Claire."

"I read that most new businesses don't even make it five years," I say.

"Yeah, but all of those people are stupid," he says, deadpan, and I almost spit out the bite of pita bread in my mouth.

He seems pleased by this. "Yours is going to make it."

I look at him. "How are you so sure?"

He stops eating and looks at me. "How do *you* feel about it?"

"Terrified," I admit. Then a smile bubbles to the surface. "But excited."

He points his fork at me. "That's how I know." He takes a drink, then adds nonchalantly, "Plus, you've got me."

Do I?

Do I have you, Miles?

A shrug. "Plus, I believe in you." He takes a bite of chicken and couscous and chews, oblivious to how these words are affecting me. How starved I am to hear someone say them. How different it feels to have someone support me and not try to tear me down.

It's this thought that makes my eyes cloud over, and I take a drink in hopes that doing so will hide all of these unwanted emotions.

That's when Miles notices.

"Wait, what's wrong?" He turns toward me, but when I don't move, he reaches over and spins me on the stool so I'm facing him.

I smile. "Nothing's wrong, it's just—"

His expression holds—serious, concerned.

"I just appreciate you believing in me," I say.

At that, his brow quirks. "Oh *no.* Are you getting sentimental on me?"

I give his shoulder a shove, and he catches my wrist in his hand and holds it for a moment that feels like an eternity. My breath is trapped in my throat as I meet his eyes, surprised to find that the concerned expression has shifted into something else.

Something unreadable.

Something that looks—dangerous.

His grip loosens and slips from my wrist to my hand. "I do believe in you, Claire. I think you're amazing."

My laugh is nervous.

"You're so used to being overlooked, you don't realize it, but . . ." He twines his fingers through mine and looks down at our hands.

But what? Why did he stop talking?

His thumb moves slowly across the side of my hand, and my

skin tingles underneath his soft touch. I lift my chin to look at him and find his eyes trained on me. My mind floods with fear—the way I felt when I had to attempt a cartwheel on the balance beam in gymnastics when I was a kid. I stood there staring at the beam, then at my foot, certain there was no way for me to stay safe if I tried it.

That's how I feel now. A little unsafe. A little uncertain. Trying to figure out how *not* to fall.

My heart is at risk here, but the logical part of me seems to be out of the office.

Miles draws in a long, slow breath, moving forward on the stool and letting out a quiet, husky "Claire" before he takes my face with both hands and kisses me so fully I feel it in every nerve ending in my body.

My breath catches as I feel his lips on mine—soft, sweet, firm lips that are hungry for more. Of me.

More of me?

Miles is kissing me. And I'm kissing him back. And it's good. It's *really* good.

My body rises off the stool, moving closer to him, our chests touching as my hands wrap up around his back, pulling him closer and savoring every sweet second of this kiss.

I'm lost in it. Drunk on it—on him—and that realization is the thing that finally brings me back to my senses.

"Miles, I—" I pull back, my forehead pressing into his, hands on his chest as my gaze falls to the floor.

"Oh man, Claire, I'm so sorry—" He takes a step back, pushing the stool out of the way. "I crossed a line. I—" He drags a hand down his chin.

I shake my head. "No, it's—" I close my eyes, battling the ridiculous desire to do that again and the commonsensical realization that I absolutely cannot.

Only . . .

"You don't do relationships," I say, a reminder to myself more than anything. "That hasn't changed, right?"

He exhales and gives his head a quick shake. "No, it hasn't."

"Okay," I say. "That's good to know. Important to know." I smile, but I want to hide. I move away from the counter, away from him. I need air. And space. And distance.

"I screwed this up," he says.

"No, not at all," I lie. Because how do we go back to the way things were after this? Am I supposed to pretend it meant nothing to me when it meant everything?

"It's fine," I say. "Just a moment that . . . got out of . . . you know, a blip that sort of . . ." But it's not fine. And this is obvious by my very visible spiral.

"I really like you, Claire," he says. "You're funny and smart and you have no idea how gorgeous you are. I don't know anyone else like you, and—" He turns away, making an embarrassed noise. "I made it all weird."

"No," I say, still lying. "It's fine. I mean, seriously. It's not a big deal." I'm moving around the space as I say this, grabbing my bag, stumbling to put my shoes back on. "I'm going to go."

"No, please don't—" He moves toward me, and I hold up a hand to stop him.

"I have to go," I say, hoping he understands that him kissing me like that—like he wants me more than air—is not something I'll easily recover from.

That kiss came with feelings. Mine—not his. The kind that I've been actively burying because I know that he and I can never, ever work.

Because Miles doesn't do relationships. And I don't do casual.

We want very different things.

I walk to the door, but before I open it, I turn back and look at him, terrified that this night will mark the end of what we have—a complicated but beautiful friendship.

I frown.

He frowns.

"I don't want to stop being friends with you," I say.

"Good." I hear the relief in his voice. "I don't want to stop being friends with you either."

"But that can't happen again," I say. "I'm not . . . It's a . . . My heart isn't strong enough."

He nods. "Understood."

I smile. It almost feels real. "See you tomorrow?"

He keeps nodding. "Definitely."

My gaze dips from those icy-blue eyes to his full, kissable lips, and the charged air between us sparks.

"I don't do friends with benefits," I say, but my voice is weak. Because for a fraction of a second, I sort of wish I did.

"Good to know." He laughs lightly. "For the record, I didn't think you did. I just—" He pushes a hand through his hair, leaving it messy and disheveled and . . . sexy. "Lost myself for a minute. I promise it won't happen again."

I nod, open the door, and step out into the courtyard, trying really hard to silence the voice at the back of my mind that says, *Darn.*

* * *

Unknown Number: Claire, this is Dr. David Fitzsimmons.

Lorraine Ashby gave me your number, I hope that's okay?

Claire: Right! The dentist! Hi!

Unknown Number: People usually call me Duffy.

Claire: Right! Lorraine told me!

Duffy: It took me a little while to work up the courage to reach out. I saw you in that video, and you're just . . . magnetic.

Claire: 😳 Aw, that's really sweet.

Duffy: I'd like to take you out this weekend if you're free?

Claire: I'd love to. Saturday? I was thinking about visiting the zoo?

Duffy: Perfect. I'll do a little planning and send you the details.

Claire: Sounds great. I'm looking forward to it.

* * *

Minnie: Are you still on a dating break?

Claire: Actually, I'm going out with a dentist on Saturday.

Minnie: Really? Did Miles set this up?

Claire: Nope. This isn't an app match. He found me through a neighbor.

Minnie: Oh, wow. Okay.

So, since we haven't vetted him, we need safety protocols. I'll text Miles.

Claire: NO!

Sorry. No. Don't text Miles.

Minnie: ☹ Okay . . . someone needs to make sure this guy isn't a serial killer.

Claire: Follow this link: www.happyteeth.org

Does this look like the face of a serial killer?

Minnie: <photo of Ted Bundy>

Claire: It's a day date. In public. We're going to the Lincoln Park Zoo.

Minnie: Fine. But please make sure someone knows where you are at all times.

And don't try to pet the giraffes again.

Claire: That was one time. Leave me alone.

Minnie: 😂👦👋🦒🚨

CHAPTER 21

It has taken a considerable amount of effort to put Miles—and that kiss—out of my mind. It's stuck on a mental loop, replaying over and over.

If I close my eyes, I can still feel his lips on mine, even now, days later.

I'm determined to be as normal as possible with him. To put things back the way they were and pretend that I'm completely unaffected by all of it.

That's a lot of pretending. And I'm not a good actor.

The memory of it blindsides me when I'm not expecting it. Pouring cream in my coffee—oh! There are Miles's lips. Sprinkling salt on my eggs, and . . . his hands are on my face. Up to use the bathroom in the middle of the night—and there he is, looking at me like if he doesn't close the gap between us he might actually pass out.

Which is why the knock on my door Saturday morning, almost a full week after the kiss, is like a speed bump for my heart. I'm standing in the kitchen barefoot, holding a coffee carafe filled with water that's about to get the glow-up of a lifetime, and at the sound of it, I stare at the door.

Another knock.

I meant what I said. I don't want to lose his friendship. It's not a big deal. It was a kiss. Kisses happen all the time.

Only . . . they don't happen to me.

It's not a thing. Don't make it a thing.

I pull open the door and smile a little too big. Paint me purple because I might as well be the Cheshire Cat.

I force my face to *calm the heck down.*

"Good morning," I say.

"You've been avoiding me."

"I have not," I say, even though we both know I totally have been.

He studies me for a beat, and it's enough of a pause to trigger my overwhelming need to fill the space.

"Okay, maybe I have," I admit. "But I don't want things to be weird." I step aside to let him in. I do this without thinking—it's almost like muscle memory at this point.

"Then don't make things weird." He steps into my apartment, the same way he's done so many other times. Only this time . . . it's different.

Because he kissed me.

And I kissed him back.

And there is a very real part of me that wants to do it again.

"I don't think we need to talk about it," I say, meeting him in my kitchen. "Do we?"

He shrugs. "I mean, if you don't want . . ."

I overlap him with, "I'm not sure it's . . ."

We both stop. And smile.

"We're adults," I say. "Why is this so difficult? Can we just be adults about it?"

He nods. "I agree. Adults it is."

"It's just—" I shift my weight from one foot to the other. "It is kind of a big deal. Like . . . it's kind of monumental for me."

"Kissing?"

"Yes. Do you know the last time I kissed someone other than John?"

He smirks. "Is this you not talking about it?"

I make a face, pick up my water bottle, and take a drink.

I don't intend to voice all the things I've been thinking since that kiss happened. But I have had lots of thoughts. It's different than it was for me in my twenties. There's so much more at stake.

I'm not interested in casual. I wasn't even *looking* for anything until Minnie signed me up with Matched.

Along with the typical swoopy, swoony feelings, there is also a certain amount of pragmatism. I just can't afford to start over, pour out feelings just to get them stepped on again.

I know what's at stake here.

"That was my first postdivorce kiss," I say. "You are the first man I've kissed who isn't John in over twenty years."

He doesn't say anything.

"I have no idea what I'm doing in that area. Baking? Easy. Kissing? Romance? Who knows? Was it good? Did you enjoy it?" I feel my face heat as soon as those words are hanging in the air between us.

He cocks his head and smiles, looking like he's holding back a laugh. I pull a face. "Wait. Why aren't you saying anything?"

He chuckles. "I'm just enjoying this moment."

"Wait," I say. "Was it . . . okay?"

His eyes widen. "The kiss?"

"Yeah."

"You want my opinion?"

Oof. Maybe I don't. He's probably kissed *lots* of women.

He leans against the counter and crosses his arms over his chest. "I think I'd need to do it again to know for sure."

I shoot him a look, then chuck a kitchen towel at his head. He catches it, his casual smile hanging loose on his lips.

I match his posture, leaning on the counter opposite him and crossing my arms over my chest. "So?"

He stares back. "So what?"

"Kissing feedback?" I prompt.

His eyes narrow. "For not wanting to talk about the kiss, you sure are bringing it up a lot." His gaze falls to my lips, and my heart sputters. The assault on my senses intensifies as I remember every single second of that kiss. As I chew on my bottom lip,

Miles's focus zeroes in on the movement, and I have to wonder if he's remembering it too.

"I just think it could be informative," I say, eyes fixed on his.

"Informative," he repeats, taking a step closer.

"Educational," I say, still holding his gaze.

"Oh, educational, for sure." Another step coupled with the slight rise of his eyebrows.

"Are you going to repeat everything I say?" I ask, exasperated.

He's standing mere inches away from me now, and there's nowhere else for me to go.

"Maybe."

I lift my chin and find him watching me, cool and calm as ever, and it's the exact reminder I need that Miles is accomplished at this. He does this all the time. He makes women feel things so he can get what he wants—casual, easy, no strings attached.

And that's not me.

He's dangerously close to me again. So close that if I wanted to, in just a simple move, I could be back in his arms.

"Claire," he says softly. "You do not need any help in the kissing department." His eyes turn serious. "Any guy who gets to kiss you is very, very lucky."

When I swallow, I wonder if he can hear a cartoon sound effect. *Gulp.*

I'm frozen for a few seconds, and then I find my voice again. "You're just saying that." I give him a playful shove, but there's no trace of amusement behind his eyes.

"I promise I'm not," he says.

I resist the urge to ask him to go into detail as the air thickens between us, but if we keep talking about it, it's going to happen again.

It cannot happen again.

I clear my throat, hoping to cut the tension. "Well, thank you."

He gives me a quick nod and steps back a bit, as if to say, "You're welcome," and I realize broaching this topic with him was a little like stepping on a hornets' nest.

"Now . . . we'll never talk about it again," I say.

"You got it."

"We're good."

"Totally."

Thankfully, the moment passes, and things get a bit less electrically charged.

I take a breath, noting my own hesitation at what I'm about to say. "I . . . um . . . I have a date. Today."

It feels weird to say it. Miles and I aren't dating, so why does it feel like I'm betraying him a little?

"A date?" His demeanor changes slightly and his jaw twitches. "I thought you were on a dating app pause."

"It's not through the app," I say. "It's Duffy, the dentist that found me through Lorraine's video."

"Oh, you're doing that."

I shrug. "He seems really nice."

In the three text exchanges we've had, that is.

Miles nods. "Okay."

"We're going to the zoo." As if this is proof that he's a good guy.

"He's taking you to the zoo," he says.

"It was my idea, Mr. Judgy," I say, feeling personally offended. "I love the zoo."

He nods again, and I can't read his expression. "Okay."

"We'll get food or something too, probably." I hear myself saying the words, but I'm having trouble figuring out why I'm saying them.

"Were you asking about kissing because you're planning on kissing this dentist?" he asks.

I open the refrigerator and pull out a carton of coffee creamer. "No, but . . . it's not as scary to imagine as it was before." I close the fridge. "Thanks to you."

He looks slighted. "Wow. Glad I could help."

His tone is off. I'm not sure what I said.

I grin, trying to lighten things. "It's nice of you to use your powers for good."

He frowns, still seeming put off. "What do you mean?"

I pull the coffee beans out of the cupboard and measure them into the grinder. "You know . . . you've dated a *lot*—probably all kinds of different women—and in this case, it paid off." I glance over at him and see that his frown has deepened. "What?"

"That's not what I do," he says, like he's trying to make sense of my comment.

I laugh. "Miles, you go out with women all the time."

"Not as often as you think," he says.

"But enough," I say, confused. Does he not want to admit this? What am I missing? "You tell them you're not looking for anything serious. They inevitably think they can change you. You spend some time with them and, I don't know, just move on after a while. Right? You told me yourself you're not interested in long-term stuff." I chuckle, but the mood has gone sour. He's back to leaning on the counter. He's gone from casual to rigid, the frown still firmly in place.

I freeze. "What? What did I say?"

"Uh, nothing. Just your take on me is . . . interesting."

I set the coffee beans down. "Miles. Come on. You're anti-relationship but not anti-dating. It's pretty easy to fill in the blanks."

He nods slowly, considering.

I look at the coffee on the counter, then back at him. "Wait, did you want to go on a coffee walk?"

He pushes himself up to standing and shoves his hands in his pockets. "Uh, no. I actually have some work to do today. The playground project—it needs a little oversight."

"I'd love to see it," I say. "Just, you know, whenever."

"Yep." He starts for the door, and before I can say anything, he's opened it and walked out.

CHAPTER 22

Duffy and I agreed to meet at the entrance of the zoo.

It's early May, and Chicago weather is showing off her sunny side, so I decide to walk. On the way, I try to think of conversation starters for this date, but "What made you want to become a dentist?" or "Why in the world are you watching Lorraine on YouTube?" are the only questions that pop into my head.

Two questions and Miles, who seems to have taken up permanent space there.

I still don't know exactly what I said that rubbed him the wrong way. I was only saying things that he's said himself.

Right?

So maybe I filled in a few blanks where Miles's love life is concerned, but it's only with things I've actually seen.

The real issue is that there are actual feelings there. On my part. About him.

What am I supposed to do with those?

Stop dwelling, Claire. Think of Duffy. He probably has great teeth.

Plus, I've been wanting to visit the Lincoln Park Zoo since I moved here. I used to love taking Minnie to the one in Denver when she was little, and I haven't been to a zoo in years.

I spot Duffy standing at the entrance, recognizing him from his photo. When he looks at me, I wave.

His wave back is enthusiastic. He grins wide and starts walking in my direction. He's taller than I expected—clean shaven and preppy.

I smile when I reach him. "Duffy?"

"Claire! Hi!" He holds out a hand for me to shake it.

No slobbery kiss. Bonus.

"Hi," I say, taking his hand. "It's nice to meet you."

"It's nice to meet me too." He frowns. "Meet you—" He shakes his head. "Sorry, I'm nervous. You're even prettier in person."

"Oh, thanks." There's something endearing about Duffy, and I pick up on it instantly. I'm betting he's been friend-zoned a lot.

"Should we—" He motions toward the zoo, and I nod, falling into step beside him.

"Have you been here before?" I ask.

"Not since I was a kid," he says. "I *loved* coming here. I used to love the monkey habitat. Oh, and the penguins. They have the best personalities. Are you an animal person?"

"Sort of," I say. "I've always loved the zoo." As we walk, I tell him about the time I chaperoned Minnie's fifth-grade field trip to the Denver Zoo. I was wearing my hair in a ponytail, and apparently I got a little too close to a baby giraffe because it reached over the enclosure and grabbed onto my ponytail. And wouldn't let go.

Duffy's eyes are wide. "No way."

"The kids thought it was hysterical," I say. "But I genuinely feared for my life—or at the very least for my hair."

"So what happened?"

"After a couple minutes, it finally lost interest, but I swear it laughed at me as it sauntered away, leaving me traumatized and slobbery." I smile at the memory. "You'd think that would've soured me on giraffes, but the truth is, they still fascinate me."

This triggers a plethora of "getting to know you" icebreaker-type questions, and through these I learn that Duffy grew up in Ohio and attended an all-boys Catholic high school, where he played the tuba and led the debate team to a state championship. He moved here after dental school, and he's been here ever since. He's never been married but was engaged once, has an extensive

Lord of the Rings collection, has been to Comic-Con, and cosplays as Aragorn whenever he gets the chance.

Which is more often than one might expect.

He's quirky. But also, he's kind. It's obvious he has a really good heart. I knew it when he asked me a thousand questions about myself, then responded to all of them with:

"You're so lucky to have a daughter, Claire. I always wanted kids."

We are standing in front of the hippos when he says this. I'm holding popcorn, and he's holding a large soda. When he catches me watching him, he smiles, but there's sadness behind his eyes. He quickly brushes it off, though, turning toward the hippos, studying them thoughtfully.

"They are funny looking, aren't they?" He tilts his head, staring at the large beasts. "Did you know the name 'hippopotamus' means 'river horse'?"

"Uh, no, I didn't."

"Odd, though," he says. "They don't look like horses at all."

I smile at how seriously he's thinking about this.

"Also, they can hold their breath for five minutes straight," he says, facing me. The enthusiasm on his face falters for a second, and then he adds, "I was on the swim team in middle school and never got past seventy-two seconds."

"That's still pretty good."

He laughs. "I promise it's not. You know what else isn't good—wearing a Speedo in the seventh grade."

Swim team. Band. Dentist for kids. Animal lover. Keeper of hippo trivia.

Duffy is kind of wonderful.

We keep walking. In the lull, I search for things to say, landing on, "You know, you could still have kids." Not exactly sure why that's what I decided to say . . . "But you may want to date someone younger than, you know, me."

"I've tried," he says. "I'm an old soul, so it's hard for me to connect with younger women." A shrug.

If I were making a "Duffy pro-con list," that would definitely go in the "pro" column.

"I do the Big Brother mentorship program, though," he says. "My little brother, Dom, is such a good kid. We play chess together. Do you play?"

I scrunch my nose. "No, I've tried, but I don't really understand the strategy. My pop and I played checkers, though."

He smiles. It's a nice smile. "Ooh, checkers is good too. And Scrabble. Maybe we can play board games next time."

I look over at him warmly. "I'd love that."

"Yeah?" His face brightens.

"Yeah. That sounds fun." And I mean it. No, Duffy isn't setting off any fireworks, but he's sweet, and I've been back at this long enough to know that sweet goes a long way.

I tell him about Minnie and how she'll be back from Oxford soon, about how I moved here because I always wanted to live here, and then I say, "And I just leased a storefront to open my own bakery." My eyes go wide. "I haven't said that out loud very much." I look over at him. "It's really new."

New and vulnerable and scary.

Just saying the words, sharing it with a stranger, I run the risk of hearing a list of reasons why this was a terrible idea.

The taxes are crazy in Illinois. Starting your own business is crazy in this economy. How are you going to run a bakery with no formal training and no business experience?

But Duffy doesn't say any of those things. The exact opposite, actually. He looks genuinely excited—thrilled even—by this news.

"Claire! You're a baker? I had no idea." He takes a step back. "I love to eat, so if you need a taste tester"—he bows in my direction—"I'm happy to volunteer."

Instantly, I can see why Duffy chose to work with kids. And

I'm struck with unexpected sadness that he doesn't have any of his own.

He holds the door open for me to an indoor African exhibit—and I'm hit with that dusty, musky, earthy, familiar zoo smell.

"I think we can make that happen," I say. "I always love to try out new recipes."

"Perfect." He grins, then itches his nose with his palm. "Then for our second date, I request your specialty."

"Wouldn't you rather request *your* favorite?"

"I would much rather find out what you love." He scrunches his nose a few times in quick succession, like he's warding off a sneeze.

He looks away, in the direction of the lion exhibit we're standing in front of. The majestic cats are in an enclosure, panting and staring. "Did you know almost all of the earth's lions live in Africa?" He moves closer to the enclosure. And then he sneezes. Loudly.

"Bless you!" I say.

He sneezes again. Two more times.

"Are you okay?"

He sneezes two more times, and it's so disruptive that people start to look at us.

I rummage through my bag and come up with a travel package of tissues. I pull one out and hand it to him.

"Thank"—*ahhhchoo!*—"you." He blows his nose, then starts moving away from the lion enclosure and toward the exit.

"Oh my goodness, my allergies—" He sneezes again. "I didn't think—sorry."

I'm doing that thing where you hold a hand over someone's back, mostly because you have absolutely no idea how to help them.

Another sneeze, and then Duffy pinches the bridge of his nose for a few seconds before taking off his glasses and rubbing his eyes.

"Let's get outside," I say.

He nods, and we exit the habitat into the fresh air.

He starts to calm down a bit, but the damage is done. He's wheezing, eyes watering, nose running.

He blows his nose again and shoves the tissue in his pocket. "I'm so sorry, Claire. I"—another sneeze—"I'm terribly allergic to cats, but I never thought in a million years that would include"—*sneeze*—"lions at a zoo."

"I'm so sorry," I say, handing him the travel package of tissues in case he needs another one. "We could've gone somewhere else. The aquarium or something."

He looks at me, splotchy and smiling. "Yeah, if I had a seafood allergy, it would only trigger if I illegally ate the fish."

I smile. Another bonus that he still keeps a sense of humor through this.

He shakes his head. "Besides, you love the zoo." *Sneeze.* "I wanted to take you to the"—*sneeze*—"zoo."

I wince. "Well, I appreciate that, but I would never ask you to put yourself through this on my account."

He blows his nose again, retrieves a new tissue, then holds the package out to me.

"No, you keep them." I hold up a hand. "And we should probably call it a day. You need to go get some Benadryl or something."

"But we haven't had lunch yet." *Sneeze.*

I smile at him. "It's okay. We'll eat on our second date."

At that, Duffy smiles. "You'd go out with me again? After this?"

I laugh again. "Sure. It's not your fault. We'll go somewhere fun with no lions."

"Mini golf, maybe," he says. "Or a similar feline-free environment."

I laugh. "Sure."

He sticks his hand out for me to shake, then looks at the balled-up tissue he's holding and pulls a face. "I'll call you."

I nod. "Sounds good."

He sneezes again, then walks off in the direction of the parking lot.

Not a single butterfly flapping a single wing in my rib cage, and yet . . . I agreed to a second date.

Because after getting swept up in Off-Limits Miles, maybe someone like Duffy is what I need. Someone grounded who knows what he wants. An old soul, like me.

Does he spike my heart rate? No. But that's okay.

I'm too old to be swept off my feet and too realistic to know how that ends. I don't want to live in a world without the promise of love, but love comes in many forms. It doesn't have to be earth-shattering, heart-stopping love. It can be kind and quiet. A promise to take care of each other. To rummage for tissues in the middle of a sneezing fit.

Or to cheer on the other person when they decide to sink their savings into a bakery with no business experience whatsoever.

And Duffy seems like a good cheerleader.

Right. Yes. This is good.

I'll go on a few more dentist dates and maybe, just maybe, these pesky feelings I've been having for Miles will finally start to go away.

* * *

After the sound of Duffy's sneezing disappears, I head out onto the street in the direction of my apartment and realize I'm starving. I duck into a little café with street seating, admiring the casual décor, and immediately start thinking about my bakery.

I order a chicken salad sandwich—a tried-and-true favorite, because not every meal needs to be an expedition—along with a bag of chips and a Dr Pepper, then find a seat outside on the patio.

I pull my journal out of my bag, open it up, and turn to the pages where I've been writing down ideas for the bakery. I feel inspired and don't want to forget what's swirling in my head.

Monday, I'm meeting with a contractor who is going to help with the projects around the space, and I want to make sure I have everything ready to maximize the time with him because I'm planning a grand opening in a month, when Minnie is back in the States.

I still haven't figured out how I'm going to find people to attend—I make a note on the middle of the page:

> *How do I spread the word about the grand opening?*

I add:

> *Ask Lennon? Miles? Lorraine?*

I take a bite of my sandwich, crunch a chip, and keep writing, flipping around from page to page.

> *Porch swing benches. Rocking chairs. Make the space feel like a summer evening on the farm.*
>
> *Porch Sips & Sits: A community table for people to sit and chat with strangers. Make it easier for people to connect and make new friends.*

Some of these are written in the margins at odd angles, so I have to turn the journal this way and that to keep reading and adding to them.

> *How much staff do I need? Actually—how many people can I afford? Open for breakfast and lunch, then only open for special events in the evening?*

I pause and look up as a horn honks down the block.

All around me, the city lives. There are people biking, driving, walking, jogging. I hear snippets of conversation and see evidence of real life happening all around me. Only I'm not on the perimeter. I'm right in the thick of it.

I flip the page and see my original list, and I smile.

Because I didn't even hesitate to walk into this café, get a sandwich, and sit down at this table and eat it. Alone.

I confidently turn to my list . . . and cross it off.

- ~~Have a meal by myself. In public.~~

Look how far you've come, Claire.

* * *

John: Claire, moving to Chicago was one thing, but Amelia just told me you're opening a bakery?

Claire: <photo of empty storefront>

I'm meeting with a contractor this morning.

John: Are you nuts?

Don't tell me you sunk the profits from the house into a bakery, Claire, for Pete's sake.

Claire: 

John: You don't know how to run a business.

Do you have a business partner? Investors?

When this goes under, you'll have nothing left—and then what?

Claire: Gotta go, contractor is here.

John: Call me when you're done.

* * *

I'm doing it.

I'm actually doing it.

I met with the contractor, Pete, who is a jack-of-all-trades Lennon knows. He's going to paint and hang my porch swings and build me a counter.

I found a secondhand bakery case at a restaurant supply store, where I also found dishes and silverware.

Yesterday, Lennon and I met for lunch, back at the fancy food court in the mall, so we could brainstorm ideas.

The grouchy woman was there again, book in hand, sitting at a four-top table all by herself. I smiled at her.

She did not smile back.

Lennon and I talked the entire lunch, mostly about the business, but also about my date with Duffy. I told her he's the first guy I'm going to go on a second date with, and she stared at me so long, I felt like I had lettuce in my teeth.

"What?"

"What about Miles?" she said.

"What about him?"

"You like him."

"As a friend."

She rolled her eyes. "Pretend all you want, Claire, but you're not fooling anyone."

When she said that, I changed the subject, but here I am thinking about it again. Because if I'm not fooling anyone, does that mean Miles knows? I mean . . . we did kiss.

I'm trying really hard to act like everything is completely normal between us. And if he starts to think I have actual feelings for him, then nothing will ever be normal again.

Stupid Miles.

Stupid crush.

Stupid kiss.

CHAPTER 23

The open-air flea markets in Chicago are insane—a barrage of amazing pieces full of character. Tables, chairs, benches, and something called a crumb butler, which I'm absolutely incorporating somehow.

Thursday, after a successful day of shopping, Contractor Pete, who has a truck and trailer, is nice enough to help load and transport my haul back to the space. If I did the spatial math right, I think I got all the furniture I'll need. I also found cupcake stands, cake stands, and several pieces of art—a cool black-and-white charcoal piece of sunflowers in a vase, and another with a blue barn and a faded red truck in front of it—to hang on the walls.

It was a full, wonderful, creative, successful day.

I've only been back at the apartment long enough to drink a bottle of water and eat a Scotcheroo when there's a knock on my door.

My heart flip-flops. It's been days since I've seen Miles.

I don't like how we left things. I feel like I messed up.

Also, apparently, my heart misses him.

When I pull open the door, it's not Miles standing there.

It's a tall, young brunette with the most perfect skin I've ever seen in my life.

I'm confused. "Hi. Can I help you?"

Her smile is wide, showing off a perfect row of bright white teeth. "No, but I think I can help you. You're Claire, right?"

"I'm sorry—who are you?"

"Oh, I'm Zoey," she says. "I'm here to set up all the social media accounts for your new business."

"Okay . . ." I look around, confused. Is there a hidden camera somewhere? "Uh . . . who sent you?"

"Miles? Miles Westbrook?" Her smile fades just a little. "He . . ." And then, as if realizing, "He didn't talk to you about this."

"Uh, no, he didn't," I say, confused. He hired her? What for? "How do you know Miles?"

"I work for him," she says.

"You work for him."

"Yes." She nods, eyes bright, like being here is the best thing she's done all week.

And that's when I realize that this isn't the first time I've seen her. The first week I moved in, *this* is the brunette I saw leaving his apartment.

Did he really send one of his women to my apartment?

She's even younger up close than she was from a distance, and knowing that she *works* for Miles and he had her there, at his apartment . . . Good grief, he's crossed so many lines. My mind starts down a path but is interrupted when she says—

"I mean, full disclosure, he's also my dad." Zoey scrunches her nose. "I never like to tell that part because, you know, nepotism—but I promise, I'm good at my job. And also, you don't really have to worry about it because I'm on my dad's payroll, and I just do what he tells me. If you hate it, you don't have to use it, and I'll still get paid." Her laugh is light.

My brain is still stuck on *"He's also my dad."*

"Wait." I hold up a hand. "You're Miles's daughter."

She nods. "Zoey."

"Zoey."

I pause. "His daughter."

She smiles. "Yes, I'm still his daughter." And then her expression shifts. "Is that weird? I know you guys are friends, and I don't want you to be uncomfortable—"

"No, not at all." But it *is* a lot of information to process. The woman I saw leaving Miles's apartment wasn't his employee or his date—it was his daughter.

His beautiful, sweet daughter.

"My older sister, Ava, also works for him," she says. "I know how it looks—like we took the easy road or whatever, but he's a really good boss, and it's a great work environment, so . . . we stay."

My brain is *still* stuck on *"He's also my dad."*

"Is your sister tall and blonde?"

Zoey's expression goes mock-annoyed. "Looks like a supermodel." She rolls her eyes. "I'd hate her if I didn't love her so much."

I sit with that information . . . then let out a rueful laugh. "He never told me . . ."

"He doesn't talk about himself a lot," she says. "He'll never say, but the divorce was really hard on him. People don't always realize it because he's so upbeat all the time. He doesn't like to be negative." A pause. "I think he's been doing better lately."

At that, I go still. Because I haven't heard this story. Also because I can't let her be the one to tell it to me.

I open the door a little wider. "Good grief, I'm so sorry . . . please, come in. Let's talk about my nonexistent social media."

She laughs. "Oh, it won't be nonexistent for long."

"So, I don't know how much you know about the bakery," I say. "It's called The Porch, and the concept is—"

She silences me with an upheld hand. "My dad already filled me in, and it sounds *adorable*. He said you're an amazing baker."

"He's being kind," I say.

She shakes her head. "He is kind, but that's not what this is. He's genuinely so excited about the idea I'm surprised he hasn't tried to become your business partner."

I laugh. "He did offer to be a silent investor."

Her eyes go wide. "I hope you said no. There is no way he will be silent."

Another laugh. It feels good to connect with someone in Miles's life. Someone important to him. It's like seeing another side of him completely. "Please, sit." I motion to the couch, and Zoey sits down.

"I'm going to grab some snacks," I say.

"I never turn down snacks."

I smile as I pull out containers of various baked goods that have helped relieve the stress of the week. I place cookies and bars and muffins onto a plate, grab a couple bottles of water, and walk back into the living room, where I find Zoey clicking around on her laptop.

I set the plate in front of her and hand over a bottle of water, watching as she eyes the treats. "Is it too late to change the terms of our agreement?" She looks at me. "I want to be paid in baked goods."

I laugh. "Like father, like daughter."

She nods. "That tracks. He's always had a sweet tooth." Zoey scans the plate, almost like she's not sure how to decide what to try.

"Whatever you don't eat now, you're taking home, so no need to be choosy," I say.

"Phew. Okay." She picks up a lemon bar and a napkin and takes a bite. "Oh my gosh, Claire." She chews. "This is amazing."

"Thanks," I say.

She swallows the bite and picks up her computer, balancing the bar in her hand. She turns the laptop around to face me. "I mocked up a few logos for you. No pressure, but I just wanted to offer them as part of the branding package."

My eyes go wide as I look at five different logos, and I realize there is no way I'm going to be able to choose just one—and unlike my baked goods, I can't save the others for later. "Oh my gosh, Zoey. These are amazing."

She pushes the laptop closer and takes another bite while I study them.

"Dad said your tagline is 'Sit, sip, and stay awhile,' so I built on that." She smiles. "Great tagline, by the way. I love the whole concept. I think it's going to be a huge hit. There's nothing like this anywhere—not that I've seen."

"Thank you for saying that," I say, looking at her screen. "Oof, I'm starting to get nervous."

"Good. That means you care." She smiles. "You don't have to pick one right now, and if you need me to tweak anything, I can do that too."

"I love them all." I try to imagine the logo on bakery bags and coffee cups. Or on a sign out in front of the shop. "I really love this one—" I point to a hand-drawn image of a big wraparound porch and the silhouette of two people sitting on a swing. "It reminds me of my grandma."

She smiles. "I like that one too."

"But the one with the wooden signpost is so great too," I say.

Zoey opens her water bottle. "They were fun to create, but this is your business, so be picky."

I laugh. "Okay. I will."

"I've been given strict instructions to handle your social media for the next six months," she says. "So we can take our time with some of this stuff. But the sooner we start building excitement, the better. Dad said you're opening in June?"

My eyes go wide. "Wait, six months?"

She goes still. "Is that okay? That's usually where I start with a freelance branding package to get a good idea of how things are working. Once you pick a logo and a theme, I'll get to work on setting you up on all major platforms. Dad mentioned you might also need help building your website. He has a guy for that too. Actually, I have a guy for that—my fiancé." She pulls her bottom lip in like she's trying really hard not to smile. She's failing.

I glance down at her hand and notice the beautiful diamond solitaire on her ring finger.

"Oh my goodness, congratulations," I say, picking up her hand.

"Thanks. It's still kind of new," she says, holding her left hand out to admire her ring. "I mean—he's not new, but the engagement is new-ish. Six months. We're hoping to get married at Christmas."

I look at her—so full of hope and excitement for the future—and I'm struck by how happy I am for her. How hopeful and excited *I* am. How nice it is not to begrudge someone else their joy, though I'm ashamed to think of the months I spent wallowing and doing just that.

"I'm really happy for you, Zoey."

"Happy enough to make cupcakes for the big day?" She turns her laptop around and closes it. "Dad said you're the best." She nods at the tray of treats. "And I agree."

My cheeks heat. Just how much has Miles told his daughters about me? He's told me almost nothing about them.

"I would be honored," I say.

She nods. "I'll talk to Kevin about website ideas once we have a direction, and we'll be good to go."

"I can't believe you're doing this for me," I say. "You have to let me pay you."

"Dad's paying me." She grins. "And there's *no way* he'll let you pay him."

I laugh. "Well, the cupcakes will definitely be free."

"No they won't." She raises a brow. "You've met my dad, right?"

Lucky for me, I have.

"This is how he is. Mr. Nice Guy." She sighs. "Too nice if you ask me. He makes business decisions like that too. His big heart is always messing with his bottom line. That's why my mom walked all over him."

The comment catches me off guard.

She rolls her eyes, and I get the impression she thinks I already know this story.

"Sorry." She shakes her head like she's shaking away an unwanted memory. "I promised him I wouldn't go there." Her phone buzzes on the table. "Oh, shoot. I'm going to be late." She looks at me. "Wait. Do you want to go out tonight?"

I frown. "With you?"

She laughs. "With a bunch of us."

That . . . actually sounds fun.

"Dad will be there," she says. "And you can meet Ava. And Kevin."

"Is it, like, a family thing?"

"A work thing," she says. "Trivia night."

"Trivia night," I repeat.

She nods. "Once a month, my dad takes the entire staff out somewhere fun. He says it's good for morale."

"I bet it is." I think about John and how he treated his employees. It was the opposite of fun. It was never about the person as a whole, only about what they could do for the company.

"You should come." She stands.

"I don't want to intrude." I stand and start for the door.

"Don't be ridiculous," she says. "Everyone would love to meet you!"

At that, I frown. How does *everyone* even know who I am?

"You can ride with me," she says. "We're all meeting in half an hour."

I give myself a quick once-over. "I've been at flea markets all day. I need to change."

"I can wait." She's beaming, and for whatever reason, all I can think is that Minnie is going to love this girl.

And I like that idea more than I should.

"Okay," I say, relenting. "I'll come."

"Are you good at trivia?" she asks. "I just need to know if I should keep you on my team or send you to Dad's."

CHAPTER 24

When Zoey and I walk into the bar, my nerves kick up like a swirl of leaves in a fall breeze.

Miles is here. Somewhere.

I haven't seen him since the night I offended him.

The bar is dark and crowded and loud, and a Billy Joel song plays in the background. Something nostalgic and heartfelt about turning lights back on.

We make our way through the throng of people, toward the back of the space where tables and chairs are set up to face a small stage in the corner.

It's slightly less crowded back here, and I follow Zoey straight over to a large rectangular table.

That's when I see him.

Miles is standing with his back to us, talking with a few other people. I want to either turn around and run straight home or keep facing forward and run into his arms, but I'm not sure which.

I had him pegged all wrong.

Those women were his daughters.

His divorce was ugly, and it didn't make him less kind.

"Hey, everyone!" Zoey says as we reach the little group.

There's a round of hellos and a few curious glances in my direction as Miles turns to face us. At the sight of me, his expression softens. "Claire."

I don't know what my face is doing—probably some weird hybrid of a wince and a smile—as if I'm aware that I'm intruding but also trying to be polite but also mentally shouting an apology but also trying not to swoon.

It's a lot.

But then the softness disappears, replaced by a single arched brow and a grin that seems to issue a challenge. "Did you come to get your butt kicked?"

Something inside me switches.

Game. On.

I slowly widen my eyes, then look at Zoey. "Definitely put me on your team. I need to show your dad how this is done."

There's a chorus of *"Ooooh"* and *"Let's go!"* from the group, but I can't seem to look at anyone but Miles.

He holds eye contact for several long seconds, then a tall blonde clears her throat. "Introductions, please."

"Right." Miles shakes his head a little, then backs out to the edge of this little circle.

"Claire, these are my people," he says. "You know Zoey." He points at her.

"I do. She's amazing." I give her a wave, and she makes a show of bowing in my direction like I'm royalty.

"This is Kevin." Zoey grabs onto the arm of a lanky-looking guy with glasses wearing a Nintendo T-shirt and a pair of jeans.

Kevin shakes my hand, and the blonde steps forward. "I'm Ava. The favorite daughter."

"Oh, whatever." Zoey smacks her across the arm, and they make ugly faces at each other playfully.

"I'm Claire," I say. "It's so nice to meet you."

There are three other people in the group—a woman named Kendra, her husband, Brandon, and another woman named Talie, who gives me the chilliest greeting of the bunch.

I'm put on a team with Zoey, Kendra, and Kevin, while Miles has Ava, Talie, and Brandon on his team. As we get situated around the table, a waitress appears and hands me a drink. "Oh, I didn't order this."

"I got it for you," Miles says. "It's a Dr Pepper."

Zoey and Ava exchange a glance, pursing their lips and raising their eyebrows, but I pretend not to notice. Instead, I pick up the drink and cheers Miles. "Thank you."

He nods and gives me a thumbs-up.

If there's any sign that he's still offended, he's not showing it.

The waitress also hands Zoey a drink, and then a woman with pink hair jumps on the stage and taps a microphone. I take a drink and listen to her as she explains the rules of trivia, which is apparently a call-and-response activity.

It's obvious to me that everyone at our table has been here before.

Round one starts, and Miles looks directly at me. "You're going down, Cake Boss."

If I had my Cubs hat on, I'd turn it backward and wipe my nose with the back of my hand. Instead, I narrow my eyes, glare at him, and say, "Bring it on, Lawn Ranger."

Best I could think of in the moment. Nicknames for a landscape architect don't just roll off the tongue.

By his expression, he's still impressed.

The pink-haired woman, whose name is Gina, is the owner of the bar and an enthusiastic host. She's also clearly obsessed with three specific trivia categories: the TV show *Friends*, the Chicago Bulls, and rom-coms of the early 2000s.

Lucky for my team, I'm an expert on two out of three of those categories.

There are other categories—geography, history, pop culture, music, science, and it seems, a whole lot of wild card questions that have nothing to do with anything, like "What was the first brand of bubble gum to hit the shelves?" (Dubble Bubble, for anyone who cares.)

After three rounds, our team is winning by one point.

That's when Gina tells everyone it's time for a break. "This is when you all go buy drinks and where I make some money. We'll be back in ten!"

Everyone starts mingling, moving around the space toward the bar, the bathrooms, or outside for a little fresh air.

I don't move and neither does Kendra, who's been sitting beside me this whole time. Miles is talking with Brandon and Kevin and a few guys from other teams, and I get the distinct impression that this man has never met a stranger.

"He's pretty great, huh?" Kendra is watching me watch Miles, and I feel like I've just been caught.

"Miles?" I know it's stupid for me to pretend her comment needs clarifying, but I do it anyway. "Yeah, he's a good guy."

She goes back to looking at him. "Everyone loves Miles."

I can see that. There's a crowd around him, and he's telling a story that has both the men and women around him completely engrossed.

I know she doesn't mean for it to, but the comment is a welcome reminder for me. The wake-up call I need to keep my feelings in check.

He could be with any single woman he wanted, but Miles doesn't do relationships.

Think about Duffy. He's perfectly nice. And stable. And kind, and nerdy, and endearing. And so very enthusiastic.

I look back at Miles.

Duffy doesn't make my insides hum.

"Do you all work for him?" I ask, taking the last drink of my soda.

"Yep. Everyone except Kevin," she says, nodding. "Brandon and I have been with him the longest, but the company keeps growing. Miles takes on so many charity projects, he needed a bigger staff to handle the ones that pay the bills, so he's hired a few more people the last couple years." She glances across the room. "A lot of the people at that table also work with us, but they have an *actual* trivia league, so they refuse to play on our teams."

I chuckle. "There's a league for trivia? With teams?"

She laughs. "Yeah, and apparently *we* don't take it seriously enough. One of them told me that we laugh too loud and we disrespect the game."

"They have matching shirts," I say, noticing that every person at the table is wearing a red shirt with the words *Risky Quizness* on the front.

"Oh yeah. They don't joke about trivia."

One of the women glances in our direction and waves. Kendra waves back.

"That's Julia," she says as the woman stands and starts walking toward us. "She's married to Bennett, the guy sitting next to her. They've been friends with Miles since before his divorce."

I glance at Miles just as he looks my way, lifting his chin and mouthing, *You good?* He's checking on me like Lloyd Dobler in *Say Anything*.

I nod back and give him a thumbs-up.

"So . . . you're the infamous *Claire*." Julia slides in and blocks my view of Miles. "Bennett is convinced you're going to take Miles off the market, and every woman who's been carrying a torch for him is going to be in mourning." She laughs and looks at Kendra. "Hey, Ken."

"Hey."

My laugh is nervous. "No, Miles and I are just friends."

Julia glances over her shoulder to where I can only assume Miles is still standing, then turns back to me. "All I know is he's turned down three plus-one dates in the past month—"

"Plus-one dates?"

"Oh yeah, Miles is the perfect plus-one," Kendra says.

"I don't understand."

"He didn't tell you." She smiles and shakes her head. "Of course he didn't."

My frown deepens. "Tell me what?"

"He's a plus-one," Julia explains. "It's a specific designation for people to attend social events without the worry—"

"—or the baggage," Kendra interjects.

"And he lays everything out ahead of time, so people know what to expect. So if you're single and of a certain age and you have a work function or a family event or a wedding or a fundraiser or something, he's the guy you bring with you. He'll keep his hands to himself, and he's so outgoing, he could make conversation with a houseplant."

Kendra twists her glass in her hands. "But in the last few weeks, he hasn't made himself available for anything."

"Well, it's not because of me."

The two women exchange a look, but they don't say anything else.

"Miles goes on a lot of dates," I say, certain of this.

"Yeah," Julia says. "As a plus-one."

"And because the women he helps pass his name around to their friends," Kendra adds.

This can't possibly be the only reason Miles dates. Right?

"He's online. I've seen his profile on Matched," I say, not quite ready to admit how wrong my impression has been.

Julia laughs. "Because Zoey and Ava put him on there."

I had all the pieces, but I just crammed them together and made the completely wrong picture. Why didn't Miles correct me?

"Miles doesn't date for real," Kendra says.

I knew Miles doesn't do relationships, but I assumed he was a player. I assumed a lot of things about him, and I'm rethinking every single one.

"Not since Elizabeth," Julia adds.

Another knowing look and slight nod pass between them.

Elizabeth.

So she has a name. "We probably shouldn't talk about her." I lean to the side hoping to catch a glimpse of Miles, but he's not standing where he was before.

"Why?" Kendra frowns. "She's not dead."

"Though she *deserves* to be after what she did." Julia closes her eyes and holds up a hand. "Sorry. Sorry. I crossed a line." She opens her eyes, puts her hands together, and looks at the ceiling. "Sorry, Jesus." Then back to us. "I promised God I'd do better. I have a serious catty streak. Especially when it comes to that woman."

I laugh, but there's an unsettled feeling inside me.

I want to talk to Miles. I want to know what happened. But also? I want to apologize. No wonder what I said offended him.

His past is not my business, and he already told me he doesn't talk about it, but it would be so much worse for me to ask his friends to fill me in. I won't betray him like that.

These people were in his life when it all happened. Maybe he doesn't tell new people the gritty details because he doesn't want their pity. Or maybe he doesn't want what happened to shape anyone's opinion of him.

I understand that logic better than most people.

I hesitate to tell anyone anything about John. Sharing that kind of rejection is vulnerable. Will admitting it make people wonder if there's something wrong with me? Will they start looking for reasons to walk away?

But I can't imagine Miles has these same insecure thoughts . . .

"I'm going to run to the bathroom before we start back up," I say.

Julia scoots to the side, and I spot Miles across the bar, standing beside a tall table talking to a few people who aren't here to play trivia.

I keep my eyes on him as I make my way through the crowd, thankful it's thinned out a little. Just when I'm about to reach

Miles, I hear a man say, "Oh, it's you!" And for reasons I can't explain, I sense that he's talking to me.

I turn in the direction of the voice and see Barry, my horrible improv date, standing in a clump with two other guys. He's holding a beer and looking slightly unsteady on his feet, but he steps in front of me, blocking my path.

"You're the chick who didn't put out!" He says this so loudly, it draws the attention of everyone in the immediate vicinity.

"Excuse me." I try to maneuver around him, but Barry isn't done.

He looks at his friends, slaps one on the chest, then points to me. "Don't let her hotness fool ya. She's an ice queen."

They laugh, and I find myself getting impatient. I don't have time for this.

"A guy spends money on a ticket to a show, *plus drinks*, and she won't even give it up." He leans in so close I can smell the alcohol on his breath. "I didn't know I was going out with a nun." He barks out a laugh, then takes another drink.

I try to sidestep him, but he moves with me.

"You can make it up to me now."

Now I'm uncomfortable. All of a sudden the bar feels way smaller. People are too close.

"Whaddya say?" His words are slightly slurred. He leans in. "I never leave a woman unsatis—"

"Hey, buddy."

Barry turns toward Miles's voice.

"How about you apologize to the lady?"

Barry laughs in Miles's face. "Why would I do that? I have a legitimate complaint."

"Apologize or leave."

Barry looks at his friends, the smile fading from his face. Without a word, he turns back and raises a fist, but Miles ducks out of the way. Barry stumbles forward but quickly rights himself and takes another swing. Miles dodges it, but when it's clear Barry isn't going to stop, he hauls off and clocks him, full on his jaw. It sounds like a punch from an action movie—a cracking thud—and Barry spins around and lands chest first into the bar, spilling two drinks.

"You should watch what you say to my friend," Miles says coolly, shaking out his fist.

Barry scrambles to his feet, now with a bloodied lip that's already starting to swell. He takes a wild swing at Miles, who sidesteps it easily, puts his foot in front of Barry's, and pushes him, tripping him to the ground where he lands face-first in a crumpled pile.

"Hey!" The female voice comes from across the room.

Miles lifts a hand. "Sorry, Gina!" He looks at Barry's friends.

They look back, unsure what happens next.

Miles points to the floor. "Get him out of here."

They scramble to pick Barry up. As they pull him toward the door, Barry starts shouting that he's going to call his lawyer or the cops or someone to throw Miles in jail, all of these threats littered with expletives until, finally, they get him outside. And the door closes behind them.

As it does, the people in the bar cheer.

A couple of people pat Miles on the back as they pass by, calling him "Champ" and saying things like "That guy deserved it."

Everyone slowly goes back to doing whatever they were doing, but my feet might as well be glued to the floor.

Miles looks at me, wild-eyed, still wired from what just happened.

I have no words. But then I look at his hand and blurt out, "Ice!" I grab him by his good arm and pull him over to the bar. "Can we get some ice in a bag?"

Gina, who has yet to return to the stage, looks at Miles, rolls her eyes, and points to a door behind the bar. "Go get some out of the cooler."

I lead him through the door and into the kitchen, then point to a stool. "Sit."

"You're so bossy," he says.

"Yes, I am. Especially when people do stupid things." I walk around the kitchen, searching for any kind of plastic bag.

"Hey."

I turn and find him holding a large, empty freezer bag. I walk over, grab it, and point at the stool again. This time, he sits.

I fill the bag with ice and walk back over to Miles, then carefully pick up his already swollen hand and gently set the ice on his bright red knuckles. "Why did you do that?"

He moves slightly, his body angled directly in front of me. "Was that one of your app dates?"

"Miles, it's fine." I go quiet. "You shouldn't have done that."

"It's not fine." He stands, eyes fixed on me.

A heat-filled moment passes between us, laced with the emotion of unsaid words. I can't think of a time when someone stuck up for me like that, and I don't know what to make of it.

All I know is that it's getting more and more difficult to remember that he and I are just friends.

Miles inhales a slow breath as if he's trying to slow his pulse, then reaches up and gently brushes my hair away from my face. "You should've told me."

I can't look at him. I don't trust myself. "It's not your job to protect me."

He twirls a strand of my hair around his finger, lets it go, then makes a fist and pulls his hand away. "What if I want it to be?"

I can feel his eyes on me, though I'm doing everything I can to not look up at him. Because if I do, every ounce of my resolve will disintegrate into thin air.

The bag of ice is sitting on top of his swollen hand, which is pressed against his chest, and I reach over and move it, just a little.

I don't know how I manage to get the words out because I'm

pretty sure I'm holding my breath, but I find a way to ask, "What are you saying?"

At that, he angles away from me, dropping down onto the stool. "I don't know. I just—" He drags his hand across his forehead and sighs. "I'm sorry."

I move an inch closer. "We talked about this—"

"I know, Claire." He looks at me and shrugs, resigned. "I know. But when I saw that guy messing with you, it just"—he blows out a breath—"made me crazy."

I think about everything I learned about him tonight.

The way he donates his time and skills to help make this city beautiful.

The way the women in his orbit trust him enough to ask him to be their plus-one.

The way he always says yes, always takes time, always helps.

He takes care of everyone—he can't help it. It's just who he is.

That's all this is. Miles doing what he does—swooping in to help.

Maybe he's just confusing that innate need with feelings . . . but the way he's looking at me right now makes it really hard to believe that.

There's a beat of silence, and I search my mind for a way to keep the moment from getting even more awkward and end up saying the only thing I can think to say. "Why didn't you tell me the women I saw at your apartment that first day were your daughters?"

He half laughs. "You didn't ask."

"I actually thought you were dating women half your age," I say. "And you didn't correct me." I go quiet. "I didn't mean to be so judgy."

He shrugs. "It's okay."

"It's really not," I say. "And it's also not okay for you to keep sending me mixed signals, so you have to stop that."

"I know." He looks at me, apologetic. "I swear it's not on purpose. You just—" But he doesn't finish the sentence.

I hear Gina call for teams to return to their tables.

I look up at Miles.

He looks back at me.

He narrows his eyes.

I narrow mine right back, thankful for the levity.

"Winner pays the next time we try a new cuisine?" He raises a single eyebrow.

I stand, not breaking eye contact, then say with confidence, "I haven't tried Japanese hibachi. Bring your wallet."

I just wish I was as confident with my heart.

* * *

The Porch is now on social media!

THANK YOU, ZOEY!

We're meeting this week to talk about branding and messaging and all kinds of things, but it's really happening.

I'm going on date #2 with Duffy. He's picking the place. I'm betting it won't be anywhere with cats.

I hired two people! I'm officially an employer. I'm going to start off doing all the baking myself, but I have two college students helping me at the counter. They're really sweet and make me miss Minnie, but since she's coming home in a few weeks, I guess that makes sense.

Oh.

It's been three days since Miles punched Barry at the bar—and since our team won at trivia—but I haven't seen him since.

CHAPTER 25

I'm doing a Duffy double down.

All in on the date with the dentist. There are definite feelings there for Miles—ones I can't lie to myself about anymore—but I'm so conflicted. He's taking up a *lot* of mental energy, and I need a break.

I need stability. No drama. Someone to go to the art museum with or to try new restaurants with. Someone who doesn't make my insides tumble around like fake snow inside a snow globe.

I suppose one could argue that snow-tumbling is *exactly* what one needs in a date . . . but I've had my fill of butterflies and electrically charged moments as of late.

So when Duffy shows up at my apartment on Sunday for the date he planned, I'm more determined than ever to try to make this work. A nice, dependable guy is exactly what I need right now.

I open the door and am shocked to find him posed, dressed in an Aragorn costume, holding a plastic garment bag.

My determination slips.

"Duffy? Hi . . . uh . . . what's all this?"

He holds up the garment bag.

It's another costume.

For a woman.

I'm a woman.

Oh no.

"Surprise!"

I half laugh, but when I catch movement in the courtyard behind him, I grab onto his arm, pull him inside, and close the door.

The last thing I need is for anyone to see my date has shown up *in a costume.*

"I'm taking you to your first comic convention!" He holds up the dress. "I've always wanted to be Aragorn *with* an Arwen!"

I never read *The Lord of the Rings*, but I did watch the movies. Sometimes I play the soundtrack when I'm baking. I know which characters he's talking about, but never in a million years did I ever think about dressing up as one of them.

I didn't even go trick-or-treating when I was a kid. I hung out with Gram and made popcorn balls. It was one of my favorite nights.

Duffy holds the dress out and shakes it at me with a huge smile on his face.

He's clearly incredibly excited. "Have you ever been to a convention?"

If I act anything other than just as excited, I may as well grab a balloon and a big knife and pop it right in front of him. But still—this is really not my scene. I try to think of something—anything—that will get me out of this. A fake migraine? A bakery emergency? Teleportation?

"Does everyone dress up?" I ask tentatively, taking the gown, not even sure it's going to fit me.

"Well, no, not everyone, but most people," he says. "We'll fit right in."

I look at the dress, then back at Duffy, who is oblivious to the fact that this is so far out of my comfort zone I might as well be in Kuala Lumpur.

"I didn't enter us in the costume contest, though," he says. "The people who win those are artistic geniuses. Our costumes are a little basic. I wanted to ease you in."

My stomach tightens because that suggests there will be more of these events in the future.

"Okay." A root canal sounds better at the moment. I start walking toward the stairs, still trying to find a way out of this.

"Oh, do you have shoes? Brown flats? Something that looks a little woodsy?" Duffy asks as I go.

"I'll check," I say as I rush into the bathroom, close the door, and open my phone to call Minnie. I pull up her number but don't hit Call.

This is *way* out of my comfort zone. But aren't I supposed to be doing things that are *way* out of my comfort zone?

What happened to making this work?

I look at myself in the mirror. "You said you wanted adventure, Claire," I whisper, then lean in closer. "You said you wanted to try new things." I narrow my eyes. "Here's your chance."

"Do you need help lacing up the dress?" Duffy calls from the bottom of the stairs.

"No! I've got it, but thanks!" I unzip the bag, pull the dress out, and hold it up in front of me. I look at my reflection, reminding myself that before he got here, I actually thought Duffy was the solution to my Miles problem.

But replacing that crush is going to be a lot more difficult if I have to wear a medieval gown to do it.

I take a breath, push my hair out of my face, and change out of my sensible outfit and into an elf costume.

An hour later, I'm walking into a convention center with hundreds of other people. The costumes are otherworldly. There are nine-foot-tall aliens, girls sporting spiky hair and carrying swords (anime, Duffy explains), and lots of Spider-Men who seem to point at one another whenever they get in groups of three.

In spite of all this creativity and color and commotion, I still feel like I'm on display.

Duffy, fully in character, stops in front of a quartet of hobbits. He then kneels in front of them, loudly proclaiming, "If by my life or death I can protect you, I will. You have my sword."

A voice from behind me says, "And my bow," and I wheel around to see a slightly overweight middle-aged man with a long blond wig, dressed in green.

"And my axe!" is shouted from across the hall, and a hairy, battle-clad, axe-wielding kid no more than about eighteen, trundles over and joins the group.

They all look at one another for a moment, then burst into loud admiration, pointing at each other's costumes, shaking hands by grabbing forearms—and not a single one breaks character.

They part, and Duffy gives some kind of farewell in what sounds like a different language, then turns to me.

"This might be the best day of my life." He pulls out our tickets and hands one to me. "Your ticket, m'lady."

Nothing could've prepared me for what I see after they scan my ticket, and we walk into the huge convention center.

The scale of the room is almost too much to take in. And there are costumed people *everywhere.*

A tall, buxom woman in a tight, red-sequined dress holding what appears to be a rabbit.

A family of five, one in a stroller, all dressed like the Incredibles, complete with masks and wigs.

Several men dressed as the Joker, wearing what look like custom-made suits, chatting up an older woman with multicolored pigtails.

I stifle a giggle at a grown man, hairy-chested with a full mustache and beard, sporting a Wonder Woman costume. It's clearly tongue in cheek, because he's posing for pictures, sticking out his tongue, and making a rock 'n' roll symbol with both hands.

Orcs, superheroes, cartoon characters, they're all here, and it's almost sensory overload.

Someone rushes over to us, dressed in a trench coat, 3D glasses, tie—and a fez, for some reason—and demands that we tell him what year it is. Once he has his answer, he pulls out what appears to be some kind of light-up screwdriver out of his pocket, points it at us as it whirs, then sprints off in the other direction.

There are rows of special displays and booths with comic books, toys, and artwork as far as I can see.

It's its own world, its own culture, and I'm gobsmacked by all of it.

There's a buzz of excitement as we slowly walk from booth to booth, interacting with other people, looking at new games and movie merchandise and comic book art.

It's obvious that Duffy is not a stranger at this event. He knows his way around and has mapped out our entire day, sort of like I would if I were taking my child to Disney World. And in some ways, I can see that this convention requires similar planning.

Duffy has an app, and he's marked key events that he doesn't want to miss "so we can stay on schedule." People stop to talk to him because they remember him from past conventions.

We're walking down one of the aisles when Duffy stops dead in his tracks. "I can't believe it."

I stop and look around, trying to figure out what Duffy is looking at. Because, frankly, I can't believe most of what I've seen today.

"He's right there." Duffy is transfixed on something—or someone—in the distance as he reaches into his leather bag and pulls out a small journal. He starts flipping through the pages. "He's right there, Claire. I knew he was coming, and I'm still not prepared to see him."

"Who's right where?" I follow his gaze and see a long line of fully costumed people, waiting for a book signing, but I can't see the sign announcing who the author is.

"It's Reggie Maxwell, the most influential graphic novelist of our generation." Duffy's tone is slightly frantic. "You know, *The Riftwalkers*," he says.

I shake my head. "I don't."

"*The Riftwalkers*," he repeats, as if that's an explanation.

"Sorry," I say. "I haven't read many comic books."

"Oh, Claire. It's not *just* a comic book. It's *so much more* than a comic book." He steps into the line as several other people gather behind us. "It's an experience. A journey. It's about this group of space rebels who have to slip through dimensions to seal unstable rifts." He gets more animated with every word. "It's a whole thing with alien races and interdimensional planets and—"

"Wait, someone doesn't know *The Riftwalkers*?" A guy dressed like some sort of alien spins around and looks at us. "How is that possible?"

"It's her first time," Duffy says, sounding like he's making an excuse.

"No way! Your first con?" A girl wearing a long white gown, white wig, white contact lenses, and white painted face looks at me with wide eyes.

"Yep! My first one," I say.

There's a slight pause, then both erupt in congratulations, hugs, over-the-top welcomes. These people have their own culture, but not a single one has been condescending to me as a newcomer. They're just excited to share what they love. It's refreshing.

I'm feeling slightly on the spot, but then the alien sighs and says, "I wish I could go back to my first time. There's *nothing* like the first one."

The line moves forward, and we all move with it.

"My first one was in San Diego ten years ago," the woman in white says. "This is my thirty-second."

"Your thirty-second?" I ask. "Wow."

"I'm only at eighteen." The alien gives her a nod. "But I'll catch up."

"Do you wear the same costume every time?" I ask.

"I do now," the woman says. "I'm sort of known for this one." She picks up the skirt and holds it out. "Do you like it?"

"It's really beautiful." I have no idea who she's supposed to be, but I'm not about to admit it by asking.

She smiles. "Thank you. It took me weeks to make it."

I'm impressed. "You made that? Yourself?"

"Yes! Most of the people here make their own costumes," she says.

Wow. I had no idea.

"*The Riftwalkers* is a classic," Duffy explains. "They made a movie a couple years ago. We'll have to watch it."

I get a mental picture of what life with Duffy would be like.

Conventions and costumes and Crest.

I shove the thought aside.

"Have you guys met him before?" a guy wearing an Ironman costume asks from behind us in the line.

This sparks a whole conversation about Reggie Maxwell, the creator of this *graphic novel* I've never heard of, a point that gets brought up three more times as more people join in. Duffy looks for ways to include me in the conversation, stopping to explain phrases I'm not familiar with or characters I don't know.

It's interesting to see how easily they all become friends. These people don't know each other, but they're all bonding over a shared passion. Minus the costumes and the character voices, these are regular people.

The thought takes me back to the day I met Lennon. I'd been so scared to strike up a conversation with anyone I didn't know, and rightfully so, it turned out. But what I'm seeing play out in front of me is that most people want the same thing—to connect with other people.

And while this wouldn't be my first choice for a date venue, I get the sense that Duffy is super excited to share this part of his life with me. It's important to him, and he's intent on helping me understand it.

It's sweet.

When it's our turn to meet the author—a young guy with dark, greasy hair and an unfortunate mustache—I try to step aside. But Duffy pulls me over to the table to stand next to him.

"This is my girlfriend, Claire."

Reggie could not be more disinterested. I, on the other hand, am slightly stunned. First, because I think I'm too old to be anyone's "girlfriend." The word makes me think of middle school. Second, because . . . *girlfriend*? Aren't we supposed to discuss labels before giving them?

Duffy hands over his comic book and his scrapbook, launching into a gushing display of admiration. Reggie isn't rude exactly, but he does seem like he'd rather be anywhere but sitting at this table. He hands Duffy's books back and thanks him with a forced smile.

"No, thank you, Reggie, really. I can't wait to see what happens next." Duffy presses the books to his chest. "Thank you."

We say goodbye to the colorful characters we met in the line, and despite the "girlfriend" snafu, I have to smile. Because these people are more excited about being here, about these costumes and their subculture, than I've been about anything in a very long time.

"Hey, Duffy," I say as we walk down the carpeted aisle. "About the 'girlfriend' thing . . . ?"

He stops. "Oh yeah, sorry about that. It sort of popped out."

I smile. "I just didn't think we were at that stage yet."

He pulls me off to the side, out of the foot traffic. "If I've offended you, please forgive me." I can't tell if he's still playing a role or if this is actually the way he talks.

"No, I'm not offended, I just—" I smile. "I want to take things slow."

"Slow is good," he says. "I'm great with slow."

I nod. "Good."

"Good."

We start walking again, joining a crowd in front of a large stage where we listen to two actors from a superhero movie talk about what's next for the franchise—something exciting judging by the reactions of the crowd. When the event is done, we weave our way through groups of video game characters come to life, visiting every single exhibit in the huge space.

By the time we reach the end, my feet are sore, my stomach

is growling, and all I can think is—mac 'n' cheese sounds really good right now.

Mac 'n' cheese. A lifetime ago.

Still, I'm really glad I came. And nobody is more surprised about that than me.

Sometimes, things are better than you imagine.

As we leave the convention center, Duffy is practically walking on air. "That. Was. *Incredible.* Wasn't that incredible? That might've been my best con yet." He grins over at me. "Did you have an okay time?"

"I did, actually," I say. "Thanks for bringing me."

"I'm glad you came." He reaches over and takes my hand. "I've never brought a date to one of these before. But my friends told me that any woman I'm going to date deserves to know what she's getting into." He gives me a quick side-eye. "Not everyone is as cool about it as you are."

He squeezes my hand and I hold my breath, searching for any sign of flutters.

There are none.

"I didn't mean to stay so long, and now we don't have time for dinner." He opens the door to his sensible Toyota Camry.

"That's okay," I say. "It was worth it."

He closes the door and runs around to the other side and gets in, pulling on his seat belt and adjusting every mirror like he wasn't the last one to drive this car. "I have a Sunday night ritual I can't break."

"You do?" I'm imagining meal prep or laundry or something practical.

He starts the car and backs out of the parking space.

"I moderate an online forum," he says. "And we have weekly discussions."

"What kind of forum?"

"Conspiracy theories mostly," he says. "Like things the government doesn't want you to know. Alien abductions. Elvis sightings."

He pauses for a three-count, then chuckles. "Just kidding. We know Elvis doesn't go out anymore." He goes silent for a beat, then starts laughing again. "You should see your face. I'm kidding!"

After today . . . that was not obvious.

My laugh is strained. "Oh." I mean to say more, but I can't find any other words. Duffy is kind, but he is odd.

Can I get on board with "odd"?

"Actually, I go over the schedule for the week, pull up patient charts, and make sure I know every kid's name. I try to make it all as laid-back and easy as I can because kids are usually terrified of the dentist."

"Some adults too," I add.

"True." He smiles. "I find that if I know a little something about them, it helps. So we ask the parents a few questions when they make the appointment. You know, 'What's your kid into right now?' 'Is there anything they might be able to talk about that would put them at ease?' That sort of thing."

I look at him. "That's really sweet."

A self-deprecating shrug. "My patients are really important to me."

He reaches over and takes my hand.

Not a single flutter.

Duffy turns on a jazz playlist, and the sound of mellow music fills the car. We drive back to my apartment, and he parks in the little lot at the end of the street, then shuts the car off.

"I'll walk you in."

"Oh, you don't have to," I say, not wanting to face the lingering at the door.

"Don't be silly," he says. "I'm not sending you out into the darkness alone. *There could be orcs out there.*" He laughs quietly and opens his door, meeting me around the other side of the car.

We walk in silence toward the building, and I say a silent prayer that nobody is in the courtyard, thankful to find it empty. The white string lights and exterior building lights cast a warm glow over the space, and in different circumstances, this might actually be a very romantic setting for the end of a date.

In these circumstances . . . in this dress . . . I'm just anticipating an awkward Middle-earth goodbye.

It's taking a lot of effort not to look at Miles's apartment, and eventually, my willpower fails. I'm part disappointed, part relieved to see that it's dark.

We reach my door, and I pull my key out of my bag, then look at Duffy. "Thank you for a very unique date."

He doesn't respond.

"Are you okay?"

"I want to kiss you." His eyes are locked onto mine. "I really like you and you're beautiful and you're the perfect Arwen to my Aragorn."

I smile. "Thank you, Duffy. I like you too." Though, maybe not romantically. Still, when he steps closer, I don't move away. Maybe there is something here? Maybe I should at least see?

Or maybe I just need Miles to not be the last man I kissed.

I can tell when I look at him that he's waiting for my permission, and while that's incredibly sweet, it does nothing to stir any kind of swoony feelings inside me.

He reaches for my hand. "Thank you for the honor of escorting you out this evening."

I press my lips together to hold back a smile. I'm not sure if I'm horrified or charmed by Duffy's quirks. I decide to roll with it. "The honor was all mine."

He reaches up and touches my cheek, then leans in and presses his lips softly against mine. He holds the kiss for three short seconds and then pulls back, smiling. "I'll call you."

I didn't even close my eyes.

* * *

It turns out a chaste, end-of-the-Hallmark-movie kind of kiss does nothing to erase the memory of a toe-curling, stomach-swooping, makes-you-forget-your-name kind of kiss.

Darn.

* * *

I signed up to have a booth at a farmers' market!

My first public business outing. My debutante ball.

I'm going to crush it.

I've been working with Zoey on social media photos and videos, something strange and uncomfortable but, according to her, necessary.

Inspections, permits, checking that things are built to code, all underway at The Porch. Now that I have a logo (it's so cute!), I've been able to order paper products, the sign for the window, and T-shirts for our staff. (I have a staff!)

I've been so busy I've hardly been able to think about Miles at all.

Which is a lie.

I do wonder what's been keeping him busy. I haven't seen him in days.

CHAPTER 26

"Okay, why are you with this guy again?" Lennon closes the door of my Jeep and meets me at the back of it.

I'm parked in the alley behind the bakery after purchasing all the groceries I need to make samples from my menu for the farmers' market this weekend.

And I just told her about my date with Duffy. And the good-night kiss.

In retrospect, I could've made it all sound a little better than it was, but I didn't have the energy.

Since the comic convention, we've been texting back and forth, and while Duffy might not be an obvious choice, I really do like him. Which is what I tell Lennon as I slip plastic bags onto my arms. "He's really nice. He makes going to the dentist fun. I know, because yesterday, he invited me to his office for a teeth cleaning."

She stops moving and stares at me. "He cleaned your teeth."

"It was very pleasant." I start marching toward the door. "He has a great chairside manner."

"This guy's hands have been in your mouth?" She winces.

"Well, when you put it like *that*," I say.

"Claire, you can't be serious."

I unlock the door and walk in, hauling the bags up onto the brushed metal counter at the center of the space. "I am serious. I've given this a lot of thought."

Because I am trying really hard *not* to think about Miles, which I think but don't say.

I slide my arms out of the bags and look at her. "He's successful and smart and quirky and kind. And he likes me. A lot. He told me so. Several times."

She looks unconvinced.

Same, actually.

I press on. "There are no games, no big mysteries. He wants to be in a relationship. With me. Do you know how refreshing that is?"

"Okay, but . . ." She puts her hands on my arms and waits for me to look at her. "Do *you* want to be in a relationship with *him*?" Her eyes are wide. "Does he make you feel tingly inside? Do you think about him when you're not together? When he holds your hand, do you feel like someone flipped a switch and everything is just a little brighter?"

I stare at her.

"Yeah. I thought so." She shakes her head slowly. "That's what you deserve, Claire."

The words hang there, true as steel.

"You deserve all the things," she says, dropping her hands from my arms. "Passion, and nervousness, and excitement, and butterflies, and all of it." She pauses. "That's not this guy."

I close my eyes and draw in a slow breath. "I can't hold out for all of that, Lennon. I'll end up alone."

She crosses her arms and frowns. "What about Miles?"

I start pulling ingredients out of the grocery bags. "What about Miles?"

"There's a lot of tension between you two—"

"You've been around us once."

"And there was tension." She walks around to the opposite side of the counter and opens one of the bags. "The good kind." She shoots me a look. "I just kind of thought, you know, you guys needed some time to figure it out."

Oh, I figured it out all right.

I shake my head. "Miles isn't on the market."

"Oh." She frowns. "Is he with someone?"

I stop moving and look at her. "He's off-limits. He's made that clear, and it's totally fine. And understandable. Something happened to him, something in his marriage, and he doesn't want to be in a relationship ever again."

She eyes me for a long moment, tilting her head slowly like she's reading my mind. "Something happened between you two."

I freeze. There is no way I'm going to be able to open my mouth to say a single word where it won't be obvious to Lennon that I'm lying. "It was nothing."

"Oh my gosh, it was totally not nothing," she says, a slow smile creeping across her face. "He flipped your switch." She wags her eyebrows at me.

I bark out a laugh. "What? No, he didn't." I pull two boxes of baking soda from the bags and walk them over to a shelf that I've only just now decided will be where they will live.

She follows me.

And stares.

I make a face.

She tilts her head toward me with her eyebrows raised.

It's weird—she's not saying anything, but I feel the increased pressure, and I can't stand it anymore, so I blurt out, "Fine. Yes. We kissed."

"Ha!"

"*Once*. It was . . ." I sigh like a lovesick middle schooler.

She leans back, eyebrows still raised.

I find the only word to describe it. "Amazing."

"I knew it."

"Nobody's kissed me like that in . . ." I pause, trying to remember. "Nobody's ever kissed me like that. But immediately after, we both agreed it was a mistake and it can't happen again."

Lennon rolls her eyes. "Oh, please."

"Which is why I am throwing everything into making this thing with Duffy work."

"That's the dumbest thing I've ever heard." She walks back to the counter and pulls out a bag of lemons and two cartons of strawberries.

"It's not dumb," I say. "It's self-preservation."

"More like self-sabotage," she says. "You're settling. You like Miles. You're both adults—why is it so complicated?"

Yeah, Claire, why is it so complicated?

I go still. "You don't know how hard it was to recover after John left." I look at her. "I didn't leave my house. I got really angry and depressed. I didn't take care of myself . . ." My gaze falls to the floor. "I can't do that again, and if I let myself fall for Miles, *who does not want a relationship*—" I snap my jaw shut and look away, a traitorous tear giving me away.

She drops a carton of blueberries and walks around the counter and pulls me into a tight hug. "I am so, *so* sorry for what you went through, Claire." She squeezes me so tight, I'm stunned frozen.

"Hug me back," she says over my shoulder.

I laugh through fresh tears, then bring my arms up around her. I can't remember the last time I hugged anyone or the last time anyone hugged me.

She pulls back and looks at me. "I understand your hesitation. I really do. Every time I saw a negative pregnancy test, I wanted to quit. It felt too painful to try again. But, Claire, I have to point out the obvious here."

A tear streams down my cheek.

"You survived it," she says. "You made it. You're still here. More than that, you're thriving. I mean, look at you. You gave your body and your mind and your heart time to heal, and you made a decision to start again. Do you know how amazing you are?"

I stand there dumbfounded, sitting in the remnants of her words, not sure how to process what she's said.

"You don't," she says. "I can see it in your face. What you did is incredible." She looks around. "What you're *doing* is incredible. Why would you take all these amazing risks in every area of your life except the one that makes the most difference?"

I wipe my eyes, not sure how to feel about any of this. "I'm convinced that I can be happy with a safer kind of love. That's all." I look at her.

She smiles. "But denying yourself the happiness of falling in love—really *falling* . . . it's like driving home just when the fireworks are about to begin."

I lean against the counter. "I don't need fireworks. I'm okay with safe. I'm okay with *fine*. Duffy is a good man." I look at her. "And he would never cheat on me."

Lennon's eyes go soft at the corners as she studies me. "You can't possibly know that, Claire."

"He's just not the type," I say, defensive.

"Nobody is the type," she says, "until they are. You can't keep yourself in a box. There's no reward without the risk."

She steps closer and takes my hands.

"Love is worth the risk."

I shake my head. "Spoken like a woman who is married to the best man on the planet."

She grins. "He really is." A pause, then she leans toward me. "What if you let yourself believe that maybe it's all going to work out exactly as it's supposed to?"

I think about my journal. I crossed off "I don't knows" and replaced them all with "what ifs." But was that only symbolic?

"Just think about it, Claire." She opens the refrigerator and sticks two gallons of milk inside. "You might be pushing to make it work with Duffy because you're too afraid of your feelings for Miles."

"That's *not* what I'm doing."

That's exactly what I'm doing.

"Good," she says. "Because that wouldn't be fair to him. And it's really not fair to you."

* * *

John: My lawyer did some digging. He thinks he can get you out of the lease on that bakery.

Claire: Please stop digging, and please stop helping.

John: You're making a huge mistake.

Claire: It's mine to make.

John: Seriously. It's madness.

Oh, and did you come up with anything idea-wise for the account?

CHAPTER 27

It's a perfect day for a farmers' market.

I arrive early with the cutest booth setup inspired by my "Porch Palette" and Zoey's branding. I have a big banner to hang in the back of my booth, flyers to give out to anyone who so much as glances at my table, and what has turned out to be an absolutely adorable display.

After my conversation with Lennon, I buried myself in baking, but I struggled to divert my attention to the tasks at hand. Her words had landed a little too hard.

I set up the kitchen, arranging canisters of staple ingredients around the workspace and figuring out the best workflow. And trying not to think about the words *"Do you want to be in a relationship with* him?"

I turned on my Bluetooth speaker and found my favorite band on Spotify. Their folksy, acoustic, earwormy music drew me in, but the story of how the band formed when two guys sent a Facebook message to a singer in England made me love them even more. I was hoping that if I played their songs on a continuous loop it would drown out the noise in my head.

All it did was make me think of Miles.

Because lyrics about stealing away, and butterflies, and moments in the sun will do that.

I mixed and measured and poured and baked, and somehow I ended up with a nice assortment of cookies, cupcakes, bars, and muffins, all meant to give the general public a sneak peek into what they can expect when the storefront is ready, when I open in two weeks.

Looking at it now, I'm still not sure how I got everything done. The last forty-eight hours have been a bit of a blur.

"This. Is. Amazing!" Lennon walks up carrying the cutest little toddler I've ever seen in my life, Daniel behind her, pushing a stroller.

"Is this Eve?" I rush to her, anxious to meet the other love of her life. "Good grief, Lennon, she's beautiful."

The little girl has Lennon's big blue eyes and Daniel's dark hair, only hers is curly. She smiles, and my teeth ache from the sweetness. A few minutes later, I see Zoey walking in our direction. Behind her, Kevin and Ava.

And behind them, Miles.

My insides decide at that precise moment to discombobulate, and my mouth goes dry.

"Claire! It looks amazing!" Zoey rushes straight to me, looking around at the reality that she helped me dream up. She did an amazing job getting my social media up and running, helping design the flyers, and getting the word out about The Porch. She took the idea and boiled it down into an easily digestible mission—one that people could get on board with. One that I could execute.

In some ways, today is as much Zoey's triumph as mine. Her fingerprints are all over this place.

"Hey, Zoey!" I look past her at the others. "Hey, everyone. Thanks for coming."

"We were promised cupcakes," Miles says.

Zoey smacks him across the chest. "Work *first*, Dad." She rolls her eyes.

Miles smiles.

And part of me relaxes.

"We're here to help wherever," Zoey says. "If you need it."

They all look so happy to be here—I'm not sure how to process the kindness.

"Oh, do you all know Lennon and her husband, Daniel?" I motion over to where my other friends are standing, pausing as the thought hits me—*my other friends.*

But I don't have time to linger on it or continue the introductions because a man walks up to my booth and starts looking around.

"Claire," Zoey hisses, giving me a wide-eyed look that's clearly meant to remind me I'm not here to socialize. I step back behind the table as the group—my group—moves away from the booth, giving people space to browse.

Miles doesn't move. Instead, he looks around at everything I've baked, eyes lingering on the Scotcheroos. He glances up and finds me watching him when I should be talking to my potential customer.

I force myself to get to work, thrilled when the man decides to buy a package of lemon bars. As he's leaving, Zoey hurries over and gives him a flyer, telling him the details of the grand opening. "Two weeks. The perfect neighborhood bakery. Sit, sip, and stay awhile."

Once the man has gone, she shoots me a look. "Sell yourself a little, Claire."

Miles strolls up beside me, wearing one of my extra aprons. "She's not going to do that," he says to Zoey.

I frown. "How do you know?"

"It's not your style," he says. "There's not an arrogant bone in your body."

"It's not arrogant to want to share the things you're good at," Zoey says.

Miles points to her, then to himself. "We know that." Then he hitches a thumb in my direction. "She's still learning."

"I resent that," I say. "I used to put together huge fundraisers all by myself. I was good at that."

He crosses his arms and looks at me. "But did anyone know you were the one who did all the work?"

I fold my arms back, defiant, but finally admit, "No."

"I thought so. Can you tell the next people who walk in here that your snickerdoodle scones are incredible? Or that the cookies are the perfect balance of crispy on the outside and soft in the center? Or that your lemon cake will make them want to be a kid on a trampoline again?"

I'm struggling to defend myself, because he's right. "I . . . will . . . have a hard time with that."

"So." He makes a motion like he's rolling up his sleeves, even though he's wearing a white, short-sleeved Henley shirt with three buttons at the top. "Let us do it for you."

Zoey's eyes brighten. "Yes! We'll be the cheer squad!"

An older woman walks up to the table and starts looking around. Miles grins. "I've got this." He walks right up to the woman, who's carrying two crocheted bags, one empty, one with vegetables in it. "Good morning!"

She looks up and, not surprisingly, seems instantly charmed by him. "Good morning."

"You've made the best decision of the day stopping here in our booth," Miles says. He launches into a spiel about my baked goods that is so perfect it sounds rehearsed, only without the stiff delivery. He's so natural with everyone, and he has no problem selling her on the half dozen sampler—a box of six different treats, perfect for the indecisive and nondiscriminating sweet tooth.

As he's ringing her up, he tells her where the bakery is located and when we're opening, then leans in closer and says, "And she's kind of shy, but that's the baker right there." He points to me. "She's *very* talented."

The woman looks at me and smiles, then hands her money over to Miles, pats his hand, and tells him to keep the change. She waves the flyer in my direction. "Can't wait to come by when you open!"

"Thank you!" I call out as she walks off.

I turn to Miles, but before I get a word out, two more people step into the booth, and he starts the spiel all over again. He begins by asking them questions about themselves, and he actually seems interested in their answers. This appears to hook them. After that, he tells them about the bakery.

Despite what I thought of him when we first met, Miles is one of the most sincere people I've ever known.

He's also one of the most enthusiastic fans of my baked goods.

Still. Fan or no, genuine or dishonest—he doesn't do relationships.

Never mind that sometimes I still catch him looking at me like he's remembering the night we kissed.

Like maybe he wants to do it again.

I'm lost in thought when Lennon steps right in front of me. She's been at the market for over an hour, and I've seen her walk by my booth at least three times. I notice that she's carrying a stack of flyers, and I'm pretty sure she's been handing them out to everyone here.

She gives me a knowing look, makes a point of moving her eyes over to Miles and then back to me.

I frown.

She slowly lifts her shoulders, as if to send me a message telepathically.

I shake my head and go back to the customers. Because she is making a point that doesn't need to be made.

Around noon, when things finally wind down, I look around the booth and realize . . . I'm practically sold out. I'm just finishing up with a sweet young mom who bought a big sugar cookie for her little boy. She gives me cash and hands the boy the cookie. His eyes go wide.

"We're going to share that." She looks at me. "He'd live on cookies if I let him."

I smile, remembering those days. "Have a great weekend!"

As they walk off, Miles comes up next to me. "Well, I'd say that was a huge success," he says, looking around at the empty display.

"Thanks to you guys," I say. "I never could've done any of this without you." I go quiet. "And I can't believe you gave up your Saturday to do this."

He shrugs. "I'm just here for the Scotcheroos."

I grin, but then a yell cuts through the noise of the market, followed by a loud, "It's too yucky, Mommy!"

I turn and see the young mom and her son only a few feet away from the booth. He's holding out the cookie, spitting the bite out onto the ground. "I don't like it!" He bursts into tears.

I frown. "Oh no."

"Don't sweat it," he says. "Kids are picky."

"But kids love my sugar cookies," I say.

But then Zoey rushes into the booth. "Hey." Ava is right behind her.

I frown. Because they both look panicked. "What's wrong?"

She pulls me toward the back of the booth, her face serious. "Claire, did you *taste* the stuff you sold today?"

My stomach drops. "Of course, I know all my recipes by heart."

"No, but like"—she presses her lips together and looks around the empty booth—"as you were baking *these* things, did you taste them?"

I feel like she's coming at me with kid gloves when I need her to sock me in the face and tell me what's going on.

"What's wrong, Zo?" Miles asks calmly.

"This." Ava holds out her phone, and Miles clicks on a paused video, moving beside me so I can watch it too.

On the screen, there's a video by a girl whose social media account is Shannon in Chicago. She's standing in the midst of the foot traffic of this very farmers' market, and now that I look at her, I remember her buying a sampler box.

"Good morning, Shan-fans, we are here at the Lincoln Square Farmers Market, and we've just stumbled across a brand-new bakery coming to the neighborhood in just a couple weeks. You know we are all about supporting small-business owners here at Shannon in Chicago, and we were super excited to hear the concept of a small-town, Midwest-inspired bakery right here in the heart of the city. It's called The Porch, and the whole idea is that you come in, and you feel like you're spending time relaxing on the big, cozy porch of an old farmhouse."

My stomach sinks because I know there's a "but" coming—a "but" that's going to feel a lot like an anvil being dropped on my head.

Zoey turns away, and Ava chews her thumbnail.

"So I was excited to try it. You guys know I love my sweets. But . . . something is really off with this stuff. We ordered the sampler pack, a box of six signature treats that are going to be featured at The Porch. The Scotcheroo, Porch pecan bars, snickerdoodle scones, oatmeal cream pie sandwiches, lemon bars, and your traditional sugar cookie.

"They all look amazing." She holds them up to show the camera. "But I took a bite of every single one, and I can tell you, without hesitation, that these are"—she walks over to a trash can and tosses the whole box inside—"garbage. I'm pretty sure that the baker at The Porch needs to get back to basics and learn the difference between salt and sugar." She laughs. "Now I'm going to go find something to drink to get the horrible taste out of my mouth."

The video ends, and I stand there unmoving, my vision cloudy and out of focus.

"Claire," Miles says.

My mind races. What went wrong? What did I do?

"That can't be right," I say, hands shaking. "I need to get back to the bakery. I need to check on this." I look around. "There's no way I made such a basic, simple mistake." I look at Miles. "Are we sure this woman isn't just trying to sabotage me? Maybe she's another bakery owner or something?"

"She's not the only one talking about it," Zoey says softly.

My eyes fill with tears. "No."

She looks at me. "I'm so sorry, Claire."

"Let me see," I say.

Zoey's holding her phone, but Miles puts a hand on it before she can show it to me. "No."

"I need to see what they're all saying."

"You don't," he says firmly. "We're going to break everything down, and we're going to come up with a plan."

"What kind of plan could possibly make this okay?" I ask, tears spilling down my cheeks. "I sank everything into this business! Everything! This was supposed to work out, this was supposed to show everyone that I—" I can't even finish.

I know how negativity travels on the internet. And I also know that launching in two weeks in the wake of this mess is going to be an absolute disaster.

And there's no one to blame but myself.

A single, horrible, unwanted thought drops into my mind.

John was right.

CHAPTER 28

Claire, it's going to be okay." Lennon is outside my bathroom at The Porch, and I've locked myself inside. I'm doomscrolling through the comments on videos I've been tagged in.

And I'm crying.

After we packed up the booth, I refused to go home without inspecting my kitchen. And Shannon in Chicago was right.

I guess I was so distracted when I was unpacking groceries and setting up the kitchen that I poured the giant bag of salt into a canister and the giant bag of sugar into an identical canister and then mislabeled them.

In a true rookie move, I didn't bother to check either one when I was baking. I was in a hurry to get everything done and packaged and ready for the market.

I rushed, even though this was my debut event.

I rushed, even though this was the first time the good people of my new city were going to be introduced to the bakery.

The bakery that I decided to start with my entire savings and a loan from the bank.

This is what I get for thinking I could pull this off.

I hear the outside door open and someone enters the kitchen. Then I hear quiet conversation. It's a man's voice. Probably Daniel. Probably came to collect his wife and save her from her disaster of a friend. *"Get out while you still can, Lennon,"* I imagine him saying. *"This woman is a mess. And nobody needs more mess in their life."*

But then there's a soft knock on the door. "Claire?"

It's not Daniel. It's Miles.

My heart clenches with wretched embarrassment.

"Can you unlock the door?" he asks calmly.

I don't move right away. This feels like such a punch in the gut. The second chance I've been building so meticulously is about to implode, and it's completely my fault.

John was right.

The thought makes me feel even smaller.

My phone buzzes with a text.

Miles: Hey, let me in.

Claire: I think I need to be alone.

Miles: No, you don't.

Claire: . . .

Miles: Don't make me pick the lock.

Claire: Do you know how to pick a lock?

Miles: No.

But I'm smart and persistent. And there's probably a YouTube video I can watch.

I stare at the words. Why is he here? Why does he care?

I reach up and unclick the lock, but I don't open the door.

After a beat, Miles opens it and steps inside. When he sees me sitting on the floor, he closes the door, locks it, and sits down next to me, his shoulder pressed into mine, legs stretched out in front of him.

It's like he doesn't want his presence to be a disruption. It's thoughtful, and it makes me want to cry again.

I sniff. My cheeks are tearstained, and I'm sure my eyes are puffy. "You know this floor is probably filthy."

"Yep," he says.

In the pause that follows, I wipe my cheeks with the balled-up toilet paper I've been squeezing in my hand.

I shut my eyes and softly hit the back of my head against the wall behind me. "Why are you here, Miles?"

"Came to check on you."

I look at him. "But why?"

He looks back. "Because that's what friends do."

I quietly scoff, gaze dropping to the ball of toilet paper in my hands. "Friends?" I sniff. "Is that what we are?"

"I mean . . ." he lilts, "at the *very* least, yeah."

I turn back, trying to read his face.

"We can't get into that right now." He smirks.

I sigh a tired sigh and bring the already-used tissue up to my nose again. "I don't know what I'm going to do."

"We'll figure it out," he says.

I shake my head. "There's no coming back from this."

He reaches over and takes my hand. "There is. We just need to find it."

I look at him like he's nuts.

He pats my hand. "Okay, here's what we're going to do. You're going to rage out for, like, three minutes. In that three minutes, you're going to voice every single negative thought you're thinking right now. Okay?"

I frown. "Why three minutes?"

"Because I don't want to listen to you for five."

I snort out a laugh, and Miles's mouth twitches up in a tiny smile. He lets my hand go, pulls out his phone, and sets the timer for three minutes.

"You're serious," I say.

"Always serious about raging out," he says.

"Is this some trick you learned in therapy?" I swipe my nose with the back of my hand.

"No," he says. "I'm just spitballing here. I have no idea if this is going to help. But it's the verbal equivalent of a punching bag, so it seems like it would."

"A punching bag might be better."

He eyes me for a beat, thumb hovering over the start button of the timer. He shakes the phone as if to ask if I'm ready.

I sniff and wipe the last of my mascara off my face. I nod. "Ready."

"Okay . . . go."

When I close my eyes, the floodgates open, and I decide not to censor myself at all.

"When I decided to move here, John told me it was a terrible idea. He said I'd never make it without him, even though, if I'd stayed in Colorado, I would've had to move out of our house and figure out a way to make it without him anyway. But that planted this little seed that moving here was stupid. A bad idea. That I wasn't going to be able to hack it.

"Then I got here, and I was terrified. And I was afraid he was right. Afraid that I couldn't do this. Who am I to even try?"

I draw in a breath, thinking back on those first weeks here in the city. Thinking back on the app dates that were terrible, but slowly helped me build my confidence. The walks around my neighborhood that started to get more familiar. The people who had come into my life along the way.

I look at Miles.

"I was on a mission to find the thing that made me excited to get out of bed in the morning. And no, I'm not saving lives with muffins or whatever, but I thought maybe I could put some joy into the world. Because that's what my gram did for me. When everything was hopeless, she showed up with biscuits. And my world wasn't bleak anymore."

Miles reaches over and takes my hand.

"So I decided to go for it. To sink everything I'd saved into this place because I was so smitten with this crazy idea. To bring that front-porch feeling to people who've been running around, searching for human connection without ever meeting a human face-to-face. The apps made me more aware than ever that people and relationships have become disposable, and I wanted to create a spot where they were celebrated.

"But I failed. Royally. In the worst way. Before I even started, really. I couldn't do the one thing I do well. I didn't even give myself a fighting chance," I say, voice rising. "And that's my greatest fear! The thing I poured everything into, the thing that was supposed to help me rebuild my life"—I shake my head—"I screwed it up! John was right! *Again!* I don't know what I'm doing! I'm not qualified for any of this!"

I feel heat and anger and embarrassment and frustration, all rolled together in a tangled mess, and I go quiet for a few moments.

Miles just sits. Patient.

My emotional RPMs rev down out of the red, and I say the one, familiar, horrible coincidence that has hit me the hardest.

"The worst part of all of this?" I take a deep breath, because saying this is so humiliating. "Once again, my failure is plastered all over the internet for everyone to see."

"Again?" Miles asks.

"Yeah. *Again.* These Porch videos? They now have thousands and thousands of views. You know what else has thousands and thousands of views?" I pull out my phone and search "Messy drunk falls into fountain at charity gala" on YouTube. And hand the phone to Miles, sniffing. "It's a riot."

His phone chimes. The timer is up.

I feel empty. Hollowed out. But strangely not the same as three minutes ago.

I look at him. "Why are you friends with me again?"

He chuckles to himself, clicking the timer off. "I'm starting to wonder . . ."

I sink back against the wall, thinking that this exercise was oddly cathartic. Like an out-loud journal.

In front of Miles.

Who, I only now realize, is still holding my hand.

Miles sets his phone on his lap as the screen on mine goes dark. "Well done. Perfectly timed, actually. Do you feel better?"

I nod. "Yeah, I do, actually."

He rubs a thumb across my knuckles. "All right." He stands, then holds his hand out in my direction. "Come with me."

I frown. "Aren't you going to contradict everything I just said? Tell me all the reasons I'm awesome and give me some sunny pep talk about how I can't quit now?"

He frowns back. "Why would I do that?"

"I thought this was the pep talk part."

"I'm not going to contradict your feelings. They're feelings." He shakes his hand in my direction, a reminder that he's waiting for me to take it. "Come on."

"Where are we going?" I eye the hand suspiciously.

"You'll see," he says.

In the silence that follows, he stands there, hand still stretched out in my direction, patiently waiting until, finally, I slip my hand in his and let him help me to my feet.

Once we're face-to-face, he scans mine and his frown lines deepen. "Oof. You look terrible."

I smack him across the arm, but then I catch a glimpse of myself in the mirror, and I have to laugh. Because he's right. I do look terrible. Puffy and pale with streaks of black still on my cheeks. I walk over to the sink, splash some water on my face, then turn to find him holding out a paper towel.

"This is all so humiliating," I say. "I swore I wouldn't let this happen again."

"I do feel the need to contradict *one* thing you said," he says as he opens the door to the bathroom. "You said *your* failure was plastered all over the internet." He looks at me, forcing eye contact with a kind and quiet intensity.

"But the cheater is the failure, Claire. Not the one who got cheated on." He flips the light off and steps out into the kitchen.

The simple movement reminds me of Lennon's words—*"He flipped your switch"*—and I have to breathe in a very long, very slow breath to calm the nerves that have bubbled up inside me.

CHAPTER 29

Fight or flight. Everything within me is shouting for the latter.

I sit in the passenger side of Miles's Range Rover, trying to keep my lower lip from quivering.

I want to tell him to drive me home so I can crawl into my bed and stay there for a year.

My default is to retreat. But I've done that before. A part of me knows it won't help, but right now I don't care. I finally know what I want. Screwing up and not being able to have it is ten times worse.

After fifteen minutes of driving in silence, Miles parallel parks his SUV—and I have no idea where we are. Miles turns off the engine and gets out of the car without a word. He walks over to my side and opens the door.

"Where are we?" I ask.

"I'll show you."

I step out onto the sidewalk, and Miles closes the door, then starts walking down the block. We're in an area of the city where I haven't been before, so I take a second to look around. There are tall apartment buildings lining the street and a parking garage at the end of the block.

We cross the street, and I hear the sound of kids playing in the near distance. Miles leads me around the corner, revealing a large playground nestled at the back of two perpendicular buildings.

Half of the space is a playground. Rounded wooden structures, short climbing walls, rope bridges, all themed around what looks like a pirate ship. There's a taller platform on one end with multiple ships' steering wheels and a circular "crow's nest" platform in the center, complete with several telescopes on stands.

The other half is open green space. Bigger than the quad at my college. Families on blankets pepper the grass, and I can see two dads with dogs who have seemingly just met each other.

Kids are running around, chasing each other, shouting, maneuvering their way through tunnels and on top of spring-loaded mushrooms. A small group of tiny humans is jumping on large, painted circles lining a sidewalk that runs the perimeter of the whole park.

The entire area is brightly colored with pockets of plants and flowers, and there's plenty of space for parents to sit and watch their kids play.

The park is interactive and obviously meant to encourage kids to use their imaginations, intricately planned and executed with children in mind.

I follow Miles straight to the center of the park, a divide between the open space and the playground. Colorful, comfortable benches face both directions, toward the kids and toward the grass, and he sits on a bench facing the playground, motioning for me to do the same.

We're both silent for a few long moments.

There's a little girl who climbs a rope ladder to the top of a slide and scream-laughs the whole way down. Over and over again.

A trio of boys are taking turns crazily jumping off a mushroom into the mulch, where each one tries to land in a superhero pose. They laugh every time, because they fall over every time.

A dad gently pushes his small daughter in a swing—but the thing that strikes me is that his daughter is in a wheelchair, and the swing is a larger platform that the wheelchair expertly fits on. It was built and designed specifically for kids like her in mind. She throws her hands in the air on every push, and the look on her face is pure joy.

For a second, I forget that my life is falling apart.

Again.

"A couple years ago, I almost sold my business," Miles says, eyes trained on a man throwing a Frisbee to a golden retriever in the distance.

My gaze latches onto him, but I don't say anything.

"I found out my wife, Elizabeth, was having an affair with my VP. Brent." Miles says this quickly, like it's a memorized line and not the first time he's explaining the source of so much pain. "He was the guy I'd hired straight out of school and mentored, thinking that he could keep things going while Elizabeth and I traveled, you know, after the girls grew up and moved out. I had a whole plan."

I shift slightly, angling my body toward him, resisting the urge to reach for him even though I know reliving this cannot be pleasant. I think of the night I told him about John and Misty. How hard it had been to get the words out—and how Miles wasn't ready to do the same.

Somehow it makes this moment feel even more important.

"I came home early from work one afternoon," he says coldly, shaking his head. "I didn't usually come home early, but it was the day before our anniversary. Thought I'd surprise her by taking her out." He goes still. "I was . . . definitely surprised."

He doesn't look at me. "They were there in our house, together. In our bedroom. *In our bed.*" That last sentence has a twinge of hurt and anger in it.

I immediately recognize that tone. It's unfortunately familiar.

My stomach twists, and in the back of my mind I see the silver sequins of Misty's skirt and John's hand on her thigh in the shadowy corner of that country club lobby.

"She immediately launched into some kind of, I don't know, speech? That she worked out in her head. She was feeling this way for a while, it just kind of happened—"

He stops mid-sentence, making a fist and clenching his jaw.

"They were planning to tell me, they just hadn't found the right time . . . or whatever."

He scoffs softly but otherwise keeps his tone mostly emotionally detached, almost like he's spitting out facts without letting a single one penetrate through the wall he's built around himself.

"I fired Brent. I packed a bag. I moved out. I wasn't sure what I was going to do, or how I was going to do it." He looks at me, half smiling. "I know you know how that feels. Directionless. Rudderless."

I nod, hoping he can feel my empathy.

"A few days later, my accountant called me. She'd noticed some strange activity in one of the business accounts," he says. "The account she was concerned about was one I used specifically for pro bono projects for underserved communities"—he looks around—"like this one."

A little girl runs past us, kicking a soccer ball, her laughter filling the air. And I understand what he isn't saying—this park started as a dream in his head.

Just like my bakery.

"It turned out Elizabeth had been funneling money out of that account into a new account so she and Brent could start a business of their own."

"Oh my gosh." I instinctively reach for his hand and squeeze it firmly.

While I understand the pain of an affair, this betrayal crossed a different line. I can imagine how much it hurt.

"We had joint accounts, and she had access to everything, so technically, she didn't do anything illegal. Morally? Ethically? She broke every single rule."

"Miles, I'm so sorry," I say.

He avoids my eyes. "For a long time, I thought it was my fault. I should've known what was happening right under my nose. I should've paid closer attention."

"I know how that feels," I say quietly, not wanting to make this moment about my pain, but wanting him to know he's not alone.

"It broke me. And my business. I was so embarrassed, I almost quit." Now he glances in my direction. I meet his eyes for a flicker of a second, then look away.

Because I understand what he's doing.

I understand why he brought me here.

"And I could've. Easily. But then one morning I went for a walk. And after two hours of aimless wandering, I ended up here. Only this entire block was just an open lot at the back of two stores. There are apartments around, so I knew there were families in the area, and I thought . . . *These kids deserve a safe place to play.*" He does a quick scan of our surroundings. "And then I thought . . . *I'm going to make them one.*"

At one end of the park, there are three tiny wooden huts surrounded by bushes, and all I can think when I see them is that any kid would love to get lost in this park for a little while.

He created something special where there was nothing.

"This was the project that brought me back to life," he says.

He turns his body toward me.

"Like your bakery."

I think about the new friends who've shown up to help me, and their genuine excitement for my project. I think about the life I'm building, a life I desperately want to work.

"Are you really going to let a little salt ruin all your plans?" His eyes smile, and there's a lilt of lightness in his tone.

At that, the tears are back, and I pull my hand from his to quickly wipe them away. "It was more than a little salt, Miles." I cringe to think of the cups and cups that had gone into those desserts.

"Life has a funny way of showing us what we're made of and of bringing us exactly what—and who—we need."

My gaze travels from our hands to his face, stopping when I meet his eyes.

"I'm terrified," I say.

"So was I," he says. Then, slowly and firmly, he says, "But you're not alone."

He's right. I'm not. The thought is humbling, and I feel undeserving somehow.

"You think doing this big thing, on your own, means handling everything by yourself, but it doesn't. It's okay to ask for help." He puts a hand on my shoulder and gently squeezes. "That's what friends are for, you know?"

I draw in a breath and look around, thinking about everything Miles has been through. I'm amazed that he's come out of it strong enough to create something as beautiful as the park we're sitting in.

But I'm not sure I have the same strength.

Miles pats my shoulder twice, then reaches into his pocket and pulls out his phone and what looks like a blue hockey puck. "Okay, so I have a confession."

"Not the greatest way to start a sentence with me."

He winces. "Ope. You're right. Sorry. It's nothing bad. Just . . . when everything happened earlier, I reached out to Minnie."

"You did not," I say, instantly embarrassed. "Did you tell her what happened?"

"She already knew," he says. "She follows all your accounts, and she has it set up so she's alerted every time someone mentions your name or your business."

I close my eyes and groan, hoping that John isn't tech savvy enough to do the same. But as soon as that thought enters my head, another one replaces it—*Who cares what John thinks?*

He clicks around on his phone, then sets the hockey puck—which I now see is a small Bluetooth speaker—down on the bench. "She told me that when she was little, if she ever had a bad day, the two of you had a tradition."

His phone. A speaker. My eyes widen.

"And since *she* can't be here, she made me promise that I'd do it with you."

I think back to the years I spent dedicating every free second to being Minnie's mom.

I'm momentarily struck with a wave of sadness that this time in my life has come and gone, in some ways, when I wasn't even looking.

But then I hear the familiar a capella opening of ABBA's "Take a Chance on Me" on the speaker.

I'm instantly transported back to Minnie's very torturous middle school years. They were marked with mean girls and first crushes and embarrassing puberty mishaps, and somehow, showing up in her room, blasting ABBA and forcing her to get up and dance with me, was usually all it took to shift the mood.

In spite of everything, I smile.

Miles looks right at me, holds up his phone, and clicks the volume all the way up. It's loud enough now to where people around us hear it.

He stands and offers me a hand. "Dance with me?"

I look around. "Here?"

He shrugs. "Why not?"

"There are people," I say dumbly.

"Who cares?" He shakes his hips as the drums kick in, and he starts to sing along—badly. A few of the kids notice him and start laughing, but Miles doesn't seem to care. He starts doing a strange disco move, pointing his fingers and undulating his shoulders, first to one side, then the other.

Immediately some kids start mimicking him, doing the same moves.

"Come on, Claire." He picks up the speaker and backs up, eyes locked onto mine, and points, beckoning me over with his finger.

I stand up, laughing, covering my face with my hands, and as the chorus kicks up, fueled by happy memories of my daughter and the pure joy on Miles's face, I start to sway to the music. Miles dances around me as two little girls point and laugh, their mothers on a nearby bench smiling at the sight of his genuine happiness as he dances around the playground with reckless abandon.

Little by little, I start to loosen up, remembering moves I'd perfected all those years ago in Minnie's lavender bedroom. Because it was always this song that cheered her. And now she was using it to cheer me—from thousands of miles away.

I begin to throw myself fully into the song, singing the words, dancing along, using my thumb as an air microphone and laughing as Miles and I dance around the whole playground.

At this point, most of the little kids have joined in, forming a crazy jumping, dancing conga line behind us. Even some of the parents are dancing with each other or showing off disco moves. Miles picks me up and twirls me around, eliciting shouts and whoops and hollers from the kids. He jumps up on the mushrooms and starts to make his way around the wooden jungle gym, with dozens of kids in tow.

I follow behind, climbing all the way up to the top of the structure, laughing all the way through the slow fade at the end of the song.

And when it ends, the kids all cheer, and the parents even applaud. My spirit is lighter, with a fresh wave of laughter rolling over me.

We're standing on top of a wooden rope bridge, swinging slightly as kids run around us, shouting and cheering, and I meet Miles's happy gaze.

"Feel better?" he asks.

I nod. "Yeah, I do."

"Good," he says. "Now let's get to work."

* * *

I've never really thought about the lyrics to "Take a Chance on Me."

They're incredibly fitting right now.

I was feeling down. The birds had all flown.

Then . . . Miles.

His playground made a great point.

And he's right. I'm not about to let a little salt stop me.

I flip over to my list and confidently cross things out. Because I believe I've found them.

1. ~~*I want a job or career I love.*~~
2. ~~*I want friends. Real ones.*~~
3. ~~*I want to live in a new city.*~~
4. *I want a dog.*
5. *I want to figure out who I am—apart from a wife and a mom.*
6. ~~*I want a place where I fit in. I want a place where I belong.*~~
7. *I want a hobby.*
8. ~~*I want to do the things that scare me.*~~
   - ~~*Have a meal by myself in public.*~~
   - ~~*Strike up a conversation with a stranger.*~~
   - ~~*Try new foods I've never had or can't pronounce.*~~
   - ~~*Download dating app.*~~
9. ~~*I want to fall in love again.*~~

I stare at the last one. My instinct is to erase the line through it . . . but I don't.

Not yet.

CHAPTER 30

"Where have you guys been?" Zoey asks.

Miles and I have just gotten back to The Bexley, and the courtyard is buzzing. All of my people (except Minnie) are here, and when they see us, they all stop what they're doing.

Lennon's eyes are wide, hopeful, and she looks a little smug. Definitely reading into the fact that I spent the whole afternoon with Miles. Maybe also reading into the fact that he was the one who got me off the bathroom floor.

"We, uh—" I glance over at Miles.

"We had a few things to take care of," he says.

"Okay, well, we got hungry, so we're grilling out," Ava says. "Everyone brought something, and it's almost ready."

I look around at this hodgepodge of people. One of our quieter neighbors, a young investment banker named Tim, is here, along with the crew from the farmers' market.

Lorraine bustles out of her house carrying a platter of meat, and Daniel is at the grill, ready, complete with a black apron with white letters reading: THIS IS A MANLY APRON FOR A MANLY MAN, DOING MANLY THINGS, WHILE COOKING MANLY FOOD.

There's a picnic table covered with trays and bowls of food, and standing next to it is Duffy.

Duffy? What is he doing here?

He lifts a hand in a polite wave, eyes drifting over to Miles, and I'm sure he's drawing a conclusion about what he's seeing. There's a gnawing in my belly that tells me I need to make this right.

When Miles sees him standing there, he walks off toward the grill, pats a hand on Daniel's shoulder, and picks up a spatula.

"We came up with a brilliant idea," Zoey says before I can move. "We've all been brainstorming since we left the market."

"You have?"

"Heck yes," Ava says. "We're invested now."

Lennon hands me a glass of lemonade. "You have a lot of people in your corner." She squeezes my arm. "And we all want to help."

The words zip straight to my heart.

These are my people.

The gravity of that hits me—hard. Because nobody has ever shown up for me like this. Not even the people who should've. Not in a million years.

"We'll talk about it after we eat," Ava says with a smile. "But we think you're going to love it."

"We *hope* you're going to love it," Zoey adds.

"She will," Lorraine says. "It's a brilliant plan."

I'm curious what they're going to propose, but I'm also hungry and exhausted, so I let it go for now and make my way over to Duffy, anxious to do the right thing where he's concerned.

He's a good person, and if today has taught me anything, it's that Lennon was right—holding on to him while I try to sort out my feelings for someone else really isn't fair.

And as much as I wish I didn't have feelings to sort, I do. That may mean I have to put some distance between me and Miles—or *close* the distance, which terrifies me—but regardless, there's no room for Duffy in my romantic life.

And it would be so cliché to ask him if we can be friends, even though I really hope we can.

I walk over to him. He doesn't know anyone here besides the online version of Lorraine, and I'm filled with a strange mix of gratitude and dread. I really don't want to hurt this man.

"Hey," I say.

He shoves his hands in his pockets. "I heard about what happened. I'm sorry I wasn't there today."

"Oh, it's okay," I say. "It was really good . . . and then it really wasn't."

"I, uh . . ." He glances over at Miles, then back at me. "I had a date."

I can't see my face, but I'm pretty sure it's showing my surprise. "Oh!"

"I know you and I are not exclusive, but I still wanted to be straight with you about it." He's nodding as he says this, and then I realize that Duffy is trying to work up the courage to let me down easy.

A flood of relief washes over me. "That's so great, Duffy," I say. "Did you have a nice time?"

He seems to be trying not to smile, but he's failing. Finally, he gushes, "A really nice time!"

"I'm so glad." And I really am.

"Actually, you met her—Sonya? She was White Diamond from Steven Universe?"

I frown.

"The woman in the book signing line—the one in all white."

"Oh, right!" I say, remembering. "She was beautiful!"

"We connected later on a message board," he says. "And realized we'd met that day." He grimaces. "I wasn't sure how you'd feel about it."

I cross my arms over my chest and smile up at him. "I feel pretty awesome about it actually, because it looks like you're really happy."

The smile is back. "I am."

"Good."

His eyes dart over to the grill, where I know Miles is standing. "What about you?" He brings his attention back to me. "Are you and your neighbor . . . ?"

I shake my head. "Oh no, we're just friends."

Duffy's grin turns goofy. "*Ohhkay.*"

I shove his arm, and we seem to settle into a playful sort of platonic friendship. "We are."

He leans forward. "Then why does he keep looking over here?"

I glance over my shoulder, and when my eyes meet Miles's, he smiles but quickly looks away. A flutter of hope fills my rib cage.

But then I remember his perfectly understandable and valid reasons for not wanting a relationship ever again. His very brutal divorce and all the hurt his ex-wife caused have irrevocably broken him. I understand that more than ever now.

And I can't even blame him. I get it. More than most.

Strangely, though, I'm willing to try again. To open up again.

If someone asked me about that possibility even three weeks ago, I would've said no way.

But I am.

And Miles isn't. I want to respect that, but a flurry of words rushes back at me. His speech in the park . . . it was all about getting kicked and not staying down. About getting back in the fight after a loss.

Miles isn't following his own advice. When it comes to relationships, he's taken himself out of the game completely. Sidelined himself with an injured heart.

Well, well, well. Pot, meet Kettle.

I sit with the revelation for a few heavy seconds, then Duffy says my name.

"What?" I blink a few times, hoping to reenter this conversation.

"I said, is it better if I go?" he says. "These are your friends, not mine."

I look around, choosing to tuck away my thoughts about Miles, at least for now, and I squeeze Duffy's arm. "*You* are one of my friends too."

He grins. "You mean it?"

"Of course." I smile at him.

"Good," he says enthusiastically. "Because I'm starving."

"Okay, it's ready!" Daniel says over the chatter. "Come eat."

We all move toward the table, piling plates with food, and I remember I have a sheet cake that I made sitting on the counter in my kitchen. "I'll be right back." I can't be the only one who shows up empty-handed to this impromptu gathering, especially when I'm the reason for it.

Though everyone will probably be terrified to eat anything I baked.

I'm standing in my kitchen, cutting the cake into squares, when I hear movement in my living room. I turn and see Miles standing there, backlit by the dim light outside.

I gasp. "You scared me."

"Sorry, I tried to be loud when I came over." He takes a few steps toward me, and I can see a pensive look on his face.

I set the knife down and turn to face him. "You okay?"

He looks at me, frozen. "I don't want you to be with the dentist."

I go still. "You don't?"

He shakes his head.

"Why not?"

"Because he's wrong for you," Miles says.

I frown. "How do you know that? You don't even know him."

"But I know you," he says. "Or I think I do."

At that, I smile. Right now, he might be the one person who knows me the best. I've told him things I haven't told anyone else.

He inhales a deep breath and says, "I know I've given you a lot of mixed signals."

I scoff. "You think?"

He pushes a hand through his hair, visible angst on his face. "I know. And I'm sorry."

I wait, hoping he'll go on. Hoping he's about to tell me that he's ready to try a relationship. That he wants to. Because of me.

But he goes silent.

"Duffy is seeing someone else," I say.

Miles's face brightens, and he looks almost happy. "He is? What about—"

I shrug. "He's really nice, and kind, but we're not a good fit."

He nods but still doesn't say anything.

He looks like he wants to—but he just doesn't.

I narrow my eyes, then move toward him, wanting, for once, to be bold—to say what I need to say. "You know, I was thinking about the park. About what you said."

He shifts his weight.

"You were so inspiring, and I'm guessing it wasn't easy to tell me the things you told me."

He makes a face. "Yeah, it's not my favorite topic."

"You were hurt. Like I was. But the way you've picked up the pieces of your life and moved forward? It made me want to try to do the same."

He doesn't move.

"But that was about your job," I say. "Not your heart."

He looks right in my eyes.

"I realized that you're just as scared as I am." I pause. "You're too afraid to really put yourself out there because what if you have to feel that pain again? You want to talk about mixed signals? You kiss me, then agree it can't happen again. You punch a guy for insulting me and tell me you want it to be your job to protect me, but then you say you don't do relationships and that we need to just be friends."

I sigh. "And now you say you don't want me to be with Duffy . . ." I pause for a beat. "But we both know that's not the same as saying you want to be with me."

His face falls. He starts to say something but stops.

I reach up and touch his face, and he turns into my hand for a fraction of a second, then his gaze falls as he inches just a little closer.

"Miles, what do you want?" My voice is low, our faces so close that if I moved an inch, we'd be kissing.

But neither of us moves.

And he doesn't say a word.

We're held in place by a current of electricity that's buzzing and about to snap.

Finally, after a long, tense—and silent—moment, I smile, softly nod, and walk back into the courtyard, leaving him standing in the darkness of my apartment.

CHAPTER 31

"This is the brilliant idea?"

It's two days after the farmers' market disaster, but the saltiness of that event is still bitter in my mind.

I'm standing in the kitchen at The Porch, trying to wrap my head around the redemption plan Zoey and Lennon have just pitched.

"Self-deprecation is your natural language," Lennon says. "You can do this."

"And then we bring in our secret weapon." Zoey grins.

"Lorraine," I say dryly, because apparently, my redemption is in her hands.

"Lorraine." Zoey nods.

"How is Lorraine going to help get me out of this mess?" I groan, wiping down a clean counter because I need something to do with my hands.

Zoey pulls out her phone, unlocks it, and hands it to me.

"What am I looking at?"

"That's Lorraine's channel," she says.

I look down at the page she's pulled up, and I see a little drawing of a cartoon Lorraine in a circle with a pink background. Underneath is the word *HeartSmart*.

Zoey taps the screen, and I finally see what she wants me to see. Lorraine's follower count.

It's almost four million.

I look at Zoey. "She has four million followers?"

"Yes," Zoey says. "I did her branding last year around the time her account blew up. She just keeps growing."

Wow. I assumed Lorraine had a couple of random subscribers. This is . . . unexpected. Yet another assumption I'd made that had been completely wrong.

"What does she talk about?" I ask.

Zoey clicks on one of the videos. Lorraine is sitting on the little bench outside her apartment. She looks up into the camera and adjusts her glasses then, like she's only just realized it's recording, and she smiles.

"Good morning, HeartSmarties! Today I'm back to answer another one of your questions. You know I can't be anything but honest, so I'm going to tell it like it is. This question comes from StrawberryLongcake03. She says, 'I started dating a new guy a month ago, and I've started to notice that he only texts me back late at night. Should I be worried?'"

Lorraine looks at the camera and laughs. "Oh, sweetheart, there's a fine line between a butt dial and a booty call. If he's only texting you after hours, it's not because he wants to be your pen pal. It's time to tell this guy he can take you out on a proper date, when the sun is up, and if he doesn't want to do that, then move on. Life's too short to waste your time."

Hearing the words "booty call" come out of Lorraine's mouth is hilarious and jarring. I'm surprised she even knows what that is.

Zoey clicks the phone off, and the last bit of Lorraine's blunt advice hangs in the air.

She's right. Life's too short to waste my time.

"Go over the plan again," I say, feeling a bit more determined than I was ten seconds ago.

"So you make a video." Zoey hands me an iPad. "I wrote out some bullet points. You simply tell your fans that you made a mistake." She shrugs. "Mistakes happen. Just be honest. You were so excited about the market that you mixed up the salt and sugar, and you want to make it up to them. Then announce your plan for 'Porch Swing Sidewalk Samples,' a chance for them to *swing* by next weekend for a free treat. Your way of making it up to them and proving to them that you *do* know how to bake."

I sigh. "This feels humiliating."

"It's not," she says. "It's honest. People respond to honest."

Me included.

Lennon nods, bouncing Eve on her hip. "She's right. People will love it."

This makes me think of my old life.

The one I never fit into.

I realize that they're right. I don't want to pretend to be something I'm not. I screwed up. I'm going to own the mistake.

And people will forgive me.

Hopefully.

"Okay, what do I need to do?"

* * *

@theporch

<Owner of The Porch, a soon-to-launch bakery in Chicago, Claire Karedec, addresses viral video and ill-timed salt/sugar mix-up>

Have you ever made a giant, colossal, HUGE mistake? Well, I did. You might've heard about it. I was so excited to unpack my first round of supplies in my brand-new commercial kitchen that I did the thing my gram said to never do. I rushed it.

I can still hear her getting onto me about that. "If you rush, Claire, you defeat the purpose of baking. If you go slow, it'll calm you down. And all the noise of the world will just . . . fall away."

I wanted The Porch to honor her memory, and what did I do? I forgot one of the most important lessons she taught me before I even opened the doors.

I mixed up the salt and the sugar.

It was a terrible mistake. And one I really regret, not only because I let you down, but because I let her down. And because . . . in a lot of ways, baking has saved me this past year. I got divorced, moved to a new city, and took a huge gamble on opening my own bakery. One that will bring all the things I love about life in a small town right here to the heart of the city.

I get that you're probably scared to give me a second chance, but what if I told you that second chance will cost you nothing?

This Saturday, we'll be serving Porch Swing Sidewalk Samples all morning. Free treats the whole family will love . . . sure to get that salty aftertaste out of your mouth.

I truly believe that life is built on second chances . . . so come on out and help me build mine!

* * *

Minnie: Have you recovered?

Claire: Not really, but I will.

Minnie: I'm glad you didn't quit.

Claire: Me too. But nervous for Saturday. What if no one comes?

Minnie: For free desserts? I don't think you have to worry.

Claire: 🤞

Minnie: I saw you deactivated your account on Matched.

Claire: Yeah, I think maybe I need to spend some time on the relationship I've neglected the most over the years . . .

Minnie: The one with yourself?

Claire: Yep. Tomorrow we're going to the art museum, just the two of us.

I hope she likes me. 

CHAPTER 32

The last time I looked, which was about five minutes ago, the video had 325,620 views.

Lorraine shared it with her massive following, and all kinds of messages of love and support have flooded in. Zoey and Lennon were right—people respond to honesty.

It makes sense. I respond to honesty too. After everything I've been through, I crave it.

The main storefront is so close to being finished, but my focus is on the food. There is no room for error, only meticulous precision.

Which is why I spent the entirety of Wednesday morning in the kitchen, reorganizing, cleaning, and *making sure the ingredients were properly labeled.*

I also painted a wall by the bathrooms with chalkboard paint and wrote in big, swoopy letters: *What Do You* Really *Want?* It's a place for people to write it down, even if they aren't ready to say it out loud.

Somehow I think it's going to be a focal point of this whole business.

After spending hours with flour and dough, icing and glaze, I give my brain a break and take myself out to the art museum.

There's a Degas exhibit—the rooms are filled with his work. Such artistry and passion and color.

It's so freeing to walk around and enjoy paintings I've only ever seen in photographs. When I'm thirsty, I get a drink. When I'm hungry, I head down to the cafeteria and order a sandwich and a bag of chips.

I feel comfortable being by myself. And that's new.

For years, I took care of John. And Minnie. I put on costumes and plastered on fake smiles and tried to make sure everyone else was okay.

I never really took the time to take care of myself.

Today, though? I take a bit of time for Claire.

And it's nice.

My thoughts turn to Miles, as they often do of late when given space to roam. He decided to take back something that was stolen from him.

And I'm doing that too, but in a different way. For him, it was his business.

For me, it was my whole identity.

Which is maybe why, as I finish the turkey sandwich I ordered at the counter in the lower level of the art museum, I start to think of who I am, how I got here, and where I'm headed.

Maybe it's the drawings and sketchbooks of Degas that are prodding me to be so introspective. You can actually see his process, from scattered lines, to formed sketches, to *Seated Dancer.* You can't help but marvel at it.

I pull out my journal, a constant companion now, and I wonder, in the context of my life now, what it all means. I flip through the pages, remembering how this whole journey started—finding this abandoned book in the cushions of my chair.

I peer back through the memories, wondering where dreams start, how they're formed, and how they are breathed into existence.

I think about the girl I used to be when I was younger.

Born in prison to a drug-addicted mother, she didn't stand a chance. She shouldn't have stood a chance. But she was fearless, certain that she could do anything and fueled by the world's belief that she couldn't.

And stand she *did*. Because people around her helped her learn how. People like my grandparents and my first real friend, Libby.

Later, when life threw her another curveball and knocked her down—I think of Lennon and Lorraine and Zoey and Ava and Miles—more people were there to show her how to stand back up again.

I don't know much, but I've learned that I'm not defined by other people's expectations anymore. I'm not trying to be something I'm not. I've learned that it's not selfish to take care of yourself—it's critical.

I'm my own person. I'm a friend. I'm a person who likes new foods. I'm a great texter. I enjoy the occasional comic book convention. I'll stand on rocks and dance with kids. I'm a mom to an amazing daughter.

I'm a baker.

I'm a business owner.

I don't wonder anymore who I am without the traditional labels. And even though I'm still learning, I believe in myself a little more than I used to. I believe that I can survive when things get hard because I've proven it.

I flip to the page with my list, take my pen, and draw a line.

1. ~~I want to figure out who I am—apart from a wife and a mom.~~

Then I smile, satisfied, close the journal, and head upstairs to spend a little more time with Degas.

* * *

It's Thursday now, and I'm in the middle of kneading a loaf of sourdough when the back door that leads to the alley behind the storefront flies open and Miles walks in.

He's out of breath and immediately starts pacing. A full minute goes by, and he's yet to look at me.

I'm about to ask him what he's doing, but he huffs out a breath and scrubs a hand down his face.

"So it turns out that I'm a total hypocrite," he says, still not looking at me.

My hands are in a big bowl of half-mixed ingredients, and I'm not sure what he's talking about.

"Because I gave you that big speech about picking yourself up and trying again, and I refuse to do the same thing. With . . . people." He puts his hands on his hips. "With you—"

"I never said that," I say.

"It was implied."

I press my lips together, but I don't respond.

"You asked me what I want."

I stop kneading.

"I did."

"And I didn't say anything."

I nod. "You didn't."

"Well, now I'm saying it. Something. I'm saying something. Now."

I hold my breath.

He looks up, right in my eyes. "It's you."

I slowly let out my breath.

"I want you, Claire."

My heart lurches.

He moves toward me. "Did you hear me? I'm not confused. I know what I—"

But I don't let him finish. Instead, I grab his face with my floured hands and kiss him so fully my own knees go weak. It's fevered and frantic, a dam that's finally split in half as his arms pull me close, pressing my body against his. I inhale his familiar, comforting scent, paying close attention to the way his skin feels under my fingers, the way his lips feel against mine—firm but soft—and I melt a little as my mind zeroes in on it all.

But then I pull back, releasing my grip on him with wide eyes. "I just made a mess of your face." There's a dusting of white flour on both of his cheeks as I pull my hands away and take a step back.

The corner of his mouth inches up, and he shakes his head. "I really don't care about my face right now." He reaches for me, pulling me back to him by the belt of my apron. He takes my face in his hands and studies my eyes.

"Is this crazy?" I whisper, certain I already know the answer.

He shakes his head. "The only crazy thing is pretending I could ever be happy just being your friend." He brushes a thumb across my cheek and smiles. "You're gorgeous, you know that?"

I try to look away, but he forces my gaze.

"I'm crazy about you, Claire."

I hold him a little tighter, but I don't respond. I'm still wondering if this is a dream.

Then, as if he's just remembered something, he pulls his hand away and my skin goes cold in the absence of his touch.

"I want to take you out." He stuffs his hands in his pockets, and I watch a little bit of his confidence slowly fade. "On a not-boring date." He gives me that trademark smile, a little of the urgency of this confession dissipating. "I'll plan everything, and all you have to do is show up."

I take a second to pretend I'm thinking about this, even though he could've stopped talking after *"It's you,"* because that's when he had me. Maybe I should be more hesitant. Or cautious. And tomorrow, maybe reality will kick in. But right now—with the way he's looking at me—I couldn't walk away from him if I tried.

I chew the inside of my cheek. "Okay."

"Okay, you'll go?" He dips down a little, hands stretched out in front of him.

I nod. "Yes. I'll go."

"Are you free Saturday night?" he asks. "After you run out of food and have a massive success with the samples? I know the timing isn't great. You might be too tired."

"I won't be." Maybe I should play it cool, but after he just kissed the heck out of me like that, the only thing I'm really thinking about right now is, *When can I do it again?*

His mouth twitches, like he's trying not to smile but decides to anyway. "Okay."

I smile back. "Okay."

An actual date.

With Miles.

Without the barrier of *just friends* or *off-limits.* Without the desperate attempt not to feel all the things I've been feeling since the first night we kissed.

"Okay, now go and let me do this—" I nod toward the dough.

"All right." But he lingers, full lips teasing in a lazy grin. "I'll see you tomorrow." He leans in and kisses me gently on the cheek, squeezes my hand, and walks out.

As he leaves, my heart sputters because tomorrow, when I'm decorating and baking and filming videos for social media, when I should be concentrating on redeeming my name, all I'm going to be thinking about . . . is Miles.

CHAPTER 33

Friday morning, I grab my bag and open my apartment door, stopping short when I find Miles sitting in the courtyard facing my apartment. He stands.

"Are you stalking me?" I ask.

"Yep." He grins.

I frown and hold up my phone. "Do you have one of these?"

"If I called you, I wouldn't get to see your face."

I bite back a smile. "Is this how you're going to be? Totally sappy?"

"One hundred percent." He sticks his hands in his pockets and grins. "Coffee walk to start your day?"

"I was going to get coffee on the way in, so I *suppose* you can tag along."

"Can I hold your hand?"

"Do you want to carry my books too? Write 'TLA' in my yearbook?"

He laughs. "That's a deep cut. I may as well tell you to keep in touch over the summer."

The comment makes me wonder what Miles was like when he was younger, and I realize I want to know. I want to know all of his stories and share all of mine.

"Are you nervous?" he asks.

I nod. "I am. I feel like I have a lot to prove."

"You're going to be amazing. You're ready, Claire," he says.

"I hope so. I tasted everything twice. Made more than I need. I checked the sugar before I poured it in every single time I used it." My laugh is nervous.

"I think it's going to make a great story on the back of your menus ten years from now," he says.

I glance over, thinking about the night we met. Me in my alien face mask and him with his casual charm. I think about the way he'd said, *"When people ask us how we met, I'll tell them the story of the half-naked woman stalking me in the bushes."*

I'd been so sure nobody would ever ask me that question.

I'd been so sure of so many things I'm not sure of anymore. In the very best way.

We stop off at a coffee truck and Miles orders my coffee without asking what I want. "I'd order something to eat, but I'm fully expecting to raid your stash when we get to The Porch."

"Hmm. I'll consider it." I take my cup from him, then lead us away from the truck and down the street on the now-familiar route to the bakery.

"I want one of the scones," he says. "And maybe a lemon bar—did you make lemon bars?"

"So this is why you're coming with me," I say, teasing. "I'm just the food lady."

"Eh." He shrugs as if to suggest he agrees.

I smack him, and he apologizes. "I'm coming with you because I want to show you something." He takes a drink of his coffee.

"Something on the way to the bakery?" I ask.

"More like something at the bakery." He doesn't look at me, but I can see him smiling.

I eye him for a few seconds, but he keeps his gaze focused ahead. "What did you do?"

The smile widens. "You'll see."

Excitement bubbles up inside me, though I have no idea why. I was literally at the bakery last night, and I didn't notice anything out of the ordinary.

I have no idea what he possibly could've done . . . only that I can't wait to find out.

I've always loved surprises.

We cross the street and head toward the entrance to The Porch, but instead of going through the front, Miles turns to the right, then down the alley in the back. Since I walk to the bakery, I go in through the front door, and I've only used the alley entrance when I've had a lot of stuff to haul in.

I've only been out there maybe four times.

It's an alley.

I slow my pace as Miles steps to the side, more intent on watching me than where we're going. I look at him and see anticipation on his face.

"Miles, what did you—?" I realize as the full area comes into view that while I've been baking and organizing and painting and decorating inside my shop nonstop for days, Miles has been working on turning the exterior of the bakery into a fully functional—and amazing—extra dining area.

It almost doubles the space.

It adds so much to what we've been doing inside, but . . . how did he pull this off?

There's a stand with "Fresh-Squeezed Lemonade at The Porch" painted on it in my branded colors. There are whimsical, colorful garlands hanging in swaths over a mix of picnic tables with benches and tall tables for people who prefer to stand. Outdoor rugs are neatly positioned all around the space, and there are potted outdoor plants of varying sizes that breathe life into an otherwise drab area. He's taken a blank, urban, concrete canvas and turned it into something small town, inviting, and warm.

My favorite part, though, is the sign hanging on the back wall of the building. It reads: THE BACK PORCH.

"The storefront is kind of small." He steps over to the lemonade stand. "And I thought it would be cool to have spillover seating for the nice days. You could take orders out here—or not. And there's"—he walks over to a small area in the corner right up against the building and pulls out a large wooden square—"corn hole." He picks up a bag of beanbags and shakes it.

"We used to play that on the farm," I say, doing nothing to keep the wonder out of my voice.

"Didn't every kid who grew up in the Midwest?" He tucks the board back where it was and walks over to me.

"When did you do all this?" I ask.

"I've been working on it off-site," he says. "At my office. And we installed everything overnight last night after you left. It's a small space, but I think we're maximizing it. I was thinking we—"

I hold up a finger to shush him, turning to set my coffee and bag down, then spin back and throw my arms around him, pulling him close in a tight hug.

I put my mouth close to his ear and whisper, "Thank you."

His arms come up around my back, and I feel him settle into the hug.

"You're welcome," he whispers back.

We stand like that for a long moment, the sun starting to heat, and I pull back and look at him. "Nobody has ever been this excited about one of my crazy ideas before."

"It's not crazy," he says, pushing a strand of hair behind my ear. "It's going to be incredible. *You* are incredible."

I search his eyes for any trace of insincerity—anything to indicate he's playing an angle here—but I don't find one. Only genuine excitement and admiration.

"I should go," he finally says. "You have work. I have work. Boring adult stuff."

I smile up at him, looking around at this incredible gift he's given me. "I really don't know what to say, Miles."

His smile goes soft, and he moves toward me, leans down, and kisses me on the cheek. He pauses there, face pressed to mine, and I close my eyes and inhale a deep breath. Time seems to stop with the realization that if I turn just a fraction of an inch, we'll be right back where we were in the kitchen. But the moment is here and gone in a heartbeat.

When he pulls back and looks at me, heat rushes through my body, and I do everything I can to try to pretend I wasn't just thinking about kissing him.

"You were thinking about that kiss," he says, never one to miss a chance to make me squirm.

"What?" I look away. "I was not."

"I was."

My eyes snap to his. "You were?"

He lets out a low laugh. "Uh, yeah. I think about it nonstop."

I subconsciously press my lips together, then realize I'm doing it to try not to smile. "You do?"

His eyes search mine as the smile falls from his face, a serious expression replacing it. "Yeah, I do."

The mood shifts, a heavy tension threading the air between us.

"I think about how soft your lips are and how you tasted like strawberry ChapStick," he says. "And how that kiss woke up something inside me that I put to sleep a long time ago." He reaches up and touches my face, fingers sliding down to my neck. And then, in a simple, casual move, he leans in and brushes the softest, sweetest kiss on my lips. So quick I can barely respond, and yet, it leaves behind a longing I can't quite process.

"But today, we both have to work."

His words are an unwanted wet blanket and a much-needed wake-up call. "Right."

He smirks, probably knowing that this whole brief encounter made me feel like a walking ball of exposed nerves.

"Have a good day." He backs away, then turns and walks down the alley, leaving me standing there, stunned at how easy it was for him to turn me into a gooey mess before nine in the morning.

Imagine if I were with him for a whole twenty-four hours.

CHAPTER 34

I've always been a bit of an overachiever. So, in typical Claire fashion, I decided to attempt two huge things on the same day.

Turn my business around and turn my dating life around.

One I'm confident about my part in and the other I'm a nervous wreck.

You could apply that description to either.

When I walk out of my apartment, I half expect to find Miles there waiting to walk me to the bakery, but instead I get a text message:

Miles: I already got coffee. I'm setting up the Back Porch. See you when you get here.

My heart swells, and I take off in the direction of the bakery, the Pointer Sisters version of "I'm So Excited" racing through my mind. I pick up the pace. It's nice to have so much to look forward to.

I bypass the front entrance and head a block over, making my way down the back alley. When I get there, it's not just Miles working to get the space ready—Daniel, Kevin, and Duffy are there too.

I stop moving and stare at them. "What are you guys all doing here?"

"Crowd control," Daniel says.

I laugh, but they don't.

Miles, who was bending over the corn hole boards, situating

them in a spot that's away from the tables, stands. "Did you walk by the front?"

I frown. "No, I got the green light, and I knew you were back here, so I came straight back."

"Come here." Miles motions for me to follow him into the bakery. I'm expecting it to be dark, but the kitchen light is on—Lorraine, Lennon, Zoey, and Ava are all bustling around the space. The two girls I hired are also here, wiping things down, setting things up.

Lorraine sees me and grabs my to-do-in-the-morning list from the counter. She waves it at me. "Claire, is there anything else? We did all of this." She looks at it again. "Oh, wait, did anyone get the lemon bars out?"

"I did!" Zoey spins around, and I see that she's wearing a tray, held on by a neck strap. On it are individually packaged versions of my baked goods.

"What in the world—"

"We got the idea from old-timey cigarette girls," Ava says. "We figure this way, we can serve more people—we'll walk up and down the line and let people pick what they want. Then we'll restock while someone else goes out with something different."

"And we'll serve the ones that aren't individually wrapped on the Back Porch," Zoey adds, and I love that this space Miles created for me already has its own name.

"I'm going to man the lemonade stand," Lorraine says. "I don't do walking."

"And I'm going to hand out invitations to the grand opening next week." Lennon picks up a stack of postcards and waves it at me.

"I didn't even think you could come today," I say. "I know you have pickleball."

She shakes her head. "Oh, please. You're more important than pickleball, Claire. I wouldn't miss this for the world."

And I wonder how I became important to her so quickly—though I suppose maybe it was in the same way she became so important to me. It's like that with some people. You just instantly know they're meant to be in your life, and you treat them like they always have been.

"I'm going to film you interacting with the people," Zoey says. "For social media."

"When did you all get here?" I ask. "And how did you get in?"

"Miles let us in," Lennon says.

He holds up a key. "Swiped your extra one yesterday."

"Thief."

He grins.

"I don't know what to say." And I really don't. I'm shocked they're here at all. I didn't ask them to come because they've already done so much for me, but I guess they're the kind of people who don't wait to be asked.

They're the kind who just show up.

Haven't had those kinds of people in a really long time.

Certainly not John and his parents. Once, when Minnie was a baby, she was colicky and wouldn't sleep more than ten-minute increments for a solid forty-eight hours. John was on a trip, and I was exhausted and hungry and losing my mind.

I called Marilyn just to see if she might be able to relieve me for a couple of hours—sit with Minnie so I could take a nap. She told me she'd already planned a day at the spa, and this was what motherhood looked like so I'd better get used to it.

Looking around this kitchen, I'm confident that if I had a colicky baby right now, each one—or all—of these people would offer to take a shift so I could sleep, and I'd do the same for them. Without hesitation.

And we've only known each other for a few months.

My heart is so full.

"Claire, what happens if you run out?" Lennon asks.

"Oh, I won't. I made tons," I say. "Practically had to take out a second loan." I chuckle to myself, but they all stare at me blankly.

I frown. "What's wrong?"

Miles pushes open the door that leads into the main space. "This is what I wanted to show you."

Out the front windows, I see a line of people, three across, stretching past where I can see down the block.

For a second, I'm confused. "What are they all doing?"

Behind me, Lorraine laughs. "Waiting for you to feed them."

I spin and face her. "Are they all here for the bakery?"

"Yep. All here for you," Miles says.

"We have a sandwich board to put out front," Zoey says, pointing at it. "It's got all your social accounts listed so people can tag you and spread the love."

"So, again I ask," Lennon says, "what happens if you run out?"

I spin around to face them. "I'm going to run out."

"Good thing you know the owner," Miles chips in.

"I printed up tickets," Zoey says. "In a few minutes, we're going to go out and give one to each person. We'll collect them and make sure nobody comes back for seconds."

"I didn't even think of that," I say.

"I know. I'm awesome." Zoey wags her eyebrows and grins.

"You're the baker," Miles says to me. "We took care of some of the other stuff so you could bake."

I have friends. They feel like family. And they all showed up.

I look at Miles, tilt my head down and smile, and say, "Let's get to work."

* * *

And work we did.

We finished all the last-minute prep, handed out tickets to the people in line, and then, right at 10:00 a.m., I opened the door and walked outside. When they saw me, everyone standing in line cheered—loudly—and the noise grew as more people realized why it was happening.

Zoey filmed the whole thing.

Ava came out with a tray of baked goods and moved through the crowd. I introduced myself to countless people, shook dozens of hands, and felt a little out of place with so much attention.

But as I stand now, at the end of the day, encircled by everyone who helped, I can't help but think of the connections I made.

One woman told me she saw one of my videos and it inspired her to get back to doing what she loves—ceramics. And another woman grabbed my hands and said that she was going through a terrible divorce, but seeing me gave her hope that one day, she would be okay. I told her to come back if she ever needed a friend.

I met a foursome of older people who made a pact to come back for the grand opening. And a guy who confessed he was trying to figure out how to ask out a woman a little bit ahead of him in the line.

This story—my story—and my little bakery were already connecting people, and The Porch wasn't even officially open yet.

Invitations for the grand opening went out to everyone we met. I was interviewed by six different Chicago-based influencers—two of whom review new restaurants around the city—and I directed three different people to the lemonade stand for autographs with Lorraine, who I suspect is a big part of why this crowd showed up in the first place.

The whole morning felt like a really fun block party, and in rare moments when I wasn't chatting or laughing or talking to the camera on someone's phone, I stood back and marveled at the entire scene.

This was what I wanted to happen.

People coming together to be there for each other.

Connecting.

And it happened because of a giant mistake.

Now that it's all over and we've torn everything down, I gather everyone together around the counter in the kitchen, pour out cups of lemonade, and retrieve a sampler tray I'd hidden in the pantry. I set it down in the center of the little circle.

They all take a cup, and I raise mine.

"A toast," I say as everyone lifts their glass. "To my friends—" The word lodges itself in my throat, and I have to swallow it to go on. "Thank you for showing up."

I look at Ava. "Thank you for helping."

I look at Zoey. "Thank you for sharing your creativity."

I look at Lorraine. "Thank you for your influence."

I look at Lennon. "Thank you for your friendship."

I gesture to all of the men in the room. "Thank you for your muscles."

A quiet laugh filters through the space.

I look at Miles.

My list of things to thank him for is long.

The way he sat with me on the bathroom floor. The way he shared his own story to convince me not to quit on this dream. The kind words. The encouragement. The Back Porch. Erasing the security camera footage. The dates. I turn to look at him more fully, and I can feel everyone's eyes on me.

"Thank you for believing in me. For doing so much—too much—to help make this dream come true." I hold the cup up a little higher and scan the circle again. "Without all of you, I would've given up. So . . . thank you for not letting me."

There's a chorus of "Cheers!" and everyone takes a drink, then Lorraine holds her cup up again and says, "And to Claire! For finally figuring out the difference between salt and sugar!"

Laughter and words of agreement fill the air.

I take out my phone and hold it up to take a selfie of the whole room. This is definitely a day I never want to forget. "Everyone get close!" I wait until we're all squished into the frame and snap three photos, then smile down at the image on the back of my phone.

The day I discovered my husband's affair, I thought my life was over.

But it turns out, that was simply the first day of the next chapter.

And I can't wait to see what happens next.

* * *

Claire: Minnie, you won't believe the day I had! Look!

<Inserts 11 photos from the day>

Minnie: Redemption, baby!

Claire: 😆

T-minus one week until the grand opening!

I can't wait to see you!

Minnie: Jokes aside, Mom, this is incredible. I can't wait to celebrate with you!

I hope you know how amazing you are.

Claire: Love you, Min.

Minnie: See you soon!

CHAPTER 35

A knock at my door.

A jolt of electricity.

Wow, it's been a long time since I've felt like this.

It's a date. It's a date with a guy. It's a date with a guy I like. And he likes me too.

I pull the door open and find him standing there, looking as handsome as ever. "Hi."

He smiles. "You look beautiful."

"Thanks. I think I tried on everything in my closet before I landed on this." I glance down at the long, flowy skirt that took me an hour to settle on. "It's hard to plan for a night out when you don't know where you're going."

"You chose well." He gives me an approving nod. "But you'll probably need a jacket."

"Still not going to tell me what the plan is?"

"And ruin the surprise?" He pulls a face. "No way."

I grab a jacket and my bag, then join him outside in the courtyard. Lorraine is sitting at one of the tables with two other older women. When she sees us, she stands and rushes over. "Claire, congratulations on your big success today! You must be so happy."

I reach for her hands and squeeze them both in my own. "Thank you so much for everything, Lorraine. I know people showed up because you told them to. And also because they wanted to meet you. Did I see you signing autographs?"

She chuckles a little. "Yes, for a sweet little thing named Ruby."

"Right . . ." Miles puts a finger to his temple, searching the air like he's trying to remember something. "You told her a man who makes you guess isn't mysterious—"

"He's immature!" Lorraine says, in unison with Miles. She laughs, then inches back. "Wait a minute. Are you two going on a date?"

"We are," Miles says.

She blows out a breath. "Well, it's about time!" She turns back toward the table. "These are the two I told you about." She starts walking away. "I guess they finally figured it out—we don't have to intervene after all."

I look at Miles, and we both laugh. "She's the best. I can't believe how happy she was to help me."

"That's what she does," he says. "When I moved in, I was kind of a wreck. She brought me dinner every single night after work. I mean, she dished it up with a side of snark, but she's a big part of the reason I survived all that."

"I hate that you went through what you went through," I say.

"I hate that you went through what you went through too." He glances at me. "But isn't it interesting that those disasters led us both here?"

I smile at that, because a year ago, I couldn't have imagined feeling happy again. And now I can't imagine feeling sad. I suppose that's how life goes, though. It's not all peaks and it's not all valleys. Not all joy or sadness. It's everything all at once, sometimes in drips and sometimes in waves.

We reach the sidewalk, and I expect him to walk over to where his car is parked, but he turns in the opposite direction.

"We're not driving?"

He pauses and looks at me. "You like to walk."

"I do like to walk," I mimic.

"Unless you're too tired. It was a long day."

I shake my head. "No, I'm good. It's a really nice night."

He stretches a hand in my direction, and after a beat, I take it, loving the way it feels wrapped around mine. John wasn't a hand-holder. Not that I want to compare everything about Miles to John. He's not John.

It's nice.

The area around The Bexley is more familiar to me now, and even though I don't know where we're headed, I'm comfortable here. And Miles makes me feel safe.

We walk in comfortable silence, catching snippets of conversation on the street as we pass by other people out for the night. A group of guys talking about where to go next after a game. A couple, one trying to talk while the other seems to be in a daze. We both stifle a laugh when an older woman on her phone says, "Well, did you try the Miralax? How long has it been stuck?" as she passes by.

So many people with so many stories. We all share joy and elation and darkness and grief. That's the human condition.

That's what being alive is really about.

I checked out of it for a long time, but I'm glad to be back now. Because I've learned that I appreciate the highs so much more because of the lows.

Just because I wouldn't have chosen this outcome for my life doesn't mean my life can't become something beautiful.

Maybe it's my mood. Things haven't gone this right for me in years, and now *everything* feels bigger and brighter and more beautiful.

We stop at a red light, waiting to cross the street, and the pause pulls me from my thoughts. I glance over at Miles and find him watching me.

"I have a confession to make," he says.

"Miles, I've *told* you that's a horrible way to—"

He laughs. "I know, I know, I'll get better, I promise."

I look at him expectantly.

"Well?"

"I might've texted Minnie and told her we were going out."

"You did?" I ask, smiling.

"Yeah. I wanted some dirt."

"Dirt? On me?"

"I'm a landscape architect," he says dryly.

I make a face at him. "If we're going to make this work, your jokes are going to have to get a *lot* better."

He laughs.

"Not *dirt*, exactly. I needed some ideas," he says. "She told me that for years you tried to get your ex to take you guys to Epcot so you could ride some ride . . . ?"

"Soarin' Around the World," I say without hesitation. "Have you been?"

He shakes his head. "I haven't. But I'll go with you if you want to."

I grin. "John hated everything Disney. The crowds. The heat. The prices. I love it because it makes me feel like a kid." I shrug. "I don't think I felt like a kid even when I *was* a kid."

"You're an old soul," he says.

I nod. "Why did Minnie tell you about my Disney obsession?" I laugh.

"Because of what we're doing tonight," he says.

"Well, the airport is in the opposite direction, so if we've got a flight to catch, we should probably get an Uber."

He laughs. The light changes, and we cross the street.

"When you first decided to give the dating app a try, you mentioned that you wanted to explore the city," he says.

"Right."

"Touristy things and not-touristy things," he says. "Which made it hard for me to choose. There are lots of things I want to show you." He glances at me sideways. "But if I have my way, we're going to be spending a lot of time together, so we can go slow."

My pulse races. *Spending a lot of time together.* I like the way it sounds.

I'm a little taken aback by how closely he seems to have paid attention to the silly little things I've said—mundane, seemingly pointless things.

Maybe this is how you fall in love. Maybe it's not a big, grand gesture that sweeps you off your feet . . . maybe it's the little things that are going to be hanging around long after the zips and zaps are gone.

Like listening. Caring about someone's dreams. Doing what you can to make them happy. I suspect I've been falling inches in love with this man for quite some time.

Up ahead, I see one of Chicago's most well-known attractions—the Ferris wheel at Navy Pier. I glance over at Miles as the wind off the lake whips up, tousling his hair, leaving it disheveled and sexy.

I want to run my fingers through it. My heart flips at the thought, the memory of the way he kissed me as fresh as if it happened only moments ago.

"Have you been here yet?" We slow down to allow for a crowd of teenagers to step in front of us on the sidewalk.

"No," I say. "But I've wanted to."

"Good," he says. "There's a lot to do here . . . Maybe we can bring the group back here next week after your successful grand opening."

I glance over at his profile, admiring the sparkle in his bright blue eyes. "There you go believing in me again."

He shrugs at me as if to say, *It's easy.*

"Are we riding the Ferris wheel?" I ask.

"We can if you want to," he says. "But . . . I planned something else I think you're going to love." He points up, and I see three screens on the outside of a building and a man standing behind a podium with the word "Flyover" on it.

Miles walks over to the podium and pulls out his phone so the guy can scan our tickets. Then we walk into what I think is a ride.

I stare up at it and realize—it's just like my favorite ride at Epcot.

The second he clocks my realization, he says, "I sent Minnie my list, and she helped me decide."

"You have a list?" I ask. "Like, an actual list?"

He pulls out his phone, clicks a few buttons, then hands it to me. I'm looking at a note in his Notes app with a bulleted list of places in and around the city under the heading "No Boring Date Ideas for Claire."

"Full disclosure? I started the list when we were setting you up on app dates," he says. "But I realized I was saving my favorite ideas because I wanted to be the one to do these things with you."

I press my lips into a concealed smile, then hand his phone back. "Good. Because I can't imagine doing something this cool with someone like Barry."

He tucks the phone away. "Let's never mention that guy again."

"Deal."

About twenty minutes later, we're strapped into a ride by the shoulders. When it starts, we're lifted up off the ground, our feet dangling in the air to create the feeling of flying while we're surrounded by a huge, wraparound movie screen playing a video of an aerial view of Chicago.

I feel like Wendy on my way to Neverland as we dip through neighborhoods and swoop through skyscrapers, fully giving in to the sensation of flying. The wind whips through my hair and as we fly over Lake Michigan. I even feel a mist on my face.

Every single second is a multisensory experience that shows me my new city from a completely different view.

There's something about feeling weightless that's equal parts exciting and peaceful, and as I listen to the narration, I decide I definitely need to get a Chicago-style hot dog, go to a Cubs game, see the river turn green on St. Patrick's Day, and visit every single museum in the city.

It's exhilarating, and it takes my breath away.

At the end of the ride, when my feet are back on the ground, I realize I smiled the entire time. The shoulder harness loosens, and we stand and look at each other.

"So?" Miles watches me.

"Can we do it again?"

He laughs. "We can do it as many times as you want. But . . . maybe dinner first?"

I nod. "Definitely."

"Okay, good, because we're moving into the non-touristy part of the night."

"Ooh, I'm intrigued." I loop my hand through Miles's arm, and he pulls me close as we leave Navy Pier and pick up dinner at a small local market. He called ahead, and our order is waiting for us in two large brown paper bags.

We walk a few more blocks, then Miles stops in front of a tall, nondescript brick building that's a little less sleek but far more charming than the ones surrounding it.

He walks up and rings a bell by the door, and a few seconds later, I hear the buzz letting us know the door is open. In the lobby, there's a man at a counter who gives Miles a wide, conspiratorial smile, then tips his hat. "Good to see you again, Mr. Westbrook."

"Good to see you, Charlie," Miles says. "Everything good to go?"

"All ready and in working order." Charlie tips his hat in my direction. "Ma'am."

I smile, unsure what we're walking into but oddly excited to find out. I follow Miles into the elevator, and as the doors close, he gives Charlie one more nod before turning to face me. "I wanted to show you a spot in the city that most people don't know exists."

"Hidden Chicago?" I say as the elevator dings with every passing floor. "Ooh. I like it."

It all feels like a delicious secret, and when the doors open, I realize we're on the roof. In a garden. Surrounded by plants and flowers and twinkle lights.

On one side is a seating area with velvet cushions and strands of white lights strung in swaths overhead. At the center of the seating area is a makeshift table, created out of empty crates that have been screwed together for an interesting, eclectic look. In the distance is the most stunning view of the Chicago skyline I've ever seen.

Miles walks over to the seating area and starts to unpack containers of food while I stand there gawking. It's like we've entered a secret space, one where we're really and truly alone while the city below buzzes and thousands of people move through their lives having no idea that we're here.

"I know you're all about trying new foods, but tonight we're sticking with classic deli fare." He glances up at me. "I know the owners of the deli, and I wanted to share some of my favorite things with you."

I walk over to where he's standing between the table and a stack of velvet floor cushions. "You designed this space, didn't you?"

He kneels down beside the table, then looks at me. "Maybe."

I take a long beat to appreciate it.

He continues, "The owners of the building are artists. And they wanted to create something warm and inviting right in the heart of the city. Like an escape from the madness."

Chicago is all clean lines and crisp visuals, but this space—it's entirely different. The opposite of neutral, it's filled with rich jewel tones and contrasting pops of color.

"It's amazing," I say, still trying to take it all in.

He motions to a mustard-yellow cushion on the opposite side of the table. "Sit."

When I do, I realize there's a sheet strung up, creating what looks like an outdoor movie screen. "Are we going to watch a movie?"

"If you want to," he says. "Or I have some favorites from my vinyl collection." He nods over to a record player and a stack of records. "I wanted us to have options."

"You put a lot of thought into this."

"I really wanted to get it right." He hands me an empty plate, then takes one of his own. "And I've been planning it for a while."

I smile at the thought. "For how long?"

He pulls a face. "Since Roger?"

"Roger!" I bark out a laugh. "I almost forgot about him." I pick up a sandwich and set it on my plate. "Or maybe I blocked it out." I meet his eyes. "But Roger was my first app date. That was weeks ago."

He scrunches his nose. "Every time you went out, I thought about how it should be me going out with you."

"And you still took this long to admit it to me." I shake my head, feigning disappointment.

"And to myself, honestly." He pulls a face. "I can be pretty dense. Plus, I had some issues to figure out. It was Zoey and Ava, actually, who finally talked some sense into me."

I go still. Because it's a big deal to know that his daughters—and mine—approve of this. When you lose your partner and you have kids, they become the most important thing in the world. "What did they say?"

"They pointed out that I'm happiest when I'm around you," he says. "And that you're worth the risk. They also said their mom sucks, but that was a whole other conversation." He laughs softly.

"I can't wait for them to meet Amelia," I say. "I hope they all get along."

The corner of his mouth twitches. "I have a good feeling." He pulls a Dr Pepper from the bag and sets it in front of me, along with a few bags of chips. "Options."

He's thought of everything. Covered everything.

I take a bag of potato chips and open it. "When I first moved here, it was barely spring, and on the nice days I noticed all the people out, like they'd been cooped up for months and just needed to feel the sun on their face."

"We *were* cooped up for months," he says. "There is nothing like sunshine after a Chicago winter. It turns fifty degrees and we're all out here in shorts."

I laugh. "I sort of think this whole experience of dating was like that for me. I had to go through the harsh winter of Roger and Barry and pervy old Freddy to really appreciate *this*." I look at him.

He shakes his head. "I hate the thought of you dating any of those idiots." He leans across the table and brushes my hair away from my face, letting his hand linger on my cheek as he studies me with a quiet, burning intensity.

"Are you sure you want to do this, Miles?" I ask, because I suddenly feel like I need to give him a way out if he wants one. "We can stay friends. We're good friends. We can still go on coffee walks and—"

"I've never been so sure of anything in my life," he says, silencing me.

"I'm only bringing it up because—"

He stops me. "From the second I met you, I knew I was in trouble." He inches closer. "I've been really good about keeping everyone at an arm's length, but you? You made me want something more." He tips my chin up and draws my gaze. "When I look at you, I imagine the rest of my life. It's not big or flashy. It's easygoing and peaceful. It's long walks around our neighborhood on Saturday mornings. It's slow cups of coffee in our bathrobes. Trying new restaurants, hanging out with our girls, maybe getting a dog? It's all of that and everything else."

My eyes fill with tears, and I have to blink to keep them from falling.

I take his hand in both of mine, tracing the line on his palm with my thumb. "You make me feel safe, Miles, and I didn't know if I'd ever feel that way again."

He closes the gap between us, pulling me close as he takes my face in his hands and kisses me softly, tenderly, like he's memorizing every second, so I do the same. I move in closer, the warmth of his body radiating straight through mine, as I give myself over completely to the euphoria of falling in love.

Falling in love.

So. This is how that feels.

CHAPTER 36

We walk back to our building hand in hand, chatting quietly and basking in the glow of a perfect first date.

Miles tells me about his parents, who are happily retired and living in Florida. We swap Christmas traditions and spend a long time contemplating names for a dog we don't have.

"I'm not naming a dog 'Stay,' you lunatic," I tell him.

"No, no, hear me out. It's perfect. We'd be like, 'Come here, Stay! Come here, Stay!' The dog would be totally confused."

All in all, it has been a perfect night. And a perfect end to a truly unforgettable day.

Next week is my grand opening, and I'm more excited than ever at how things have fallen into place.

Which is why, when we walk into the courtyard, I'm completely knocked sideways to see someone I know sitting on a bench outside my apartment, a suitcase on the ground beside him.

It's John.

Miles's arm is draped around me, and at the sight of my ex-husband, I go rigid, feeling for a second like I'm doing something wrong.

Like I've been caught. And then I remember.

John stands.

"Oh my gosh," I say so only Miles can hear me.

"What is it?" Miles asks, his eyes drifting through the courtyard to where my gaze is parked.

I step away from him. "John?" My eyes dip down to his familiar suitcase, and I think of all the times I packed it. Business trips.

Vacations. Golf weekends with his father or the guys from the office. I planned his wardrobe. Packed his clothes. Made sure he had all the toiletries he'd need for the number of days he'd be gone.

"What are you doing here?"

He looks at Miles, then back to me. "Hey, Claire."

I go cold as Miles steps up beside me, hand on the small of my back. He reaches across me with his other hand, extending his toward John. "Hey, man."

John looks at his hand, pauses, then shakes it. "Hey."

"I'm Miles—I'm Claire's—"

"What are you doing here?" I cut in because it's really none of John's business who Miles is to me.

"Can we talk?" John asks. Another pointed look at Miles. "Alone?"

I inhale a slow breath, then glance at Miles. He shifts, a little uncomfortable, then nods. "We'll talk tomorrow." He kisses my cheek, squeezes my hand, then walks away.

I miss him immediately.

I didn't want this beautiful, perfect, wonderful night to end this way. I wanted it to end with me in Miles's arms.

Instead, I'm standing here, instantly on edge, trying to figure out why—and how—my ex-husband is here.

"Is there somewhere we can go?" he asks.

I glance over at my apartment door, then back in time to see Miles disappear behind his. I don't like this. It feels unfair for John to just show up here, dropping another grenade into my life.

I walk past him and pull out my key, unlock the door, and walk inside.

John follows, setting his suitcase up against the wall in the entry.

"You can't stay here," I say.

"I got a hotel."

"You should've told me you were coming." I walk over to the refrigerator and pull out a bottle of water. I hand it to him.

"Thanks."

"So?" I cross my arms and look at him.

"Who's the guy?" he asks as if he has the right to know.

I shake my head. "We aren't talking about my personal life."

"Okay . . ." He opens the water bottle and takes a drink.

"Just tell me why you're here," I say firmly but semi-cordially. "Do you have another campaign you need help with?"

He half scoffs. "I'm not the one who needs help, Claire."

I frown, already exasperated. "What are you talking about?"

"I saw the video, Claire," he says. "Everyone saw it. Even my mother, and she's hardly ever online."

My stomach rolls, knowing that all those people I used to call friends have been discussing my giant salt disaster. It feels like I'm standing in the freezing cold water of that fountain all over again.

It seems he doesn't know the rest of the story.

But I do. And I'm over it.

"So?"

He puts on a pitying expression. "Look, I'm risking a lot to be here. Misty was less than thrilled about me coming here, but I still feel some obligation toward you."

I frown. "Why?"

He scoffs. "Because I was the one who kept you from doing these sorts of crazy things over the years. I mean, if it weren't for me, you would've tried to become a wedding planner when Amelia was in grade school. Or a flower arranger when she hit seventh grade. You always had these ridiculous ideas that I knew would never amount to anything, so it was left to me to talk sense into you."

I'm stunned silent.

The words hit me sideways. I think about all those other ideas I'd had over the years, the ones I'd dreamed of and never pursued—the times I'd wanted to get a job, to go out into the world and meet people and do something meaningful with my life.

And then I think about all the times John had told me no. Not a harsh, cruel no, but a no just the same.

One that was disguised, as this is, as a redirection "for my own good."

"This is what happens when I'm not around." He scoffs. "Throwing all your money down the drain to open a bakery? I mean, really, Claire?"

I drag my eyes up to his, and I feel the prickle of self-doubt on the back of my neck. "So I called my lawyer. We can't get everything back, but he thinks there are a few options—"

"Wait, what?" I cut in. "You did what?"

"Bankruptcy *might* be the smartest at this point," he says. "You wouldn't have to pay everything back right away."

Anger and disbelief start to rise. "I can't believe—" And I stop.

If he's saying what I think he's saying, he's even worse than I thought.

"I'm here to help, Claire," he croons. "Don't worry, babe, I'm going to figure out a way to help you out of this."

I stare at him for a long moment, trying to make this make sense. It's like scales falling from my eyes. This is how he did it. All those years of keeping me small. All those years of disregarding my creativity but benefiting from it when he needed to.

How had I never realized it before?

And then I have the most freeing thought I've maybe ever had in my whole life. I just don't care.

I don't care what he thinks. I don't care if he's marrying Misty. I don't even care if they have babies and he's an old grandpa kindergarten dad.

And the not caring—it's downright exhilarating.

"Claire?" He's staring at me while I'm having this epiphany, and I can't help it—I start to laugh. It's small at the beginning, just a sort of disbelieving giggle, but it quickly grows into something else, something wild and a little manic.

"What's so funny?" John sticks his hands on his hips, looking like a father who can't control his toddler.

The thought makes me laugh even harder—the kind of uncontrollable, shoulder-shaking laugh you have when something strikes you funny at a totally inappropriate time, like at a funeral or in church. And judging by the sour expression on his face, I'd say John does not think it's funny.

And I don't care about that either.

"Claire, get ahold of yourself, for Pete's sake," he hisses.

I hold up a hand. "Sorry." I walk over to the counter and grab a tissue, dabbing the tears from my eyes and drying my cheeks. "Wow, I haven't laughed that hard in—" It starts up again, but I manage to lasso it in a little more quickly. "Okay, sorry. You were saying?" I stifle another giggle.

This time, his sigh is doubly heavy. "I was saying, I'm here to help save you from yourself."

"Yeah, that's what I thought you were saying." I close my eyes and will myself to be serious. "But I don't need saving, John. I'm great. My life here is wonderful."

"I saw the video, Claire. You don't have to pretend."

I slowly shake my head. I actually feel a bit sorry for him, that he still doesn't get it.

"I'm not pretending. I *am* fine, and my life is mine to make whatever decisions I want to."

He starts to say something but quickly snaps his jaw shut.

"I've been fine for a while," I go on. "Better than fine, actually—I'm really, really happy."

He almost looks pained by the words.

And I don't care about that either.

"Look, I admit, for a long time I was angry, and I was bitter," I say. "And I *really* hated what you did to me."

"Claire, I—"

I hold up a hand and he shuts right up.

"But I'm not angry anymore. I'm doing really well. I'm happy here. I have great friends. An incredible relationship with someone who actually values me *and* my ideas. This new life suits me. I appreciate that you think you're here to take care of me in the only way you know how, but I don't need taking care of."

He stills.

And it's in that moment that I feel it—the knot that's been in my stomach since the day I caught him with Misty unravels, and in its place, I imagine all the seeds of possibility sprouting and growing and winding and weaving like they're finally, finally free to do so.

"My business is going to be a success," I say. "But even if it wasn't, that's not your problem. It's mine. And either way? I can handle it."

I lean in just a bit closer.

"And I will."

He draws in a breath and blows it out, almost like he's not sure he should believe it.

"You still think of me as that lost, brokenhearted woman you left standing in the fountain all those months ago. But she's not here anymore, John."

He inhales a sharp breath. "Does that mean you forgive me?"

"Does that mean you're apologizing?"

He blows out a breath. "Yeah. Yeah, I am."

I narrow my eyes, searching for the honest answer. "No, honestly. I don't think I've forgiven you yet," I say. "But I will. I'm working on it. You put me through hell, but I've started to realize that good things grow out of pain."

Good things grow out of pain. The words were out before I even thought about them, spoken from a well somewhere inside me. They give me the confidence that one day, maybe soon, I will fully forgive John for what he did. It won't happen all at once. It'll be a small decision every day until eventually, the pain will lose all its power.

There's no room for grudges in my heart when there's so much love growing every day.

I resist the urge to tell him that his apology skills need work.

I don't want to get mired in the injustice of the way he treated me or wallow in the self-pity I sometimes feel no matter how much I deserve to do so.

Not anymore.

I want to look at the beautiful things life has brought me and not focus on what it has cost me. I want to learn from the past without letting it destroy me, to focus instead on all the good that's coming my way.

Because there's *so much good.*

And even in the dark moments, because I know there will be more, I'll tip my face toward the sunshine and remember that every storm has an ending.

Somehow, my life now is even brighter than before.

I look at John. Someday I'll forgive him. For now, I'll choose kindness. Even though he doesn't deserve it.

But it's what I want.

CHAPTER 37

I made this.

A week later, I'm sitting alone in the bakery. I look around at this thing I created. With the help of my friends.

It's the morning of my grand opening—early, the calm before the storm. I've baked all the treats, stocked the display cases, swept the floor three times, folded aprons and towels and T-shirts with The Porch logo on them in our little retail corner, and now I'm going to take a moment to appreciate where I am . . . and all the things that got me here.

Before he went back to Colorado, John stopped by the space. After giving me a list of things I needed to think about or change, he looked at me, almost like he was seeing me for the first time. Or at least the first time in a long time.

"You're . . . different," he'd said.

I thought about all the reasons why I'm different, and I smiled. "I know."

He nodded, studying me for a second, and then his phone rang, and when he stepped outside to explain to Misty why he wasn't on his way to the airport yet, I went back into the kitchen and let out a relieved breath.

Because I don't care about that either.

My new world? Filled with my new people?

In a word—*sweet.*

Lennon brought Eve by three different times this week, and while she never stayed long, she always made it clear she's in my corner. Lorraine interviewed me for her YouTube channel, which

I took very seriously now that I know how influential she is, but also just because she is delightful, and I'm lucky to know her.

And Miles? He's been an ever-present constant in the chaos.

Every morning before work, he walks me to the bakery. We pick up coffee, and I thank him in baked goods and brief make-out sessions in the pantry, hidden away from the eyes of the employees who started this week.

And after work every night this week, he's picked up or made dinner, rubbed my shoulders, and kissed me senseless, though not always in that order. Tuesday, the kissing started the second he walked in the door.

I've wondered if I could cross out number seven on my list and count kissing him as my new hobby.

On Wednesday evening, Miles drove me to O'Hare where we were yelled at three different times by security because "You're not allowed to park here! Move on out or I'm gonna have you towed!"

"My daughter's coming home!" I yelled back as Miles dutifully vacated the curb.

When I saw Minnie walk out of the terminal, I rolled the window down and started yelling for her. Miles rolled his window down too, then blasted "Take a Chance on Me" through the speakers as he pulled over and put the car in Park.

I grabbed onto my beautiful daughter and pulled her into the biggest, tightest hug, and after a long minute of that, she started shaking her hips and dancing just like she did when she was little. ABBA hit the chorus, and we both shout-sang the words at the top of our lungs.

And the pieces of my world fell back into place.

The security guard started blowing her whistle, so Miles jumped out and grabbed Minnie's bags. He stuffed them in the trunk, and we all piled back into the car, laughing and singing and honking as we drove off.

It was one of the happiest moments of my life.

I've made a point to pay attention to those moments, thankful to have so many to discover.

Minnie and Miles chatted the entire way into the city. We met Zoey, Ava, and Kevin for dinner, then all headed back to The Bexley to sit in the courtyard, drinking wine and catching up. Minnie, Zoey, and Ava were instant friends, and even though they connected by swapping embarrassing stories about their parents, I couldn't have been happier.

Miles and I sat at the table holding hands, both of us smiling at the scene unfolding in front of us, and I wondered—not for the first time—how I got to be so lucky.

Scratch that. It wasn't luck that brought me here at all.

In fact, it was the opposite.

And yet, here I am . . . thriving.

I finish off my coffee and stand, ready to get to work as Minnie and Miles arrive through the back door. They're deep in debate about which is better—*Attack on Titan* or *Avatar*, neither of which I've seen. They both grab aprons from a hook in the pantry and tie them on as Zoey and Ava enter talking about a particular episode of *Only Murders in the Building*.

I'm standing off to the side, thinking that these moments—the mundane, ordinary, sweet moments—are just as special to me as the big ones, like the grand opening of my bakery.

There's a line gathering outside, and I know better than to assume every day will be like this—I'm just happy that today is. I even recognize a few of the people from the sample day, and I suppose this is how customers become loyal.

Last night, Minnie and I wrote conversation starters on paper cups, and I can't wait until this place is filled with chatter.

Connection.

I walk out into the bakery, smiling at the hand-lettered menu board behind the counter and the sign with my motto—*Sit, sip, and stay awhile*—above it. I flip on the white twinkle lights and give the whole space one last quick look. Minnie and Ava brought tables out onto the sidewalk a few minutes ago, so there's just one thing left to do.

Like my heart, I flip over the sign in the door.

It says "Open."

EPILOGUE

The grand opening was an unbelievable success.

We ran out of almost everything, and the stuff we had left over, Miles ate.

I'll have to add a line item in the budget just for that man's metabolism.

All day he was there—in my space but not crowding me. He let me be the star of the day, and it felt amazing to know he was in my corner, not the least bit threatened by the idea of me succeeding.

In the following days and weeks, I've baked more than I ever have in my entire life. I've given away hundreds of samples, and it hasn't hurt my profits one bit. Zoey and I have filmed content for my social media accounts, sharing the whole process of starting this business. She told me to be honest about my feelings, to talk about the thoughts and fears and excitement—the good *and* the bad—reminding me that the world is craving connection and honesty. Sometimes those things are so hard to find.

And now, three and a half weeks in, I'm still floored that every day has brought a line of people outside, cheering when I flip over the sign and swing open the door.

It's become its own tradition at this point.

And today, in the quiet hours of the evening, after the sun and the people and the craziness have subsided, I prop up my phone and hit Record.

"I'm sitting in the middle of the most surreal dream ever," I say, looking at the tiny version of myself on the screen. "At a table. In the middle of *my* bakery."

I look around the room, then back at the camera.

"I still can't believe it."

I pick up the phone and move around the space slowly.

"This was a dream of mine, on a page in my notebook, and now it's here. And it's succeeding in a way I never even hoped or thought possible." I pause and smile. "And now that it's been a couple of weeks, I thought it would be appropriate to ask you to join me for a porch talk. Kick off your shoes, gaze up at the stars, and share secrets until we're too tired to keep our eyes open."

I turn the camera around and head to the Back Porch, where the twinkle lights are on but dim, the air is crisp, and the sounds of the city are alive but faded.

I sit, point the camera forward, and lift my feet, kick off my shoes, and then cross my ankles on the bench of the table in front of me.

I swing the camera back around and say, "I didn't think before I did that. I hope you don't think my feet are gross."

I settle back into the chair. "These are the kinds of nights I had growing up on my grandparents' farm. The kind of nights that inspired this business in the first place. My gram was a kindred spirit right from the start. She was the one who taught me how to bake."

I pause to look around. "I wonder what she'd think of all this."

I smile back at the camera. "I was challenged by my therapist a little over a year ago to ask myself a very simple question: What do I really want?" I shift in my seat, then lean in a little. "And I couldn't answer it. At that time, I didn't know. All I knew was that my whole world was collapsing around me, and I was perfectly fine letting life pass me by."

I catch my own sad smile on the screen. "It's a strange thing to be a human, isn't it? Contradicting emotions and layers of feelings? You can be ready to conquer the world one day and just want to hide in your bed the next."

I look up, and even through the lights I can see a clear sky.

"There's a lie that we're told," I say, looking back at the camera. "That we have to have everything figured out. That we have to have all the answers, and even if we don't, we should 'fake it 'til we make it' and pretend we do."

I shake my head. "I couldn't disagree with that more.

"What happens when the best possible outcome turns out not to be so great? Or when someone else decides you aren't their best possible outcome? A very important person once told me that life has a funny way of showing us what we're made of. I understand what he meant now. It'll push you to your limits, then shove you off a cliff. Sometimes life is a schoolyard bully daring you to get back up.

"But sometimes . . . it's so beautiful it'll take your breath away." I go still.

"I used to really resent getting pushed off that cliff—" I pause. "And then I realized that it's the only way you can soar."

I pause to think about all the beauty in my new life. From springtime cherry blossoms and skyline views to the many, many people who've come into my life since I moved here.

"And I guess that's the whole point, isn't it?" I look into the camera, feeling the excitement, the energy of this new life seeping in at my edges. "The world is always changing. Just when you get comfortable, it changes again—shakes things up—just to see if you're paying attention.

"It's going to stretch you and challenge you and try to make you think you can't do the things your heart is telling you to do. That if you pick yourself up and move forward, you're going to fail.

"It's going to terrify you because that's what life does. But what I've learned is that bravery feels a lot like fear." I smile right into the camera. "And it's *never* too late to begin again."

I pan around the space just as Miles appears in the doorway holding a bag of takeout and looking like a whole other dream come true. He must've come in through the front.

Caught in the frame, he freezes, lifts a hand in a slight wave, and smiles.

I turn the camera back on me. "Oh, look. A very good-looking man has brought me dinner."

"It's good too," he says from off-screen. "Chicago-style hot dogs from Vinnie down the block."

I make a face at the screen.

"I've never had a Chicago-style hot dog before. There's ketchup on it, right?"

He turns to leave and calls from the other room, "Forget it, I'm eating it all. You can't be trusted." He walks away muttering. I hear the words "ketchup" and "sacrilegious" but then he's gone. And all I can think about is how much I want to be wherever he is.

I stand. "So no matter where you are in your journey . . . if you feel like you're too old or too young or too unqualified or too *whatever*, just know that the only thing stopping you from changing your life . . . is you." I lean in. "Beautiful things happen when you get out of your own way."

After I film my video, I add captions and post it. If I'm going to be on social media, I'm going to share all of it—unfiltered.

I just don't have room in my life for anything phony anymore.

I tuck my phone away and meet Miles near one of the tables. He's smiling.

"What?"

He shakes his head. "Nothing. Just . . . you're incredible."

I try—and fail—to hide a smile. "Is that why you've been hanging around here all week?"

"Yes." He sets the bag down on the table and takes me in his arms. "I have a confession to make."

I try to push him away. "For the love of all that is holy, that is *not* how you start a conversa—"

He plants a kiss on my lips mid-word.

I stop talking.

He pulls back and says, "Sorry, I stopped listening. What were you saying?"

I roll my eyes and pull him close, resting my head on his chest.

I feel him draw in a breath. "I love you, Claire."

"Oh, is that all?" I look up at him.

He laughs. "Is that all? That's, like, huge."

"Oh, right." I grin up at him. "I love you too."

"Yeah?"

I nod. "Yeah. I tried not to, but you wore me down."

"I'm pretty persistent."

"And it's a shame you have no personality."

He smirks. "I could ask Roger for some tips."

I laugh at that.

He takes my face in his hands, and I close my eyes and close the gap between us, pausing for a beat to capture this moment in my memory, where I know it will live for the rest of my life.

And whatever else that life decides to bring me, I know now I can handle it. And during the downs, I'll remember how I discovered what I really want. I'll remember how I decided to take a chance on myself.

And I'll never forget the people who helped me along the way.

I'll sit.

I'll sip.

And I'll stay awhile.

* * *

<Insert photo of adorable shelter dog>

Meet Harley

4. ~~I want a dog.~~

AUTHOR'S NOTE

Every time I write a new book, I think about the tribe of people who've shown up along the way. During the time I was writing this, they found a tumor in my son's leg (benign, thank you, Jesus), which led to his third surgery on this leg, followed by extensive physical therapy, and a whole lot of emotions. It was only seven years ago they found a tumor on my daughter's thyroid (not benign, sadly,) so walking through this medical crisis with another one of my kids was hard. Exhausting. Frustrating.

But it also helped me reframe a lot of old beliefs I'd been holding onto. Some anger that had seeped in, along with that self-pity of "why us?", "why them?", even "why not me?"

As a parent, I would've loved to take on these burdens for them, but that wasn't our story.

It was strange how in a way, this situation with my son, reminded me of all the things I have to be grateful for. All the ways God showed up for us. Even though these weren't the paths I wanted for either of my kids, He never once let us down or broke a promise. In fact, He carried us through what turned out to be incredibly hard months and years.

During all of that, I was writing this book. A book about starting over, something that is often romanticized in fiction. And while I have no desire to start over when it comes to my family/career/kids, etc., I did have some baggage to lay down.

Claire is braver than I am. The things she tackled are things I still haven't found the courage to do. Making a new friend. Eating at a restaurant by myself. Unearthing a buried dream.

Little things and big things that maybe I haven't even admitted out loud.

I think writing her journey was my way of testing the waters a bit. And I have to say, I want to challenge myself to do some of these things. To not let myself feel obsolete because my kids are older now and need me less. To remind myself that if I don't like something about my life, I can change it. It was informative and inspiring in ways I hadn't expected.

I hope, no matter where you are in your life, that some of her story inspires you too, and more than that, I hope it made you happy. I always want my books to feel like a light-hearted escape from reality because life is so heavy all on its own.

Thank you for choosing to read one of my books. You are the reason it's possible for me to keep writing, and I know you have endless options, so when I tell you it means the world to me, I really, really mean it. Please don't hesitate to reach out to me any time on social media or through my website! Connecting with readers is one of my favorite hobbies. :) And of course, if you liked this book, I hope you'll pass it on or review it online. Your recommendation is an absolute gift.

Thank you so much for reading,
Courtney

ACKNOWLEDGMENTS

It truly takes a village to bring a book to life, and I have the best village an author could ask for.

Adam, thank you so much for keeping my world plenty bright. I am so grateful to have a partner who believes in me, who doesn't let me quit, who forces me to slow down, who celebrates me, and who refuses to read the kissing scenes I write. You are my favorite.

To my kids, who will never read this. I'm so grateful I get to be your mom. The older I get the more I think I'm the luckiest because I actually really *like* you. Thanks for not being jerks. ;)

To Becky Monds, wow. I don't have words. For your encouragement, your kindness, and your creativity—thank you. I'm so incredibly honored that I get to work with you.

To Amanda Bostic, thank you so much for being so kind and encouraging to me. I am so thankful for you. Still pinching myself that I get to write books for you.

Kristy Cambron, thank you so much for believing in me. I don't have the right words to explain to you how much your support and encouragement meant to me. You are the best.

Katie Ganshert and Becky Wade, your friendships are one of my life's greatest gifts. I only wish we lived closer, but then I'm pretty sure none of us would get anything done. Thank you for being my safe space.

Tarah Curry, thank you for helping me behind the scenes. I couldn't do this stuff without you, and I'm SO grateful!

Halie Cotton & Sandra Chiu, for the stunning cover art. I have no words. THANK YOU.

To the entire TNZ team, you guys are truly the best of the best. I feel like the luckiest author around that I get to work with such an amazing team. Thank you so much for making my books the best they can be and for helping get them out into the world. You all have my eternal thanks.

DISCUSSION QUESTIONS

1. "Good things grow out of pain." How does this quote from the book describe Claire's journey?
2. The characters in the book find meaning through the expression of their art. (For instance, Claire expresses herself through baking; Miles expresses himself through creating outdoor spaces.) How does artistic expression shape their individual journeys?
3. Discuss this quote from Claire's therapist that appears early in the story: "Nothing about your life is going to change if you don't change it." How does Claire put her therapist's advice into practice?
4. Perfection is a theme that appears throughout *Brighter Than Before*. Is striving for perfection always a negative thing? How do various characters embrace or reject perfection or imperfection?
5. Claire misjudges Miles based on her own experiences. Why is this such a common mistake, and what can be done to prevent it?
6. When she's feeling frustrated, Claire asks herself, "What do you really want?" How did she answer this question throughout the novel? What obstacles prevented her from really knowing what she wanted? What enabled her to figure it out?
7. Claire's experience with dating apps provided humor throughout the story, but also valuable insight. What did Claire learn about herself from these disastrous dates?

8. What characters and situations shed light on the importance of commitment–in romantic relationships, in family relationships, and in friendships?
9. Claire is a list maker. How did her lists help her navigate a new life? Are lists always a good thing, or can they sometimes prevent growth?
10. Individuals like Claire, who have spent their life supporting others, can sometimes lose themselves in the process. What helped Claire discover who she really was—and who she wants to become?

ABOUT THE AUTHOR

COURTNEY WALSH IS a novelist, theater director, and playwright. She writes small-town romance and women's fiction while juggling the performing arts studio and youth theater she owns with her husband. She is the author of thirteen novels. Her debut, *A Sweethaven Summer*, hit the *New York Times* and *USA TODAY* bestseller lists and was a Carol Award finalist. Her novel *Just Let Go* won the Carol in 2019, and three of her novels have also been Christy Award finalists. A creative at heart, Courtney has also written three craft books and several musicals. She lives in Illinois with her husband and three children.

* * *

Connect with her online at courtneywalshwrites.com
Instagram: @courtneywalsh
Facebook: @courtneywalshwrites
X: @courtney_walsh